SUMMERTIME, ALL THE CATS ARE BORED

Philippe Georget

SUMMERTIME, ALL THE CATS ARE BORED

*Translated from the French
by Steven Rendall*

Europa
editions

Europa Editions
214 West 29th Street
New York, N.Y. 10001
www.europaeditions.com
info@europaeditions.com

Translation by Steven Rendall
Original title: *L'été tous les chats s'ennuient*
Translation copyright © 2013 by Europa Editions

Library of Congress Cataloging in Publication Data is available
ISBN 978-1-60945-121-9

Georget, Philippe
Summertime, All the Cats Are Bored

Book design and cover photo by Emanuele Ragnisco
www.mekkanografici.com

Prepress by Grafica Punto Print – Rome

Printed in the USA

Notice

Resemblances with landscapes that exist or have existed are in no way accidental: on the contrary, they result from my imagination's complete refusal to conceive a more appropriate and beautiful setting than I found in Roussillon. On the other hand, those who think they recognize in this book persons who exist or have existed are the victims of an overly excitable imagination.

SUMMERTIME, ALL THE CATS ARE BORED

Chapter 1

Robert got up at 4:00 A.M. As he had every day for the past forty years.

For him, it was neither a choice nor an obligation. It was just the way it was. It didn't matter to him whether it was daylight saving time or not: at 4:00 A.M. he woke up and immediately slipped out of bed.

He poured himself a cup of cold coffee. Added a drop of milk. Then he set the crossword puzzle aside so he could put his cup on the little table.

All his life, Robert had worked as a tool and die maker for a firm that manufactured agricultural machinery near Gien, in the Loiret region of France. He got to work at four-thirty on the dot and he had never been even a minute late. Well-regarded, valued by his superiors, not unionized, and polite. A model worker. Laid off as a result of down-sizing as he approached the age of fifty-five.

He sat down on the narrow bench and drank the bitter, cold coffee, grimacing with distaste. He could have warmed it up, but he couldn't be bothered. In any case, he wasn't allowed to put sugar in it, so he might as well swallow it as fast as he could. At one point he'd tried drinking tea but found that too severe a punishment.

Although he'd stopped going to work, Robert had not been able to re-set his internal clock. It drove his wife Solange crazy that he woke so early in the morning. So at the beginning of his involuntary retirement, he'd tried to stay in bed. To sleep in, at least until six o'clock. But he tossed and turned, wrapping himself in the sheets, so that his wife finally told him he could get up as soon as he woke. And then she had left him. A few months later. Bone cancer.

Robert poured the dregs of his coffee in the sink and rinsed his cup. The water pump was humming in its cabinet under the bench. He put the cup in the drain rack and walked out of the trailer.

It was the middle of June, and The Oleanders campground in Argelès was still almost empty. A few retirees like Robert and a handful of foreign tourists. The Dutch always got there first, then the Germans. Robert went directly to the toilets. The day before, he'd used the second stall from the left. Today, it would be the third. It was Wednesday.

He urinated slowly and voluptuously in a clean basin. A sweet odor of lavender filled the shack. That was what he'd liked right away about The Oleanders: the toilets were immaculate. They were cleaned regularly, and especially one last time late in the evening. Robert appreciated not having his nostrils brutally attacked first thing in the morning by the odors of the other campers' piss and shit.

He enjoyed it right down to the last drop that splashed against the smooth and still clean side of the urinal. When he'd finished, he looked at his watch. 4:19. He washed his hands, as he had the day before, at the nineteenth sink in an endless row. Then he wiped his hands on his pants. He was ready for his daily walk.

He had a feeling it would be the most difficult of his life.

The white gravel of the lane that ran down the middle of the campground crunched under the leather soles of his sandals. Usually he liked that delicate little sound, but this morning he paid no attention to it.

Robert and Solange had discovered The Oleanders in 1976. Earlier, they'd camped by the side of the road, or even simply slept in their old Dyane. But after their son Paul was born, they wanted more comfortable arrangements. Then Gérard and Florence had come along. The children had made friends in the campground. They were happy to see them again every summer. Robert and Solange had also formed habits. The parents of their children's playmates had become their friends, and vacations passed pleasantly, with games of *pétanque*, barbecues, and marathon card-playing tournaments.

Robert stopped by his trailer to be sure he'd locked the door. A mania of his. While his wife was alive, he'd controlled himself. But Solange was no longer there.

He turned the handle. The door resisted. It was locked. Of course.

Robert was proud of their campsite. The best set-up in the whole campground. There were two awnings that connected the trailer with a wooden deck next to a stone barbecue that he'd built himself in 1995. The year he was fired. The whole thing was enclosed by a wooden fence on which a dozen flower pots hung. Before, it was Solange who took care of them. The first summer after she died, the pots had remained empty. Then Robert had picked up where she left off. He liked putting flowers on the fence more than putting them on a grave.

Exposed to the sun and salt air, the green paint on the wooden posts was beginning to peel off. He'd planned to repaint them. He doubted that he could do it this summer.

The site was rented by the year. At the beginning of his retirement, they lived almost seven months a year at Argelès. Now the summer season exhausted him. He was sixty-five years old, and he felt tired. He would have preferred to spend the summer along the Loire River, but it was the only time when his children and grandchildren could come to see him.

He crossed the campground, walking slowly and silently.

A ray of light was coming through the crack under the door of a neighboring trailer that was registered in Germany. It belonged to a couple in their sixties. The man was tall and fairly bald. The woman was petite, heavy, and had a permanent. They'd argued loudly as they maneuvered the trailer into its spot. At first, Robert had laughed at them. Then he'd felt very strange. He missed arguments since he'd been living alone.

Just next door to the Germans, in the tent occupied by the young Dutch woman, there was neither sound nor light.

Robert arrived at the little gate that opened onto the beach. It was closed but he had the key. Charles and Andrée, the managers of the campground, knew his early morning habits, and had long ago given him a spare. Over time, they'd gotten used to each other. Robert sometimes gave them a hand doing maintenance work during the off season. A little job here and there. A sink to unstop, a part of the lawn that needed reseeding, a barbecue to be repaired. He liked doing that kind of thing, and in his trailer he didn't have much to do. Robert and Charles chatted as they worked and that occupied their minds. And then, contrary to what is often said, men are more likely to talk openly around a faucet they're changing than over a glass of anisette. Charles was the only one to whom Robert had been able to confide his distress when Solange died.

One time he had even gone so far as to shed tears.

He started down the path that crossed the Mas Larrieu nature preserve. The birds, indifferent to his torments, were chirping their eternal hymn to life. Behind their songs, the hoarse voice of the sea could already be heard.

The sea breeze was slowly rising, bringing with it a wild aroma of iodine and faraway places. The path led prudently between two wooden posts that were supposed to hold back the sand and channel the tourists. On both sides, flourishing prickly pears were vigorously growing their Mickey Mouse ears.

As he approached the beach, it became more difficult to walk, and Robert's feet sank into the sand. He kept as close as possible to the fence in order to put his feet on the meager tufts of grass. Near a thicket of reeds, he hesitated. Then he decided to walk down to the sea first.

After a few dozen yards he came out on the beach. The wind grew stronger, the aromas more intense. The surf was high this morning. On the horizon, the sky was already clearing. Life would go on. Imperturbable.

Robert walked as far as the changing line of the waves. He contemplated the somber mass of the sea and the white line of its crests. No sea would ever again carry his body, he told himself sadly. An immense loneliness invaded him. A total despair. His knees bent under the burden and forced him to suddenly sit down on the damp sand.

How he would have liked to turn the clock back a few hours. Yes, only a few hours . . .

Thoughts struck his mind without ever sticking. A wild seaswell washing over the rocks. Solange, Florence . . . the only women in his life. Fragmentary memories of happy vacations surged up and were immediately wiped away by images of fury and blood. The storm was raging in his skull. He knew that it would stop only on the day of his death. As soon as possible . . .

He remained prostrated for endless minutes. When he raised his head, a red line was cutting across the horizon. The sun would soon be up. The first children were running onto the beach, laughter, life . . . With difficulty, he decided to return to his trailer.

He planned to go back to bed. To pull the covers over his head like a kid. Childhood was so far away, and he felt so old. People say that someday we fall back into childhood. If only that were true. To rediscover joy and innocence just before dying . . .

But the hour of freedom had not tolled for him.

Back in front of the thicket of reeds, he imagined he heard a slipping sound. A strange noise. He moved cautiously forward through the tall grass, following a trail of broken stems. And it was there, in a minuscule clearing made by the mortal struggle of two bodies, that he found the bloody corpse of the young Dutch woman.

CHAPTER 2

A gentle breeze cooled his chest, made sweaty by the heat. At a glance, he could take in the whole plain of Roussillon as far as the blue of the Mediterranean. To the north, the crest of the Corbières slowly descended toward the bay of Leucate; to the south, the Albères range hid Spain from his dazzled eyes.

The sun blurred the different shades of green but made the red roof tiles gleam. Every year, urban growth stole a couple of hundred acres of land from the vineyards and orchards. Subdivisions were slowly spreading over the plain. They surrounded the villages, submerging them and leaving no trace of their past except the silhouette of their old serrated Romanesque church towers. The population had grown continually over the past fifty years and the new arrivals eager for a pleasant way of life had to be housed.

Gilles was having a hard time catching his breath. He'd left the medieval town of Castelnou forty-five minutes earlier and slowly climbed the path that led to the Sant-Marti de la Roca chapel. The hill was steeper toward the end and it had forced him to stop and rest. Earlier, he hadn't had to do that.

From the rocky outcropping where he was resting, he couldn't see the Têt, but he could easily follow its course through the villages that bordered the river all the way to Perpignan. He could list the names of these villages, one by one.

He, too, had been a new arrival a few years earlier, one of those immigrants from the north that the Catalans received with a mixture of fellow feeling, pride, and resignation. Fortunately, he had a job. A trade he was no longer crazy about but which provided him with a sufficient salary at the end of each month.

He opened his canteen and drank two little gulps of the already-lukewarm water. He sprinkled a little on his head. The water ran onto the nape of his neck and then slipped down his back.

He shivered.

The sounds of human activity reached him diluted in a steady drone. Only the buzz of the fire department's Cessna, which was keeping the mountain ranges under constant surveillance, could be distinguished against the background noise.

Sebag thought again about Léo, his son.

That morning, the boy had cleverly avoided hugging him in front of the high school. The car had hardly stopped before he jumped out, mumbling something inaudible that probably meant "Bye" or "See you tonight." He'd been doing that for more than a month. It was his age. He was in tenth grade. High school. He was an adult now. He had no desire to show the slightest affection for his father within sight of his buddies. That's life, get used to it! Sebag tried to be philosophical about it. He'd always known that the time of hugs and kisses wouldn't last forever. With Léo as with Séverine. And he'd enjoyed each second, hugging their bodies to his, closing his eyes the better to imbue himself with their smell. He remembered the time, not so long ago, when Léo used to put his arm around his waist and leaned his head against his chest for a few moments before disappearing into the schoolyard. That time was over. Forever. The kid had fuzz on his chin and he was almost five feet eleven. In a few months, maybe a few weeks, he'd be taller than his father.

Nonetheless! Gilles felt a void. A lack. Physical. Stopping smoking wouldn't have been any harder.

He got up, stretched the muscles in his arms, and shook out his legs. His back was stiff and sensitive. A little more than usual.

He had to make up his mind to go down. To dive back into that turbulent world. And even if at the moment he didn't have much to do in the office, Sebag couldn't be away all day.

He put on his T-shirt and went toward the Sant-Marti chapel. A little break that he allowed himself.

It was open. He went in. Silence reigned in the chapel.

He took off his cap and held it over his belly in his crossed hands. He walked along the row of benches. Through a square opening in the west façade, he contemplated Le Canigou. The Catalans' sacred mountain was trying to retain in its hollows the last marks of winter. Spring had come late, and now, at the end of June, there was still some snow. Clinging to the mountain's folds, it made its relief more noticeable. Le Canigou, veined in white under the sun, was more majestic than ever.

It was time to leave.

Sebag didn't feel like going to work. He was finding it increasingly difficult to put up with the routine of his job.

Outside, the blazing sun forced him to close his eyes.

He took a last drink from the canteen and returned it to the pocket on his backpack. He set the chronometer on his watch. It would take him about half and hour to get back to the car. Twenty minutes' drive to reach Perpignan. Fifteen minutes more, long enough to take a shower in the locker room at the university's stadium.

He would be at police headquarters around eleven-thirty.

CHAPTER 3

She was floating between consciousness and somnolence without being able to reach a shore. She couldn't move, paralyzed by an excessively deep sleep. Her numbed limbs permitted no movement. She was not in a hurry: the sun would come up soon enough.

She felt her dreams slowly slipping away from her. Already, she had only fleeting impressions. Warmth, a little tenderness, sweetness. Far, she supposed, from what awaited her upon awakening. No sound reached her. No image. The void. Night. Silence. She existed only through a transient thinking that refused to settle down.

As the cold spread through her body, she felt the pain growing. She hurt all over. Her legs, arms, head. Her back, too.

Her limbs were—she was beginning to understand—firmly bound. Her feet and hands were tied and attached by a rope behind her back. She couldn't move. At most, she was able, for a moment, to raise her heavy, feverish head. Her face seemed to be half-buried in a mattress that smelled of mildew.

She must have gotten involved in a very strange game. She no longer remembered the rules.

In addition to the contact with the damp mattress, she perceived another sensation on her face. A kind of cloth. Over her eyes, to be precise. Her eyes had been masked. She now realized that the sun would not come up. That it would never come up again, perhaps. This wasn't night but horror.

She tried to struggle against the immense terror that came over her.

It wasn't a game.

After finding it so difficult to emerge from the dense mist that had anesthetized her consciousness and her body, she would have liked to go back to sleep now. Maybe she would succeed in waking up somewhere far from here. In the snug comfort of a guest room, for instance. But her mind was becoming more and more lucid, stimulated by the throbbing pain that was rending her body. A word formed in her head, impossible, incredible, a word that she rejected.

She tried to remember. Nothing precise came back to her. Just the sensation of having gone to sleep with her head leaning against the window of a car, gently rocked by the curves of a country road. A recent memory or a distant reminiscence? As a child, she liked to let herself fall asleep like that on her way back from a delightful Sunday spent at her grandparents' home. Once again, she saw the light of the headlights piercing the pitch black of the Dutch countryside. She remembered the hum of the motor and her parents' quiet conversation. This time, she hadn't fallen sleep on the back seat of the car but on the passenger seat, to the right of the driver. That memory was at least precise.

She hurt but couldn't remember any violence. She plunged into listening to her body. The pain was coming chiefly from the bruises caused by her bonds. Then she focused on her limbs stiffened by a position that was growing more and more uncomfortable. Still proceeding mentally, she examined her head. Her pain felt like a headache, not like something caused by a blow. She had not been struck. Her mind slipped down to her vagina. No pain in that damp place, not the slightest burning. She had not been raped.

The word suddenly forced itself on her. There was no possible doubt. A kidnapping! It was a kidnapping.

But why?

She moved her head, rubbing her face on the mattress to try to move the damned cloth that was hiding the light from her. Then she held still. Memories of cop shows came back to her. If the kidnappers had blindfolded her, it was so that she couldn't recognize them later on. After they had released her.

So they were expecting to release her.

When?

For the moment, that didn't matter. She had glimpsed a hope. A light. So it *was* a kind of game. A cruel game. She wanted to see it that way. She was prepared to play earnestly. She'd learn the rules, and respect them scrupulously.

Everything was going to be all right.

In a few days at most, she would return home. She would go back to her little apartment in Amsterdam and give her parents a big hug.

Just as she was formulating these reassuring thoughts in a low voice, she heard a key turn in a lock.

Who could have kidnapped her? She had an idea but rejected it with horror.

The door creaked. Ingrid's tears soaked into the rough cloth that masked her eyes.

CHAPTER 4

"Could you please do me a favor, Gilles?"

Perceiving his colleague's hesitation, Jacques Molina conspicuously looked at his watch. He was late for work.

"Provided you do me one in return, of course," Gilles replied.

Jacques Molina had been working with Gilles Sebag for four years. They shared the same office and often conducted investigations together. They got along well but were not friends. Too many differences. They put up with each other; they respected each other. They both thought that was good enough.

"What can I do for you?"

"A young woman came in to report her husband missing. It's a case that seems . . . interesting, but I absolutely have to leave. I'm in a hurry. I've got an important meeting at noon. If you could keep this warm for me, I'd be eternally grateful."

"What do you mean, 'keep it warm'?"

Molina gave him a complicitous wink.

"I just had time to take down the main points of her deposition. I'd like you to get the details and give me your impressions. I'll take over the case afterward."

Sebag heaved a long sigh.

"No problem. I'll take care of it."

Molina was delighted.

"I knew I could count on you! We'll both put our signatures on the report, as if we'd spent the whole morning working on it. As usual."

"As usual," Sebag replied wearily.

He wasn't very proud of himself. Not very proud of them.

"Go ahead, hurry up. You're going to be late."

"Thanks. See you later."

Molina was already on his way. He was going out the door when Sebag shouted after him:

"Brunette or blonde?"

Molina waved his hand and answered without turning around.

"The meeting is with a blonde, the deposition with a brunette."

"So . . . your name is Sylvie Lopez, née Navarro. You're twenty-four and live on Vilar Street in Perpignan. You work as a housekeeper for an industrial cleaning firm. You've been married for . . . three years, and you have a little girl born last January."

Sebag looked up from the notes his colleague had taken and looked at the young woman. She was in fact a brunette, with a Louise Brooks–style bob. She had a pretty, sad face, lit by two large, dark, and glistening eyes. Tired eyes. Sebag understood what Molina meant by an "interesting case."

"Your husband is named José. He's a cab driver. And he hasn't come home for two days. Is that right?"

She nodded timidly.

"Tell me everything," Sebag went on. "The last time you saw him . . . What you said to each other . . . When you started to get worried, and so on."

The young woman smoothed out her skirt with her right hand and started in.

"The last time I saw him was Tuesday noon. I was leaving for work and he had to leave too. We both work afternoons and evenings. Actually, I'm the one who works like that, he has adapted to my schedule. That's easier in his trade, you know, as an independent cab driver, he's freer . . . "

She pulled a thread on the hem of her skirt and continued.

"I came home around ten-thirty, after I went by my parents' place to pick up our little girl. I put her to bed and made dinner while I watched television. Normally José gets home around eleven-thirty. He waits for the last train at the Perpignan rail station."

She looked up slightly and glanced at the inspector from below. Sebag said nothing. Didn't move. You had to let them talk.

"At midnight, he still hadn't come home. I told myself that was good news: it meant that the last customer had asked for a long trip. At that hour, it's nighttime rates, and long trips bring in a lot of money, you see. José hasn't been driving a cab for very long, and it's a little difficult. He has to make payments on the car, pay for his license, gas, it's really hard. But then my parents help us . . . "

Sebag allowed himself to nod his head to encourage her. The minimum. She had opened a parenthesis regarding their financial and familial situation. It was up to her to decide whether she should close it right away.

"Finally, at midnight I decided to eat dinner. I mustn't go to bed too late. Our daughter wakes up every morning at six, and often she even cries several times during the night, so, as far as sleep is concerned, you understand . . . "

He understood, yes, and he told her so with a flick of his eyelids.

She didn't go on immediately. She returned to the hem of her skirt, seeming to check its condition. Pauses, like digressions, could be significant.

"Jenny . . . Jenny is our little girl, her name is Jennifer but we call her Jenny, she didn't cry at all that night and she woke later than usual. Just before seven o'clock. That hasn't happened more than once or twice since she was born."

She seemed proud of her daughter. So proud that she dared to stop examining her skirt and raise her eyes toward Sebag.

He smiled at her. He too remembered the first week with Léo, how a child's sleep and meals could determine everything in a household.

"I . . . I took care of Jenny," the young woman went on. "I gave her a bottle. And since José still hadn't come home, I decided to call him on his cell phone. But I got his voice mail."

"What time was it when you called?"

"Uh, I'm not sure. Maybe eight or nine in the morning."

Sebag sat up and put his elbows on his desk, his hands folded in front of his mouth. He asked, as if it were the most natural thing in the world:

"Did you leave a message?"

"Yes . . . No," she finally stammered. "That is, not right away. I had housework to do, ironing. I was busy. I played with Jenny."

"You weren't concerned?"

"Not very . . . Not yet, really."

Sebag tried to imagine what would happen at his house if he didn't come home one evening. Claire wouldn't have waited until the next morning to call him. She would have called before going to bed and she would have left messages on his cell phone. She would have quickly gotten worried, and she would probably have slept badly. Being a policeman was a dangerous occupation, but not as dangerous as being a cab driver. The road kills more people than hoodlums do.

The situation in his marriage wasn't comparable. Sebag would never have stayed out all night without letting his wife know.

"When exactly did you start to get worried?"

The question seemed to destroy the trust that had been established between them.

Sylvie Lopez looked down again at her hem.

"Well, uh . . . In the morning. I'd called his cell phone, I'd left a message, and since he still hadn't called back, then I got worried."

"And what did you think then?"

Sebag didn't want to rush the young woman. He was an advocate of painless births.

"I don't recall, precisely," Sylvie Lopez went on after a few hesitations. "I was annoyed: it was getting late and I had to leave for work."

"You weren't worried all that much, in fact."

She suddenly stopped fussing with her hem and starting smoothing her skirt again.

"Not all that much, no."

Sebag looked at her. He waited a few seconds until she decided to raise her eyes to him. He spoke in his warmest voice, in his most understanding tone. Even during a painless birth, there comes a time when the baby has to be pushed out.

"This wasn't the first time he'd stayed out all night that way?"

The young woman's chin began to tremble. She looked at him with her dark eyes shining with shame.

"It wasn't the first time, was it?" he repeated.

"No," she admitted in a whisper.

Tears welled up and rolled slowly down her hollow cheeks. She sniffled. Sebag opened the top drawer of his desk and took out a package of Kleenex. The last one. He'd have to buy some more, he said to himself. The administration provided free cartridges for revolvers but hadn't thought of Kleenex. They were, however, more useful on an everyday basis.

Sylvie Lopez blew her nose for a long time. Sebag waited until she had finished.

"Does your husband have a mistress?"

She jumped. The word offended her. As if he'd shown a spotlight on a situation she had pretended she didn't know about. So long as we don't name things or people, we don't bring them to life. And we prevent them from taking too much power over us.

"No . . . I don't think you could say that."

She looked for words, and would have liked to clarify her thought, but first she needed to get things straight in her own head. She had to begin by looking the truth in the face.

"I think he's had . . . flings that didn't go anywhere. I don't think he has an, uh, ongoing relationship . . . I would have noticed."

She dried her eyes with the Kleenex. Her mascara had run and left marks on her cheeks. She wasn't able to wipe it all away. Sebag would have liked to get up and help her.

"Have you spoken with your husband about his . . . flings?" he asked.

She shook her head. Sebag didn't try to hide his astonishment.

"You seem to have accepted this situation pretty easily . . . "

She shrugged.

"What good would it have done to talk about it?"

She blew her nose again and, confronted by Sebag's silence, felt obliged to explain.

"I believe men sometimes have needs that women don't have. And then I think being a father scared him a little. Maybe he needed to reassure himself, I don't know. Do you have children?"

Sebag did not answer.

"And then so long as he came home and was nice to me, to us, I didn't have any reason to complain, did I?"

Sebag found her touching in her old-fashioned naïveté. She'd said that as if it were a commonplace. Her husband was really the worst of jerks. You don't leave a woman like her. He scribbled a few key words in his notebook. A little blue notebook with large squares. These notes would later be valuable for re-transcribing the interview as accurately as possible.

"What made you think your husband hadn't simply stayed out two nights in a row?"

"Since I hadn't heard from him, I called some of his colleagues, I know two or three who've come to the house. I said that our daughter was sick and I had to get in touch with him right away, but he'd lost his cell phone. But nobody had seen him all day Wednesday."

Sebag weighed his words so as not to hurt her.

"He could also have stayed out all day, so to speak."

She shook her head vigorously. A lock of hair stuck to her wet mascara.

"That seems impossible to you?" he asked.

"He would have called, asked about Jenny . . . "

"He might have been afraid."

Her big, somber eyes grew round. They looked like two black marbles.

"Afraid of what?"

"Afraid of you."

"Why, since I don't ask anything of him?"

"You wouldn't have made a scene? And you would have let him leave again without saying anything?"

Her two black marbles caught Sebag's eyes. She wanted to convince him.

"What good would it have done to make a scene? We would have risked losing him forever. And then if he wanted to leave us for good, he could have come back to tell us, couldn't he?"

"Even the best of men are cowardly sometimes," Sebag said ironically. "Maybe he didn't dare tell you?"

She thought about the inspector's arguments for a moment, and then rejected them with a vigorous shake of her head.

"No, I really don't think so. You have to believe me, Inspector. Something has happened to him. I know it, I can feel it. Something serious."

After lunch, Sebag reread the missing person report Sylvie Lopez had filed. They had filled it out together, sketching a quick description of José: In his thirties, 5'9, heavy-set, dark eyes, thick brown hair and eyebrows, a mole on his neck. They had mentioned the clothes he was wearing on the day he disappeared—light brown slacks and a sky-blue shirt. Then Sebag had had her sign the report before he sent her home with a few reassuring words that hadn't reassured her at all.

He remained perplexed.

The young woman's concern had ended up contaminating him. He couldn't extinguish in his memory the wet and imploring flash of jade in her soft eyes. He wondered what was leading him to pursue this case. Was it the intuition that this disappearance was in fact concealing something serious, or was it the sympathy he felt for this young woman?

He was dialing the number of the husband's cell phone when the land-line on his desk rang. It was Superintendent Castello. His boss.

"Ah, Sebag, finally . . . Could you come see me?"

He added, but Sebag had already understood from his tone: "Immediately."

The superintendent's office was on the fourth floor, right over his. Sebag quickly climbed the stairs. The door was open but he waited prudently on the threshold.

"Come in," Castello said, "and close the door behind you, please."

Sebag obeyed. Fearing a dressing-down for being absent that morning, he tried to forestall his boss.

"So, how's the training going? Are you in good shape?"

The inspector and the superintendent had met several times at foot-race competitions. At first, Sebag, who was younger and in better condition, ran far ahead. But Castello, despite being in his fifties, continued to make progress. He hoped to run a marathon someday. Paris or New York, in a year or two. Sebag offered him advice and encouragement. He'd run three marathons.

Castello didn't allow his subordinate's question to distract him.

"Listen, Gilles, I couldn't find you this morning."

"Did you need me?" Sebag answered evasively.

"Yes, I had a telephone conversation with Captain Marceau, the head of customs, about this matter of contraband cigarettes, you know . . . "

"Are they getting anywhere?"

"Slowly, but Marceau is thinking all the same about raiding a warehouse near the Saint-Charles Market and also a few bars in Perpignan. They will probably need us."

After a couple of fruitful confiscations the preceding spring, the customs men had noticed that a small gang of local criminals was setting up a regular network for the clandestine sale of cigarettes, taking advantage of the enormous disparities in price on the two sides of the Pyrenees.

"Isn't it a little early for a raid?" Sebag asked with concern.

"Probably. But the prefecture is putting pressure on us. The government wants quick results."

The subject was politically sensitive. Since the increases in cigarette prices in France in the early years of the decade, tobacconist shops were closing one after another in Roussillon, whereas cigarette sales had doubled in the border village of Le Perthus. Those mainly to blame were not the smugglers, however, but rather private individuals who bought their cigarettes in Spain. They saved twenty euros per carton, and that quickly paid for the trip. Since they couldn't stop the smokers, the prefecture had decided to set an example by putting an end to the smuggling.

"If customs acts too quickly, it may end up being a waste of time," Sebag observed.

"I know, and I said that to Marceau. But when politics get involved . . . "

"We have to look active, right?"

"You might put it that way," Castello smiled.

Sebag shook his head resentfully. If the politicians really wanted to do something about the problem, all they would have to do is harmonize the two countries' fiscal policies. The smuggling would cease immediately. Then customs could concentrate on more dangerous schemes and the police could concentrate on real crime. The kind that can't be dealt with by a simple ministerial decree. The thefts, violence, and car-burnings. The kind that really affect people's lives.

"Marceau told me that our minister was planning to take advantage of the opportunity to bring a public relations campaign here," Castello added.

"I can already see the spiel," Sebag grumbled. "They'll set up a great show: joint operation with the police, customs, and maybe even the gendarmes. They'll talk a lot, arrest a handful of smugglers, and seize a few cartons of cigarettes. And what will matter is not the result of the operation but its coverage in the media."

"Well! It's not by making remarks like those that you're going to advance your career."

Sebag refrained from snickering. He'd given up hope for his career long ago. Or rather he'd been forced to do so.

"Don't you regret now the choices you've made?" the superintendent suddenly asked him.

Sebag crossed his arms nervously. He didn't feel like talking about that. Castello caressed his graying beard. It was a little too long. His hair, too, for that matter. It was beginning to go down his neck. The chief grabbed a pen on his desk and put it in a terra cotta pot that Sebag knew well. He'd received one just like it for his participation in the *Ronde cérétane*, a famous race in the region.

"I've never had a chance to tell you, but I think it was a very courageous choice."

The remark surprised Sebag. It was the first time he'd been congratulated on this. Up to now, he'd had more the impression that he was considered a pariah. From one day to the next, he'd passed from the status of a promising young cop to that of an ugly duckling. And all this without anyone saying anything at all explicit about it.

The chief went on in a serious tone:

"When I began to understand things, it was too late."

Castello lived apart from his wife. She'd refused to follow him to Perpignan, preferring to remain in Paris. Sebag had sensed that divorce proceedings were under way. Castello had two grown sons; one was studying medicine, the other was still in high school, a senior. Until now, Castello had never shown that loneliness and distance weighed on him: a boss, rather like a father, had to be strong and resolute. Sebag agreed, and did not seek to elicit more such confidences.

"Your children are grown up now," Castello went on. "I thought I might give you a little promotion."

"God forbid!" Sebag said with alarm.

The chief frowned. His eyebrows had remained oddly brown, while his beard and his hair had gone white.

"You know, I already consider you to be the de facto coordinator of the team of inspectors. Coordinator and supervisor are more or less the same thing in practice, but officially they're very different. And the salary isn't the same."

Sebag avoided Castello's eyes. He didn't want this position and the responsibilities that went with it. But he had no argument to offer—at least none that was valid in his boss's view.

"I . . . The present situation suits me very well as it is."

Castello furtively scratched the end of his nose.

"Think about it. Your children will soon be going to university and then you'll see that a simple inspector's salary is no longer enough."

"Léo is still only in tenth grade. And then my wife works, too . . . "

"Time passes more quickly than we think. And by the time

your son has finished high school, the position will have already been filled."

Sebag shook his head in a manner he hoped looked grave.

"I promise you that I'll think about it," he said.

The superintendent was satisfied with this answer, but Sebag knew that he was annoyed. The following question confirmed his impression.

"By the way, where were you this morning?"

"Working on an investigation with Molina, uh . . . an interesting case, at least I think it is."

"But still . . . "

Sebag was aware that he was traversing a slippery slope.

"A taxi driver who has mysteriously disappeared."

"Mysteriously? Come on! How long ago?"

Sebag made a rapid calculation in his head. Sylvie Lopez had not seen her husband since Tuesday morning. Two days of absence were enough to cause a wife concern, but not enough to disturb a cop's routine.

"More than seventy-two hours," he exaggerated.

"Hmm. I suppose you've put out a missing person bulletin?"

The law allowed the police several kinds of action in such cases. A missing person bulletin could only be put out for an administrative investigation carried out in the local jurisdiction alone. A kind of minimum. For adults, it was the most common procedure.

"I was about to do that when you called me. I was also wondering whether I shouldn't put him on the national database of missing persons."

"Already?"

Castello automatically put two fingers on his lips.

"It's true that seventy-two hours is beginning to seem long," he went on. "A little too long for a simple matter of sex, isn't it?"

"That's what Molina and I thought. There might be something else behind it."

"What?"

"I'm not sure. There are some details, in fact, that don't fit with the idea that he just took off or simply had an adulterous affair."

Sebag hesitated. "The bigger the lie, the more people believe it," Molina always said.

"To judge by the first results of the investigation, the taxi driver was making lots of round-trips to Spain."

"You think he's involved in smuggling cigarettes?"

"I'm not sure, in fact, but there's something funny about it."

"Your instinct?"

Castello believed in instinct. Sebag preferred to speak of intuition, but the latter is associated with women, and it didn't seem to suit the superintendent.

"Yes, maybe . . . There's something wrong in this case."

Sebag didn't like lying. Experience had made him skilful but not comfortable in that domain.

"Do as you see fit," Castello said.

He put his fingers to his lips again.

"Do you have a cigarette?" he abruptly asked Sebag.

"I thought you'd quit."

"Yes, as I do every week," the superintendent grumbled. "And as I do every week, I started again the next day."

Sebag tapped a cigarette out of his pack of Gitanes blondes and handed it to him. Castello took the package and read the label out loud.

"'*Fumar puede matar.*' Do you buy your cigarettes in Le Perthus, too?"

"Like everyone else, I go there from time to time. I don't smoke much."

Castello laid the pack on his desk and put the cigarette to his lips. Sebag took out his lighter and held the flame up to him.

"As the proverb says, 'You can't smoke without fire.'"

The superintendent gave him a minimal smile. He closed his eyes and took a long, voluptuous drag on the cigarette. The smoke wrapped his face in a bluish halo.

"Man, it's good, this junk," he said, opening his eyes again. "And it's even better after a few days of abstinence. But . . . one mustn't ever become a prisoner of his vices. Nor his choices."

He slowly took another drag.

"I've already told you and I'll say it again: I respect the choice you made a few years ago. You're a good cop, Sebag, but a good cop isn't anything without a minimum of work."

Sebag put the lighter on the desk next to the pack of cigarettes.

"I'm leaving it all for you, boss. I've got dozens of lighters. They give them away free in Le Perthus."

"When you get involved in a case, you're the best, Gilles, but only on that condition."

"It's lucky that they give away lighters in Spain, otherwise we'd have to deal with lighter smuggling as well . . . "

Sebag interrupted himself. Castello was scratching his nose and biting his lips at the same time. It was a bad sign.

"I've always had confidence in your instinct and I hope I can continue to do so. I want to see some tangible evidence in this case of the "mysterious" disappearance of a cab driver, and see it soon."

Sebag acquiesced with a nod. He turned around and started toward the door. Castello stopped him.

"One more thing, Sebag."

"Yes, sir?"

"When I say soon, that means before tomorrow night. Understood?"

At his house, everything was oddly calm. He went into the living room. The French doors were open.

Gilles Sebag lived in Saint-Estève, on the outskirts of Perpignan. The house was constructed in a U-shape, and faced south toward the terrace and the swimming pool. On the east side, there was an office and the master bedroom with its own bathroom; on the west side, the children's bedrooms and a family bathroom. Between the two, there was the common space: a big living room/family room with an open, American-style kitchen. The house also had a garage, but Sebag had divided it into two parts to serve as both a laundry room and a gym area.

He crossed the terrace. No one outside. The water in the pool was rippling in the light breeze. A few apricot leaves were floating on the surface. He went back inside.

He opened the bar, took out the bottle of *pastis*, and poured himself a few drops in a large glass. He dropped in three ice cubes and then filled the glass at the faucet. He drank a mouthful. It was still too warm.

He called out:

"Claire!"

No answer. He called again.

"Claire!"

A high-pitched voice reached him from the back of the house.

"She's not here, Papa. There's only me."

He crossed the west wing—the term made the house sound big, he liked it—to Séverine's room. He knocked but didn't wait for her to tell him to come in. His daughter was sitting at her desk, doing her homework. Sebag saw nothing but her brown, curly mop of hair.

He laid a kiss on the nape of her neck.

"Mama isn't here?"

"No, she had a student evaluation meeting at school."

"A student evaluation meeting? Two days before vacation?"

"You're right, it's not an evaluation meeting. I think it's more like a disciplinary council meeting, something like that."

"I see. What about Léo?"

"Papa . . . He's playing basketball in Perpignan. Like every Thursday."

"True! Do I need to go get him, or did he go on his scooter?"

"He took his scooter."

Sebag hesitated between relief at not having to go out again and worrying about his son on the road with that damned scooter. He hadn't wanted to buy him one, but after a bitter fight, he'd had to give in to Léo's insistent requests relayed by his mother. We are always done in by those who know us best—or a breast. One night his wife had come to talk about the scooter with her blouse unbuttoned. She'd sat on his lap and ended up getting him to agree. Who will still claim that men are the stronger sex?

Séverine had gone back to her homework. She was in seventh grade. A good student. No problems. He put his hands on her slender shoulders and leaned over her work.

"You still have homework just before vacation?"

"No, not really, but I'm interested in the subject: Charlemagne and the organization of the Carolingian Empire."

"Woof! The *missi dominici*, the marches, Aix-la-Chapelle, the coronation in the year 800, the emperor with a full beard . . . "

"Hey, you really know your stuff!"

"Of course I know it . . . Who in the police hasn't heard about the Dominici case?"

She let out a little crystalline laugh. Enchanting. A few weeks earlier, they'd watched a documentary on this famous murder case. Sebag closed his eyes. He knew that his daughter wouldn't always laugh at his facile jokes.

Before leaving the room, he took a brief look around. A few stuffed animals were waiting patiently on the bed. A bear, a rabbit, a cat. The last witnesses to a childhood that was rapidly passing away. On the walls, posters showing fashionable singers were already publicly proclaiming the teenager's emotional turmoil. At least Sebag could rejoice in his daughter's preference for a more literary kind of song, the *chanson française à textes*, which he was discovering at the same time she was. With Léo, it was different. The boy's only passions were for sports and rap, two domains about which Sebag was proud to say he knew nothing at all.

He quietly closed the door.

Holding his glass, he went to the laundry room. He sorted the wet clothes in the washing machine. Claire had started a load in the morning before leaving for work. In the yard, he hung the clothes on the line. The wind out of the north/northwest—*la tramontane*—was singing in the trees and the sun was beating down despite the fact that evening was coming on. In just an hour, he would be able to bring everything in. He didn't mind doing household tasks. These repetitive acts carried out with care gave him time to think. He'd become accustomed to doing them after Séverine's birth, when he'd opted for a half-time parental leave in order to spend more time with his children.

That was the notorious career choice that had cost him dear.

However, the law had not excluded cops from the program. Everyone had the right to choose an adjustment of his work time during his youngest child's first three years, and no one had been able to oppose it at the police headquarters in Chartres where he was working at the time. But his decision had surprised and displeased people. A man who chooses his children over his profession—that was obviously not part of the habits and customs of the French police.

As a result, his career had been significantly slowed. After his transfer to Perpignan, he'd gone back to full-time work, but his name was probably on a black list in a secret file in the Ministry of the Interior. People all around him had been promoted, but he had received nothing. Until Castello took over three years earlier. Then Sebag had finally obtained a salary increase and, still more importantly, he had recovered his superiors' trust. That made his work more agreeable for him on a daily basis, but for the rest it was too late. Today, his life was outside the police station, and his only ambition was to do his job well enough, without pointlessly complicating his life.

In the laundry bag, he picked up a bra he didn't recognize. Pink. Small. It took him a moment to realize that it belonged to Séverine. Her first bra. He remembered a summer when she stubbornly refused to take off the top of her swimsuit. She kept it on under her T-shirt, even to go to school. She must have been seven or eight years old.

That was yesterday.

He picked up another bra. Larger, and with lace. It belonged to Claire, that one. The girl still had a way to go before she would have her mother's seductive figure. No need for nature to hurry. He hung the bras far from one another so as to avoid annoying anyone.

He'd worked hard with Molina this afternoon. He'd gotten them into deep shit with his stupid instinct. There was probably nothing mysterious about the cab driver's disappearance. When he found out, the boss would be furious. If at least they could bring the adulterous husband home by tomorrow night, they could limit the damage.

To ease his conscience, Jacques had also left a message on Lopez's answering machine while Sebag was calling the Perpignan hospital and then the main clinics in the area. He had even contacted the psychiatric clinic in Thuir. Without result. They had communicated the taxi's license number to the police patrols. And to the municipality as well. No trace of it on the streets of Perpignan. In the late afternoon, they had transmitted the number to the gendarmes. Jacques had gone back to see Sylvie Lopez at her workplace. She had given him a photo of her husband that she kept in her wallet. In the meantime, Sebag had gone to the train station and the airport. He'd questioned Lopez's colleagues. No one had seen him. Not today, and not yesterday, either. In theory, he'd completed his last trip on Tuesday, not at 11:00 P.M., as his wife supposed, but around 7:00 P.M. Finally, armed with Lopez's photo, together they had made the rounds of all the hotels near the train station, in case the taxi driver had taken his conquests there.

They'd come up with nothing.

Molina still had to work this evening. He would go to a bar where Lopez played billiards on Friday nights. Maybe he would meet the cab driver's friends there. For his part, the next day Sebag was supposed to resume the rounds of the hotels, extending the scope of his search. For the time being, he'd had enough.

Sufficient unto the day is the idleness thereof, that was his motto.

Before leaving work, they had received Lopez's police record. A conviction for car theft in 1994, when he was seventeen; another for assault and battery five years later. Lopez wasn't a greenhorn, that was something of a surprise. A second tangible fact, but it did not provide a new line of investigation any more than the first one did.

After he'd hung out the laundry, Sebag sat down on the edge of the swimming pool. Dangling his feet in the water, he enjoyed his iced *pastis*.

So where had this damned Lopez gone? He had a nice wife who not only pardoned him his escapades but also pretended she didn't know about them. No remark, no reproach. Why did he have to take advantage of her? Was it daddy's baby blues? It seems that these fathers often don't accept their responsibilities. Many couples split up within six months after the birth of a child.

Gilles had always found that strange.

Léo's birth had been the most beautiful day of his life. He found the expression appropriate, even if its banality weakened its force. After leaving the maternity ward after a long night without sleep, he'd wandered through the streets of Chartres, knowing that he wouldn't be able to sleep. He examined the faces of the men he met, thinking he could see in them the happiness of paternity. How could they be fathers and not shout it from the rooftops? How could they continue to live as they had before? For his part, he had such a feeling of fulfillment and accomplishment . . .

He'd taken part in the birth from the beginning to the end. He'd breathed with Claire, he'd pushed with her, they'd cried out together at the moment the baby emerged. Taking in his hands that little ball of a person curled up on itself, he'd felt strong. Invincible, for the first time in his life. Then he'd understood what no one had been able to explain to him. That if the bitter struggles of life shaped character, only the suffocating warmth of a maternity ward could make you a man. A new Gilles Sebag had been born that day.

Séverine had joined them scarcely two years later. A boy, a girl. The king's choice, as they say. Perfect happiness.

"Good evening!"

A sweet, melodic voice. Gilles extricated himself from his thoughts. He turned around.

"Good evening."

Claire came toward him. She wore a flowered dress, light on her tanned skin. Her walk was aerial. Earlier, she'd studied dance for ten years and her body remembered it. She bent over him and kissed him on the lips.

"You're beautiful."

She gave him an astonished look.

"That's kind," she said softly.

"No, it's not kind, it's sincere."

She bent down again and gave him a long, sensual kiss. Their lips lingered. Claire's cheeks were red. She must have been hot in the car, Sebag said to himself.

"You were late getting home."

The words had just slipped out of him, and they sounded like a reproach. Fortunately, Claire didn't notice. She limited herself to blowing out a long sigh.

"We had two difficult cases to deal with: students in tenth grade whose parents are refusing to let them repeat a year."

Claire was a French teacher. She taught in a high school in Rivesaltes. She was still passionate about her profession. He wished he could say as much about himself.

"What are we eating?" she asked.

"I don't know. There's a leftover tomato salad."

"Again . . . "

"We can fry up some bacon bits with little onions. That'll be something new."

She gave him another kiss on the lips. Tender.

"Can I let you take care of everything? I'd like to have a swim."

"No problem."

She let her dress fall to the floor and slowly unhooked her bra. Well! He didn't know that one. Then she took of her g-string panties and plunged naked into the water.

He contemplated her for a moment. He found her beautiful. Even more beautiful than before. He finished his glass, pulled his feet out of the water, dried them off, and went into the kitchen to make dinner.

When Léo came home, they were finishing the meal on the terrace. He was proud as a peacock and took off his helmet only when he sat down at the table.

"Great," he said.

"You think a tomato salad is great?" asked Séverine, who was sulking over her dish.

"No, basketball."

Sebag questioned him in turn.

"Basketball or the scooter?"

Léo laughed.

"Both, Captain."

"Lieutenant," Séverine corrected him. "Today, an inspector in the French police is called a lieutenant."

"Oh, yeah, that's right. I always forget."

"I do, too," Sebag assured him. "And I'm not the only one."

"Lieutenant!" Léo laughed. "That's too cool. Like in the States. Papa, are you Starsky or Hutch?"

"Neither. Inspector Gadget, rather."

Gilles and the children giggled. Claire, who seemed not to have followed the conversation, smiled to be in tune with the others.

After the meal, while they were alone in the kitchen, cleaning up, Gilles asked his wife:

"I have a feeling that you've been preoccupied for some time. Is it work?"

"Yes, a little," she replied without conviction. "I don't know. Maybe it's just the end of the year."

"Or a mid-life crisis?"

She pretended she was going to slap him.

"Oh, it's okay, I'm not yet forty."

"Getting pretty close."

"Next year."

"That's what I said: a few months."

He kissed her on the neck.

"You've never been so beautiful."

She ran her hand through his hair. Gently made him lift up his head.

"Do you love me?"

"Not yet, but I have a feeling that might happen some day."

"How soon?"

"Let's wait another couple of decades."

They kissed for a long time over the open door of the dishwasher. A little later, at bedtime, he undressed her. She seemed embarrassed. He closed the window and they made love. It was hot.

Claire's body shone in the moonlight. It was of an almost unreal alabaster color. Gilles caressed her skin. His fingers slipped over her neck, then her back, down to her buttocks.

"*J'aime le clair de lune. Et la lune de Claire.*"

He'd already told her that countless times, but you had to know how to repeat yourself. She turned her face toward him. Smiled at him with a little too much gravity. Her cheeks were red. Like a little while ago.

CHAPTER 5

She'd eaten. Pasta, cooked too long and not salted enough, but she'd eaten. And drunk, too.

Before she sat down in front of a plate and a glass, the young woman hadn't realized that she was hungry and thirsty. The fear that was tying her stomach in knots was too intense.

Her jailer had come in on tiptoe. He'd made no sound. She had simply noticed his calm breathing. Before untying her hands, he'd checked to make sure that the mask over her eyes was secure. She'd gotten the message, and assured him she wouldn't take off the mask. She had talked to him at length, moreover. At first in Dutch, and then, realizing her mistake, in French. The words had come to her all by themselves, even in that language that she still didn't speak very well. They gushed forth like a tide that has been too long held back. They let out her fear. To speak is to live, it is to remain a human being. And it is also to create a bond. She'd asked her kidnapper questions. About his intentions. His motivations. And his choice.

Why her?

But she'd received no response. He'd taken her hands and put them on the plate. Then he left.

She'd devoured the pasta, shoveling whole forkfuls into her greedy mouth. It was so good to eat. When the body is busy, the mind rests.

After the meal, she'd meekly lain on her stomach to make it easier for him to tie her up again.

He'd returned immediately.

He must be watching her from behind the door. But he'd knocked before coming in. That had astonished her. He'd come up to her, taken her by the arm, and guided her into a corner of the cellar. The cool dampness of the place meant that it had to be a cellar.

The man had made her touch something she had easily identified. A pail. He'd pushed firmly on her lower abdomen, and initially she'd mistaken his intentions; then she understood. Since he didn't move, she'd ended up lowering her panties in front of him, lifted her skirt, and sat down.

It took hours before she could let go. He hadn't said a word in protest. Just breathed. Always calmly.

Then he'd taken her back and tied her up again. First her hands. Behind her back. Then her feet. He'd stopped there. Hadn't tied her hands to her feet.

Her situation was less uncomfortable now. She saw that as a reward for her docility. The rules of the game were simple. That was a positive sign. It had to be a positive sign. She needed one. To keep from cracking. From screaming. Because at first, once her physical needs had been satisfied, she'd felt surprisingly calm. But now that she was alone again in the dark, fear was taking up all the space. It was coming back. Stronger than before.

CHAPTER 6

Sebag had been going over the cab driver's file for a good half hour when Molina appeared in the office. Jacques was holding a paper cup containing a hot, black liquid that Sebag refused to call coffee.

"So?" Gilles asked abruptly.

"None of his billiards buddies was there yesterday, but I got their names and phone numbers. We'll be able to contact them this morning."

Molina took a sip of his coffee before expressing his astonishment

"Weren't you supposed to be continuing the rounds of the hotels first thing this morning?"

"I started at eight o'clock sharp. I did a dozen of them and then gave up."

"Ah!"

The task had quickly annoyed him. Going from one hotel to another and showing Lopez's photo was already not exactly fun, but it was part of the job. What he'd found more difficult to put up with was the way he was received by the hotel staff. At the Hôtel de la République he'd almost blown up at the person on the reception desk, who'd told him, without even glancing at the photo, that he didn't recognize the taxi driver.

"If you want my opinion, we're wasting our time. The people who work mornings aren't going to have seen Lopez. If he'd been to one of these hotels, it would have been in the afternoon or evening, not the morning: he was with his little wife."

"There are also the hotel registers," Molina retorted.

When he'd tried to look at them, the other grump at the République had asked if he had a warrant. Sebag felt like making the asshole eat his register page by page. The older he got, the less patience he had in such situations.

Molina wasn't happy. He didn't like his colleague giving up so quickly.

"You know," Sebag continued, "I think we've already expanded the circle around the train station enough. Either he went to get laid somewhere right nearby or he could have gone almost anywhere else. After all, we're not going to visit all the hotels in the department. Do you have any idea how much work that would be?

That was a sure-fire argument. Molina made a quick calculation. The Roussillon plain formed a rough rectangle about twenty-five miles long by twelve miles wide and included not only the city of Perpignan but also the Mediterranean coast, with all its hotels. That made it certain . . . a job impossible to finish before evening. Especially for two such highly motivated inspectors. He leaned back his head and swallowed the last drop of his coffee, crushed the cup in his hand, and threw it in the wastebasket. Then he heaved a long sigh. Defeated if not convinced.

"So what do you think we should do?"

Sebag wasn't very happy about having won the argument.

"The usual. We poke around and see what turns up."

"Can you be a little more specific?"

"We'll do the most efficacious thing."

"And what's that?"

"No idea."

Sebag went back to reading Lopez's file. The cab driver's two criminal convictions. The first concerned a car theft in August 1994. The young José had gone out with some pals, apparently all sons of Spanish immigrants living in the Saint-

Jacques neighborhood of old Perpignan. They'd met some German girls during the day and were supposed to meet them that night in Canet. Since they thought it would look stupid to show up on motorbikes, they' simply stolen a car. It probably wasn't their first car theft, but this time they got caught. For speeding. Lopez was in the back seat and he had no police record, but he got two months in jail anyway, suspended: he'd argued with a policeman.

Molina interrupted Sebag's reading.

"Okay, I'm going to call Lopez's two billiards buddies. That's all that's left to do. I'll take one, you take the other. Unless you'd rather do it the other way around."

Since his partner didn't react, he added:

"Well, if you don't care, I'll take one and you take one . . . "

"Fine with me."

Lopez's second conviction went back more than six years. Some kind of fight outside a discotheque. He'd been flirting with a girl, and her boyfriend hadn't liked it. They'd shouted at each other in the discotheque, and then taken it outside. Lopez had won the fight. Naturally! He had a buddy who held the jealous guy while he beat the shit out of him. The victim got two weeks off work, and Lopez got six months in jail.

"That's perfect, Mr. Barrère, thanks for fitting us in so quickly. I'll send you one of my colleagues; he'll be there in ten minutes."

Jacques Molina hung up the phone; he looked happy.

"Well?" Sebag asked.

"It worked, pal. I got us two interviews this morning. I'm going to see Fabrice Gasch; he runs a security company in Cabestany, and I've got an appointment with him at ten-thirty. You're going to see Gérard Barrère. He's waiting for you. He also has a company located near the station. I didn't understand very well what he does, exactly, something in public relations. Lopez knew people . . . "

"Among professionals, that's understandable. Shall I meet you here afterward?"

"No, not here, it's too depressing. The less I'm here the better I feel. And by the time we've finished it'll be time for a drink. Meet you at the Carlit?"

"Great!"

"In fact, I hardly know Lopez."

Gérard Barrère gave him an armor-plated professional smile. He was a little hair ball, hardly over five feet tall. His flowered shirt, unbuttoned over his chest, revealed a dense, damp savanna. He was sweating heavily despite the air-conditioning, which was set for a temperature close to that of Stockholm on Christmas Eve.

"We met in a billiards hall and played a game. Which I won, moreover. Since then, we've played regularly. He comes every Friday."

His mouth opened wider, showing the little, pointed teeth of a carnivore.

"Generally speaking, I win," he added.

"When did you first play?"

"About six months ago. More or less."

Gérard Barrère had rejected his office in favor of sitting on chairs that were fashionable but nonetheless soft and comfortable. A low round table separated him from the inspector. The room was well-lighted, the walls light-colored, and the furniture made of glass. Everything gave an impression of transparency and conviviality. Gérard Barrère's gestures were ample and gentle but his apparent affability was contradicted by two bright, piercing little eyes hidden behind round glasses.

"Do you play for money?" Sebag asked.

It was a direct question, as Sebag was well aware. That was his way of refusing the crony relationship that his interlocutor was offering him. Barrère pursed his lips but continued to smile.

"Oh, Inspector, how could you think that?"

His right hand rotated the silver band on his Rolex. He was lying and didn't even try to hide it. One might even say that it amused him.

"When did you last play with him?"

"Last Friday, I suppose."

"You suppose?"

Sebag felt a tingling in his fingers. He was beginning to get annoyed.

"Some weeks I play billiards two or three evenings in a row. But if Lopez was there, I suppose it was a Friday."

"That doesn't help me much."

"I'm very sorry about that."

Sebag looked carefully, but he detected no sorrow in Barrère's eyes.

"Was he alone?"

"What do you mean?"

"I thought my question was clear enough: was José Lopez alone or was someone with him the last time you saw him?"

Barrère took his time before answering. As if he were weighing the pros and cons. His eyes left Sebag's and looked somewhere behind him.

"Yes, of course, he was alone. As usual."

Barrère was still lying, but this time trying not to show it. He turned his eyes away from the inspector again. Sebag took advantage of this to have a close look at the man. He had little, close-set eyes under thick but delicate eyebrows. His mustache looked like a freshly trimmed broom. A thick neck under a dimpled chin. The body was husky without being fat. Sebag's eyes moved down Barrère's white, hairy arms and stopped at his small hands. Manicured. Being ugly doesn't mean you don't have the right to take care of yourself.

Since Barrère was still looking behind him, Sebag decided to turn around. On the other side of the glass wall that protected the office from indiscreet ears, a pale secretary sat facing them, diligently filing her nails. When she saw the inspector looking at her, she quickly pressed her legs together.

"What exactly do you do, Mr. Barrère? I'm not sure I completely understand."

The mustache lengthened as Barrère smiled.

"I'm an event organizer," he answered, handing him a business card.

Sebag examined it closely. On it was the name—Perpign'And Co—along with the firm's address, phone number, and website.

"That doesn't get me very far," he said.

Barrère furrowed his brow and raised the left corner of his upper lip, hollowing his cheek. This meant something like: "You're really stupid, but it's okay, I'm willing to explain it to you."

"I organize events for businesses. Seminars, parties, weekend retreats. Sometimes trips."

Sebag looked doubtful.

"And you do all right?"

"I can't complain," he answered, smiling complacently and making a broad sweep with his arm to invite Sebag to admire the luxury of his place.

Objects worth their weight in cash and ostentation were arranged here and there on the glass furniture. A few old books, probably rare, a statuette in genuine ivory, numbered Tintin figurines, a coaster containing ancient Roman coins. On the desk was a miniature replica of Alberto Giacometti's *Walking Man*.

"It's a copy, but it's a real one," Barrère explained.

Sebag pointed to a garish painting, the only decoration that hung on the walls. Composed of splashes of color with a preference for blood red and goose-shit green, it reminded Sebag of the first autopsy he'd witnessed when he was a young cop.

"And that's a real what?"

Barrère had seen what he was looking at. He smiled.

"The work of a young Catalan artist. A complete madman. Very nice. When I say very nice, I'm referring to the artist, obviously. His work is a little more . . . complex and tormented."

"You like it?"

"Let's say I put up with it."

Sebag didn't hide his astonishment.

"In fact, I'm doing him a favor by displaying it. Lots of people pass through here, you know, CEOs, politicians. People who count. That's useful for a young artist."

Sebag was not fooled. Barrère's allusion to his connections was no accident. It was a kind of notice, a warning.

"Events are a big thing in business these days," Barrère went on. "It's a form of management that's currently very trendy. An event can range from a simple Christmas tree to an outing to go canyoning, by way of a weekend in Morocco, tuna fishing on the Mediterranean, or a private box at a rugby match."

"Are there many of you doing this in Perpignan?"

"No, I'm the only one. And especially, the best!"

He laughed at his own joke. Sebag, frowning, didn't even try to look amused. He looked behind him again. The young secretary had put her legs back under her desk. She was on the telephone. Judging by the excited gestures she was making, he guessed the call was in no way professional. He winked complicitly to the Perpignan king of the event.

"There are good sides to your business, it seems."

Barrère pretended to be offended.

"Don't jump to conclusions, Inspector, she's the daughter of a friend, a student whom I took on as an intern for the summer. As I was telling you a moment ago, our business concerns relationships, and we have to know how to be useful."

"All right, then," Sebag said in conclusion, "if you haven't anything else to add."

"I'm sorry, Inspector. I wish I could have been more helpful."

Barrère had stood up, ready to usher his guest out. But Sebag remained seated, flipping through the little blue notebook in which he wrote down the important points in his interviews.

"All the same, it's odd . . . "

He circled a few words written in his notebook.

"What's odd?" Barrère asked impatiently.

"Maybe I made a mistake. I probably wrote down one of your answers wrong."

Barrère's smile grew broader. A little too broad to be sincere.

Sebag turned several pages, pretending to re-read certain sentences. A petty revenge. It was amusing the way sometimes the person standing up could find himself in a position of inferiority.

"Regarding Lopez . . . "

Barrère shifted his weight from one foot to the other. Irritated. Or not very at ease.

"Yes . . . ?"

Sebag decided to try a bluff. It didn't cost anything to try. Especially when you'd arrived at a standstill in an investigation.

"Another witness told us that Lopez had someone with him the last time you played billiards."

"Really?"

Barrère changed his position again, crossed his arms over his belly and then immediately uncrossed them.

"Who told you that?"

Sebag leafed through his notebook again. Stopped at a blank page, holding his pen in the air.

"You don't want to change any of your statements?"

"My . . . statements? I thought we were just talking. My statements . . . All of a sudden that sounds very official!"

He puffed a little inaudibly and sat down again.

"Oh, and then after all . . . "

He shrank back into the cushion of his armchair.

"I didn't think that all this could be that important for you and I was afraid of getting Lopez in trouble. He's married. But . . . since you already know about it."

He hesitated a little longer, then began to talk.

"In fact, we played only one game that evening. There was a young woman with Lopez. They left together around nine-thirty."

Sebag inwardly congratulated himself.

"How would you describe this young woman?"

"Tall, blonde. Quite pretty. If you like that type."

"What type?"

"The Germanic type. Or Scandinavian. She spoke French well but with a northern European accent."

"Did this woman have a name?"

"He introduced us to her as Vanessa."

Something in his tone suggested that he was skeptical.

"That wasn't her real name?"

"I don't know. Aren't all tall blondes called Vanessa?"

"Is that what you think?"

"In a certain milieu, yes!"

"What milieu?"

He looked down at his patent leather shoes, and seemed to regret having spoken too fast.

"You know what I mean . . . The milieu of loose women and sex for money."

Sebag carefully noted down this last information.

"Anything else? Something unusual, a detail?"

"Uh . . . yes. The young woman . . . had a bird on her right shoulder. That is . . . she had a tattoo of a bird."

"And that was which evening, again?"

He seemed surprised by the question.

"Well, Tuesday night, of course. I thought you knew that already."

Leaving Barrère's office, Sebag felt rather proud of himself. He gave the young "intern" a friendly smile and almost ran into a big, crew-cut guy who seemed to be waiting. The client looked him up and down with curiosity.

In the end, he hadn't needed to bluff. Without trickery, Molina had obtained the same information from another of Lopez's buddies. It was in fact Tuesday night that the cab driver had played billiards, in the company of a blonde.

"That coincides with what I was told, and that's good," Sebag commented, "but it's still not very much. And above all it seems to confirm that we're dealing with a simple case of adultery."

"Yes and no. That still doesn't explain this two-day absence. By the way, are you drinking something?"

Molina had arrived at the bar before him, and was drinking a *pastis*. Sebag asked for a lemonade with barley water. Rafel, the bar's owner, had foreseen his order and brought it immediately.

"*Vols tambe un caf?*" ("Would you like coffee, too?")

"No thanks, not now. Mainly, I'm thirsty."

Fabrice Gasch, Lopez's other friend, ran a surveillance firm. He provided watchmen for small and large stores in the city and doormen for a few nightclubs. He recruited mainly in the department's boxing clubs, and had himself boxed with the professionals a few times, on the quiet. Gasch and Lopez had known each other since they were children; they'd grown up together in the Saint-Jacques neighborhood. Pals, they had also been accomplices: it was Gasch who'd helped Lopez beat up a rival outside a discotheque ten years earlier.

Perpign'And Co sometimes hired guards. Barrère had taught Gasch how to play billiards. One night Gasch had invited Lopez to join them and that's how the three men had gotten into the habit of meeting regularly.

"He spontaneously acknowledged that Lopez was accompanied by a young woman Tuesday night?"

"Yes, almost. First he told me that he'd seen Lopez Tuesday, and when I asked if the cab driver was alone, he admitted that he wasn't. After two or three seconds of hesitation, maybe."

"Did he know the young woman?"

"No, it was the first time he'd seen her."

"What did he tell you about her?"

"Not much. That she was blond, tall, rather pretty, with a tattoo on her shoulder. A description that tallies with the one Barrère gave you."

Sebag was pensive.

"I wonder why Barrère tried to hide the fact that Lopez was with someone. He claimed that it was to avoid getting Lopez in trouble . . . But Gasch didn't hesitate even though he was closer to the couple. He's the one who should have tried to hide his buddy's romantic affairs."

"Not necessarily."

"Why not?"

"If he knew about the relationship between Lopez and his wife, he knew there was hardly any risk in talking to you about the blonde."

"Maybe you're right," he conceded.

However, he wasn't really convinced. He had a feeling there was another possible explanation.

"He also tried to lie about the date of their last meeting. He said it was Friday and not Tuesday evening. But that's very important information . . . That said, he didn't stick to his lie, either. He gave in as soon as I bluffed."

"So?"

"So I don't know. It's a little as if . . . As if he'd been afraid, at first, of saying too much, and then later of attracting our attention by telling too big a lie."

"A little fuzzy, huh?"

"For sure. But maybe it would be worth poking around a little along that line."

"How?"

"That's the problem. We can't pick a fight with Barrère. For the moment, we're concerned only with the disappearance of an adult person: no misdemeanor has been committed, much less a crime."

"We have to draw one conclusion, however," Molina said, looking at his watch.

"What?"

"It's time to eat. You staying here?"

"No, I've got an errand to run. I'd like to buy a cell phone for Léo. He's going to a summer camp next week, and if I want to hear from him from time to time, I think I'm going to have to get him a phone."

"A cell phone? He's going to be one happy kid."

"Are you kidding? His reaction will be something like: "Finally!" All his friends have one, and some of them have had one since they were in primary school, so you can imagine . . . "

"And you've held out up to now . . . Bravo. What heroism."

"Go ahead, make fun of me. What about your sons, do they have cell phones?"

Molina had two boys. The younger was Léo's age, the elder would soon be eighteen.

"They've had them for years. After the divorce, I had to: they allow me to talk to my boys without going through their mother."

He lifted his arms toward the heavens and then let them fall back heavily. Fatalist.

"Note that it's cheaper to buy one now," he went on. "It'll cost you less."

"I don't understand."

"Well . . . when you get divorced!"

For Jacques, three things in life were inevitable: death, hemorrhoids, and, if you were married, divorce. He'd mocked Gilles ever since the latter had told him one day that in eighteen years of married life, he'd never cheated on Claire.

"You're a poor imbecile if you've never tried to see what else is out there, and a dull cretin if you think that being as beautiful as she is, your wife has always limited herself to your pretty little face. And when I talk about your face, I mean . . . "

Sebag was walking through the streets of Perpignan, looking down on the Basse. The little river ran quietly in its channel through the downtown area, below street level. Its grass-covered banks looked like nice places to hang out, but they were not accessible to the public. Planted on the lawn, pink, white, and red oleanders grew their brightly colored leaves as far as the sidewalk.

Sebag was satisfied: he'd found a cell phone that could actually be used to make calls. He'd had to wage a long battle with the salesperson, but had finally managed to get a model without too many gadgets. He'd yielded on the camera, though. He imagined that Léo would enjoy sending pictures even more than having a conversation, and the idea of receiving photos from his son from time to time during his vacation had convinced him.

The police headquarters in Perpignan was a grim building, a three-story block that looked like one of the low-cost housing towers in the working-class neighborhoods of the northern part of the city. Two sickly palm trees framed the main entrance. In the reception hall, Martine, the young policewoman on duty there, gave him a warm smile. Sebag slid his badge over an electronic reader. The door opened with a click and allowed him to push it open. He briskly climbed the two flights of stairs that led to his office.

Jacques was already back. With both feet on his desk, he was reading *L'Equipe*. A cup was sitting next to him. Sebag had wolfed down a sandwich and hadn't taken time to drink a cup of coffee. He felt a terrible craving but didn't feel like going back downstairs to drink the lousy stuff dispensed in the cafeteria.

"I asked a couple of pals at the gendarmerie to put out a search bulletin for Lopez's car," Molina told him. "I also went by the Vice Squad: they do in fact have a Vanessa in their files, a blonde but small and rather plump. I've got her address, and I'll try to stop and see her this evening."

He winked at Sebag before going back to his newspaper.

Sebag looked at his watch. It was three o'clock. They hadn't found anything. Soon, Castello would be blowing his top when he learned that they'd wasted precious time on a case that wasn't worth it. At least he might give up that stupid idea of a promotion.

Gilles was already thinking about the weekend. The last one all of them would spend together for some time. Tuesday, Léo was going to take the train to the Cévennes, where he would spend a month at a special motocross camp. Séverine was leaving the next day with the parents of a friend of hers for a vacation on the Costa Brava. The following week, it would be Claire's turn. Rather than spend her time alongside the pool with her dear and loving husband, she had decided to book a Mediterranean cruise for herself. He couldn't blame her. But he didn't at all like the idea of being alone part of the month of July.

So, what about this Lopez?

He tried to concentrate on the investigation. The difficulties they'd run into made him think that it wasn't just a banal romantic escapade; there was something else. However, no matter how much he reflected on it, the information they'd gathered up to that point in no way justified that impression. So what was it? Instinct? Nonsense. And why not simply the unconscious hope that a "great" case would soon help him forget the absence of his family members?

He went down to the cafeteria to drink a Perrier. The headquarters' break area was in fact only an old storage room whose walls had been torn down. It had been fitted with five chairs attached to the walls and two vending machines: one distributed hot drinks, the other cold ones. Sebag put a couple of coins in the cold drink machine and received his can of water. Despite the smoking ban, an odor of cold tobacco lingered in this closed space. He opened the window. The warm air that flowed in carried the acid effluvium from exhaust pipes. The headquarters was next to a highway interchange. National Route 9 came in from Narbonne over the Arago bridge before heading out toward Barcelona, and crossed the National Route 116, which wound around toward Andorra. Barcelona, Andorra . . . In Roussillon, the highway signs encouraged you to dream and to travel.

When he got back upstairs, Molina was hanging up his phone. He was beaming.

"You know the Força Real hermitage?"

"A little. I went running there once. But I much prefer the Sant-Marti chapel above Castelnou."

"Oh, yeah," Molina said, looking as if he was thinking about something else.

"Over thirteen hundred feet difference in elevation, if I remember correctly."

"For Força Real?"

"Yes. When I went there, the hermitage was closed but the view is superb."

"It's quiet up there, in any case," Molina commented, all smiles.

"That's true."

His colleague's jubilation surprised Sebag.

"Very quiet, in fact." Molina went on. "When you abandon

a car there, you can be sure that the gendarmes won't find it right away."

"Which means . . . ?" Sebag urged, thinking he'd understood.

"Which means I've got a pal at the police brigade in Millas who has just called me. Lopez's taxi has been found in the parking lot at the hermitage."

"Shit! It can't be true. And Lopez?"

"No trace of him."

"Well, well . . . "

The case was getting interesting. A taxi and no driver: so there *was* a mystery, after all. Sebag thought quickly. An hour to get together a team of technicians and get over there. Two hours there to check all the usual things and inspect the area around the hermitage. Before seven, they'd be in the boss's office for a quick summary and maybe a few congratulations. Then enough time to throw together a report and give instructions to the teams on duty over the weekend, and off he'd go! He'd be home by eight at the latest. Wasn't life great?

CHAPTER 7

"Will you play with me, Grandpa?"

The boy set his blue eyes on his immobile grandfather.

"Hey, hey, Grandpa . . . "

He put his delicate fingers in the big, dry hand of the man who was still sitting motionless in front of his glass of *pastis*.

"Will you play *pétanque*?"

Louis kept at it with the stubborn patience a four-year-old can show.

"Will you play, Grandpa?"

Despite his clear, high-pitched voice, he couldn't get his grandfather's attention.

Finally the boy dropped a ball on the table and overturned the glass of *pastis*. Robert emerged from his lethargy and seeing the damage done, swore. He met his daughter's saddened eyes and got hold of himself. His grandson's repeated questions finally made it into his consciousness. He managed a slight smile and got up with difficulty. In any case, the alcohol couldn't do anything for him.

He picked up the set of *pétanque* balls and put his hand on Louis's shoulder.

"I'll start," the boy demanded. "I get to throw out the *conchon*."

"The *cochonnet*, Robert automatically corrected.

"Yes, the *conchonnet*, and I get to throw it out first, okay?"

Robert led Louis toward the area in the campground

reserved for *pétanque*. He distractedly greeted the four vacationers who were already playing a game. He recognized at
least two of them. Jean and his son. How did he know them?
Oh yes, Patrick. It must have been twenty years ago now.
Twenty years . . . the age of the young Dutch woman.

"Are you all right, Robert?" Jean asked, looking at him over
his glasses.

"I'm all right," Robert answered without the slightest conviction.

At first, people had felt sorry for him, pitied him. More, in
fact, than the young woman, whom few of them had known:
most of the vacationers now staying in the Oleanders campground had arrived after the tragedy happened.

"Making a discovery like that, just imagine, what a shock.
It's hard to get over it, that's normal! It'll get better in a while,
you'll see. You'll forget . . . "

It was two weeks now, and he hadn't forgotten a thing.
Josetta's crushed-in face continued to haunt him. Day and night.
People had gotten tired of hearing him talk about it and had
ended up turning away. Then Robert had retreated into silence.

The local newspapers had also quickly gotten tired of the
subject. The murder of the young Dutch woman had been in
the headlines the first day. The following day, it was accorded
a less prominent place, but it was still on the front page. Then
it had slipped into the inside pages and finally disappeared.
Since there were no new developments and the investigation
wasn't getting anywhere, it fell victim to oblivion and indiffer-
ence. Argelès was preparing to receive hordes of tourists. As it
did every summer, the population of the area was going be mul-
tiplied by a factor of ten or twelve in less than a week. There was
no longer a minute to lose. Soon the tourists would be there.
Everything had to be ready. Everything had to be beautiful.

Only Robert's torments perpetuated the memory of the
young woman.

"I threw out the *conchon*, Grandpa. I've also thrown a ball. Your turn to play."

Robert looked at the playing area. He had some trouble remembering what he was doing there. The *cochonnet* had been stopped by the planks that enclosed the area. But where was the ball Louis had thrown?"

"Go ahead, Grandpa," the boy said impatiently.

Finally Robert located Louis's ball. Only a yard from his feet. He threw his ball. Or rather he tossed it. Luckily or unluckily, it struck the *cochonnet*. Louis was simultaneously dazzled and furious.

"You're cheating, Grandpa. You're bigger than I am, you should stand farther away."

He went to draw a line a good yard behind them. Robert, docile, moved back. Louis took advantage of this to advance a bit. He positioned himself right next to his first ball, which he shamelessly picked up. It's amusing, he's always been like that, Robert thought. A nitpicker and a poor sport, exactly like his father . . . He was not being fair to his grandson, he knew, and didn't care.

In fact, it did him good.

Louis threw another ball that bounced off the plank and hit his grandfather's. He shouted with joy and pride.

"I beat you, Grandpa, one point for me."

Robert accepted the rules improvised by his grandson. He picked up the *cochonnet* and handed it to him.

The police had questioned him. Briefly. They'd seen how upset he'd been by the discovery of the body and hadn't gone on. After all, he didn't know much. He'd just accidentally found the body.

The path to the beach had remained closed for twenty-four hours. The team from the crime lab had gone over the sector with a fine-toothed comb but found nothing. At least that's the impression he'd gotten from reading the newspaper. Every morning for a week, he'd gone to the closest cafe to look at *L'Indépendant*. He sat down on the seaside terrace and ordered an espresso, which he sugared heavily. As he used to do. It was good. And to hell with his diabetes! Death would come when it came. Whatever people did, whatever they said, death always had the last word.

Always.

According to the journalists, the investigation was not advancing. The police seemed not to have any sure leads, and since there was no evidence of sexual violence, they were saying that the crime might have been committed by a vagrant. Which meant they had no idea.

After the autopsy, Josetta's body had been returned to Holland, where it had been cremated the following day. A moving ceremony, to use the reporter's expression. The article was accompanied by a photo of the victim's parents and sister. Weeping.

The game of *pétanque* continued without hitches. Robert was careful to throw his balls randomly. Louis played his turn over until he'd placed his ball near the *cochonnet*. Not knowing how to count, he innocently jumped from five to ten points. Robert congratulated him.

"Ten to zero, you've won, bravo."

Louis was modest in victory.

"I can't wait for papa to come, he's better than you are, but maybe I'll beat him anyway. Shall we play another game, Grandpa?"

Robert ran his wrinkled hand through his grandson's short brown hair.

"Later, Louis, later. You're too good for me. You've worn me out."

"If you want," the boy persisted, "I can let you have a handicap."

"Thanks. We'll see next time."

"Then you have to put everything away," Louis ordered as he went off toward the campground's play area.

Robert picked up the balls and the *cochonnet*. He put them in their plastic case and went back to the trailer. Florence was waiting for him under the awning, sprawled on a seat, her legs spread and her belly full-blown.

"Thanks to him. He loves playing with you."

Robert collapsed on a chair. He took up his crossword magazine and leafed through it looking for a new puzzle. Most of them had been begun, but none had been finished. He closed the magazine, then reached for the bottle of *pastis*. He hesitated. He didn't really want any.

"You're drinking a lot these days, aren't you?" Florence said.

He replied with more weariness than anger.

"Your mother is no longer here to bug me about it. Don't feel obliged to replace her."

He poured himself a comfortable dose of *pastis* and filled the rest of the glass with the lukewarm water from a carafe on the table. Florence bit her lip to keep from crying. She'd never seen her father in such a state. She watched him drink half his glass in a single draft.

He'd changed. Paler. Thinner. Older. Alarmed by the sadness of his tone on the telephone, she'd decided to come down earlier than planned. Without waiting for her husband's vacation time. She was on maternity leave, pregnant with a little Anaïs, and had nothing to do with her days except to rest and take care of Louis. Provided the two could get along. She'd taken the night train from Paris with her son. Got off at Elne in the wee hours of the morning. Robert had come to pick them up in the car. She was startled to see his hollow cheeks, the bags under his eyes, and his wan complexion. Louis had refused to kiss his grandfather.

Robert looked up from his glass of *pastis*.

"When is Arnaud getting here?"

He didn't really care, but the tears in his daughter's eyes had struck a chord in his soul that was still sensitive. Poor Florence had nothing to do with what was happening to him.

"Not before July 10," she replied, sniffling. "He's got a lot of work."

Florence's husband was an architect in a large firm outside Paris. He always had trouble getting away for vacations.

"I'm not sure it was wise for you to come, my dear Flo."

"Why do you say that, Papa?"

Robert examined the bottom of his glass.

"I'm not an ideal companion for a woman in your condition."

Florence struggled up from her seat and came to sit alongside her father. She put her arms around his neck.

"Does it bother you that I'm here?"

He managed to smile at her. The presence of his daughter forced him to make superhuman efforts.

"No, my dear. On the contrary."

He pushed the empty glass away.

"I'm mad at myself for not being able to show you a better face. I'm trying but I just can't do it."

The last words were muffled by a repressed sigh.

"Don't worry about me, I've grown up. I know that for you I'll always be your beloved little girl, the youngest in the family. But I'm not a child any more. And haven't been for some time now . . . "

She massaged her father's neck. For a long time, they hadn't had any physical contact. She realized that they were entering new territory. The roles were being reversed: now it was she who was going to care for him.

"I think you should see a doctor."

She felt his body stiffen.

"I'm not sick," he protested.

"It's a kind of sickness," she said gently. "And like all sick-nesses, it can be treated."

He stood up.

"You want me to see a psychotherapist? At my age?"

"There's no age limit for that. No shame either. But if you prefer, first go see a general practitioner. He'll at least be able to give you some pills to help you sleep."

"Sleep? That's all I do . . . "

Her father's bad faith made her smile in spite of herself.

"You aren't sleeping, you're drowsing. You nod off a dozen times a day but you don't sleep at night. You try as hard as you can to be quiet, but trailers are small . . . I hear you."

Robert went to bed early every night. Exhausted. Sometimes he fell asleep quickly, but he never slept soundly. He woke several times during the night and finally got up to lie under the awning. There, in the relative softness of the morn-ing, he waited, listening for the campground's first sounds. Footsteps on the gravel, a toilet flushing, a toad whistling in the distance. When he heard the first movements in the trailer, he got up and went to the closest bakery. Twenty minutes round trip. Fortunately, the road ran far from the beach.

"Do I keep you from sleeping?"

She seized the opportunity he offered her.

"A little, yes. And in my condition, I need to sleep."

She caressed her round belly.

"All right, dear Flo, I'll go see a doctor. Do you remember Dr. Pascal? We used to go to him when you had earaches. I think he's supposed to retire at the end of this year. It would be a chance to say good-bye to him."

Chapter 8

Sebag knew only one remedy for Monday morning blues: work all weekend! Unfortunately, he hadn't worked the day before. Worse yet, he'd had an excellent time with his family. So he looked like Death warmed over when he came into police headquarters that Monday morning.

Before going up to his office, he stopped in to say hello to the men on duty in the *service de quart*, the equivalent of the emergency room at a hospital. He glanced distractedly at the log and then approached François Ravier, who headed the service.

"I'm working on the case of the cab driver who disappeared, the one whose car the police found at Força Real. Do you know if there's anything new on that?"

"Apparently not. But ask Ménard. He's the one that was assigned to it yesterday."

François Ménard was the officer responsible for the weekend teams. A native of Picardy. A good cop. Serious, even austere, according to some. Sparing with words, not with his work. A grind, a real one, whose example made others feel they should work harder.

In their office, Jacques Molina was on the phone. Pretty annoyed. He was talking with his ex-wife. Sebag greeted him and sat down. He was in no hurry to go to work.

The preceding day, Gilles and Claire had taken the children to the summit of Le Canigou for the first time. By way of the Mariailles refuge. Four hours up, three hours down. A marvelous hike. The trail wound through the forest undergrowth, then slalomed between broom and wild pansies. Afterward, it continued over loose stones and ended with a climb through a vertiginous chimney. Nothing insurmountable. If you didn't have vertigo.

Up there, the view was splendid. On the rocky peak, there were about twenty people picnicking around the ashes of a gigantic fire. Several years earlier, the Catalan tradition of the Bonfires of Saint John had been revived. A few days before the ceremony, the pluckiest carried logs, vinestocks, and bundles of vine shoots up to the summit. They piled them in a pyramid to make the mountain even higher. On the night of June 23, the peak was set afire and, weather permitting, the *flama del Canigo* could be seen all over Roussillon.

On the way back, they'd had a snowball fight with the last *névés*.

Molina hung up. He stirred his coffee angrily. The bitter odor dissipated the warm fragrance of the broom that the thought of Le Canigou had put into Sebag's nostrils. Jacques's face relaxed. He eyes became complicitous.

"I don't know what you did this weekend, but obviously you haven't come down again yet."

Sebag knew that he was going to disappoint his colleague. He hadn't any salacious anecdote to tell him.

"We went to Le Canigou."

"Ah . . . "

Jacques had played rugby for twenty years and during that time exhausted all taste for physical effort. His passion for sports was now expressed only on the bleachers of the Aimé-Girai stadium, the temple of Perpignan rugby.

"Have you ever climbed to the top?" Gilles asked.

"My father took me there when I was a kid. I've never gone back."

Le Canigou is to northern Catalans what Mt. Fuji is to the Japanese. A sacred mountain and a symbol of identity. A local legend says that God laid his hand on the Earth and between his fingers three mountains rose up: Sinai, Olympus, and Le Canigou. However, many Catalans seldom went up there, or had in fact never even climbed it once.

"I never get tired of it," Sebag went on with the fervor of a new convert. "The climb is worth making, and not just for the views from the summit. When you go by way of the Mariailles refuge, the whole hike is superb."

In the last part of the ascent, Léo had challenged him. They'd raced, leaving the trail and its endless switchbacks and climbing straight up the slope. The little devil! He'd pulled out all the stops but Sebag had showed him once more—probably for the last time—that he was still the boss. That night, Léo had devoured two plates of pasta and gone to bed. By eighty-thirty, he was snoring like a baby. Gilles had had a little more trouble going to sleep, and had awakened this morning with cramps and a very stiff back.

"By the way," Molina remembered, "our meeting with Castello isn't until ten o'clock this morning."

"If I'd known . . . "

Usually, the Monday meeting began at nine on the dot. Current investigations were reviewed and the boss set the priorities for the coming week. It was the only day on which Sebag couldn't come in late.

"So we're free until ten. Do you know why?"

"No idea."

"Do you know if there's something new in the Lopez case?"

"I talked with Ménard a little while ago. The police combed the area around the hermitage but didn't find anything. A search bulletin has been put out."

Sebag booted up his computer and connected to the Internet. He took out the business card Barrère had given him and copied the address of the website of Perpign'And Co. There were several rubrics. The types of organization: travel, parties, weekends; the themes: sports, culture, entertainment. He found the site attractive. A little flashy, perhaps, or even enticing. Lots of pictures of pretty girls, often not wearing much. A subliminal message?

"Incidentally, did you meet the famous Vanessa?" he asked Molina.

"No. I only saw her roommate. Vanessa is in Barcelona for the week. But I was able to see photos. She's clearly not the one who was with Lopez."

"We kind of suspected that."

Sebag started printing several pages of the Perpign'And Co. website and then moved on to other sites. He looked at the local newspaper long enough to be sure he hadn't missed any news over the weekend, and then surfed sites specializing in training advice for runners.

"Shall we go?" Molina asked.

Sebag looked at his watch. The hour had passed very quickly.

Lambert and Llach were already waiting in the meeting room. Ménard was there too. And a young guy sitting to the right of Castello. Sunglasses on his forehead, fashionable linen jacket, relaxed. He was tall, emanated a lot of energy and a little too much self-assurance. Raynaud and Moreno came in. In house, they were called the "brotherly friends" or "the duet." Because they were inseparable and their names sounded like something on a music-hall program. Behind their backs, the two of them were called instead "the laugh brigade" because of their total lack of humor and the way in which they went through life as if they were attending a perpetual funeral.

Sebag passed in front of the air conditioner, which was running full tilt. He turned it down and went to sit on the other side of the room.

The boss cleared his throat. It was serious. Everyone sensed it and silence fell immediately. Castello signaled to Lambert, who was closest to the exit. The young inspector understood and closed the door.

"Gentlemen, I'd like to introduce Cyril Lefèvre. He's a superintendent at the office of International Technical Cooperation. He's just gotten off the plane from Paris. I delayed our weekly meeting by one hour so that he could be with us."

The Technical Cooperation office is a kind of diplomatic police assigned in particular to exchanges of information with police forces in other countries.

"Cyril Lefèvre is here in connection with a case to which we will have to give priority this week. It involves the disappearance of a young Dutch woman. But I'll let Cyril tell you the facts in greater detail."

Another disappearance, thought Sebag. It's the rule of threes!

Cyril Lefèvre quickly surveyed his interlocutors and then went straight to the heart of the matter without any polite preamble. He was the direct type.

"Ingrid Raven is a Dutch citizen, nineteen years old. A university student, she was vacationing in the region. She was traveling alone. She took a flight from Amsterdam to Gerona on June 10, a Sunday, and then got on the train to Perpignan."

He took an electronic organizer out of his hip pocket. He turned it on and continued his narrative while it started up.

"She usually called her parents every evening, but they have had no word from her for a week. Her last call goes back precisely to the evening of June 26. They have left her numerous messages on her cell phone but there has been no reply."

Glancing from time to time at his agenda—which he seemed to use mainly as a notebook—Lefèvre outlined the case for the Perpignan police. Ingrid Raven was studying history of art, he told them, and had chosen fauvism as the subject of her thesis. Hence her stay in the region. She'd reserved a room in a student residence hall but stayed there only a few days. She made friends with some local people and went to stay with them in Collioure. These friends were an artist couple who owned a house in the village: that was all she'd told her parents. Ingrid had no car and traveled by train and bus. Her parents had advised her against hitchhiking, but were not sure that she had taken their advice on the subject.

During his presentation, Lefèvre handed around photos. In some of them, the young woman's hair was red, in others blond. She had a pretty smile and emanated *joie de vivre.*

"Ingrid Raven's parents are very worried, I can tell you that. Their daughter has never gone for such a long time without contacting them. The Dutch authorities request that we look into this disappearance with all due diligence. A request relayed by the Minister of the Interior, who also wants results."

Superintendent Castello took the floor again to add something intended to galvanize his troops.

"Ingrid Raven's father is a policeman in Amsterdam."

Cyril Lefèvre typed a few notes on his electronic organizer and then laid it on the table.

"Any questions, gentlemen?" he asked.

Llach didn't hesitate. He often spoke up first in work meetings. An activist in the professional association, he had adopted above all the labor unionist's habit of making objections of principle: before attacking a problem, make sure it can't be circumvented.

"If I understand correctly, the parents are our only source of information."

"Correct," Lefèvre acknowledged.

"I ask because I've already encountered a case in which a father claimed that his son had disappeared. After investigating, we found out that in fact they had been at odds for several weeks. The boy no longer maintained contact, and he'd even moved without notifying his father. We wasted our time."

"I have to say that I hadn't thought of that possibility," Lefèvre admitted. "I suppose our colleagues in Holland made sure the parents were reliable before alerting us."

"Let's hope," Molina muttered.

Castello spoke again to reframe the discussion.

"There are no grounds for entertaining such a hypothesis. We have an official request from the Dutch authorities and we will investigate. With all our diligence and experience."

There was a pause. As there was every time the superintendent allowed himself to be carried away by a certain bombast.

"Our first task will be to draw up a detailed account of this young woman's activities," Castello went on. "We have to find her room in the residence hall and her friends from Collioure. Since she was working on fauvism, we can also assume that she went at least once to the museum in Céret."

"Collioure and Céret are under the jurisdiction of the gendarmes," Llach noted.

Lefèvre looked at him like an explorer in an equatorial jungle who has just discovered a tribe that still practices cannibalistic rites.

"Is that a problem?"

"We have excellent relationships with the department's gendarmes," Castello assured him. "If I am not mistaken, what concerns Inspector Llach is whether the work load that you're asking us to take on will be equitably distributed among the various services."

Llach scowled at this ironic presentation of his thought but did not contest it.

"That question does not fall within my domain," Lefèvre explained. "It will be up to you to make the arrangements, but it seems to me preferable that the responsibility not be shared. And I even think it should remain in the hands of the local police. It's a matter of efficiency, I'd say!"

Sebag sensed his colleagues becoming less reserved as Lefèvre's flattery began to take effect. He met the young superintendent's eyes. They made him think of sparrows: always alert, they fixed on people only reluctantly, and flew away at the first sign of danger. At first, he'd taken that for modesty; now he knew he'd been wrong.

The discussion went on for a good quarter of an hour. Sun was pouring into the room, which the presence of so many people had already made warm. Lambert quietly got up and put the air conditioning back on maximum.

Sebag decided to speak up.

"The photos of Ingrid Raven that the superintendent has shown us suggest that the young woman likes to change her style. Is it possible to know how her hair was done and what color it was when she arrived in France?"

"Photo no. 1 is the most recent," Lefèvre said. "It was taken just before she left Holland. Her hair was blond then—that is in fact its true color—and it was cut short. That's interesting because it implies that she couldn't have changed her hairdo that much since then."

The photo was handed around again. The young woman was posing in front of what must have been the family bungalow. She was wearing a loose tank top over light-colored, close-fitting pants. The inspectors examined the image attentively in order to memorize the young woman's features. Lefèvre seemed to be looking for something else in his electronic organizer.

"Your question makes me think of an important fact that I forgot to mention, and which does not appear in the photos. Before leaving Amsterdam, Ingrid got a tattoo, a real tattoo, not one of those decals that are so fashionable among the young."

Gilles Sebag felt a shiver run down his back.

A tattoo . . .

He thought quickly. A young blonde, tall and pretty. Another disappearance. It was probably just a coincidence. He consulted his little blue notebook. Sylvie Lopez hadn't heard from her husband since last Tuesday. June 26. The date of Ingrid Raven's last telephone call to her parents. He turned over a page and reread the notes on his interview with Gérard Barrère. He had written: "northern European accent, Nordic or Germanic." There were getting to be a lot of coincidences.

With the tattoo, too many.

He went for it:

"Her tattoo was on the right shoulder, wasn't it?"

Lefèvre confirmed that it was, without trying to hide his surprise. Everyone turned toward Sebag. Molina was also beginning to make the connection.

"And it was a bird, wasn't it?" he went on.

CHAPTER 9

Her physical situation was improving day by day.
The young woman was now free to move around. Her hands were no longer tied. She could dry her tears with the back of her hand, wipe her nose with her fingers, and above all scratch herself. She could tell that her body was covered with bumps; it was being bitten by the minuscule but countless insects that were swarming in her prison. When she thought about it, a long shiver ran along her spine.

This morning, she'd taken off her mask. She didn't know whether she was allowed to do that. But she'd made up her mind to do it anyway. She'd dared. During the first days of her captivity, her jailer checked her bonds every time he brought her something to eat. Then he'd stopped doing that. Before coming into the room, he took care to knock three times, then waited a few seconds. As if he wanted to give her time to put her mask back on.

After having imagined her universe for a long time she had finally seen it.

It didn't amount to much, really.

Her prison was a cellar. Dark and sinister. At the end of the room there was a small window near the low ceiling. It was blocked from the outside by a pile of planks and cardboard boxes, but nonetheless let a little air and light into the room. She stood on tiptoe. She could clear the obstruction with a single vigorous blow of her fist. Then she could take a deep, intoxicating breath of fresh air. Dazzle her eyes with daylight.

But then what? What would her kidnapper's reaction be? She couldn't bear being punished. Being tied up again and plunged into darkness. Still, if only she'd had some hope of escaping through the opening. But it was too high and too small.

Now she could count the days.

She remembered falling asleep in José's taxi. It was a Tuesday evening. She must have slept until the next day.

How many days had she been held captive? At least a week, she guessed. She imagined her parent's concern. Her mother's tears, her father's worried silence. My God, what a terrible week they must have endured. Had they continued to work or had they stayed home all day waiting for a telephone call that became less and less likely? She knew that they were not sleeping, or if they did, only for a few minutes here and there, prostrated by fatigue and fear. She was their only daughter, their "angel," their "pearl," "the apple of their eyes." Earlier, that had pained her. As a teenager, she'd even come to envy her friend Mary, who had been orphaned at birth. What a marvelous feeling of freedom one must feel when one didn't have to bear on one's frail shoulders the hopes, worries, and ambitions of a mother and a father! At times, she still felt that way: everything would have been so simple if she hadn't had to worry about anyone but herself. And then at other times, when she was seized by despair and feared she would go mad, she clung fiercely to the memories of her father and mother. If she could no longer fight on for herself, she had to fight on for them. They would be too miserable . . .

Tears rolled down her cheeks.

José . . . She never stopped wondering what role her lover had played in the kidnapping. The deep sleep that had overcome her during the trip in the taxi was not natural. She'd been drugged. She remembered the way José insisted that she drink a beer when they got into the car. "That'll give you courage," he'd said. She'd ended up agreeing to do it. She was about to do something she'd never done before.

Her parents must have quickly notified the Dutch police. But how long would it take the French police to start looking for her? And how long before they found her?

She thrust her hands into a basin of cold water. From the beginning, he'd put one there every morning, on a stool next to the pail where she relieved herself. She could clean up. And each time she was gripped by fear, she came and washed her face.

Despite these repeated washings, a strong, rancid odor persisted around her. Her skirt and blouse were imbued with it. Not to mention her underwear. It was warm enough in the cellar for her to go naked. She'd stayed in nudist campgrounds and had never felt embarrassed. She was not prudish, and was in fact proud of her body. But she wasn't in a nudist camp and she sensed that to be able to continue to consider oneself a human being it was sometimes better to wear clothing that stank rather than go naked.

She felt that she was under surveillance. As soon as she'd finished her meals, her kidnapper came to take away the tray, as if he'd been watching her the whole time. On some occasions, she'd intentionally dawdled, chewing slowly, drinking in tiny sips. On others, she'd eaten very quickly, gulping down the food the way she had her first meal. But every time, as soon as she had swallowed the last mouthful, he'd come in.

She constantly talked to him. Even when he wasn't at her side. She told him about her childhood, her city, her parents. She talked about painting and film. She asked questions about what he liked or what the weather was like outside. She adopted a light tone, that of a conversation among friends. She knew he would never reply. Besides, she didn't want him to reply. She didn't want to know things that would allow her to identify him someday.

CHAPTER 10

The machine had gone into high gear.

Castello had grabbed the telephone and called the prosecutor, who had immediately decided to open a preliminary investigation. However, by lending support to the hypothesis of an amorous adventure, the simultaneity of the disappearances of Ingrid Raven and José Lopez might have been considered reassuring. But the magistrate had preferred to play it safe in this matter that involved a foreign national. He'd also asked that the cab driver's home be searched.

Sebag and Molina had gone to pick up Sylvie Lopez at her parents' house. The young woman had insisted on taking her daughter with her. She held her tightly in her arms and patiently put up with her screams. Above all, the child's presence allowed her not to think, and provided an outlet for her fear. Now she was afraid for her husband. Afraid that something serious had happened to him. And afraid that he'd done something stupid. She didn't know which she should fear more.

Gilles Sebag thought again about his little minute of glory. His boss's proud smile and Lefèvre's surprised one. Also the frowns of some of his colleagues. Generous in triumph, Sebag had let Molina set forth the main lines of the case they'd been working on for several days. Jacques had done that very well, giving a great deal of importance to their insignificant advances and emphasizing particularly the facts that had made them suspicious. Sebag himself had ended up thinking they'd been very shrewd.

The Lopez family lived in Moulin à Vent, a neighborhood built in the 1960s on the heights above Perpignan. The apartment buildings were a little dilapidated but the whole still looked pretty good. Vigorous palm trees and svelte pines prospered over well-tended lawns. Loggias with wooden railings decorated the façades of the buildings, while open-work brick screens concealed the poverty of cluttered sculleries. Finally, red tile roofs lent these blocks of buildings a certain village quaintness. The neighborhood had initially housed the hundreds of thousands of *pieds-noirs* who returned from North Africa with heavy hearts and empty hands. Then, with the rebirth of the university system toward the end of the 1960s, it had begun to be a place for nice, quiet students.

"We moved in when José started driving a taxi," the young woman told them. "Before, we lived in a low-cost housing development in Bas-Vernet. It was less expensive, but José was too afraid something would happen to his car. You know, these days young people don't respect anything. José used to sleep in the taxi at night. We couldn't live that way."

The elevator took them to the fourth floor. Jacques offered to carry Sylvie's daughter for her. He held out his arms but the girl immediately began to scream. The young woman politely declined the offer.

"Jenny's a little shy. She doesn't do well with new people."

In front of the door to the apartment, Sylvie, her hands full, handed Jacques her purse.

"The keys are on a big chain with the Perpignan rugby team's logo on it," she told him.

Suddenly overcome by a young man's timidity, Molina carefully probed for the keys with his big fingers, hardly daring to move the various objects in the bag. He put out his tongue and two big beads of sweat appeared on his furrowed forehead. Sebag thought with astonishment that some men felt more uneasy putting their hands in women's purses than they did putting them in their pants. After a few seconds of superhuman effort, the inspector held up the keys with as much pride as a Perpignan rugby player raising the championship trophy in Paris. He immediately put the key in the lock and opened the door on a cool, dark apartment.

Sylvie opened the shutters in each room. A kitchen, living room, two bedrooms, and a bath. Molina noted with satisfaction that the search wouldn't take long.

Their hostess offered them a drink before they began their search. Jacques opted for a beer, Gilles for a simple glass of water. Astonished by his frugality, the young woman insisted on flavoring his water with fruit syrup or even a little anisette. He refused, but managed to satisfy her by asking for a few ice cubes. Outside, the sun was already high in the sky and the *tramontane* had stopped blowing. It was going to be a hot day.

Sylvie Lopez put her daughter on a play-mat in the living room and headed for the kitchen.

"Does your husband keep his personal things in some special place?" Sebag asked her from the living room.

"His clothes are in the bedroom closet."

Gilles waited until she came back with the drinks before explaining what he meant.

"By personal things, I meant papers, documents, files . . . "

The question seemed to surprise the young woman. Her husband wasn't the kind to like paperwork. She finally pointed to the PC that stood on a desk in a corner of the living room. Right next to the play-mat.

"José spends lots of time on the computer, but it's mainly to play with CD-ROMs or on the Internet. I don't think he has many personal things on it."

"What about the accounts for the taxi?"

"All that's on the computer, yes. But I'm the one who handles it. José hates bookkeeping."

Sylvie Lopez dropped two ice cubes in a glass of water and handed it to Sebag.

"Would you like a glass?" she asked Jacques.

"No, I prefer it this way. Out of the bottle."

"José does too," she replied, not without pride.

Once they had finished their drinks, they divided up the work. Sebag took the living room, Jacques the bedrooms. Sylvie Lopez hesitated a moment, then decided to follow Molina.

Gilles gave little Jennifer a friendly smile, but prudently kept his distance.

"Where would you begin?" he asked her.

The little girl let out a little chirp.

"Really? You think?"

The furniture was modest and disparate. Sebag chose to examine first a strange pile of gray wood boxes that claimed to play the role of a bookcase. The latter was not large, and the books, not very numerous, included a few recent best-sellers, an older volume that had won the Goncourt prize, and a handsome work with aerial photographs of Roussillon. At the very bottom there were three photo albums, which he ignored. He had a feeling that the solution to the case was not to be found in the Lopez's family life.

He set aside the book that had won the Goncourt, lifted up a colored candle, and ran his finger along the shelf. No trace of dust. He flipped through the books one by one and shook them. A piece of paper fell out of *The Da Vinci Code*. He picked it up with care. It was a page torn out of a notebook with small squares. A telephone number was written on it. A cell phone number. Nothing else.

He started to explore the family address book lying on the desk. It bore names, sometimes just first names, and also a few nicknames—Jeff, Fred, Lulu—but no esoteric signs, abbreviations, or even initials. Nothing obscure or suspect. Nonetheless, Sebag found no trace of the mysterious cell phone number. He took a plastic bag out of his pants pocket and carefully put the paper in it.

"Watch carefully what I'm doing, okay Jenny? I need a witness. It's the law!"

He went up to a piece of furniture in Formica that held the television. Underneath was a DVD reader, and under that, two drawers containing films: American TV series, a complete collection of *Star Wars*, French comedies, two or three little romances. Then he went through the couple's CD collection. Popular television singers mingled unabashedly with English and American hits. Sebag noted the impressive collection of Barry White CDs. He took one at random, put it into the CD player, and turned the sound down low. The American crooner whispered his sugary songs in his ear.

He ran his finger over the television screen. Still no dust. His suspicions were confirmed. Sylvie Lopez was assuredly a meticulous housekeeper. Maybe even a maniacal one.

Sebag went back to the desk. He stepped over the play-mat. Little Jennifer followed him with her eyes. A pungent odor was emanating from her.

"Oh, don't you smell good," he said, holding his nose.

He switched on the PC. It was a new one with a flat screen. The home page showed two accounts. One under the name of Lopez, the other under the name of José. Sebag clicked on Lopez. A photo of a baby appeared in the background. It was without any doubt Jennifer Lopez—he now noticed, for the first time, that she had the same name as the actress—scarcely a few minutes after she had appeared on Earth. A woolen bonnet protected her head and forehead, but could not conceal the birthmark that decorated one of her eyelids.

Sebag looked deep into the baby's dark eyes.

Séverine had also had very dark eyes when she was born. Her skin was red and wrinkled, her hair was already thick and brown. An adorable little Inca doll. He saw her again just after the birth, lying all flushed on her mother's white, round belly. That was thirteen years ago.

A heartbeat, an instant.

The screen went dark. It had taken advantage of the inspector's reveries to put itself to sleep. Sebag hit a random key. The screen jerked and agreed to wake up. Sebag surveyed the icons. The usual programs installed on the computer at the factory. A shortcut led to the taxi's books. He had no time to waste on that for the moment.

He exited the family account and tried to open the husband's account. Impossible. It was blocked. He called on Sylvie Lopez for help. The young woman came in three seconds. She smiled when she recognized the music.

"Do you like Barry White, too?" she asked.

"Yes. Well . . . a little," he replied politely. "I don't know him very well. I've often heard his songs on the radio. Like everyone else."

"José is a real fan. Absolutely. There are CDs he sometimes plays over and over. It seems odd to me . . . to hear them when he's not here."

To hide her embarrassment she bent over her daughter, sniffed her, and then took her in her arms.

"Is she bothering you?"

"Not at all. We've been talking. She's charming."

Sylvie Lopez gave him her most radiant mother's smile.

"I called you in because there's a password on your husband's account. Do you know it?"

"A what?"

"A password."

She seemed still not to understand. He explained.

"There's free access to the computer but your husband's account is protected. It can be opened only with a code, a password that he put on it."

He pointed to the flashing cursor.

"Look. Here, you have to write a secret word, a name, nickname, anything. Afterward it simply opens."

She leaned over the screen despite the burden in her arms. He pitied her back. He'd always admired women's ability to hold a child in their arms for hours and to go about their business as if it were nothing at all.

"Haven't you ever used the computer on your husband's account?"

She looked perplexed. Still leaning over the computer, she was holding the child's bottom near the inspector's nose.

"I think there's a little problem," he dared to say.

She stood up.

"I'm sorry. I use the computer only to do the bookkeeping for the taxi, and I don't need a password."

He sighed.

"Too bad. Thanks all the same. You can go back to my colleague now."

After a short hesitation, he added, pointing to the diaper:

"The little problem I was talking about was, uh, related to the big job."

The young woman's eyes smiled. They were just as dark as Jennifer's.

"Oh yes. Excuse me. I'm going to change her."

Sebag was alone again. That's how he preferred to work, even if it wasn't altogether legal. He opened the desk drawers. The files were categorized. Taxes. Gas. Electricity. Health. Just like his. Like everyone's, he imagined. He glanced through it all rapidly. Nothing caught his attention.

He sat down on the sofa in front of the TV. The sofa was soft. Too soft, as always. It was incredible how many uncomfortable sofas could be invented. Sebag preferred chairs, but he could see the whole room better from the sofa. He silenced his thoughts and tried not to pay attention to details. He wanted to feel the soul of this apartment.

The sunlight made the stark white walls of the living room dazzling. Sebag stroked the paint with his fingertips. It was rough. A simple primer coat. The only thing that enlivened the room with a touch of bright color was a painting that hung to the right of the TV.

Despite the heat that was gradually filling the room, he shivered. Something was wrong. The furniture was disparate, the place hadn't been fully moved into, there was a total absence of disorder. Those were the objective facts. They could have been found in many other homes. But what he felt, beyond that, was a kind of . . . absence of life. That was it! That was what he felt deeply. There was no life in the Lopez's home.

"I've searched the bedrooms and the bath," Molina interrupted. "I didn't notice anything out of the ordinary."

Jacques's sudden appearance had made Sebag jump. He slowly raised his eyes and looked at him. Sylvie Lopez came in as well. With little Jennifer still in her arms. She smelled of baby powder.

"In fact, you don't spend much time here, do you?"

The apparently anodyne question seemed to hit the young woman like a sucker punch. She started breathing faster, her back hunched slightly. Sebag had wanted to be direct, not brutal, but he'd touched a sensitive spot. Sylvie Lopez shifted her daughter from one hip to the other and answered looking down at the living room's linoleum.

"We work a lot, you know, and especially we come home late. It's true that some evenings when I stop at my parents' home to pick up Jenny and I see her sleeping peacefully, I don't have the heart to disturb her. Sometimes I just lie down beside her, and at other times I go sleep in the bedroom I had when I still lived with my parents. That way, if Jenny wakes up crying it's my mother who takes care of her and I can catch up on my sleep a little."

Little Jennifer began to fuss. Her mother hoisted her up a bit on her hip.

"The first evening, when your husband disappeared, you weren't at home, in fact?

"No," she whispered. "I was with my parents."

Quiet up to now, Jacques broke in.

"So he could very well have come home without you knowing it?"

She turned her delicate face toward Molina. Her eyes detached themselves from the floor. They were darker than ever. The color of night.

"No, he didn't come home. I'm sure of·that."

"How can you be so sure if you weren't here?" Jacques persisted with a gentleness Sebag had never seen in him. "He could have at least been here briefly. That night or even another night. Or any time during the day."

The young mother's eyes jumped from one to the other of them. She didn't know how to explain. Then she took on a stubborn air.

"I'd have noticed if he'd come home."

Sebag tried to help her. He knew that the most experienced policeman's power of observation was not equal to the steely and inquisitorial eye of a homemaker.

"You think he would have to have left some trace behind if he'd been there, don't you? A footprint in the entry hall, a coffee stain on the kitchen table, a dirty glass in the sink. Or simply some object that he moved and didn't put back exactly where it belonged."

The young woman's eyes fell on the inspector and lit up for an instant. Putting his hand in his pants pocket, Sebag felt a plastic bag. He took it out and showed Sylvie Lopez the paper he'd put inside it.

"Does this telephone number mean anything to you?"

She looked at the paper attentively. Her eyebrows came

together and furrowed her forehead. Then her features suddenly relaxed.

"Where did you find this?"

Sebag didn't like it when a witness answered him with further questions, but he chose not to be offended.

"In a book in the bookcase."

"That's the phone number of a girlfriend of mine who has just come back to France after a stay in New Caledonia—her husband is in the military. I wrote it down the other night when she called me and I couldn't find it again."

She reached for the plastic bag but held back at the last moment.

"Can I have it back or is it important for your investigation?"

Sebag avoided Molina's eyes. He could imagine the laughter shaking his broad shoulders as his colleague gently made fun of him. He took the paper out of the bag and gave it to Sylvie Lopez. Another idea ran through his mind.

"Do you have a garage?"

"Yes, of course. That's why we moved here."

Molina immediately reacted.

"Will you show me the garage, Mrs. Lopez? My colleague surely has things to do here."

The young woman reflected for an instant. Sebag followed her eyes from little Jennifer to the play-mat.

"Will it take long?"

"That depends," Molina said evasively. "Is there a lot of stuff in the garage?"

"No! Just a few tools and a couple of boxes."

"Then fifteen minutes should be enough."

"Fifteen minutes? Then let's go right away."

She resettled her daughter on her hip and went off with Molina.

Sebag could now snoop around the apartment alone. The walls of Jennifer's bedroom were the only ones that were papered. Cherubs on a sky blue background. A large photo hung over the crib: papa, mama, and little Jenny. The only thing tying the three members of the family together.

Sylvie and José were clearly having problems, but had they ever really been a couple? Sebag had met many people like them in the course of his career. Far too many of them. A man and a woman meet one evening and go out together. He could have chosen another woman, she could have done worse, and they take that accident for love. One day they have a kid. Because when a man and a woman are together for a couple of years, they have a kid. Necessarily. Ultimately it's easier than choosing not to have one. The headlong rush maintains the illusion.

Josie and Sylvie Lopez no doubt met from time to time. Around the dinner table, in front of a television screen, over the crib, or perhaps simply on the landing. They weren't happy together. Or unhappy, either.

The music stopped and the room was silent again. Sebag got up, put away the CD, and sat back down.

Who was José Lopez, really, and what role did he play in all this? That of a man in love who'd run away? He no longer believed that. The hypothesis didn't fit with either the abandoned taxi or young Ingrid's profile. She could have gone off to the other end of the world with her cab driver, had a perfect love affair with him, and continued to call her papa and mama every evening. He probably had to assume that the worst might have happened. Was Lopez a victim or a murderer? His convictions, including the one for assault and battery, meant that he wasn't gentle as a lamb, but to jump to the conclusion that he was a killer . . . The fact that someone will break an egg doesn't necessarily mean that he would kill an ox. And still less a young woman.

The door at the end of the hall opened. Molina came back in and found him sitting on the sofa. Lost in his thoughts.

"Are you falling asleep?"

Jacques turned to Sylvie Lopez.

"Trust my colleague, madam. He looks like he's sleeping, but he's thinking. Me, it's the other way around . . . "

He thought it necessary to add:

"I look like I'm thinking, but I'm really sleeping."

Sebag got up.

"Did you find anything?" he asked.

"Negative. The garage is almost empty. That's normal, since the car is . . . elsewhere."

Sebag looked again at the reproduction of the painting that hung on the wall. He went up to it. The canvas was signed "Derain." A classic of fauvism.

He took the frame off the wall to check out an idea.

"This picture is recent, isn't it?"

"Absolutely."

"It was José who brought it here a few days ago, right?"

"Yes, how did you know that? Is it related to his disappearance?"

"No. That is, not directly."

He didn't have the heart to tell her about Ingrid and her studies in art history. When he called earlier, Molina hadn't been very specific. He'd just told her that José's disappearance had disturbing resemblances with that of a young Dutch tourist and that this coincidence required them to pursue the investigation further and thus to search the apartment.

"Did you know that your husband has a police record?"

"It was just a fight. He was young."

"Has he seemed worried recently?"

"No, not at all. On the contrary. He no longer seemed concerned about his taxi. He still had loans to pay back, but he said we'd be able to manage somehow.

The inspectors thought about these answers. Then Sebag gave the signal to leave.

"I think we're done here. We've bothered you enough for today."

She assured them that they hadn't bothered her, that there was nothing worse than waiting without anything to do, and that at least she'd felt for a short time as if she was helping them in their investigation. She offered them another drink before leaving, and when they refused finally asked the question she was dying to ask:

"Do you think something serious has happened to José?"

The two men looked at each other in silence. They were playing for time and each hoped the other would take the lead. Sebag was better at this little game.

"It's too early to say," Jacques explained. "Every year many people disappear in France, and most of the time, things turn out okay."

Statistically, Molina was right. What he deliberately failed to say was that these were usually minors who'd run away or senile old people. In cases of adults who had disappeared, the outcome was often more complicated.

The sun lit up a star in the young woman's dark pupils. Sylvie Lopez sniffled. The star was soon washed in tears.

Jennifer put her hand on her mother's cheek. She was astonished to feel the wetness under her little fingertips.

"Everything will be all right, you'll see," said Jacques, putting his hand on her frail shoulder.

The young woman was polite enough to be satisfied with these banal words. Before leaving, Sebag and Molina picked up the computer and had Sylvie fill out the usual form. As they were carrying the PC to their car, she wrote down, as they had asked, a few possible passwords. Their daughter's first name and her various nicknames, the names of her parents-in-law, her husband's birthplace, a place connected with some memory . . . everything that occurred to her. Sebag sensed that she was willing but doubted her inspiration.

The engine was idling and the air conditioning made him

forget the early summer heat. Parked in front of a gym, he was watching a magnificent parade of girls. Some were amazingly beautiful. They knew it and weren't afraid of going out in leotards. It was enough to make you want to get involved in sports . . .

Sebag and Molina had been the first to return to headquarters. That might be a good sign, so far as the other teams were concerned. They'd find out soon. There was a meeting at the headquarters in the early afternoon.

Sebag had two hours free, and wanted to take advantage of them to surprise Claire. To stop and pick her up after her gym class and take her to a little restaurant that Jacques had recommended. It was twelve forty-five and Claire still hadn't come out. Her step aerobics class had been over for a good quarter of an hour. Long enough to take a shower, do her makeup; she should have already come out.

In front of Sebag's car, two enormous turbines were sweating dirty, stale water as they pumped out into the street the saturated air from the gym. Air conditioning is a soft drug that is spreading throughout the world, he said to himself.

In a gesture he considered heroic, he cut off the motor. The fan pumped out a little more cool air but it was a matter of seconds. It was time to leave his precarious oasis and confront the world.

A long counter of light-colored wood received members of the club. Behind it, a tall brunette smiled at him. She was Claire's teacher. Last spring the three of them had had a drink together. She'd asked him to fix a ticket for her. He'd refused. She hadn't liked that.

"Hello."

She had short hair, and was muscular and high-waisted, but didn't have much of a figure. Most of her charm consisted in her hoarse voice punctuated by a melodious intonation.

"Hello. I'm Claire Sebag's husband."

"Yes, I remember well . . . "

She'd almost said "the cop," but had managed to stop herself.

"I stopped by to pick up my wife. Has she already come out?"

She was surprised.

"I haven't seen her this morning."

"Ah."

He smiled. Stupidly, it seemed to him. A husband always looks stupid when he doesn't know where his wife is. He felt obliged to explain.

"Something must have come up. Anyway, I didn't tell her that I'd come to pick her up."

And he went out. In the street, he called to cancel the reservation and quickly headed for the nearest fast-food place, determined to stuff himself on fries and burgers.

The windows were still closed and the shades were down, but the sun nonetheless crept into the meeting room. People's foreheads were damp with sweat, and so were their underarms. The air conditioner had died. It had to be replaced, but probably wouldn't be before fall. Sebag sniffed. The odor of sweat would soon mask the aroma of fried food that he was carrying in the fibers of his clothing. Raynaud and Moreno were absent; it seemed they were on a case. As usual.

At the end of the table, the boss had taken off his jacket but hadn't yet undone his tie. At his side, Lefèvre remained impeccable. Colgate smile and fresh breath. Slicked-back hair. He looked like he'd just gotten out of the shower.

"All right. Gentlemen, who wants to begin?"

Superintendent Castello was playing it "serious and solemn." The inspectors got the message. As in school, Sebag thought, it was best to begin with the last. And he volunteered. He summed up their few discoveries. A computer hard disk that was being examined and the confirmation of the idea that part of Lopez's life took place outside his family. The harvest was meager. Castello wasn't upset.

"That was predictable, but we had to carry out that search. You didn't find anything that could show that Lopez was involved in smuggling cigarettes?"

It took Sebag a moment to understand. He'd already forgotten what he'd invented four days earlier to awaken Castello's interest.

"Uh . . . no . . . we didn't find a stock of cigarettes at his place and, uh, his wife doesn't know anything about it."

"Too bad . . . "

"What's all this about cigarettes?" Lefèvre asked.

Castello gave him a brief account of the case. Lefèvre looked puzzled.

"And you think this might have something to do with Ingrid Raven?"

The question was addressed to Sebag. He met Molina's amused eyes.

"Ultimately, no."

To Sebag's great relief, the superintendent turned to Llach, who immediately began describing his morning. With Lambert, he'd visited Fabrice Gasch, José Lopez's other friend and the owner of Securita Catalana. Gasch had immediately recognized Ingrid Raven in the photos. It was in fact she who had been with Lopez on the evening of June 26, and she had called herself Vanessa. Gasch had rapidly admitted that he played billiards for money with Barrère and Lopez, and that the latter often lost. Sometimes a hundred to two hundred euros in an evening. He'd claimed he had no idea where this money came from. He'd just said that his friend—like all independent businessmen—must have put aside a little cash. He'd even added that that was understandable.

"What he needed was a good tax audit," Castello grumbled.

Questioned about his friend's disappearance, Fabric Gasch had expressed "sincere concern." He had no idea where Lopez might be and rejected the idea that he'd run off on an amorous adventure. This wasn't his first extra-marital affair, and never, absolutely never, had he shown any desire to leave his wife. In any case, still according to Gasch, if he were to leave Sylvie, he wouldn't do it that way.

Then Castello called on Ménard, while Lambert seized the chance to slip discreetly away. Ménard had talked with Barrère. The owner of Perpign'And Co. had also recognized Ingrid in the photos. And this time he had admitted employing Lopez several times in the evenings, to drive certain persons around and give them a tour of the department.

"It seems that's often done when there are big contracts to sign," Ménard explained.

Molina laughed.

"Perpignan by night: night-spots, private clubs, and little old men. It's true that people say that makes it easier to get signatures. There might be something there that we should look into. The other day Gilles and I already said that Vanessa was a pseudonym widely used by call-girls. In any case, there are more Vanessas than Martines or Brigittes."

"And what conclusions should we draw from that, in your opinion? That through Perpign'And Co. Ingrid Raven found a new way of financing her studies?"

"Why not?" Molina replied.

"That might explain certain things, then," the superintendent said enigmatically.

He stroked his beard. That morning it had still been long, but since then it had been carefully trimmed. He'd also had his hair cut.

Lefèvre was tapping on his electronic organizer.

"Personally, I had the impression that Barrère was still hiding things from us," Ménard went on. "He didn't seem really at ease during our interview. He was exasperated but also tense. I think he was just dribbling out information, and that he didn't want us to dig around too much in his affairs."

"However, that's what we're going to do, and soon," Castello announced. "There are a number of corroborating facts that put this case in a new light."

He took the time to observe his audience before adding:

"Because I, too, have something new! This morning I re-examined Lopez's car. The routine inspection done this weekend hadn't yielded anything but a lot of fingerprints, especially in the rear seat, of course."

Lambert timidly came back in and took his seat, not without trailing behind him the aroma of cheap cologne. The young inspector, fearing that he was giving off too strong body odor, regularly sprinkled himself with perfume. And that was the chief reason his colleagues didn't want to be near him.

"In view of the new importance this case has taken on," the superintendent went on, "this morning I asked our technical team to completely dismantle the vehicle, as our colleagues in customs know so well how to do. And here's what they found."

From a briefcase he took two plastic bags, one containing a roll of bills and the other a foil-pack of blue pills.

"By taking apart the driver's side door, we found almost two thousand euros in cash and twenty Viagra pills."

The inspectors leaned over the table to see better. Only Lefèvre didn't budge. He'd closed his electronic organizer. No need to take notes. He'd clearly been the first to get this information. Castello circulated the plastic bags.

"Thus it seems that José Lopez succeeded in making a little pocket money without his wife's or the taxman's knowledge. First, all the night-time drives he made for Barrère were certainly not declared. Second, he undoubtedly took advantage of these evenings to sell Viagra to Barrère's clients. And finally, though this remains to be proven, he might have envisioned the possibility of being Ingrid Raven's pimp in this milieu."

"Cab driving, prostitution, drugs. Lopez is a real specialist in transports of all kinds," Molina joked.

"In any case, he's far from being an honest businessman and quiet family man, that's for sure."

Castello loosened his tie and then grabbed the telephone in front of him. He asked his secretary to bring them some water. Lambert, leaning back his chair, moved discreetly closer to the air conditioner. He pushed all the buttons but the machine for creating cold didn't respond.

"We've made some real progress on this case today," Castello continued, "but let's not kid ourselves: nothing that we've found tells us what has happened to Ingrid since she disappeared."

He cleared his throat before going on.

"This afternoon we're supposed to receive the young woman's fingerprints and DNA analysis from the Dutch police."

Three timid knocks on the door. Jeanne, the superintendent's secretary, appeared with her arms full of bottles of mineral water. She was a petite brunette with an alluring figure. Tight khaki green pants showed off her ass perfectly and the cream-colored T-shirt claimed she had been a "White House Intern." Sebag didn't get it until he saw the wink Molina gave him. Then he remembered the Clinton–Monica Lewinsky affair and couldn't repress a smile. He admired the boldness—or obliviousness—of this young woman who was moving from table to table with ease and confidence while flaunting that delightful joke under the noses of a good half-dozen males. She was playing with fire because, contrary to what she liked to suggest, she was not a loose woman. According to Molina, who had tried and failed.

"Still concerning young Ingrid," the superintendent went on after the departure of his secretary had focused his team's attention on him again, "we are also expecting that the gendarmes will succeed in identifying the artist couple in Collioure who are supposed to have put the young woman up. We are hoping that this, too, will provide us with new information this afternoon."

He opened the bottle of water and filled a plastic glass. The signal was given, and everyone did the same. The water was cool. Pleasant.

Molina got up to open the window behind him. A breath of hot air blew into the room. The good feeling that followed was as ephemeral as it was relative, but Molina seemed satisfied. But then he was seated next to Lambert.

Castello put down his empty glass and cleared his throat again. The afternoon was already half over and it was time to distribute the work to be done next. As he had feared, Sebag was assigned to examine Lopez's books, while Ménard was to examine Barrère's. Lambert was given the mission of finding Ingrid Raven's room in the student residence hall and Llach was to make the rounds of the museums that she might have visited.

Castello turned to Molina.

"Have you got something on for this evening?"

"Nothing much," the inspector replied worriedly.

"You don't mind doing a little overtime?"

"I don't especially go looking for it . . . "

"You don't? Too bad . . . I was planning to ask you to pursue our investigation in the call-girl situation. You'd have to find and question the ones who participated in Barrère's evenings with Lopez. But I can give that job to someone else . . . "

"Don't bother," Molina interrupted. "In this line of work you sometimes have to be able to go the extra mile."

"My view entirely. And you also have to know how to make the best use of each individual's skills, right?"

"Oooh . . . A cell phone, that's so cool! You finally made up your mind . . . "

Léo's gratitude was very qualified, but it was a pleasure to see him so happy. He'd understood even before he opened the package. Sebag could see that in his eyes.

"And you can make an unlimited number of calls," he added perfidiously.

"Unlimited? I can call as much as I want?"

"Yup."

The kid couldn't get over it. Sebag waited a few seconds, long enough to let him enjoy his illusions. Claire was staring at him.

"On the condition, however, that you call our home number or our cell phones, your mother's and mine. For all other calls, of course, you're the one who pays."

"Oh, yeah, okay. I wondered . . . "

He dialed a number and went off to be alone at the back of the yard while Séverine finished clearing the table. Claire and Gilles were the only ones who kept their seats. They'd dined on the terrace. A tomato salad, accompanied this time with pine nuts collected under the trees in the neighborhood and spiced with a few leaves of marjoram from the garden. It had been an outstanding evening. The last one they'd spend together for a long time. The next day, Léo was leaving for that summer camp in the Cévennes, the one whose theme was motorcycles and ATVs. His father would have preferred rock-climbing, hiking, or even kite- or wind-surfing, but Léo went in only for mechanical sports. Séverine, for her part, was leaving to spend the month of July with that girlfriend and her parents on the Costa Brava. Gilles hoped she would at least take advantage of the opportunity to review her Spanish.

During this time, Claire would work on her tan, between the pool and the sea. First in Roussillon, then on her cruise ship. In August, they'd see what they wanted to do. Depending on their desires, their means, and the children who agreed to join them. This was the first summer they were likely to spend entirely alone. That should have been an opportunity for them to get re-acquainted. To make a new start. To imagine and prepare for a future for two people and no longer for four.

"You're very pensive," Claire said, passing the back of her hand over his cheek.

It was getting late, but it was still warm. Léo and Séverine were playing noisily in the pool. The solar lamps that dotted the yard were coming on one after the other.

"Is it this missing person case that's preoccupying you?"

He seized the pretext she offered him.

"I sense that it's going to be a long and difficult investigation. I don't know why, but that's how I see it. You scratch a little saltpeter off a wall, and you think you're making progress, but behind you're going to find concrete. Too solid to demolish, too smooth to climb."

His wife's hand caressed his chin and his raspy whiskers, which by this hour were growing out again.

"You know I don't always follow you when you speak too metaphorically."

He picked up a piece of bread that had fallen on the tiles and put it on the table. He'd pored over Lopez's books until 6:00 P.M., and had found nothing significant. Three cab trips for Perpign'And Co. were in fact listed as credits, which suggested, as Castello had indicated, that others had been paid for in cash. So far as he could tell, none of his colleagues had made any progress.

"I don't know how to explain it, but I've got a bad feeling about this."

On the dinner table, there remained only his half-full glass of wine. He took a swallow of it.

"Right now, we're scratching at the young Dutch woman's

activities and some money found in Lopez's taxi. We'll gradually move ahead and end up putting the puzzle together, but the picture we'll form may well tell us nothing."

"I still don't understand."

"The disappearances don't necessarily have anything to do with Lopez's illicit dealings. As for what Ingrid was up to, once we've filled in all the gaps, we'll arrive at the point where she disappeared without having a single serious lead."

A shrill cry exploded, followed by a resounding splash. Léo had just pushed Séverine into the water. Claire kindly told them to hold it down: it was late, and the neighbors had a right to expect a little peace and quiet. Hardly had she finished speaking when another splash was heard over the laurel hedge. Things were hot tonight for the neighbors as well. And too bad for those who didn't have a pool.

"Aren't police investigations always like that?" Claire asked, lifting her husband's wineglass to her lips.

He shrugged.

"Yes, probably. But in this case, I'm not so sure. I can't get a handle on this case."

Claire grabbed his hair and shook his head:

"My poor Gilles . . . You really aren't getting any better as you age. Hasn't experience taught you anything? Ever since you've been in the police, you've always been like that at the beginning of an investigation. You worry and get discouraged by the size of the task. But you inspectors always end up finding the right thread to unwind the ball."

She took the time to meet his eyes.

"And you know too, don't you, that most of the time, you're the one who finds that thread?"

In his heart of hearts, he knew she was right. But this time, it was worse than usual. He also sensed that not all his doubts had to do with the investigation. His attack of late-evening pessimism had other sources.

"That's not true," he insisted, "we don't always find the thread."

Especially not in missing person cases.

Claire got up and went back into the house with her graceful walk. She came back shortly afterward dressed in a swimsuit. She turned on the light in the pool and slowly went down the three steps that led into the water. The children understood and got out of the pool. Séverine wrapped her long brown hair in a towel. She walked past her father, kissed him on the forehead, and announced that she was going to bed. Léo approached in turn and laid his hand on his father's shoulder.

"We're leaving at seven tomorrow morning, don't forget."

"I won't," he assured him. "I've already set my alarm. You'll be on time."

Gilles put his hand on his son's. He didn't dare ask for a kiss. Tomorrow, maybe when he was saying goodbye . . .

Claire slipped through the water without apparent effort. When she arrived at one end of the pool, she dove and came out again at the other end. She was capable of doing that for hours. And Gilles could follow her with his eyes just as long.

Night had now fallen. Gilles didn't need to get into the water himself; he already felt refreshed. Claire came out of the pool. She took off her swimsuit and hung it up to dry. She knew that he was looking at her and she took her time. She knotted a sarong around her waist. Her breasts swung when she began to walk. She leaned down toward him. She ran her hand through his hair again.

"Are you coming to bed? I'm exhausted."

"Was your session at the gym tiring?"

He'd promised himself he wouldn't ask. And certainly not in that way. Was it a sudden attack of jealousy or an inappropriate professional reflex that led him to set this idiotic trap for her? He'd never know. To his great despair, Claire dove into the trap head-first.

"I don't know what was wrong with the teacher today. She must have gotten up on the wrong side of the bed. She made us sweat more than ever before."

And then she left him alone with his gloomy thoughts. The water in the pool still remembered her swimming movements and stupidly continued to ripple. Its bluish light made the branches of the palm tree dance stealthily.

As the old proverb had it: He is trapped who thought he was the trapper.

CHAPTER 11

The girl is playing along. She has understood. That's good. It will be easier. He was reassured. Up to now, everything had gone well.

She was eating, drinking, washing herself. She no longer cried much and seemed to be resigned. Perfect. There would be no pointless violence. He didn't like violence, but he wouldn't hesitate.

The kidnapping had been disconcertingly easy. The young woman was asleep in the car and hadn't awoken when he transported her. The hardest part had been convincing the taxi driver to make her drink the drug. But he'd turned out to be more venal than clever.

Everything was going according to plan.

A cool obscurity reigned in the house. It was agreeable. He didn't like heat. He didn't like summertime. In the past, during all the long vacations, he never left the house. Despite his mother, who badgered him about it. From the high window, she showed him the neighbor's children in the distance who were amusing themselves in an inflatable pool. They were yelling and jumping around, gesticulating, fighting. "Go play with them, at least once, you'll see, they're nice," she kept repeating all day long. She got tired when evening came. He preferred to read adventure novels and watch the Tour de France on television. He had no friends; he didn't need any. He didn't like the games children his age played.

And he didn't like to please his mother.

He was going to have to go to work. Nothing had changed

over the years. He still found it difficult to leave, even for a moment, the calm of this house. Each time it was a rupture, a divorce, a painful childbirth. Soon he was going to be able to enjoy peace. Finally. Stop this circus, these pretenses, this masquerade. Move once and for all to the other side of the world.

He mustn't change his habits in any way. Mustn't appear suspect. They'd never be able to identify him without his help. He had no ties, or almost none. He held all the cards in his hand. He was going to deal them out as he wished, cleverly mixing them up. He'd foreseen everything, but he hadn't yet decided everything.

Only the outcome was inevitable.

He'd been afraid for a moment when he met a policeman at that idiot Barrère's place. It had in fact been a policeman. He'd had no difficulty confirming that. God, how much he'd loved that short moment of fear. It had reminded him of games of hide-and-seek. The delicious shiver when his father approached the closet where he knew he was hiding. The hope when he pretended to go away. And the immense joy when he finally caught him.

They hadn't played often. In any case, most of the time his father wasn't playing. He was looking for him so he could punish him. For his thefts, his lies. Why was it always necessary to be naughty in order to be able to play?

He'd found the policeman nice. Firm gestures, dark eyes, assertive, with something about his mouth, childlike and fragile. An intelligent cop, sensitive and perceptive. It looked like the game would be amusing.

He was surprised by the silence in the newspapers. It saddened him. The young woman's disappearance hadn't been reported anywhere. Were reporters even stupider than the police? They would probably also need a little help.

Regretfully, he got up. He had to go out. Confront people, the heat, the light. It was getting harder and harder.

Courage, he said to himself, it will soon be over.

CHAPTER 12

Sebag didn't like Collioure.

The "Jewel of the Vermilion Coast." Flower-lined lanes leading down to the sea, where many-colored boats bobbed drowsily. A few painted façades. A strange round church tower that looked like a minaret. And an astonishing light that had attracted a handful of unknown painters at the beginning of the last century.

It was pretty, okay, but enough!

When he landed here in 1905, Matisse didn't imagine that a century later the picturesque village would have become a major tourist site on the Mediterranean coast and that mediocre copyists with long, greasy hair, long beards, and dirty jeans would be pretending to be artists and luring customers with loud canvases that were to fauvism what punk was to Bob Dylan.

Sebag really didn't like Collioure. And even less in the summertime. In the fall, on the other hand, in the streets one met only a few old Catalans and a small number of real talents. In the fall, the light was soft and caressing.

Gilles had dozed off during the trip from Perpignan to Collioure. He was tired. The preceding night, he'd ruminated for a long time on his dark thoughts, while Claire was sleeping like a baby next to him in bed.

He'd caught her in his trap, and that hadn't helped him at all. On several occasions, he had been on the point of asking her where she was at the time of the gym class. But the fear of seeming ridiculous had held him back: did a little lie necessarily conceal a great deception? He didn't know what to do, and that made his bad mood even worse.

And then, Léo had left this morning.

They'd gotten up early to go to the train station. Gilles had accompanied his son as far as the platform. Before getting on the train, Léo had casually offered his cheek. Sebag had had only time to give him a rapid peck. He would so much have liked to hug him!

Although the summer season was still just getting started, the sign on the parking lot at the royal chateau in Collioure said it was full. Fortunately, the gendarmes had agreed to meet them on the little parking lot above the Port Avall beach. Jacques parked the car next to the gendarmes' blue van.

Sebag and Molina greeted Lieutenant Cornet of the research squad in Perpignan. He was a young, lanky guy. He had to be almost six feet three and his slenderness made him seem taller still. The young man shook their hands with pride and enthusiasm.

"We had no difficulty identifying the couple that was putting the young woman up. Their names are Gérard and Martine Revel. They live in the Port Avall neighborhood, a little away from the tourist part of Collioure."

"That's surprising, for painters," Sebag said, puzzled.

"Not necessarily for real painters," Cornet replied, thus completely winning over Sebag. "Gérard Revel was born here, he's a real native of Collioure who has been able to gain a small following in Spain. Or rather . . . in South Catalonia. His wife is also a painter."

The lieutenant led them into a winding lane that started up the hill. They soon stopped in front of a white house and knocked at a door painted apple green.

"They know we're coming, and are waiting for us," Cornet explained.

There was no name on the door, just a metal plaque the size of a school ruler, on which were engraved two very stylized silhouettes. A man and a woman looking at each other.

The door opened and Sebag saw the man's silhouette. His nose, long and prominent, contrasted with his other features, which were gentler, almost feminine. He had a shaved head. His massive figure and muscular arms held apart from his body showed that he'd spent hours in body-building gyms.

Gérard Revel moved aside to let the policemen enter. He pointed to a door at the right in the narrow hall. Cornet went first into a vast room, a sort of kitchen-dining room. They sat around a large table of worn wood blackened by time or by the perverse activities of a clever craftsman.

"I have to ask you to excuse my wife. She's finishing a water color and will join us in a few minutes."

As if to justify what he'd said, he put five large cups on the table.

"Can I offer you coffee?"

They all accepted his offer and their host filled four cups with black, fragrant coffee. Revel set in front of them a bowl containing rough cubes of brown sugar.

The room had the strange and calming charm of those old places that seem to have lived for a thousand years. The thick stone walls isolated them from street noise and the wooden furniture muffled fragments of voices. Fragments of life. The enormous fireplace with a stone mantel demanded respect. Behind the little windows with lace curtains, conversations had to be both trivial and essential. Muted and confidential. Here you didn't chat, you spoke. And if you had nothing to say, you let the pendulum of the tall clock fill existence. These old clocks from Franche-Comté used to play the role now played by television. Less the stupefying effect.

"I'm ready," Revel said, sitting down across from them.

Molina started the interview. Sebag observed. That was

their technique when they worked together. Jacques conducted the conversation, while he attended to what the people said. Gilles tried to concentrate on "how they say it."

"So you put up a young Dutch citizen named Ingrid Raven here for a few days?"

"That's right."

Molina took color copies of the photos of the young woman out of his hip pocket. He laid them out on the table among the cups.

"Is this her?"

Revel looked at the photos carefully. He pointed to one in which the young woman had blond hair.

"That's her. And when we met her, she looked more like this photo than the others. But she also had a kind of tattoo on her right shoulder."

"Do you remember what it was a tattoo of?"

During an interview, certain questions were asked to determine the reliability of the witness.

"It was a somewhat stylized swallow in flight."

"You are very observant," Jacques said, complimenting him.

"In my trade, that's as useful as it is in yours," Revel replied modestly. "And then Ingrid served as a model for me during her stay here. That helps."

"How long was she here, exactly?"

"Four days and three nights. From Tuesday the nineteenth to Friday the twenty-second of June."

"You're not only observant . . . "

Revel shrugged his broad shoulders.

"The gendarmes told my wife and me about your visit this morning. It didn't take us long to check the dates."

"How did you meet Ingrid Raven?" Molina asked.

"It was my wife who met her. Martine does guided visits at the museum in Céret. Ingrid was part of the group she guided on Monday—June 18. They talked for a long time afterward.

My wife is a specialist in fauvism, and so is Ingrid. We continued the discussion over this same table at noon on Tuesday; Martine had invited her. Since she was nice and a little short of cash, we wanted to make her stay in France easier by putting her up."

Sebag wrote in his little blue schoolboy's notebook all the details about the young woman's activities. There were still four days left unaccounted for.

"Did her stay go well?" Molina continued.

"More or less . . . "

"Meaning?"

Revel spread his arms and put his hands flat on the table in a gesture of openness and sincerity.

"She's a pretty girl, with a very pleasant figure, and not only for a painter. She's also a person who is . . . how to put it . . . rather forward."

"Did she make advances to you?"

Jacques was a good interviewer, but Gilles sometimes reproached him for being too directive. He thought that during an interrogation the silences and hesitations lied less than the words.

"Not just to me."

Molina met his colleague's eyes and held back the question he was about to ask. Revel took the time to drink a bit of coffee. Sebag did the same. It was tonic, strong, and slightly acidic. With delightful notes of cocoa and almond.

"She posed nude for us," Revel went on. "For both of us at the same time. She made it clear that she was attracted to both of us."

He drank the last drop of coffee, then picked up the pot and offered it to his guests. Cornet and Molina declined with a gesture; they hadn't yet finished their cups. Sebag gladly accepted.

"This is a Central American coffee, isn't it?"

Gérard Revel did not hide his astonishment and pleasure.

"It's a mixture of coffees from Guatemala and Antigua. Congratulations. It's rare to find a true coffee lover."

"It's also rare for a coffee lover to drink such good coffee."

"Thanks."

"You're welcome."

Faced with this exchange of worldly remarks, Molina grimaced with annoyance. For his part, Sebag found this pause necessary before beginning a more intimate phase of the interview. He decided to re-start the conversation himself.

"And how did you react to Ingrid's advances?"

Once again, Revel spread his arms wide.

"What man hasn't fantasized about sleeping with two women at once?"

Sebag wondered whether women had the same desires. All night, he'd imagined Claire in the arms of a lover. Why only one, after all? Did women deceive their husbands more when they slept with two men at the same time? Or with a man and another woman? He forced himself to drive away these inopportune thoughts.

"So you agreed?"

Molina had taken over again.

"No. And I don't know if I'd have done it. Fantasies are not necessarily meant to be realized. In any case, I didn't have time to say anything at all."

"Why?"

"You wouldn't ask that question if you knew my wife. She didn't appreciate the proposition, and even less my hesitations. She threw Ingrid out of the house."

"Do you know where she went?" Jacques asked.

Revel suddenly crossed his arms and stared at his coffee cup.

"She called a taxi and left. Afterward, I don't know . . . "

His arms tightened even more. His right hand was rubbing his left bicep. For the first time, he was not entirely at ease. Sebag guessed that he needed a little help.

"Did she find the taxi's number in the phone book?"

Revel looked at Gilles but didn't answer.

"She didn't call a taxi at random, did she?"

The painter silently shook his head and looked at Sebag. Then he made up his mind.

"Since you seem to be well-informed, I have no reason to hide anything whatever from you. After all, I don't know anything about this guy."

In the doorway behind Revel a pretty brunette appeared. Her wild mop of hair was streaked with strands of auburn. Her figure was feline, her profile Greek, her eyes severe and lively. An image faithful to the engraving on the front door. Revel told them what they already knew:

"This is my wife Martine."

Martine Revel had come in at a bad time. Sebag half stood up as a sign of politeness.

"Please sit down, madam, your husband was telling us about Ingrid Raven's departure."

The pretty brunette sat down cross-legged on an ottoman. Molina took the lead again, addressing himself to Revel.

"You were saying that Ingrid didn't call just any taxi."

Revel looked at his wife out of the corner of his eye. Sebag divined that he was embarrassed to have already arrived at the point of giving the police names. Even in serious matters such as disappearances or murders, there was always a certain uneasiness when the time came to implicate other people. A complex about betraying someone. Revel would have liked to resist longer. Not for glory but to avoid burdening his conscience.

"As you seem to know already, a man named Lopez came to get her. He really is a cab driver. He'd met Ingrid at a party we'd taken her to. Wednesday or Thursday evening."

"Wednesday evening," Martine Revel said.

Her tone was firm. She had no hesitations, and she was not embarrassed about informing the police.

"Which party exactly?" Jacques asked.

"A vernissage for an exhibit in Perpignan," Revel replied.

"Ingrid came to France to study fauvism but she is also interested in contemporary art."

"Contemporary art, my ass!" his wife interrupted. "The psychedelic delirium of a young Spanish painter puffed up with pride and cocaine . . . "

Revel coughed and squirmed on his chair. His wife's critical comments on art seemed to him inappropriate.

"And what was Lopez doing at this exhibit?" Molina went on.

Martine Revel was laughing openly but it was her husband who answered first.

"I think he works for the man who organized the exposition. A certain Barrère, who's in public relations. All the important people in Perpignan were at that vernissage."

"Lopez seemed completely out of place and uncomfortable," Martine Revel explained again. "Like a eunuch in a sex-shop."

The image was bold but clear. Martine Revel was natural. Spontaneous.

"Maybe that's what attracted Ingrid to him," she added.

"Because she was attracted to him?"

"She liked Lopez right away, and she didn't try to hide it. Ingrid is no prude, you know."

"Yes, we've gathered as much," Jacques summed up, eager to return to a subject that interested him. "Your husband has told us what happened here, but we would like to have your version of the events as well."

"'Event' is a very big word," she said evasively.

She ran a finger splotched with blue paint over her upper lip, lingered over a little sensual sniff in the middle of it. Martine Revel didn't really want to talk about the circumstances of Ingrid's departure again. Her husband was watching her furtively. Uneasy, he occupied himself by pouring her coffee. The young woman took her time: she tossed a sugar cube in her cup and slowly stirred it.

Molina was getting impatient.

"Well?"

"Well, what?" she answered, abruptly putting her coffee spoon back on the table. "I don't really see how what happened here can help you find Ingrid . . . "

"Please allow us to decide what's important in this case, madam."

The atmosphere was becoming electric. Sebag knew from experience that when his colleague said "madam" in that tone, "bitch" was the word he would have liked to use.

"I know it's not very pleasant to talk about such personal matters in front of three strangers," he said, adopting a conciliatory tone. "We take no pleasure in asking you to return to that moment, but I remind you that we are investigating Ingrid's disappearance."

Martine Revel wavered for a few more seconds. She took another slow swallow of coffee, then started in. Not without having shot her husband a glance as dark as her coffee.

"The day after she arrived, Ingrid proved to be very different from the shy little student I thought I'd met. She went around all morning in scanty clothes: a little skirt and a T-shirt that was too short. And she had something sultry in her gestures, a come-hither look in her eyes. And then on Friday we made the error of asking her to pose for us, I don't know what we were thinking, it was as if we blundered straight into it . . . Anyway, we needed a model, she was there, she was pretty. There you have it."

The clock loudly struck four. Gilles could not help thinking about his son for a moment. By then, Léo should have arrived at his vacation camp. He might already be on a motorcycle. Happy as the kid he still was.

"She was nude," Martine Revel continued, "and she very quickly took poses that were . . . suggestive. Very far from what we were asking of her. What we were looking for was something like Renoir's bathers. She took herself for a pin-up in a men's magazine. She started asking us questions about our love life. She wanted to know if we were swingers—I was amazed that she knew the word in French—if we'd already done a threesome. Instead of relaxing during the rest period she came and walked around us."

She would have much preferred to stop there, but the policemen were careful to say nothing, to give no sign. Another glance at her husband.

"I recognize that I acted rather brutally. I ordered her to get dressed, and while she was doing that, I went up to her room. I put all her things in her bag and threw it out the window."

Her cheeks had grown slightly pink but her green eyes had gotten darker. This woman was a volcano. Capable of erupting but also of collapsing.

"Do you think something serious has happened to Ingrid?"

"At the moment, we have no reason to say that," Sebag said. "What we do know is that it was not a simple disappearance."

"You think she might have been . . . ?"

Sebag didn't try to reassure her. A little dose of concern often proved necessary to make witnesses talk.

"I reacted too harshly, I don't know what got into me," Martine said regretfully. "Now I'm angry at myself for it. If Ingrid had stayed here, nothing would have happened to her."

Her husband leaned toward her. He put his big paw on her frail hands splattered with paint.

"It was mainly because of me that you got angry, you know that."

He added, for the benefit of the others:

"I couldn't move while she was walking around us. I was . . . fascinated."

With the nail of his index finger he was mechanically trying to remove a red splotch on the back of his wife's hand.

"Don't blame yourself, you did what had to be done," he

said. "And whatever might have happened afterward is not your fault."

Martine Revel rested her forehead on her husband's shoulder. The heavy tick-tock of the clock resounded in the room. It slowly dissipated the moment's emotion.

Sebag took the coffee pot and poured the remaining coffee into the cups as equitably as possible. Molina roused their hosts.

"Would you have a little brandy or something to go with the last drop of this excellent coffee?"

Molina's savoir-faire in matters of psychology was limited to old-fashioned recipes, but when properly applied, it could be effective.

Revel was the first to move and waited for his wife to raise her head from his shoulder before rising heavily to his feet. He took a bottle without a label from an old cabinet and poured a colorless liquid into the cups. Cornet politely declined, putting his hand in front of his cup. Martine pushed hers forward to make sure her husband didn't forget it.

"This is a grape brandy my uncle makes," he explained as he sat down again. "It's all right in coffee, but alone it's pretty strong."

"A drink for real men," as they say," Jacques remarked. He knew his classics.

They took little sips. Sebag could hardly repress a grimace, Jacques loved it, and Martine Revel choked, seeming to confirm Molina's remarks about males. Putting down his cup, Gilles asked:

"Do you have any idea where Ingrid might have stayed between the time she left your home and her disappearance?"

"No, none at all," Revel replied.

"Did you question this Lopez guy?" his wife asked.

The three men looked at each other and for a moment hesitated to answer.

"Is there a problem?"

"José Lopez disappeared at the same time as Ingrid," Molina replied.

"You don't think it might be simply two lovers running away together?" ventured Martine Revel.

"If we thought that, we wouldn't be here," Molina said evasively.

Sebag decided it was time to leave. He finished his fortified coffee. Yuk! To spoil such nectar with a rot-gut barely good enough to make a tractor cough! Molina might sometimes show a talent for psychology, but he would definitely never have taste.

When they got back to police headquarters the meeting was already over. However, they found on their computers a summary of the proceedings rapidly written up by Ménard.

Sebag skipped the passage concerning the work done by Jacques, who had already told him about it that morning. At least one call-girl he'd talked to had admitted having met Lopez at parties organized by Barrère. She even said that she had had "paid sexual relations" with the cab driver. The expression the young woman used had made Molina laugh.

For their part, the Raynaud-Moreno pair had gone to Toulouse to talk with Charles Got, who'd been beaten up by Lopez outside a night club a few years earlier. Got had left the Perpignan area in 2003 and moved with his wife and children to the suburbs of Toulouse. He seemed to have retained no hard feelings about their argument. "Lopez paid, the whole business is forgotten," he'd told the inspectors. Moreover, he had an excellent alibi for the night of June 26: along with a dozen other people, he'd been helping prepare for the village fête.

Lambert had found Ingrid's room in the student residence hall, a very small studio with a kitchen near the university. In it he had found nothing belonging to the young woman except a tourist folder about the museum in Céret and an open tube of mayonnaise in the refrigerator. At the museum in Céret, Llach had dug up a signature reading "Ingrid from Holland" in the guest book, dated June 18, thus corroborating the Revel couple's assertions.

Ménard had come up with the day's most important information. In Barrère's account books he'd found the record of a check made out to a fancy hotel in Canet-Plage, curiously annotated "paid for JL," JL like José Lopez, as Ménard judiciously noted. He had immediately looked into the matter: the hotel's register bore no trace of the taxi driver, but on the other hand it did mention Ingrid Raven, who arrived Friday night—the day she left the Revel's home—and left Tuesday morning. Four nights in all: Lopez had paid in cash for the last two, but Perpign'And Co. had in fact paid for the first two. Castello had immediately decided to bring Barrère in for questioning the next morning. The interrogation was to be conducted by Ménard under Lefèvre's supervision.

Just as Sebag was about to exit his e-mail, a new message appeared on his screen. It came from Castello's office and ordered all inspectors to be at the headquarters at six o'clock the next morning for a raid organized with the customs men and directed against contraband cigarettes. All officers were to be armed with their service weapons.

"Damn it to Hell," Molina swore. He'd discovered the message at the same time as Sebag. "Six o'clock in the morning! . . . And I had a date this evening! I'm too old for this shit . . . "

"Yes, I think you are," Sebag joked. "You're too old to go out with twenty-year-old girls. Watch out, your heart will make you pay for that someday."

"Go ahead, laugh. Everybody isn't lucky enough to have a wife who gets younger every year."

This jibe, which was intended to be friendly, plunged Gilles back into his dark thoughts. He tuned out of the conversation for a few seconds but sensed that Jacques noticed. He had to get it together. Put Jacques off the scent.

"Tell her that you're not a womanizer and you never sleep with a girl the first night, as a matter of principle."

"And you think that women like that sort of talk?"

"I've already used it several times, you know. In the past."

"And it worked?"

"I didn't sleep with them the first night, if that's what you want to know."

"What about the other nights?"

"What other nights?"

There was a short silence during which Molina looked at his colleague without seeming to understand. Then he burst into laughter. Satisfied that he had distracted his attention, Sebag clicked on a game site. After all, it was only six-thirty. Claire could wait a little this evening. One little game would do her no harm.

"Do you remember where you put your gun?" Molina asked.

Sebag answered without looking up from his computer screen.

"It's supposed to always be in the second drawer of my desk. That's where I put it the last time. In 1957, I think."

He didn't like firearms and took out his revolver only when the order to do so was precise and imperative.

"I hope you still know how to use it, just in case."

"I hold out my arm, the elbow slightly bent, I close one eye, and pull the trigger. No problem. How about you, do you remember what you're supposed to do if I use my weapon?"

"Shoot in the same direction as you and try to hit the target you've missed?"

"That's the second thing you're supposed to do. But you can do that only if you've properly carried out the first assignment, which is far more important."

"And what is that?"

"Always back me up, you imbecile! . . . And damn! You made me lose with your bullshit. I was about to break my record."

He was far from having gotten his best score, but Sebag was one of those who believe that a little deception from time to time doesn't hurt anyone.

"Sorry," Molina said, though he wasn't. "See you tomorrow."

He left and Sebag took a deep breath. He was happy to have a few minutes to think before going home. For the first time, he wasn't in a hurry to leave the office. Tomorrow Séverine was leaving with her girlfriend's parents. Claire and Gilles would be alone. It would be time to sort things out.

Gilles was perplexed and worried, but he couldn't feel angry. Maybe it was because the presumption of guilt wasn't strong enough. After all, Claire wasn't obliged to tell him everything; she could have her little secrets and even lie to protect them. Just because she'd missed a gym class didn't necessarily mean that she'd spent that time in a lover's arms: she must have had another reason for lying to her husband.

Okay, but what?

He would have much preferred not to reason like a cop in this matter. But his name was Gilles Sebag and Gilles Sebag was a cop. At least for the time being.

Unconsciously, he argued both sides of the case. On the one hand, Claire's repeated absences and her lie. On the other, her expressions of love and their passionate love-making despite twenty years of living together. And then her happiness. Her happiness to be living with him, he was convinced of that. Or else everything was just a lie.

His mind was spinning. He could feel a headache coming on.

He took out his telephone and dialed Léo's number. At the second ring, his son answered. There was music in the background.

"Hi, it's Papa. Did you get there okay?"

"Yeah, yeah, no problem."

"Are you having good weather?"

"It's sunny but it seems cooler than in Perpignan."

"Did you already ride a quad this afternoon?"

"Just a little bit, to see what level people were at."

"Do you like it there?"

"Yeah, it looks like it'll be fun."

Léo interrupted himself. He was speaking to someone in a low voice. Behind him, the music grew louder.

"Have you eaten?" Gilles asked.

"No, not yet. We're going to eat soon, I think it's dinner time."

"Well, then I'll let you go . . . What's on the program for tomorrow?"

"We have a quad lesson in the morning and in the afternoon we'll do motocross."

"Great . . . "

He almost told him not to go to bed too late, but stopped himself.

"Okay then, see you, son."

"See you."

"Don't hesitate to call, okay?"

"Yeah, yeah, I promise, papa."

He hung up, frustrated. He recalled the pleasure they'd taken in talking on the phone when Léo was a child spending his vacations with his grandparents. The boy never knew what to say when Gilles tried to make him talk about the little joys of childhood. The pebbles and bits of wood collected in the fields, the games he'd made up with Séverine, the cartoons on television. The words didn't matter much. What mattered for the father as well as for the son was prolonging the moment.

Sebag tried to concentrate on the case. He opened his notebook to write down the results of his reflection. Gérard

Barrère's conception of public relations activities was clearly too flexible for the tax authorities and the vice squad. But Sebag couldn't imagine him being involved in Ingrid Raven's disappearance.

Besides, "disappearance" was not a legal offense.

If the hypothesis of a voluntary act was definitively set aside, a disappearance could be the consequence of two kinds of crimes: a kidnapping or a murder. Sebag wrote down and circled the two words. He connected them with a third expression that he wrote just under them: criminal court. Barrère's lies were too fragile and too easily discernible to stand up to an extensive police investigation. And then when you're getting ready to kidnap or murder a young woman, you don't pay for her room in a hotel with a check that has your business's name on it.

The telephone interrupted his reflections.

"Hello, Gilles?"

It was Claire.

"Are you coming home soon? Should we go ahead and eat or wait for you? Séverine and I would like to watch a film on television tonight."

He looked at his watch. It was almost eight o'clock.

"Excuse me, I had work to do. I'll be there in fifteen minutes. Just go ahead and begin without me. What's the film?"

"*Les Choses de la vie*. It's a film by Sautet made in the 1970s. I'd like Séverine to see it, but I'd be surprised if you liked it . . . "

"Doesn't matter. Go eat. I'll be there soon."

He got up with difficulty. Last night he'd slept badly, and he had to get up early the next morning. He felt tired just thinking about it.

CHAPTER 13

S ebag checked to be sure he'd taken off the safety. He knew from experience that when you decided to carry a gun, it had to be ready to fire.

The warehouse they were surrounding looked just like the other warehouses in the Saint-Charles Market. Except that behind these metal doors there were hundreds of cartons of cigarettes. If they got lucky, there might be thousands of them. Superintendent Castello had tried to postpone the raid but the prefect had insisted on it. He needed something to brag about. Fortunately, there was no longer any talk of a visit by the Minister of the Interior.

Castello had sent Lambert, Molina, and Sebag, along with a dozen other uniformed officers, to help out their colleagues in Customs. Ménard and Llach had remained at headquarters to question Barrère. Ménard, because he was not comfortable with this kind of raid; Llach because he was too well known in the neighborhood to take part in a surprise operation.

They were waiting for the signal from Captain Marceau of French Customs. They arrived in the area at 7:00 A.M. A first van had arrived at about eight o'clock. The warehouse door had slid open just far enough to let the van enter. Then it had been immediately closed. A second van arrived shortly afterward. Neither of them had come out again. They estimated that there were five or six people inside. They'd taken up their positions surrounding the warehouse at 8:20.

In his headphone, Sebag heard Marceau's low voice.

"We're ready, we have them surrounded, let's go."

Marceau had hardly finished speaking when Sebag saw far away on the highway interchange two cars and a dark blue van with rotating lights flashing on their roofs. They roared up to the parking lot, their sirens blaring. Eight customs men spurted out of the vehicles. Two of them placed themselves on either side of the big metal door to the warehouse; the others, holding their rifles to their shoulders, took up positions behind the cars. They pounded on the door while the usual orders were barked out. The operation might seem excessive for the arrest of a handful of amateur smugglers. But in every raid, you had to be ready for trouble: you could never tell when one of the criminals might be a hothead prepared to fire on a cop to avoid going to prison.

The wait seemed to Sebag interminable. Gripping the handle of his revolver, his right hand was getting sweaty. His fingers were all white. He loosened his grip. The metal walls of the warehouse revealed nothing about the hesitations and probable discussions among the smugglers.

The door slowly slid open. Silently. Just as a few men started to come out with their hands in the air, a side door suddenly opened. Right in front of Lambert. A young man rushed out, a revolver in his hand. Stunned by the presence of the police, he froze. Only his haggard eyes moved, jumping from one cop to another without stopping on any of them. He gripped his gun more tightly. Sebag saw Lambert, who was also scared, straighten his arm slightly to aim better. Somebody had to speak. Right away. Make contact.

"Let's calm down, people, let's calm down," he said, spreading his arms wide, his palms forward.

The young man's eyes settled on him. Beads of sweat were forming on his forehead. His hand was still gripping the revolver, but he wasn't aiming it at anyone.

"There's nothing you can do, there are too many of us. Don't make it worse for yourself."

He raised the barrel of the revolver a little, but a slight flutter in his eyes betrayed his hesitation. He'd understood the situation. Sebag sensed that he had to be given time to come to an agreement with his pride. He had to maintain contact.

"There are about fifty cops here, and the whole area is surrounded. You know it isn't worth it. You have no chance."

Without taking his eyes off Sebag, the young man slowly lowered his gun.

"Now drop it on the ground, and then slowly put your arms behind your back and turn around. Slowly, still very slowly."

The boy waited a few more seconds for appearance's sake. Sebag continued to talk as calmly as possible. The words didn't matter, the tone was the most important thing. Calm and firm. Cops should do internships with circus lion-tamers, he thought. Finally the young man did what he was told. He crouched down to drop his gun. Got back up. Turned around. Sebag put away his revolver while Lambert held a gun on the criminal. He took his pair of handcuffs from the back pocket of his pants and put them on the young man. Without his gun and the extreme tension that had filled him during the last few seconds, he looked like what he really was: a boy of eighteen at most. Just a few years older than Léo.

Lambert led the boy away and made him get into the Customs van. Sebag took a deep breath. He suddenly felt terribly thirsty.

He went into the warehouse. A bluish light fell from the skylights. He counted five men sitting handcuffed in front of a mountain of boxes. He went up to Captain Marceau, who was talking to the prefecture on the phone. He waited until Marceau had finished his conversation.

"Well?"

The leader of the Customs men looked half-satisfied.

"The catch could have been better," he said, "but it's not so bad. A few weapons confiscated, six people arrested, including the ringleaders, I think. A stroke of luck. So far as the merchandise is concerned, we're still working on a preliminary estimate."

Two Customs men in uniform were in fact moving around the pile of boxes, counting them.

"Would you say you made a forcible arrest?" Captain Marceau asked Sebag.

"Forcible seems to me an exaggeration . . . Let's say it was tense."

"A perp came out with a gun in his hand, I'm told?"

"True, but he didn't really threaten us."

Sebag guessed where his interlocutor was trying to get him to go. Psychologically, the confiscation of weapons was more important than the quantity of cigarettes seized. It would allow them to show the public that cigarette smuggling was no longer harmless and that it led directly to major crime. The arrest of the boy was thus likely to be highlighted. Sebag knew that some people at the prefecture or the ministry would go so far as to regret—only *sotto voce*, of course—that there hadn't been an exchange of gunfire. Ah! If a cop could have been wounded in this operation . . . Sebag no longer nourished any illusions regarding the limits of his lofty, distant superiors' cynicism. But maybe that was due only to the bad mood that had settled over his tired mind. In any case, he'd do everything he could to ensure that the boy wasn't made to seem more dangerous than he was.

Superintendent Castello, who had followed the whole operation by radio from his office, appeared in the warehouse a few minutes after the operation. He greeted Marceau and then Sebag. He wore a broad smile.

"Perfect, gentlemen. This was carried out in high style, I think."

One of the two Customs men who were counting the boxes came up to Captain Marceau.

"We've counted 292 boxes, that makes almost three thousand cartons in all."

"Market value?"

The Customs man did the calculation in his notebook and gave his verdict:

"At thirty euros a carton—the average retail price—that comes to a total of 87,600 euros."

"Not bad," the superintendent commented soberly.

"It's not equivalent to a seizure of drugs in Le Perthus," the Captain said. "But for cigarette smuggling, it's not bad, in fact. We'll round it off to a hundred thousand euros for the newspapers and that will be fine."

Castello gave a crude horse-dealer's wink to the head of the Customs men.

"I'll leave you two of my men, but if you no longer need the others . . . We're planning to make raids on bars in Perpignan. We've already located three of them, but the operation will be more extensive."

Marceau approved.

"So, in the end the minister is not coming?" Castello asked.

"He's busy elsewhere, but the prefect will be here around eleven—I've just talked to the head of his cabinet. The reporters will be called in for an improvised press conference. The television crews will be allowed to film it."

It was the superintendent's turn to approve.

"I see the public relations plan is under way."

"It's part of the job," Marceau confirmed.

Castello turned to Sebag.

"You'll stay here with Lambert. Molina will join Llach in Perpignan; they'll direct the operations. I'm going back to headquarters. Ménard must be grilling Barrère."

Sebag and Lambert recorded the identities of the smugglers and began the preliminary interrogations. Two of the criminals—apparently the ringleaders—were, to use the traditional formula, known to the police for the crimes of procuring and dealing drugs. After doing time in prison, they had thought they could get away from it all by selling cigarettes. They'd made the first runs in their own car. A dozen cartons on each trip, that was almost legal. Then they'd recruited a handful of buddies who were out of work and their little business grew larger.

Three of their accomplices had been unemployed for four years. They hadn't thought they were doing anything wrong. They made trips from time to time. Brought home a little money. The first in a long time. It wasn't much at first, but it was already a lot for them. They got more and more involved and hadn't been able to quit when they should have. A single round-trip to Spain brought in more than a hard day's work in Roussillon's vineyards or orchards.

The boy had already appeared before the juvenile court judge. The theft of a scooter, burglary. He'd barely avoided going to prison, and this time he wasn't going to get off again. He'd turned eighteen two months before, and had been arrested with a gun in his hand. He was the one who would get the heaviest sentence.

"He didn't point his gun at you, did he?" Sebag asked Lambert.

"No. I thought he was going to but he stopped when you spoke to him."

"So we agree. You won't change your version of the facts even if you're asked to?"

"Uh . . . no. But why would anyone ask me to do that?"

"Who knows," Sebag said evasively.

A few years earlier, he would have found ways to make the reports less damning. He would have avoided mentioning the boy's reluctance to surrender, which would have gotten him a more lenient sentence in court. But would the kid even know how to take advantage of that? His record hardly left room for any illusions about that. Once he was back on the street, he'd start all over again. And maybe next time he'd raise his hand and fire. Sebag didn't want to take that risk. He couldn't do anything more for the boy.

They left the warehouse just before the prefect and the media arrived. They'd all gotten up early that morning. It was time for lunch. Their stomachs noisily demanded their reward.

They joined Jacques in a little restaurant in the Saint Charles Market. Gilles ordered fish *a la plancha* with ratatouille. Molina told them about the police raids in the Perpignan bars. They'd raided about a dozen bars and had found contraband cigarettes only in the three they'd already targeted.

That afternoon, everyone gathered in the meeting room. It was unbearably hot, but they'd have to bear it anyway, because the air conditioner had resisted all Lambert's, Molina's, and Llach's attempts to make it work.

After devoting a few minutes to the morning's operation, they moved on to Ingrid Raven's case.

Lopez's computer had been hacked by specialists from a computer shop who'd been brought in by Castello. It had taken them only a few minutes, the password being simply Syljenny, a condensed version of the first names of his wife and daughter. Lopez used his computer mainly to play video games, watch DVDs, and surf the Net. He often visited porno sites but limited himself to free ones. Lefèvre, who had undertaken to explore Lopez's account, had found nothing noteworthy other than an Excel file containing initials, dates, and a few figures. He handed around a few copies.

"We'll come back to this after Inspector Ménard's presentation," he explained.

Ménard was eager to report his interrogation of Barrère. He seemed satisfied with himself, which was a good sign. Barrère had begun the interview by reprimanding the policemen. He was furious to have been hauled in that way and laid out his connections the way one puts on a bullet-proof vest: the prosecutor, elected officials, the chamber of commerce, etc. Ménard had immediately countered. He'd drawn a dark picture—prostitution, kidnapping, perhaps murder. He'd made Barrère see that his famous connections wouldn't hold up for long under the weight of the facts about which he was being questioned today—as a witness and only as a witness. Barrère had quickly understood. He'd become meek as a lamb and told them everything he knew.

He admitted having occasionally organized rather unusual parties for businesses that wanted to show certain important customers a good time. It was essentially in the context of these parties that he hired Lopez to serve as a driver and a "guide." It was a good deal, because he paid Lopez in cash and won back all or part of the money when they played billiards. Lopez spent what remained to him on call-girls, because he had a hard time remaining passive during these "lively" parties. Barrère denied knowing anything about Lopez's trafficking in Viagra.

One Friday, the cab driver had called him because he needed money to pay a hotel bill for a young woman he'd met a few days earlier at a vernissage. The hotel was expensive, and Barrère didn't have enough cash on him, so he paid the first two nights in advance with his firm's checkbook, thinking that he could absorb the bill into his general operating expenses. Lopez had confided in him that he intended to get the beautiful Vanessa to take part in some sex parties in Perpignan.

Barrère had seen Lopez and the young woman—he didn't know what her real name was—again on Tuesday evening. Lopez had paid back in cash the five hundred euros that Barrère had advanced him for the hotel, explaining that he'd found Ingrid's first customer. He'd spoken openly in front of the young woman. Barrère had heard nothing further from him since that evening. And he had no idea who the customer in question was.

"What was your impression of Barrère this morning?" the superintendent asked.

"I think this time he told us everything. He said that when we first told him about Lopez's disappearance he thought he'd run off with a woman. So his sole objective was to keep us from discovering his firm's dubious practices, and since most of the information he could have given us about Ingrid Raven and Lopez threatened to lead us to examine his activities, in each case he'd told us as little as possible.

"Do you think Barrère had something to do with Ingrid's disappearance?" Castello asked Ménard.

"No, not directly, anyway."

Lefèvre confirmed Ménard's impression. Then he forked out a compliment regarding the way the interrogation had been conducted. That pleased Ménard, but his colleagues appreciated it less. Not because they were jealous but because it didn't seem right for a young greenhorn to allow himself to comment on their work.

"With your permission," Lefèvre continued, "we'll now return to the table that was found on Lopez's computer and that I distributed to you a little while ago. We think it is a kind of summary, coded account book for Lopez's petty trafficking. I say summary because Lopez wrote down only the entries, that is, the amounts received or due. Across from the amounts, there are initials corresponding to his cab customers. You'll note that the letters "GB" often come up. They refer, of course, to Gérard Barrère. This morning he confirmed that the amounts recorded generally corresponded to cash payments he'd made to Lopez.

The inspectors silently examined the table.

"I'd like to draw your attention particularly to the very last line. Across from the letters "BW," there is the sum of three thousand euros. If from that sum we subtract five hundred euros to repay the sum Barrère advanced to pay for the first two nights in the hotel, and then five hundred more to pay for the following two nights, we have two thousand euros—and that is, I remind you, the amount found in Lopez's taxi."

Lefèvre gave the policemen time to follow his reasoning. The inspectors' eyes moved from one line to another on the table. They all finally arrived at the notorious initials.

"So without going too far we can say that these three thousand euros constitute the payment made by the customer that Lopez found for Ingrid. BW is probably the last to have seen the couple. Thus at this point he is our main suspect."

Sebag nodded. The reasoning seemed to him simple and hence pertinent. The investigation had just made real progress. Maybe Claire had been right the other night when she called him an eternal pessimist.

However, they still had to find this mysterious BW.

The house was empty and silent.

Séverine had left while Sebag was playing cowboy. For her part, Claire had gone out with some female friends. At least that's what she'd said.

He found himself all alone.

On leaving headquarters, he'd gone running. He'd gotten on a bike path and followed it for the first two or three miles, doing wind sprints. Then on the way back he'd run at a steadier pace. Seven miles an hour. Running had done his mind good but exhausted his body. Not enough sleep the last few nights.

The first thing he did when he got home was take a shower. Cold water on full blast. His body stiffened under the spray and then gradually relaxed. He gave the water time to get rid of the heat accumulated under his skin. When he turned off the faucet, it was immediately silent again. A heavy silence. He put on a pair of shorts and a simple tank top.

He wandered through the soulless house. He thought he liked it, felt good in it, but it needed to resound with noise and life. Silent, he found it sinister. Glacial, despite the heat. He gazed at the pool through the living room window. The water was calm, pure, and blue. Tempting. But he didn't feel like going for a swim. There was no one to splash water on him.

He ran his eyes over the bookcase. It had been a long time since he'd sat down with a good book. He could read in the study. Or in the bedroom, on the terrace, in the living room. He had only too many choices. No need to get away from the television set, from the computer, Séverine's radio or Léo's stereo. His new freedom made him feel dizzy.

Not a single book on the shelves aroused a desire to read it.

He picked up the remote and turned on the TV. Hopped from one channel to another. No one was there to protest, and he took advantage of it. Five minutes. That was long enough to realize that nothing caught his interest.

However, he left the TV on and went to get something to drink in the kitchen. First he filled a glass with Coke, added three big ice cubes; he was thirsty after running. As he drank, he poked around in the refrigerator. There were quite a few left-overs: carrots, tomatoes, cucumbers, but nothing tempted him. Instead, he added a dash of whisky to the remains of his Coke.

He could have called a friend. Just like that. To talk. Catch up.

He didn't have any friends.

Time and distance had caused his old friendships to lose their intimacy. He hadn't been able to replace them. No pals with whom he could drink beer, ogle girls, and talk soccer or rugby. Because he didn't like beer, and liked sports events still less. Or any of the things men did when they went on a binge together. He'd never liked the company of men. Too much showing off and hidden rivalries. Too much vulgarity.

He had to put up with more than enough of that at work.

He did have a few relationships: the parents of Claire's students and her colleagues. People with whom he could have discussions but not talk. Whose fault was that? His own, probably. That's how he was, discreet and even secretive. It was also his occupation's fault. People liked to know somebody who was a cop. Like doctors and plumbers, they can come in handy sometimes. But you don't confide in a cop. Not without a summons.

He liked family outings, games of cards or Scrabble on the big table in the living room. Apart from his job and running, he had no life outside his family.

He poured himself another big glass of Coke. And put a larger dose of whisky in it.

The children were growing up, moving away. Nothing was more normal than that. They had their own lives to live. Without him. "Little by little, the bird leaves the nest." Léo and Séverine no longer needed their father. They'd been weaned. He hadn't.

It was painful. Like a divorce.

Claire had her work, her friends, her activities. Gymnastics, the chorale. She didn't seem to suffer from the situation. On the contrary. She was bursting with joy and health. Maturity suited her well.

Why wasn't she there?

He'd often imagined this moment when there would just be the two of them again. They'd sometimes even been impatient for it to arrive. They'd met at university and had Léo very soon.

Too soon?

They hadn't been kids, however. Gilles was 25, Claire 24. But they hadn't yet taken time to live. They finished their studies; Gilles had dragged things out a bit. They were just beginning to earn a living. They wanted to travel, to go around the world. They'd tried another adventure. An adventure that was now coming to an end.

They thought they could catch up later on.

Later . . .

Later should have begun tonight.

In a few days, Claire would be leaving on a cruise. Her first boat trip. With her friends. When she'd told him that she'd bought her ticket, he'd felt a twinge in his heart. He hadn't said anything. She had to keep busy. She had two months of vacation, while he had only one. She had already declined her girlfriends' proposals several times, and had limited herself to a few short trips in July with her family. But this year the children were going off by themselves, and she'd given in.

They were missing their rendezvous. As a couple, were they really so different from Sylvie and José Lopez? Were they still living together or just side by side? They saw each other in the morning and the evening; from time to time they said "I love you." More or less the way one says "hello." Out of politeness. Out of habit.

When you know each other by heart, you can read your partner's body language, smiles and grimaces. You start by no longer needing to look at each other and end up not seeing each other at all. You no longer even bother to look up.

All that was drearily banal. He knew it. But you always think: "*We'll* be different." From time to time you wake up, you want to react. You bring home a bouquet of flowers, make love on the living room carpet, suddenly decide to go to a movie.

And then one day you realize that you're alone. Still a father, still married, but a bachelor again.

That had been the part hardest to bear. And whether or not Claire had a lover was merely a detail.

He'd poured himself more whisky. Without the Coke. He was already finishing it. A last swig. He closed his eyes. Notes of smoke. Pepper, iodine. The perfume of the Scottish islands. He'd changed since his first bachelorhood. Earlier, he hadn't been able to afford to get drunk on ten-year-old Talisker.

He had a wild desire to call Claire. Her melodious voice and her joyful laugh hummed in his memory. He wanted to hear their echo in reality. He went to get his phone from the pocket of his jacket, which was hanging on the rack in the entry hall. He dialed her cell phone number and hit the call button. He waited until her name appeared on the screen, then hung up.

Where are you, Claire?

She'd told him she was going out with Pascale and Véronique. They were supposed to go to a restaurant and then to a movie. Or the other way around. He no longer knew exactly. Above all, he remembered that she'd told him not to wait up for her. That she'd probably get home late.

Grabbing the remote, he silenced the TV.

He turned on the stereo and looked for a CD. Something calm. Tender. And melancholic. He chose a disk by Cesaria Evora. *Sodade*. The languorous voice of the singer from Cape Verde rose in the deserted house.

His head was already spinning. He knew he should eat something, but he wasn't hungry. It was too hot.

He thought again about the class evaluation meetings. There had been too many of them that year, and they'd run too late. And about Claire's frequent outings with Véronique, her friend who'd been depressed since she'd been going through divorce proceedings. He kept thinking about this gym class she claimed to have attended.

How could he still have any doubts?

Claire sometimes seemed so far away. He recalled the other day. Her graceful movements, her distant smile. And especially the pink in her cheeks, the same as when they had just made love.

The clues were piling up, his suspicions becoming more precise. The cop wanted to know but did the husband? You're not a cuckold so long as you don't know it.

"Cuckold . . . " The word was enormously ugly.

Why did he have to set that damned trap for Claire?

He imagined his wife in another man's arms. He invented situations, provided them with details. Pure masochism. The pain was atrocious and he kept coming back to it. Like a tongue returning again and again to the tooth with a cavity in it.

In the end, he wasn't surprised. It was all so natural. How could a woman limit herself to being looked at by a single man for twenty years? How could she be satisfied with the same hands on her body, the same skin under her fingertips. The same cock . . . The worst part was thinking that when she prettied herself up this morning it was for another man. For another man that she hesitated between her form-fitting dress and her frilly skirt. For another man that she undid the top button of her blouse and that she allowed the lace on her bra to be seen. For another man that she emphasized her green eyes with discreet eyeliner. That was the real betrayal. The sex was merely accessory.

He didn't wait until he'd finished his glass to pour himself more whisky. He sensed that the evening was going to end badly.

But how could he stop his imagination from functioning? Would the mixture of alcohol and solitude give him a gloomy outlook on life or a flash of lucidity?

With a rolling gait, he went out onto the terrace. Night was falling but it was still hot. However, a little breeze was making things more pleasant. It was rustling the bamboos at the back of the yard.

He collapsed on a chaise longue.

Whistles repeatedly disturbed his ruminations. The neighbor was calling her cat. She'd lost two of them recently; they'd been run over by cars. She'd gotten another, but she was constantly worried. As soon as the cat escaped, she walked all over the neighborhood whistling the same two sad notes, over and over. Occasionally the tom showed up. But most of the time the old woman went on whistling in vain for hours. She got out of breath and began to cough. A hoarse cough. A smoker's cough. She was exhausting the whole neighborhood. This evening, he felt overwhelmed by a strange sympathy for the woman the children called "the crazy old lady."

Was he doomed to end up like her? Abandoned by his family and friends, and with a cat that ran away as his only companion?

No.

"Definitely not."

The words had slipped out of him. He'd shouted. He finished his glass in a single swig. Inside, he was full of new energy. He was going to resist; he was going to fight.

And if he lost anyway, he'd get a goldfish instead.

CHAPTER 14

Anneke had spent a delightful evening with her French friends at the Deux Margots bar. But she'd preferred to return alone to her furnished room. She walked rather uncertainly down the dirty, slippery sidewalks of Perpignan's old quarter. She could have been leaning on Florent's strong arm had she responded to his advances. The guy was cute, and his lively blue eyes sparkled with desire. Maybe some other time. She hadn't liked his excessive self-confidence and especially his insistence. As if Dutch girls were supposed to lie down as soon as someone smiled at them.

Nightfall hadn't cooled down the air. It was still hot. But less than in the bar. Anneke was a little ashamed of the stains on her dress below the armpits. She'd had to watch her movements all evening, and especially not lift her arms. She was afraid she might smell a little strong despite the deodorant—above a certain temperature, chemistry is powerless.

Anneke was in a hurry to take a shower and go to bed. She was tired. The evening had been a long one, and so had the school year. She was finishing the first part of her university degree in molecular biology. She was deeply interested in that field. She'd chosen to take her degree in France; these days, with European Union programs, it was easy to do that. She'd had a hard time with French. She'd been a good student in high school, but taking classes in a foreign language was really very different. Especially in French, a language that was so subtle and so complex, with all its rules and exceptions to the rule. A language that resembled the country.

She walked through the narrow, winding streets of the North African quarter, passed in front of the window, still lit, of a shop that offered cheap telephone calls all over the world. The historic center of the city had retained its popular soul. Squalid buildings still housed a mixed population of immigrants and gypsies. In Holland, the city centers now consisted only of offices and residences for young, single managers. In France as well, she'd been told. But not in Perpignan. Not yet.

She heard footsteps behind her. Very close. She now realized that these footsteps had been following her for some time. Following her . . . "Hey, girl, you're getting paranoid," she tried to reassure herself. She'd said that to herself in French. She caught herself more and more often thinking in that language. Some nights she even dreamed in French. She wouldn't have thought that possible. The week before, on the telephone with her parents, she'd had trouble finding her words in her native language. Several times her mother had had to reproach her for filling her remarks with French expressions.

The streets she was walking through were deserted. She'd met only two persons since leaving the bar. However, the footsteps behind her were coming closer. They weren't a figment of her imagination. In a shop window, she tried to get a glimpse of her pursuer, but it was too dark. She was now quite close to her room. She clutched her purse to her and walked faster.

She left the Saint Mathieu neighborhood and approached the Avenue Poincaré. She had only to follow that avenue, a gentle uphill walk. She passed a service station that had closed for the night. A few hundred yards more and she'd be there. The footsteps had stopped. Soon she'd be in her bed.

Suddenly a dark form leaped out of a doorway and slammed her against a car. A hand covered her mouth to prevent her from crying out. She felt the blade of a knife on her neck. She didn't dare swallow. The man attacking her was wearing a hood. He must be dying of the heat, she said to herself, astonished to have such thoughts at a time like this.

The man didn't move. The moment went on. Anneke was pinned between the car and her attacker. She could feel his slow breathing, both muted and amplified by his woolen hood. He still hadn't tried anything. Her fear gave way to puzzlement. Then to a certain impatience. The moment was going on endlessly. She didn't understand. If he wants to kill me, let him do it, if he wants to rape me, let him get on with it, but for God's sake let's get this over with. Headlights appeared at the other end of the avenue. A sign of life. A hope. They were like a signal for the man.

"Get into the car," he said in a hushed but firm voice.

His hand left her mouth and slipped behind her back to try to open the car door against which she was pressed. But the door resisted. Anneke noticed that the pressure of the knife blade had disappeared from her throat. She pushed the man away with all her strength and screamed. Holding her purse by the strap, she swung it in front of her. It seemed to her that she had hit her target. Then she began to run down the middle of the street toward the approaching headlights. The driver slammed on the brakes. A man got out.

"Help me, please, I've just been attacked . . . "

A woman got out of the car as well, on the passenger side. She came up to Anneke and put her hands on her shoulders, while her companion had a look around.

The woman took out a tissue and wiped Anneke's neck. The tissue was stained red. The knife blade had left its mark. The woman handed her another tissue so that she could wipe away her tears. Then she said to her gently:

"I'm calling the police."

Anneke would have liked to take refuge in her bed, hide under her clean, cool sheets. She also wanted to take a shower, a long, hot one. But she knew that she would have to wait a while yet.

The driver came back toward the two women. He'd found no one. Silence fell over the city again.

CHAPTER 15

T he alarm roused him out of a cottony fog. He slowly stood up. The solar lamps studded the yard with points of melancholy blue. An empty bottle lay next to the chaise longue. He bent down to pick it up and felt sick to his stomach. His head was spinning. He squinted to get his bearings.

Talisker. He'd finished it off under the stars. Right out of the bottle.

The alarm clock stopped ringing.

He looked at his watch. 3:20. Claire still hadn't come home. It wasn't an alarm clock ringing that had pulled him out of his coma. Not at this hour. And in any case he couldn't have heard it from the terrace.

He went back into the house. He'd left his cell phone somewhere. On the bar. The screen indicated that he had a message. Who could be calling him at this time of night? Someone from work? Or Claire?

Something had happened.

He feverishly dialed the access code for his message service. What did he fear most? A message from the hospital telling him that Claire had had an accident or a message from Claire telling him that she wasn't coming home, that she'd never come home again? Before he could muster the courage to answer that question, a strong voice with a vigorous accent assaulted his sensitive ears.

"Pardon me for disturbing you at this hour, sir, it's Ripoll, André Ripoll. I'm on night duty at the station and a letter has just arrived for you; it appears that it's important, and that's why I took the liberty of calling your cell phone. I didn't know whether I should also call you at home, I'm very sorry . . . "

He hadn't finished listening to the message when the land line started ringing in the study. Ripoll must have made up his mind. Sebag interrupted the message and went to pick up the receiver.

"Hello, this is Ripoll, André Ripoll, I'm sorry . . . "

"It's okay, get to the point," he interrupted, "I've just gotten your message. What's all this business about an urgent letter in the middle of the night?"

"I know it may seem bizarre, but first there was a telephone call, about half an hour ago, to say that a letter was waiting for you in the station's mailbox and that it was urgent. It didn't seem to be a joke, so I went to see. There was in fact an envelope in the mailbox and it was marked 'urgent'."

"Can you describe this envelope for me, what does it look like?"

"Well . . . nothing special, it's a normal envelope, that's all. White. With your name typed on it. No stamp, it must have been dropped directly in the box."

Obviously, at that hour! What was he thinking, this Ripoll? Did he think the Perpignan postmen made a second delivery every night around 3:00 A.M.?

"Is that all? No sender's name?"

"No, just a drawing on the back."

"A drawing?"

"Yes. It looks like a bird."

A shiver ran through Sebag's body.

"What does this bird look like? A swallow?"

"Maybe. I don't know anything about birds. But it might be a swallow, yes."

He dropped two aspirins in a glass of water before going off to take a shower. He didn't touch the hot water faucet and breathed noisily under the impact of the icy spray. After he'd toweled off, he put on decent cop's clothes. "A police raid, hmm . . . that's amusing." Then he quickly swallowed the two aspirins. On the living room table, where she couldn't miss it, he left a short note to Claire. Ultimately, he wasn't sorry he wouldn't be there when she came home. Maybe she'd be a little concerned, too.

The streets of Perpignan were empty, and in five minutes he was at the headquarters. As he turned into the parking lot he almost hit a patrol car that was coming out at high speed. Alerted by the flashing light, he hit the brakes at the last minute. The car was responding to a call. Not too urgent: the officers hadn't yet turned on their siren. A memo issued last year drastically limited the use of horns and sirens at night. Citizens needed their sleep. At the risk of causing an accident. Who would be considered responsible in such a case? The memo didn't say.

Repeating his excuses, Ripoll handed Sebag the envelope with his greasy hands. Sebag refused to take it.

"Don't you have any gloves?"

The guard understood too late that he should have been more careful himself. He opened a drawer in his desk and handed Sebag a pair of plastic gloves.

"I had no way of knowing . . . " he stammered.

"No, of course not. An anonymous envelope sent to an inspector in the middle of the night, there's nothing more ordinary than that, right? I get them every night."

He put on the gloves and took the envelope. It was in fact just like millions of others that circulated everyday in France. It was addressed rather pompously to "Inspector Gilles Sebag, Perpignan Police Headquarters." The address had been typed in a font that made it look like handwriting. In the upper right corner, the word "urgent" was written in red and underlined by hand. On the back, in place of a return address there was a stylized image of a swallow that resembled Ingrid Raven's tattoo.

"Are the surveillance cameras outside still not working?" Sebag asked.

"They were supposed to be repaired last week, but it didn't happen. I don't know why. I'm on night duty this week, and I wasn't told anything."

"Didn't anyone notice the person who put the envelope in the box? A patrol that was coming back just at that time?"

"Not so far as I know, but I'll ask the night teams."

"Was the telephone call recorded at least?"

"Probably, yes. Like all calls."

"You haven't checked."

"Uh . . . no. Not yet."

Ripoll was uneasy. Maybe he'd fallen asleep or had been drinking coffee in the cafeteria when the phone rang. He probably thought he'd spend a nice quiet night on duty. In the middle of the week, that was often how it was.

"You'll get the cassette and bring it to me in my office. I want it within five minutes."

He heard Ripoll grumble a few words in Catalan. He went to his office, reproaching himself for taking out his bad mood on poor Ripoll. It wasn't his way to lay into subordinates, but everyone had moments of weakness. Especially when they'd had only a few minutes to get over their first binge in twenty years.

He put the mysterious letter on his desk and sat down. The room was plunged in darkness and silence. He turned on the little desk lamp. He knew that it was preferable to hand the document over to his colleagues in the technical division, but he didn't have the patience to wait until the next day.

After all, the letter was addressed to him. And it was already the next day.

Still wearing gloves, he took a letter-opener out of his drawer and carefully slit the envelope. Inside, he found a letter written on dark recycled paper. He unfolded it. There were only three lines, written on a computer. The message was clear and direct:

We demand 150 million euros for the liberation of the young Dutch woman. Other instructions will follow.

It was signed:

Moluccan Resistance Front

A hundred and fifty million! The amount surprised him at first. Who would have that kind of money? The CEOs of multinational corporations, football players and rock stars. Maybe also a winner of the Euro Millions lottery. But certainly not Ingrid Raven's parents.

Next his eyes fell on the signature. Moluccan Resistance Front . . . Black and white images came back to him. A train. A train stopped in open country. He recalled hooded heads captured by the telephoto lens of a camera from behind the windows of a train compartment. He remembered a door that slowly opened and a body that fell heavily onto the tracks. A Moluccan—maybe even South Moluccan—commando had seized a train in Holland. That was in the 1970s, if he recalled correctly. He'd seen it on TV. People had died.

"What does this all this crap mean?"

"Excuse me? Did I screw up again?"

He hadn't heard Ripoll come in. The sergeant remained on the threshold. His broad silhouette stood out against the light in the hall.

"No, excuse me, I was talking to myself."

Ripoll approached. He set a cassette on the desk.

"I wound it back to the message that interests you."

Handing him a small tape recorder, he added: '

"It'll work better with this."

"That might be very helpful, in fact," Sebag replied, giving him his friendliest smile. "Were you able to contact all the teams?"

"Yes. But no one saw the suspect at all."

"Too bad! But thanks for your quick work."

Ripoll turned around to go, but Sebag stopped him before he crossed the threshold.

"What was your impression of the guy who phoned?"

"What do you mean, my impression? I don't know. You're going to be able to listen to him yourself."

"I will, in fact, but I won't be in the same state of mind you were. I'm going to listen to it already knowing something. I'd like to know what you felt. For example, how did you know right away that it wasn't a joke?"

Ripoll took the time to reflect before answering. Sebag couldn't see his face, which was back-lit, but he could sense that Ripoll was flattered by the question.

"He had a hollow, rather distance voice, but his tone was dry. He hadn't said more than a dozen words before he'd already hung up. People don't do that when they're joking."

"I see. What do they do, in your opinion?"

Ripoll ran his hand through his thinning hair.

"I don't know. I think, uh . . . I think they wait a few seconds, at least long enough to see how the other person reacts. If you're making a joke, that's why you do it, isn't it?"

"Very perceptive. What else?"

"Well . . . nothing."

"Thanks very much. I'll call you if I need something else explained."

"Any time. I'll be there until seven o'clock."

He listened to Ripoll's heavy footsteps moving down the empty corridor. He took a deep breath and put the cassette in the player. After a little static, a man's voice could be heard. More of a whisper.

"There's a letter for Inspector Sebag in the mailbox at police headquarters. It's urgent, very urgent."

The dial tone that followed these two short sentences split his eardrums. The caller's tone was self-assured, strong, "dry," as Ripoll had put it, almost authoritarian. The message was sober, like the letter. But it was hard to gain an idea of the voice because the caller was whispering. Sebag rewound the tape and listened to it again, taking care, however, to stop as soon as the last word had been spoken. There was not the slightest hesitation in the rapid utterance of the two sentences. No trace of an accent, either. All that didn't sound like a joke, in fact.

He got up to open the window. The air was cooler, but the temperature wouldn't go down any more now.

If only they'd been able to locate the place where the call was made! For the past two years they'd been waiting for a promised new telephone switchboard, but the delivery had been repeatedly delayed. The funds were lacking, and there were always other priorities. A patrol car parked carefully in the lot. The car that he'd almost hit as he came in. Sebag saw two officers get out. They had a young woman with them.

The outside air did him good. His headache had gone away. Claire's image tried to impose itself on him, but he refused to allow it any room. There was no point brooding on it. There was only one question he had to ask himself, and only one answer to give. Did he want to know?

He spent the rest of the night on the Internet, reading up on the Molucca Islands and their subversive movements. He took breaks in the cafeteria and reluctantly swallowed several cups of bad coffee. The grimaces he couldn't repress as he drank it helped keep him awake as much as the coffee did.

Toward five o'clock, coming back from one of his trips to the cafeteria, he met the two officers and the young woman on the stairs. A pretty blonde. Rather tall. She smelled like sweat and fear. She was crying. The end of the night must have been difficult for her. Sebag noticed that she held a tissue against her throat.

"*Bon dia,*" said Rafel Puig, the owner of Carlit. "*Com vas?* Did you fall out of bed this morning? You look beat. Don't tell me you went running before you came in?"

"No. *He treballat tot la nit*" ("I worked all night"). Sebag had been taking evening classes at the Generalitat de Catalunya, a sort of unofficial embassy of South Catalonia in Perpignan. He understood Catalan and could repeat a few simple phrases.

"*Tota la nit? Carall*, you must not do that very often."

Sebag shrugged.

"You can't always avoid it."

Rafel automatically wiped his impeccable zinc bar top with a rag. The proprietor of the Carlit always mixed Catalan and French in what he said. It was his way of propagating his country's language, a didactic and open way that Sebag liked.

"*Una tassa de cafè, com de costum?*" ("A cup of coffee, as usual?")

"A triple shot in a big cup, please. With two eggs fried hard. The night was short, and today is going to be long."

"Go on, sit down. I'll bring it all to you in five minutes."

At six o'clock, Sebag had decided to allow himself a real break. Passing by the reception desk, he'd asked Ripoll to wake up Castello and tell him what had happened during the night. Then he'd crossed the avenue and gone into the Carlit.

He picked up the morning newspaper and sat down in a corner. Their exploits the day before were on the front page of the local daily. On the inside pages, there was a big photo showing the prefect in front of a split-open box out of which Spanish cigarettes were spilling. The boxes had been spread out on the ground and presented so that the haul seemed impressive. The article referred to the seizure of more than three thousand cartons worth a total of a hundred and fifty thousand euros. The final calculation had thus been made in terms of the official sales price in France and not in terms of the black market price. That made no sense, but it did make it possible to arrive at an considerable sum. A hundred and fifty thousand euros was something. Converted into francs—a simple mathematical operation that many readers would automatically make—the total was nearly a million, a figure symbolically suitable to strike people's minds.

He did a rapid calculation: it would take a thousand confiscations like this one to arrive at the amount demanded by Ingrid Raven's kidnappers. This ransom was crazy!

A second article reported the police raids on a dozen bars in Perpignan and the arrest of three managers. In one photo, two policemen stood on either side of a man hidden in a jacket, his hands cuffed behind his back. The three managers arrested had been taken into custody. The newspaper suggested that they would probably spend the night at police headquarters. Sebag knew they'd already been released. In a box at the bottom of the page, a lawyer denounced this disproportionate operation. He wasn't wrong: the forceful arrests would probably result only in simple fines imposed by the criminal court.

Rafel set his breakfast on the table.

"*Bon profit!*" ("*Bon appétit!*").

He sat down across from the inspector and jerked his chin toward the newspaper.

"I'm lucky, after all, to be right next to the police headquarters. If half my customers weren't cops, I'd probably be selling Spanish smokes myself. I hope it wasn't because of this stupid business that you were up all night."

"No, don't worry. I'm working on a big case. With international implications. But I can't tell you anything about it for the moment."

Rafel understood that he was making fun of him and didn't persist. Sebag was able to finish his breakfast in peace. The coffee was strong, the eggs fried the way he liked them. The other stories in the paper were of no interest, however.

When he was done, he took his plate and cup to the bar. Then he went back to headquarters. Ripoll had finished his shift, but he was hanging around hitting on Martine, the cute little police auxiliary who was on the reception desk during the day. Behind the randy old guard's back, Sebag made a sign of compassion to the young woman cop, who replied with a friendly smile. Ripoll turned around to tell him that the boss had just come in and was waiting for him. Sebag stopped by his office to get the letter and its envelope out of his desk drawer. He picked them up with a pair of tweezers and climbed to the fourth floor.

Castello and Lefèvre were standing in front of the window, talking. They interrupted their conversation when Sebag arrived. The inspector put his precious items on the boss's desk and sat down. Castello and Lefèvre examined them carefully. Then they sat down in turn.

"What do you think?" the superintendent asked Sebag. "Is it serious or not?"

The inspector had thought about that question half the night.

"It's serious. Yes and no!"

Both Castello and Lefèvre started.

"Some parts of it are serious and others are less serious," Sebag began to explain. "I think the sender of the letter is in fact involved in Ingrid's disappearance. The drawing on the envelope resembles her tattoo; it's a signature we have to take seriously. I have rejected the hypothesis that it's a joker who is taking advantage of the situation: we haven't yet made any statement about this case; no one knows about it. Besides, I've just read the local press, and so far nothing has gotten out."

Castello approved his reasoning. Lefèvre remained non-committal.

"What doesn't seem credible to me is the signature. 'The Moluccan Resistance Front . . . ' I did a little research last night. The Moluccas now belong to Indonesia, and used to be a Dutch colony. The majority of the population is Muslim, but in the 1960s there was a South Moluccan independence movement that recruited members among the island's Christian minority. This movement organized terrorist actions on Dutch soil, but seems to have completely disappeared today."

"Islamist terrorist movements are active everywhere in the world," Lefèvre interjected. "Why should they be set aside from the outset?"

"I think we aren't understanding each other: I don't need to set aside what doesn't exist. As I was saying a moment ago, the only terrorist movements that the Moluccas have experienced were more connected with the Christian community. So far as I know, there has been no Islamist movement in that region."

Sebag had felt Lefèvre stiffening during his long-winded speech.

"Al-Qaeda has branches throughout the Muslim world," the Parisian superintendent retorted. "You may not be aware of all of them."

"Probably not," conceded. "But re-read the text of the demand. I think it goes in the direction of what I'm suggesting. We are being asked for money, period. Usually the demands made by Islamist movements are drowned in important religious and geo-political considerations. And although some cases of kidnapping have been settled by paying ransoms, for the most part that was done on the quiet."

Lefèvre could not repress a sardonic smile.

"Do you have special training regarding matters of terrorism or did you become an expert on geo-politics by surfing the Net?"

Sebag was getting annoyed, but he refused to rush into the

stupid and vain battle between the provincial cop and his Parisian colleague.

"Let's say that there is in fact a Moluccan Resistance Front, and that for their own reasons its activists want to attack Dutch interests; why would they kidnap a young female student, and why here, in Perpignan, in this remote corner of the country?"

He'd emphasized the last words.

"Anyway, and here I'm sure that you'll agree with me, if this international terrorist movement exists and is capable of carrying out an operation like a kidnapping so far from its bases and networks, it's hard to understand why it would send a letter demanding ransom from me, a little hick cop in the provinces."

Castello raised an eyebrow; he didn't like the terms his inspector was using. Lefèvre slowly nodded and then smiled ironically:

"I find particularly interesting the last question you raised, and I'd like to know your hypotheses about it. Why you? What do you have to do with this case?"

The question was direct. Castello reframed it in an attempt to attenuate its harshness.

"Do you have an idea, Gilles? The answer could probably guide us."

"I haven't the slightest idea. I thought about that too at length, and I have no explanation."

"In the course of your career, you've never been at odds with extremist movements of any kind?" Lefèvre asked. "Or . . . with megalomaniac and mischievous criminals?"

"Not so far as I recall."

"How long have you been in Perpignan?"

"Seven years."

"And before that, where were you?"

"In Chartres. The capital of the department of Eure-et-Loir."

"I know that, thanks. For how long?"

"Is this an official interrogation?"

Their eyes met defiantly for a few seconds. Then Sebag shook his head. He was mad at himself for getting angry. But he was tired, and Lefèvre was really being an asshole.

"Don't get upset, Gilles, and don't make things more complicated," Castello said. "This is not an interrogation, but it is important to find out why the kidnappers contacted you. You and not someone else. The answer is probably in your recent or distant past."

He paused before going on:

"We're going to have to conduct a little investigation."

"Of what precisely am I suspected?"

"That's enough, Gilles," Castello said, annoyed. "You're not suspected of anything, and you know that very well. It's one of the few leads we have, and we can't neglect it. Period."

"And who is going to follow this lead?"

The superintendent looked him straight in the eye.

"You know that, too. We have the good luck to have here a policeman who doesn't know you and knows nothing about the cases you've solved here, or about the individuals you've made it possible to arrest. He will conduct the investigation with complete objectivity, I hope."

This time it was the young superintendent from Paris whom Castello stared at.

"That goes without saying," Lefèvre snickered.

"Good," Castello concluded provisionally. "You will discuss all that together a little later."

They remained silent for a moment. The superintendent slowly roused himself. Bits of conversation reached them from the corridor, despite the closed door. Castello began to speak again.

"The sum they're demanding is insane! A hundred and fifty million euros, a billion francs."

"The Moluccan Resistance Movement may not keep close tabs on the exchange rate for the euro," Sebag said bitterly.

Castello didn't react to the jibe. Lefèvre pretended he hadn't heard anything. He got up and pointed to the letter.

"I suppose you're going to have it examined in every way by your technical team. I'd like to make photocopies of it first. I'll fax some to a colleague in the National Security Service. I'd like to have his . . . expert opinion."

When Lefèvre had gone out, the boss turned to Sebag.

"I've got a job for you, Gilles, or rather two jobs. I've already spoken to you about the first one, and I want you to answer precisely all the questions Cyril Lefèvre asks you."

Sebag nodded to signal his willingness to do what his boss asked.

"The second job will be easier for you. After your interview with Cyril, I want you to go home and rest. You look tired to me. You haven't slept much, I suppose?"

"Two or three hours."

"I want you in top form when you come back tomorrow. It's important. Because our mysterious correspondents have chosen you as their contact, you will need to be as available as possible over the coming days. As a good marathon runner, you know that to go the distance, you have to know how to economize your strength."

The house was still silent but it was no longer empty. Claire was sleeping in their bed. He tiptoed into the bedroom and lay down at her side. Sunlight was coming in around the shutters. She rolled over and nuzzled up against him. Her body had the soft warmth of the bed. Her green eyes flickered, then settled on Gilles.

"Didn't you sleep at all?" she asked him gently.

"A few hours. How about you?"

"I don't know. What time is it?"

"About eleven."

"Then I almost got my usual seven hours," she said, stretching.

She tapped her pillow and sat up. He took the opportunity to move away from this body that was burning his skin.

"What was the middle-of-the-night emergency? Nothing serious, I hope?"

He told her about his adventures that night. The ones that began with waking up hung over. He had hardly finished when she asked him *the* question. The one he'd be asked constantly throughout this investigation, and to which he hadn't even the beginning of a hypothetical answer.

"Why was the letter addressed to you?"

"I haven't the faintest idea."

She remained quiet for a few moments. Then she suggested: "Maybe he knows you."

"Who?"

"The kidnapper."

"Why the kidnapper? Why not the kidnappers?"

"I don't know. Did I say the kidnapper?"

"Absolutely."

"You must have said it yourself. Or from the way you presented the facts, it seems there could be only one kidnapper."

He thought about that remark for a while. He realized that in fact he was beginning to prefer the singular.

"You don't believe this demand, either?" he asked.

"No."

"Why?"

"Because you don't believe it," she replied with cheerful candor. She'd always shown more confidence in his abilities as an investigator than he himself did. That had often troubled him, sometimes even embarrassed him. But this time he found her confidence reassuring.

It was after two when he got up. Claire was taking a sunbath alongside the pool. She'd waited for him to eat lunch.

Her purse lay half-open at the foot of the bar. He could see her cell phone. He had only to pick it up, turn it on, and look at the last numbers she'd called. If she'd erased the last calls, that would already be a confession.

He hesitated.

The doubt was disturbing. Worrisome. Anguishing. It was rotting his mind. But the truth might turn out to be worse. Cruel and even more upsetting. And then above all he couldn't make up his mind to use his police methods against his own wife. What if, after he'd lowered himself to using such methods, he ultimately found nothing at all? He would feel ridiculous in his own eyes and he wouldn't necessarily feel reassured for all that. The absence of a proof of guilt cannot constitute an absolute proof of innocence.

Claire's telephone rang. A brief beep. There was a message. Just as he was yielding to his curiosity and reaching for the phone, his own cell phone rang. He went to get it out of his jacket pocket. It wasn't a message but a photo. Léo, all smiles, riding a quad. Sebag took the telephone to Claire.

"Your son is doing very well, apparently."

They ate lunch together in the living room. It was too hot on the terrace. Claire told him about her night out. Her scene. After the restaurant, they'd decided not to go to a movie. The film they'd chosen seemed too serious, and Véronique needed a change in atmosphere. So they'd decided to go to a night club. The Maracas in Saint-Cyprien. 1970s disco ambiance. They'd had as much fun as kids. Especially Véro.

"Did you get hit on?"

"What do you think?" she asked with a mischievous smile.

He took the time to contemplate her. Pretty green eyes that nascent wrinkles made even more sparkling, a slender, pointed nose, a saucy mouth. His eyes moved lower. The blue T-shirt she'd thrown on after her sunbath revealed the roundness of her breasts.

"You got hit on," he repeated in the affirmative mode this time.

She laughed.

"So?" he went on.

"So what?"

"So?"

Her smile slowly faded away. With her right hand, she fluffed up his hair.

"You idiot."

She kissed him tenderly to put an end to the conversation.

The afternoon was spent between the sun and the pool. His cell phone rang as he was getting ready to barbecue their dinner. Superintendent Castello gave him a summary of what had happened in the late afternoon. The anonymous letter had been closely examined. On the envelope, only Ripoll's fingerprints had been found, but in the upper left corner of the letter, there was another print. It had been compared to the one the Dutch police had just sent them. There was no doubt. It was Ingrid Raven's. The same fingerprint had been found on the passenger-side door handle of Lopez's taxi.

The first information provided by the National Security Service confirmed Sebag's view. French counter-espionage had never heard of a Moluccan Resistance Front. In any case, the Parisian colleagues did not think it likely that such a movement—if it in fact existed—would be capable of undertaking any action whatever on French soil, where it had no known connections. However, the Security Service had contacted the Dutch counter-espionage service. Its primary interlocutor in Perpignan would be Lefèvre.

"We've come to a standstill. Our only lead is this BW, the notorious customer. Maybe he's your mysterious friend," Castello said.

Sebag replied drily.

"I don't have any friends who like to kidnap young women."

"I was joking, Gilles, just joking. Do these initials really mean nothing to you?"

"Nothing at all."

Castello, having sensed Sebag's annoyance, tried to conclude the conversation on a more agreeable note.

"How are things going at home?"

"Fine, thanks. The children have gone on vacation. It's quiet, and that's nice for a change."

"Take my advice, old pal, and don't miss the opportunity. You and Claire are alone together like lovers. It's a precious moment. A new honeymoon."

Sebag did not reply. He wasn't Castello's "old pal," and he didn't want his advice. There was nothing worse than a boss who tried to play marriage counselor. Especially when he'd screwed up his own marriage.

CHAPTER 16

Robert hesitated, holding his watering can in his hand, in front of his potted banana tree.

Usually, it was his friend René who took care of the yard in the summer. He came by two or three times a week to water the lawn and the flowers. Did he water the banana tree each time?

Robert had always had trouble making decisions. Not only regarding the major choices in life but also about the smallest daily dilemmas. He relied on Solange. Gossips used to say that she wore the pants in the house. So what? She had good judgment! Even today, he still asked his wife's opinion. And sometimes she answered. She was the one who had advised him to leave the Oleanders and return to their little house in central France. Once again, she'd been right: he felt better since he'd come back.

Robert decided to water the flowers first. He had to fill the watering can three times. When only a few drops remained, he gave them to the banana tree.

He and Solange had bought the house in the early 1970s. At that time a worker's family could still afford a comfortable house. All you needed was a small down payment. Afterward, inflation would gradually reduce the monthly payments. The house wasn't very spacious but it had three bedrooms. At first, Solange didn't work. Then as the children grew up she started working as a cleaning lady, and without being well off, they finally had enough to get along easily. It seemed to Robert that the children had lacked for nothing. Neither love nor money.

They'd been able to get the education they wanted: a short one for Paul and Gérard, who didn't like school, a longer one for Florence, who had earned a Master's degree in language and literature before taking a job teaching French in a middle school. They had all been happy in this house.

Then Solange died. The illness had carried her off in a few months. A simple routine visit to the doctor, and their whole life had been turned upside down. Complicated and painful treatments, prolonged stays in the hospital; their quiet happiness had ended long before she was on her deathbed. A few days before she died, he'd taken her home. Against the doctors' advice. It might have been the only decision he'd ever made all by himself. He was proud of it. She'd died at home. In this house where he hoped to die when his turn came.

He thought about that often.

The nights were difficult to endure. During the day, he had things to do. Housework, errands, the yard, crossword puzzles, walks along the Loire, a glass of white wine at Eugène's bar. And then television in the evening. His little habits kept him going.

But at night . . .

In the darkness and silence of the bedroom, the anxiety that had lurked all day in the pit of his stomach regained its hold on him. He couldn't sleep without taking two or three sleeping pills and drinking a couple of glasses of white wine. The mixture was dangerous.

His sleep remained fitful. Full of bad dreams. He often woke up. And each time, he realized that reality was even worse than the most atrocious of his nightmares. Some of his nights were so terrible that he no longer awoke at 4:00 A.M.

He put the watering can in the garage alongside the garden tools. It was 5:00 P.M., time for the regional news. He went back into the house and sat down in his armchair. His neck on the head-rest, his legs on the ottoman, he absent-mindedly watched the images flit by. It was always more or less the same thing. The same tone, the same rhythm, the same words. Only the voices changed. The voices he was used to were on vacation.

The telephone rang right at the end of the news broadcast. Florence. He sought to reassure her. "Yes, yes, I'm feeling better." He weighed his words, trying to sound credible. "A little better." He told her once again that he'd made the right choice in deciding to go home, that he felt better in their house, that it would soon be all over and forgotten. He was already sleeping again.

"Just imagine, Flo . . . This morning I woke at seven o'clock."

He hoped he was convincing. He didn't want to worry his daughter. Florence was the baby, the daughter they'd so much wanted after having the two boys. He hadn't noticed that she'd grown up. She still seemed to him so fragile and vulnerable.

"How about you, is everything going well? Your pregnancy isn't tiring you out too much?"

It hadn't been a long time since she left home. She'd studied in Orléans, held her first teaching job in Montargis, but didn't really become independent until she got married. Her departure for Paris had been very difficult. For him and for Solange.

"Maybe I'll come back down to see you before summer is over," he said.

She seemed to believe him. For a few moments, he allowed himself to be deceived by the power of the words. He was feeling better; he might get over it and he would go back to Argelès, if not during the summer, at least in the fall, as if nothing had happened. But after he'd hung up, he suddenly felt dizzy. A shrill and harsh laugh drowned out Florence's gentle voice. Robert was forced to sit down on the cool floor tiles in the entry hall. His vision got blurry. Two blue eyes were looking at him. They were no longer those of his daughter. He could make out a face surrounded by bloody blond hair, a face that was laughing despite the horrible absence of its mouth.

Robert knew he'd never get over it.

CHAPTER 17

A t 6:00 A.M., Sebag slipped silently out of the bed, leaving Claire to sleep on. He donned his running clothes. A storm had come up during the night. The air was humid, the wind cooler. Without eating breakfast, he ran through the countryside for an hour. In the distance, the first rays of the sun were touching the summit of Le Canigou.

He thought again about the talk he'd had with Lefèvre before leaving the headquarters the preceding day. The interview had gone off without a hitch. The young cop had made an effort: he hadn't spared rhetorical precautions to ensure that their conversation didn't resemble an interrogation. It had rung false most of the time, but Sebag had also shown his good will. They should be able to put up with one another so long as this investigation was going on.

Provided that it didn't last too long.

On the way home, he stopped at the bakery to buy two baguettes.

He put breakfast on the terrace. A big cup of black coffee for himself, a small cup and a tea-bag for Claire. Bread, butter, honey. The jar of strawberry jam was almost empty. He added a line to the shopping list. Claire would see to it this morning.

He turned on the radio. This first week of July was predicted to be calm in France and abroad: the first forest fires on the Côte d'Azur, the perennial traffic advisories and public health checks regarding restaurants and bodies of water. The summer routine. Plus a few car bombs in Baghdad. Nothing likely to disturb a vacationer's peace and quiet.

He was driving tranquilly to police headquarters when his eyes fell on a poster hung on the window of a news agent. A headline from *Le Parisien-Aujourd'hui en France* shouted in bold-face type:

PERPIGNAN: Series of attacks on young Dutch girls

He double-parked and got out, paying no attention to the insults heaped on him by unhappy drivers.

"That's going like hotcakes," the news seller told him with satisfaction.

He got back in the car and found a parking place a few dozen yards farther on. There was nothing concerning Perpignan on the front page, but he found the article on page four.

The daily's regional correspondent had connected three events that had recently occurred in the department: the murder of a twenty-three-year-old Dutch woman on the beach at Argelès in mid-June; the attack on a nineteen-year-old co-ed, also Dutch, on the streets of Perpignan two nights earlier; and finally the puzzling disappearance of a third young woman—clearly the reference was to the Raven case, even though no name was given. The article mentioned certain similarities between the cases, especially between the last two, describing in fact the attack in Perpignan as a "failed attempt at a kidnapping." The reporter had cleverly avoided concluding that a serial attacker was involved, but he more than hinted at that hypothesis.

At the Perpignan police headquarters, everyone was on full alert.

"The superintendent is waiting for you in the meeting room," Martine told him at the reception desk. "He's already up there with the policeman from Paris and another one from Montpellier."

In the fourth-floor meeting room, the air-conditioner was humming. A miracle. Sebag chose a seat far from the machine. Castello handed him a file: the deposition of Anneke Verbrucke, the student attacked in Perpignan.

"We're expecting any minute another report from the gendarmerie's research team concerning the Argelès case," the superintendent explained.

Ménard was already reading the file. He'd underlined with a yellow highlighter the passages that seemed to him important. Then Llach came in. He was given a file as well.

As soon as he'd read the first lines, Sebag understood that Anneke Verbrucke was the young woman he'd seen weeping the other night in the headquarters' corridors. A complaint had been filed for assault, and not for an attempted kidnapping. The young woman had been attacked by a hooded individual near the university, at 3:00 A.M. According to the police report, she'd been threatened with a knife held against her throat. The man had ordered her to get into a car, but she had succeeded in getting away. When the anti-crime squad arrived on the scene, it had found no trace of the attacker, and no witness. The individual in question was said to be about five foot eleven and slender. Those were the only identifying elements the victim had been able to provide. In other words: nothing.

The police report had been written like all reports in all the police headquarters in France. On a first reading, it appeared to be sober and precise. Informative. But Sebag had found nothing in it that seemed to him indispensable. That was life! In reports, reality seemed to be put through a grinder, poured into a mold, and spat out again in a formatted way. Every time he read one, Sebag thought of what Alfred Sauvy had said about statistics: "They're like bikinis: you think they're showing everything but in fact they're hiding the most important thing."

Lambert and Molina came in and greeted them in low voices. Castello had gone out and Sebag still hadn't seen the other two policemen that Martine had mentioned. Lambert and Molina each took a packet of papers and started to read.

A few minutes later, Castello came back. With a new file in his hands and, on his heels, Lefèvre, in an impeccable charcoal gray suit. They were followed by an inspector from the regional criminal police in Montpellier, whom Sebag had met on several occasions. His name was Petit, Bernard Petit, and he wore a jacket in the neutral color characteristic of the local police.

The three men gave them time to peruse the gendarmes' report on the murder in Argelès. They were talking in low voices. Jeanne, Castello's secretary, brought them coffee. She put three cups on the table. She was wearing a short skirt. Her tanned legs danced between the tables. Her calves were perfectly rounded, her thighs firm and muscular. The temperature rose one or two degrees. Jeanne filled the three cups slowly, without seeming to notice the effect she was having on the men around her.

After she'd left, the movement of her legs still floated around the room, prolonging the recess for a few moments. Her vanilla-like perfume slowly disappeared, giving way to a delicious aroma of dry, strong coffee.

The body of Josetta Braun, twenty-three, had been found in a thicket of reeds near the Mas Larrieu nature preserve on June 17, around five in the morning. It had been found by an early morning walker, a retiree on holiday who was staying in a nearby campground. The young woman's skull had been fractured by blows with a stone. Three blows, according to the coroner: one on the mouth, two on the left temple. A stone stained with blood and bits of brain had been found more than a dozen meters away. The investigators had found a clear thumbprint on the stone. The report added that no information about the weapon used or about the thumbprint had been communicated to the press. The murder had occurred a few hours before the discovery of the body: probably between eleven and midnight. The young woman had been killed right there. Her blouse had been removed and she was wearing no panties beneath her skirt, but she had not been raped. She had not had any sexual relations during the hours that preceded her death.

Josetta Braun had arrived at the Oleanders campground in Argelès on June 5. She was traveling alone but, according to the deposition given by the owners of the campground, she did not spend many nights alone in her tent.

The gendarmes had questioned the young people who had hung out with Josetta since her arrival in France. None of them had a thumbprint matching the one found on the stone. In the absence of any other lead, the gendarmes had given priority to the hypothesis that the perpetrator was a vagrant. They had brought several vagabonds in for questioning, but the comparison of prints had not yielded anything there, either. They had all been released. In desperation, a call for witnesses had been put out via the press. Without result. The investigation was ongoing, the gendarmes said at the end of their summary. A gentle euphemism meaning that it was at a standstill. The family had picked up the body: Josetta was buried in Holland on June 27.

Sebag knew that, barring some unexpected development, the investigation would not continue. The gendarmes had a lot to do in Argelès during the summer. From less than ten thousand inhabitants in the off season, the population rose to a hundred thousand in the summer. The tourists were scattered over about sixty campgrounds, which had won the commune the title, not necessarily greatly desired, of the "European capital of open-air tourism." After certain excesses caused in the early 1980s by young people on vacation at the seaside, a mobile company of gendarmes was sent to Argelès every summer. Despite this reinforcement, the local police force did not have time to devote to tasks other than maintaining order.

He finished reading the file and remained puzzled. It was hard to imagine a connection between these three cases. A murder, a kidnapping, and an assault. Even if the latter were redescribed as an attempted kidnapping, it was difficult to see any link, for lack of similarities in M.O. In Ingrid Raven's case, the kidnapping had taken place in complete security in an isolated place, and it seemed to have been prepared at least a few days in advance. In Anneke Verbrucke's case, if there was an attempt to kidnap her, it had been made in the middle of the city and in an improvised way. Except for the nationality of the three victims, he didn't see how the three cases could be connected.

The murmur of conversation drew him out of his thoughts. His colleagues had also completed their study of the files and were exchanging points of view. With a wave of his hand, the superintendent put an end to the separate discussions.

"Gentlemen, you have just seen the reports on the three cases that that we now have to deal with. I'd like to have your impressions."

The question was formulated in an open-ended way. Castello didn't express an opinion.

"When you say that we have to deal with these three cases, does that mean that the police department is officially taking over the murder in Argelès? Has the gendarmerie given it up?"

It was Llach who had asked the question. He was always very punctilious about each branch's prerogatives.

"Not entirely," Castello replied. "We don't have the resources to do everything."

He pushed his chair back slightly to lend more prominence to his two neighbors.

"Even if we have received reinforcements from Paris and Montpellier, we can't operate on all fronts. Our priority remains the kidnapping of Ingrid Raven. We will work on the two other cases so long as we have not eliminated the possibility of a connection."

"So is a connection officially considered a possibility?"

Sebag had spoken up without thinking. He hadn't wanted to be the first to raise this question.

"For the moment, yes," Castello confirmed. "We can't afford to ignore it. That is, moreover, the point of this morning's meeting."

Sebag sighed.

"Do you have a problem with that?" Lefèvre said.

"No, absolutely not. If we have time to waste . . . "

Sebag bit his lip. He didn't want to seem aggressive. The truce with Lefèvre was turning out to be precarious.

"You don't believe there is any connection?" Castello asked.

Sebag glanced out the window. The wind had driven away the clouds, and the sky had become uniformly blue again. He remembered the time when he was trying to teach Léo a few rudiments of guitar-playing. He recalled how hard it had been to find the words to tell him how to tune the instrument. The note was right or it wasn't. The ear hears it or it doesn't. What can words do? It was the same today. He sensed a good half-tone of difference between Ingrid's kidnapping and the assault in Perpignan. As for the murder in Argelès, it wasn't on the same harmonic scale at all. But how could he express this feeling?

Everyone had turned to gaze at him. Lefèvre's eyes had regained their ironic sparkle. Sebag couldn't limit himself to expressing his views. He had a few seconds to construct a solid argument. He took a deep breath.

"These cases have one obvious point in common: all three

of the victims are young women of Dutch nationality. Period. And that's it. Nothing in the way these attacks took place seems comparable, and the young women did not suffer the same kind of violence."

It was a bad beginning. He didn't like this categorical tone. Usually he was able to express himself in a more qualified way.

"What basis do you have for saying that it wasn't the same kind of violence?" Lefèvre asked.

Lefèvre's arrogance irritated him, but he didn't want to start a war. He glanced at his colleagues: no one seemed about to speak up. On the contrary, they were waiting for him to respond.

"One of the three is dead, a second was kidnapped, and the third is safe and sound," he ended up saying.

"Anneke is alive and Josetta is dead, we agree about that," Lefèvre conceded. "But Ingrid? Who can say at this point whether she is lying in a ditch with her face crushed by a rock?"

"The murder of Josetta Braun was a savage attack that seems to have been committed in a fit of madness. It in no way shows the organizational ability that Ingrid Raven's kidnapper showed."

"Maybe we've gone the wrong way on this case," Lefèvre replied. "Maybe it's not a kidnapping premeditated and organized by José Lopez's customer, the infamous BW who is supposed to have paid three thousand euros for Ingrid's services. We can't eliminate the hypothesis that a murderer—a serial criminal—has passed through here."

"In the Argelès case, Josetta's body was left where she was killed," Sebag said. "Did the killer act differently in Ingrid's case, then? And what happens to Lopez in this scenario?"

Lefèvre turned to Superintendent Castello.

"Has the area around the hermitage of Força Real been properly examined?"

"Twice. Once very quickly after Lopez's taxi was discovered there, and a second time more carefully, after we'd made the connection between Lopez's disappearance and that of Ingrid Raven. I can ask the gendarmes to examine it again more extensively."

"That would be good."

Addressing Sebag once again, he went on.

"It's puerile to think that a serial killer always acts in the same way. That is true only for serious psychopaths."

Puerile . . . the adjective sounded like an insult.

"And then, after all, three young Dutch women who have been the victims of violence in less than two weeks in your department, that has got to get your attention, doesn't it?"

Sebag let a few seconds go by, but his colleagues still weren't ready to get involved.

"Frankly, no! I don't know the precise number of Dutch women currently vacationing in the region. But in my opinion there must be several thousand. If we consulted the logs of the police headquarters and all the gendarmeries in Roussillon over the past two weeks, we'd find other crimes and misdemeanors committed against Dutch women tourists: assaults, rapes, attempts to do something, steal their credit cards or even purses, who knows?"

Sebag's delivery had accelerated; his tone had become more aggressive. Maybe because Lefèvre had continued to smile. Ménard spoke up, trying to run with the hare and hunt with the hounds.

"In what Gilles says there are things we should take seriously. We have to examine more closely all the complaints filed last month. Maybe we'll find others concerning Dutch women. If there are lots of them and they are of no interest, that would tend to support Gilles's view. If we find one or two more serious ones, that might confirm the postulate of the existence of a series of attacks. And maybe that will give us additional information about this possible serial attacker. An identikit portrait, why not?"

Castello agreed.

"I'm assigning you that job, François."

From the back of the room, Llach asked:

"Where exactly are we with the terrorist hypothesis? Has it been abandoned?"

"It was never really taken seriously," Castello replied. "Neither in Paris nor in Holland."

"And the ransom demand? What are we supposed to think about that, then? We do have proof that whoever sent us the letter is holding the young woman."

"We are in fact obliged to take that demand into account. I have to say that we're not sure what to make of it."

"Does that mean that it's out of the question to pay the ransom asked?"

Castello sighed.

"A hundred and fifty million, Joan, do you realize how much money that is?"

The discussion went on for another quarter of an hour. It quickly returned to the question of the relation among the three cases. People took sides. Molina declared his skepticism in solidarity with Sebag. Raynaud and Moreno supported the thesis defended by Lefèvre and finally by Ménard. Castello took no position, and neither did Llach or Lambert. Beyond the arguments they made, Sebag sensed that his colleagues were chiefly afraid of missing out on something big. Something fabulous. All cops have dreamed of having to confront a serial killer someday or another. Of finally playing in the big leagues.

A newspaper article had sufficed to radically change the direction of the investigation. Who had dared to speak of puerility a little while ago?

The superintendent concluded by assigning tasks. They

were to pursue further the leads that had come up in the framework of the investigation into the kidnapping of Ingrid Raven: Llach and Lambert would continue to look for the store where the paper and the envelope used for the ransom letter had been bought; Raynaud and Moreno would still be working on finding all the BWs in the department. Molina received permission to go to Argelès to gather additional information regarding the murder of Josetta Braun. Finally, he asked Sebag to reinvestigate the assault in Perpignan.

"I found some gaps in the anti-crime squad's work. We have to go over everything again seriously and methodically. I'm counting on you for that."

It was a backhanded compliment, his way of letting Sebag know that he wasn't repudiating him. The inspector appreciated that.

"What's going on with Kevin Costner?"

"With whom?"

Jacques was amused by his astonishment.

"Kevin Costner."

Sebag stared at him. They were back in their office, face to face. Molina was sipping a black coffee and looking at him slyly. Sebag didn't understand why he'd suddenly started talking about movies.

Jacques decided he'd had enough fun at his colleague's expense.

"You don't think Lefèvre looks kind of like Kevin Costner?"

Jacques was very good at seeing resemblances, in both faces and voices.

"Do you think so? If you want my opinion, I think he looks like a hypocrite."

Now that he thought about it, however, it seemed to him that Jacques wasn't entirely wrong. A strong-willed and gentle face full of pent-up energy, blue eyes under straight eyebrows, a tall, slender figure. The two men seemed to be characterized by an unusual determination, a quality Sebag found attractive in Costner but that verged on smugness in Lefèvre.

"What is it about him that you don't like?" Molina asked.

"I didn't like his last film."

"I'm talking about Lefèvre."

"So am I. The scenario is weak, his interpretation a carica-ture. Apart from that, I don't have much against him. He's a lit-tle too full of himself, of course, but along the lines of 'Policeman from Paris on assignment among the hicks' I've seen worse."

Jacques agreed; they had a few memories in common.

"At the same time," Sebag went on, "as soon as he starts talking, and no matter what he says, I don't feel like agreeing with him."

"Do you really think the cases we're talking about have nothing to do with each other?"

"Yes, we're going down the wrong path, in my opinion. What do you think?"

"I don't know. It's true that it all seems pretty convoluted, but at the same time . . . "

"At the same time, jeez, a 'serial killer' in Perpignan, that would be pretty cool, right?"

"No, it isn't that. You know, so far as I'm concerned, rou-tine work suits me perfectly. I think above all that we mustn't miss out on a big deal. Can you imagine? If there really was a common attacker and we refused to follow that lead after it was mentioned by the press, we'd look really stupid."

"I see that, yeah. More than ever, then, we have to apply the famous adage . . . "

"I fear the worst . . . "

"'Prudence is the mother of security,'" in this case the Urban Security Squad."

"Yeah, I suppose . . . I didn't know that proverb."

"Okay, next time I'll stoop to your level."

Molina looked as if he were going to throw his telephone at Sebag, but he just picked it up to call the gendarmes in Argelès. In the end, Sebag wasn't very proud of his proverb.

It was definitely not his day.

CHAPTER 18

He'd arrived early and was stirring a cup of coffee. Sebag had made an appointment to meet Anneke Verbrucke in a cafe on the Avenue Poincaré, near the place where she had been attacked. The interview would be less formal that the one at police headquarters. He'd followed Anneke's route from the discotheque. Then he'd sat down in the cafe. He'd reread the night patrol's report and had in fact noted a few gaps. Oversights that were symptomatic of policemen who were tired and had no illusions about their chances of solving this case, which was commonplace enough. An aborted attack—no theft, no wound other than a scratch on the neck, no description of the assailant. The police's laziness sometimes had excuses.

A blond young woman entered the cafe. He recognized her immediately. Despite the heat, she was wearing a silk scarf around her neck. Her blue eyes looked around the cafe and stopped on Sebag's raised hand. Anneke Verbrucke came over to his table and sat down. The inspector let her order a Monaco before having her tell her story once again. She spoke French very well, with just enough accent to make her soft voice seductive. The night club, her crossing of Perpignan on foot, the attack, the knife, and finally the escape: her account added nothing to the anti-crime squad's report. It was time to make some progress on this case.

"Let's start over from the beginning, please. Precisely when did you understand that you were being followed?"

She sighed.

"I don't know, it's difficult to say. As I told you, it was when I came to the palace of the Kings of Majorca that I realized that there were footsteps behind me . . . but on second thought, it was as if they had been there much earlier and I hadn't been aware of them."

"Could you have been followed from the time you left the bar?"

"Do you think that's possible?"

"It's just a supposition. We have to consider everything. Did you notice something or someone odd at any time during the evening?"

"Odd in what way?"

"I don't know. Someone who paid special attention to you?"

Sebag sensed that she was repressing a smile.

"What does 'odd' mean? When I first came to France, it seemed to me that all men looked at me oddly. And then I understood that it was in your nature. You Latins are like that, aren't you? You aren't even aware of the insistent way in which you look at women. In Holland it's not like that. Men are more . . . discreet."

Her blond hair fell in curls on her bare shoulders. She was wearing a tank top with lacy edges. Obviously she wasn't wearing anything under it. When she spoke, a dimple appeared on her right cheek. Sebag had no trouble imagining the looks that some men might give her. Especially at late hours of the night.

The waiter set the Monaco down in front of her.

"Let me reformulate my question: have you noticed in the course of your stay anyone who looked at you in a *particularly* odd way?"

She thought for a few seconds. Her mouth grew still slimmer. It looked like a simple pink line between her nose and her chin.

It wasn't her best feature. Clearly she'd thought of something, an idea or an image, and she was reluctant to talk about it.

"Tell me everything," Sebag insisted. "From the time when that occurred to you; that may not be insignificant. I'll make the decision regarding that."

"You're probably right," she admitted. "It's . . . there was a man who stared at me for a long time. Oddly. He didn't look at me in exactly the same way as other men. I don't know how to put it, but it was . . . more coldly. A little like the way a doctor looks at you. And then he was alone at his table. All the other men were in groups, or in couples, but he was all alone."

"Could you describe him for me?"

"Do you think . . . ?"

He interrupted her with a gesture.

"Just describe him for me, please. We'll see about the rest later on."

"Okay. He must have been between forty and fifty years old. He was slender . . . maybe even thin, I'm no longer sure, and he had hollow cheeks. His eyes were light-colored . . . That's about it, I don't remember anything else."

"What did he look like? Was he tall?"

"Yes, I mean no, I don't know. He was sitting down. Oh, wait: one time he went out for a few minutes, to go to the toilet, I suppose. He was . . . of medium height."

"What time did you leave the bar?"

"At three A.M. One of my friends' watches sounded every hour—it was really annoying—and it had just beeped when we got up to leave. Afterward, I talked with a friend in front of the café for maybe ten minutes or so."

"Did anyone come out during that time?"

"I don't know. I wasn't paying attention."

"What about the guy who was watching you—did he stay in the bar?"

"No. I think he left a little before we did."

"Weren't you afraid to go back to your room alone? Couldn't anyone accompany you?"

"No, I thought it was better . . . alone."

She'd blushed. The question had been indiscreet.

"With Latins, sometimes you have to make things clear, don't you?" he asked her with a complicitous smile.

"That's one of the first things I learned in France. But at first there were some . . . misunderstandings. It isn't always easy."

Sebag took out his notebook and made a few notes regarding Anneke's description of the man in the bar. Then he drew up a quick chronology of the night. At 3:00 A.M., the young people left the bar. At 3:10, Anneke started walking back to her room. At about 3:20, she reached the Avenue Poincaré, the site of the attack made on her. 3:20 sharp was the time when Ripoll woke him after having received the anonymous phone call. Hard even for an attacker to do two things at the same time. Of course, the details would have to be checked. A few minutes one way or the other, it still worked despite everything. Especially since he thought he remembered Ripoll saying that he'd waited a moment before deciding to wake him.

The devil was in the details, he said to himself. And so were the bad guys!

"Do you think this man in the bar might be the one who attacked me?"

He put his elbows on the table and rested his chin on his hands.

"I don't know, Anneke. I haven't any idea. For the moment, I'm just gathering information. We'll filter it later on."

She'd already finished her Monaco, and he had long since given up on his coffee. Too bitter.

"Would you like something else?"

"No, thanks."

The sun was already high in the sky. It would soon be time for lunch. He'd have liked to drink a *pastis* but didn't dare.

Anneke undid her scarf. The mark made by the knife was still very visible on her white skin.

"How was the attack made, exactly?"

Her eyes turned dark blue. The severe pink line of her mouth reshaped itself under her nose.

"He suddenly appeared out of nowhere. I hadn't heard him coming. He pinned me against a car . . . He put one hand over my mouth and I felt a knife against my neck."

"What hand was he holding the knife in?"

"It was his . . . left hand that was gagging me, so he must have been holding the knife in his right hand." Sebag shrugged. The attacker was right-handed, like 90 percent of the population. Too bad!

"And what happened next?"

"Next? Nothing!"

"What do you mean, nothing?"

"He waited."

"What was he waiting for?"

"I don't have any idea. He was holding me against the car, he didn't move, he didn't say anything. I just heard him breathing. He was breathing heavily but calmly."

She put her index finger and her thumb on her neck and rubbed the red mark.

"Because he . . . waited, you must have had time to take in a few more details. I know he was wearing a hood, but what did he look like to you? Was he tall? Fat?"

She closed her eyes. Her features hardened even more and that was not because of the effort to remember he'd asked her to make. After a few seconds, she reopened her eyes.

"He was about my height, around five-eleven, I'd say. Fairly thin. Dark eyes."

"What was he wearing?"

"Uh . . . Dark-colored clothes. A jacket, maybe. Yes . . . he must have had a jacket."

"What about the man in the bar?"

"He was wearing a light-colored polo shirt. I don't know whether he had a jacket."

Sebag noted all this down alongside the description of the man in the bar. It was too thin to draw any conclusions.

"When your attacker stopped . . . waiting, what did he do?"

"He told me to get into the car and not to cry out."

Sebag turned a page in his notebook. They'd arrived at a crucial point in the narrative and he needed room: he knew that he'd have to come back to the question they were about to take up.

"Which car did he want you to get into?"

"The one he was holding me against."

"Are you sure? Do you think you were being held against *his* car?"

"He even put a hand on the door handle to try to open it," Anneke went on, "and that's when I was able to get away."

"What kind of car was it?"

"Light-colored . . . yellow, I think. Yes, yellow. With elegant shapes. Like a sports car."

Sebag scribbled furiously on his notebook. He finally had something tangible. A yellow sports car, that was not so common. But that wasn't the most important thing. That car could not belong to the attacker. Impossible, he wrote in his notebook. And he underlined the word several times before putting his pen down again.

"Which hand did he use when he tried to open the door?"

"The one that he was holding over my mouth . . . The left."

"And was he able to open the door?"

"I don't know."

She ran her fingers down the side of her empty but still cool glass.

"I think he had trouble opening it, and that's why I was able to get away from him. At a certain moment, I no longer felt the knife against my throat and I yelled. I shoved him away, hit him on the head with my purse, and took off."

"You hit him?"

"I think so, but it's difficult to say: at times like that, you're not aware of what you're doing."

Sebag pointed to a little purse in dyed fabric that the young woman had set on the table when she arrived.

"Is that what you hit him with?"

"Yes."

"Do you mind if I have a look?"

He picked it up and weighed it in his hand. A couple of pounds at most. She must not have done him much harm, he thought.

"Then what happened?"

"Then I crossed the street, there was a car coming. It stopped. When I turned around, there was no longer anyone there."

"He'd left?"

"Yes."

"On foot?"

"Uh . . . yes, I suppose.

"But you're not sure? You didn't see him running away?"

"No . . . "

"You didn't hear him, either?"

"No . . . But how else could he have gotten away?"

"In his car, for example."

"No, I'd have heard that. And then he couldn't have gotten out like that, there were cars in front of him and behind him."

"So the car stayed there."

"I think."

It took her a moment to realize.

"Oh, damn . . . "

Sebag smiled at her sadly. According to their report, the anti-crime brigade men had rapidly arrived at the scene. They had looked around but hadn't found any trace of a suspicious individual. They'd gone back to headquarters to take the victim's deposition. It was therefore only after they'd returned that they learned about the business with the car. Either they didn't react, or they couldn't be bothered to go back to the scene. The night was almost over, and so were their shifts.

"One last question, please, Anneke. This time I'm going to ask you to answer without reflecting. Tell me the first thing that comes to mind. Okay?"

Her face became concentrated and serious, like a little girl's.
"Okay."

Sebag ran a finger over his lips before he asked his question.

"You told me that your attacker waited a long time, but you didn't know why."

"That's right."

"What happened at the moment when he stopped waiting?"

She did as she'd been told and replied immediately.

"A car came down the avenue."

"Are you sure?"

"Yes. For a few seconds, I even thought he wanted me to get into the car that was coming. Until he put his hand on the car door, as I told you."

Sebag wrote this remark in his notebook. Circled it in red. There was something here that he didn't understand, either. He thanked Anneke and gave her his cell phone number in case she remembered something else. Even something that seemed to her unimportant. It was for him to decide, he said again.

Anneke took her coin purse out of her bag. He stopped her.

"Please, allow me," he said, picking up the bill. "Courtesy of the French police."

He put the money on the table and the bill in his wallet, as if he were hoping to be reimbursed for it. But the police didn't have a line in its budget for that kind of gallantry.

Claire was dozing beside the pool, her entirely naked body

exposed to the sun's caress. That evening, or tomorrow at the latest, her skin would have forgotten all trace of a swimsuit.

"Are you having a good vacation?"

Her sunglasses reflected the image of a perfectly blue sky. Gilles saw her eyebrows move and knew that behind the lenses she had opened her eyes. He knelt down beside her.

"How about you?" she asked, without turning her head. "You job wasn't so bad today. You're home early."

"Is that a reproach?"

She took off her glasses. The blue of the sky entered into her eyes.

"Why do you say that?"

"I was joking."

"It's not funny."

"I know."

He tried to laugh. It rang false.

"I'm going to make myself some coffee. Do you want some?"

"What time is it?"

"Almost four o'clock."

"Too late for me, thanks."

He bent over her. As he was bringing his lips to hers to kiss her, he put one hand under her shoulder, the other under her knees. With a sudden movement, he lifted her up and pushed her into the water. Then he went toward the kitchen, pretending to ignore her furious complaints.

In the cupboard, he chose a Guatemalan coffee. Its stimulating, acidic taste was just right at this time of day. While the first aromatic drops were flowing into the coffee pot, he went to take his swimsuit off the line near the pool. He dived in and swam alongside Claire. They did a few lengths together before getting out of the pool and sitting on the edge, dangling their feet in the water. Claire was still naked. The water was sliding off her pearly skin.

"It's nice that you came home early," she said to him. "We'll have an extra long evening. Shall we have dinner in front of the TV or a film night?"

"Neither, unfortunately. I came home early because I have to go out again. I want to check a couple of things."

"And you absolutely have to do that in the evening?"

"Absolutely."

"Too bad."

She seemed sincerely disappointed. He wrapped the towel around his waist. Then he went to get a cup of coffee and came back to drink it next to the pool. He took a first swallow.

"Is it good?" Claire asked.

"Delicious."

"Can I have a taste?"

He handed her his cup but it was his mouth that she drank greedily. She put her arms around his neck and began to hug him very tightly. He prudently put down his cup. Claire pulled him toward her and they both fell into the cool water. Gilles felt happy. Claire still seemed to be in love with him.

They climbed out of the pool. Sebag sat down again to finish his coffee while Claire lay down to finish her tanning.

"Since you won't be here this evening," she began, "I'll take the opportunity to go out with Véronique. She's not doing any better, you know."

"As you wish, my love, as you wish."

That was all he was able to say. The charm had just been broken.

Avenue Poincaré crosses a residential quarter snuggled up to the foot of the palace of the Kings of Majorca. Built in the thirteenth century at the time when Perpignan was the capital of a kingdom stretching from Montpellier to Valencia and including the Balearic Islands, the citadel dominated the city. However, all that can be seen is its thick walls. Backed up against this imposing mass, the area is quiet. Avenue Poincaré becomes calm again each evening as soon as the residents of Perpignan come home from work.

Sebag inspected all the little streets in the neighborhood, unsuccessfully, and then sat down in a bus shelter at the top of the avenue. He took out a cigarette. The first he'd had in days. Although some smokers light up more often during periods of stress, Sebag smoked much less. He forgot. He could do without tobacco much more easily than coffee.

He'd thought all afternoon about this business with the car. It couldn't have been the attacker's car. How could the man have been sure that Anneke would pass right in front of him on her way back to her room, and that the street would be deserted at just that time? Either he was very lucky, or . . .

Or what? That was precisely the problem.

A bus was coming up to the stop. Sebag signaled that he didn't want to get in. The driver looked surprised and drove on.

Sebag didn't wait long. He had hardly finished his cigarette when a yellow car came down the avenue. A yellow Peugeot 306 sport coupe. It was moving slowly. Its driver was looking for a parking place. The car passed in front of him. He had time to catch a glimpse of the owner: high forehead, turned-up nose, round chin. He saw the car hesitate, then turn right at the intersection. He left the bus shelter and went back into the side streets. The 306 came out of Lluis Espare Street and turned right. It went along the ramparts of the palace of the Kings of Majorca for about twenty yards and then stopped in front of a little area for playing *boules*. Its back-up lights came on. The driver had found a place to park. Sebag waited.

A brown-haired young man, not very tall, slightly plump, crawled out of the car. He was wearing a shirt and tie and had his jacket draped over his arm. While he was following him, Sebag got out his cell phone to call police headquarters. The young man went into a small four-story apartment building that looked out on Avenue Poincaré on one side. At headquarters,

Sebag's call was taken by the officer on duty. That was Sergis, a young inspector who had just arrived from Cahors. Sebag knew he was efficient. He gave him the car's license number.

"It's urgent," he explained.

He went to have a look at the car. It wasn't a luxury model but its interior made it look like an expensive car: seats in light-colored leather, steering wheel and gear shift knob in wood. The body was lemon yellow, clean, even immaculate, without a trace of a scratch or dust. Its owner probably went over it with a chamois several times a week. There couldn't be many yellow 306 sport coupes on the road in the department. It couldn't be a coincidence.

He went back to wait under the apartment building's windows.

The Peugeot's driver did not correspond in any way to the description of the attacker given by Anneke Verbrucke. That didn't surprise Sebag. He re-read his notes from his interviews with the Dutch student. His opinion was confirmed: the attack on Anneke couldn't have been an attempt to kidnap her.

A dog came along pulling a man in his sixties who was holding his leash. The dog sniffed Sebag's shoes. He found them so interesting that Sebag wondered if he'd stepped in something. He glanced at the dog's master but the latter had clearly chosen to look elsewhere. The inspector took advantage of that to give a gentle kick to the dog, who immediately lost all interest in his shoes. In the end, dogs are like people—it's the lack of proper training that sometimes makes them disagreeable. Sebag had always had a tendency to think that a little slap now and then would put humanity back on the right track. The problem was to know who would be capable of properly distributing the slaps.

His cell phone rang while the mutt and his master went on to bother someone else.

"Your driver's name is Marc Savoy," Sergis informed him.

"He's a sales rep for a pharmaceutical company. He's married to Isabelle Savoy and they live on Jean Rière street, at the foot of the palace of the Kings of . . . "

"I know where it is, thanks. Can you see if this guy is in our files?"

"I've already looked and didn't find anything. Do you want me to start a national search?"

"No, I don't think that's necessary. Thanks for acting so quickly."

"You're welcome. For the moment, it's a quiet night, don't hesitate to give me something to do."

Sebag went up to the door of the building. "Savoy" was the first name written on the doorbell panel. He pushed the button next to the name.

"Hello?" said a woman's voice.

"Hello. I'm a police officer and I have a few questions I'd like to ask you in connection with an investigation."

There was no answer, but after a few seconds he heard a metallic click. He had only to push the door open. In the entry hall, he found the Savoys' mailbox. They lived on the fourth floor. Sebag chose to take the stairs.

The door to their apartment was located at the end of a little corridor. He rang. The door opened immediately. Through the half-open door, Marc Savoy looked at him mistrustfully.

"What exactly is this about?" he asked. "My wife didn't quite understand."

"It concerns an investigation. I'd like to ask you a few questions. I'm a police inspector."

Savoy looked at his watch. It was almost 9:00 P.M.

"Are you allowed to do that at this hour? Do you have a warrant?"

Sebag repressed a sigh. French citizens' knowledge of the law was often limited to two or three replies they'd heard on television serials, usually American. It was disastrous.

"I don't have a warrant, but I have the right to come to your home and ask you to let me in."

"Ask me? So I don't have to accept?"

He closed the door a little more.

"No, you don't have to."

Sebag found it exhausting to have to go to such lengths to obtain what should have been taken for granted. The French did not find their police efficient, and at the same time did everything they could to make it difficult for them. What did this Savoy guy think? That he had nothing better to do than to work until nine in the evening while his wife was running around somewhere, and that he'd showed up at his house at this late hour just to annoy him? Sebag took out his notebook.

"In that case," he began, pretending to be filling out a form, "I'm going to leave you an official summons. You will have to come by police headquarters at ten tomorrow morning."

He stopped for a moment, chewing on his pen.

"'Savoy,' you do write that with a 'y,' don't you? Bring your identification papers, of course, and expect to have to wait a bit, because lines are often long at headquarters, and we've got a lot of work, you know, with all the people who prefer to go there rather than receive us in their homes for a few minutes in the evening. You'd probably better expect to be there all morning."

He put away his pen and ostentatiously tore off the sheet of paper.

"Just to be sure, it would be wise to block out part of the afternoon as well. In any case, no matter how it goes, you'll be out before five o'clock. After that, we close . . . "

"Five o'clock . . . "

The door opened again.

"What is it, anyway? Is it serious?"

"It's about your car."

Sebag couldn't have come up with a better opener. Savoy stepped completely aside to let him come in.

The woman greeted him in the living room and politely asked him to sit down on the couch. He refused to fall into such a crude trap and chose instead a brown leather chair with wooden arms. Savoy was forced to sink into his sofa.

"What were you doing last Tuesday night?"

Since his interlocutor liked the dialogue on television, there was no reason to disappoint him. Savoy opened his eyes wide and turned toward his wife.

"We didn't do anything special Tuesday night, did we?"

"No, I don't think so."

She opened a TV magazine.

"There was a Louis Funès film on channel 1. We watched it and then went to bed. Though you got up later to take a shower because it was so hot."

"Yes, I remember. It was very hot. It's a little better today. But Tuesday it was really hot."

Sebag hastened to put an end to questions about the weather. Though they could sometimes make laborious discussions go more smoothly, many interrogations also got bogged down in them.

"Do you always park your car outside?"

"Often, unfortunately."

"Even though your apartment building has garages?"

"We have one, but my wife puts her car in it. She comes home earlier than I do, around five P.M., at a time when it's still hard to find a parking spot in the neighborhood. I get home much later—if fact, I'd just come in when you rang—so I park mine on the street."

His tone made it clear that it broke his heart that his car had to spend the night outside. Even though he didn't share Savoy's concern, Sebag felt he had to show sympathy.

"Isn't it a little dangerous to leave such a beautiful car on the street?"

Before answering, Savoy glanced at his wife. His look said: "You see, he thinks so, too."

"We really don't have a choice. Isabelle comes home with our son—he's sleeping there in the other room, he's six months old—and she has to park somewhere close. We've tried to rent another garage but they're hard to come by in this neighborhood."

"And so on Tuesday night your car was outside?"

"Yes, of course. But what exactly was it that happened on that night?"

Sebag deliberately ignored the question.

"Where did you park it when you came home Tuesday evening?"

"Well . . . Tuesday . . . I don't know. Probably on Rière Street, as I do most of the time. That's where there's usually a place."

"Are you sure?"

He'd asked the question while looking at Isabelle Savoy. Women were better at remembering everyday things.

"Tuesday, your mother came to keep the baby because I had errands to do. Wasn't it that evening that you ran into her outside? She was leaving when you came home . . . "

"That's right! I waited until she left and then took her parking spot."

"And where was that?" Sebag asked.

"On the avenue. Avenue Poincaré. Right across from our building, next to the service station. I like to park there when I can, because I can see the car from the living room window. But is that really important? What exactly are you investigating? What does my car have to do with all this?"

Sebag gave them a general description of the attack on Anneke Verbrucke. They listened to him religiously.

"That's unbelievable," Savoy commented, "I always lock my car—you can count on that!"

"Someone might have tried to break into it. You didn't notice anything?"

"No, nothing at all. In any case, I've got a car alarm. This guy is sick. How could he hope to force someone to get into my car?"

That was just the question Sebag was asking himself. He felt that the key to solving the puzzle was somehow to be found in it. He drew an enormous question mark in his notebook and then bade his hosts good-bye. He had no more questions for them.

Savoy put his hand in the pocket where Sebag had put the "summons."

"So I won't need to come to police headquarters tomorrow?"

"No. We've said everything that needs to be said, I think. We can just throw that paper away." He took back the sheet of paper, crumpled it into a ball and lofted it toward the wastebasket—his form was impeccable, but he missed. On the paper was written: "Gotcha."

CHAPTER 19

P rairies in dots of orange and green tumbled down toward Collioure. Terrified by the artist's brush as by the blowing of the wind, the grasses were moving in all directions. Farther down, white houses with flat red roofs formed a barrier. They blocked the way to a sea of a dark, intense, pure blue.

To escape the shadows that populated her damp prison, Ingrid tried to think in colors. She took refuge in the universe of the fauvist painters. Revisited in her mind the Museum of Modern Art in Céret. The memory of the works by Matisse and Derain illuminated her darkness with an almost joyful light.

She also filled her tedium with memories of her childhood. Elementary school, high school. She tried to recall the names of her classmates. Those of her teachers. She remembered in particular a math teacher. He had an angelic face and long, curly hair that fell on his shoulders. Her first love. Platonic. He was flirting with the boys instead.

She perceived more and more clearly the sounds that came from outside. The distant hum of a highway that reached her on windy days. Birdsong in the gentle peace of early morning. One night, she'd heard rain falling. But from the house overhead she never heard anything.

Every day, she was allowed to take a shower. Sheer joy. The door to the cellar was cracked slightly. Toward evening, in general. She pushed it wide open. The door creaked. On the other side was a small room with a white tiled floor. An immense closet on one wall and a shower in the corner. The shower was rudimentary. A faucet and a basin. The wall was tiled up to waist level to prevent the water from splashing on the wall. No curtain. Maybe he was watching her from behind a door. She didn't care. She no longer had any modesty in front of him.

Washing herself had become as important to her as eating and drinking.

This morning, she had found clean clothes. A flowered blouse, beige pirate pants, a lacy bra and a g-string. Her own clothes, which her kidnapper had found in her traveling bag. The last time she'd seen that bag it was in the taxi. José had just put it in the car. He'd slammed the trunk shut and then come up to her. He'd kissed her. Afterward he'd opened the door and she'd taken her seat. She'd quickly fallen asleep as he drove off.

She'd never been able to resist handsome, dark-haired men. She especially liked their hairy hands on her body. But she'd never succeeded in keeping one for very long. There was something about her that attracted them. And probably something else that made them run away. She'd never had much luck with men, but this time she'd really touched bottom.

She wouldn't have thought José capable of harming her.

She ran her hand over her blouse. Her friend Rebecca had given it to her for her eighteenth birthday. The clean smell made her dizzy.

CHAPTER 20

Gilles Sebag was in a very bad mood when he arrived at police headquarters. The preceding night, when he'd returned from his conversation with the Savoys, Claire wasn't home. Around 1:00 A.M., she'd silently slipped into bed alongside him. Her leg felt for his. Half-conscious, he snuggled up to her. Her hair and body reeked of alcohol and cigarettes. The smell penetrated his nostrils and reached his brain, where it woke him up completely. He listened as his wife's breathing gradually calmed down. He didn't move. But he couldn't go back to sleep. So he got up. He drank a glass of whisky, smoked a cigarette. Then he lay down on the chaise longue in the yard. He counted the stars and dozed off from time to time.

When he got up again, she was still asleep. He hadn't taken care not to make noise, but she hadn't woken.

Or else she had pretended to still be sleeping.

It was Saturday. The superintendent had asked them to be there. At least during the morning. On Monday, Claire was leaving on her cruise: they still had a day and a half. Giles had planned a hike in the Albères.

He stopped at the *service de quart*. The officers on duty were trying to question a young man. Arrested during an ordinary roadside check, the boy had resisted the police. He was drunk and was driving without a license in a stolen car. He was only seventeen. The police had left him in the drunk tank all night, but he was still giving off bitter fumes of alcohol. He was hand-cuffed to a radiator. He replied to every question with volleys of insults and his strong foreign accent was getting on the officers' nerves. Sebag could see that soon they would start hitting him. Patience had its limits. Young people's hatred for uniforms was steadily increasing in the immigrant neighborhoods and was ultimately equaled only by the cops' scorn for these street kids.

Which came first, the chicken or the egg?

"What's new, this weekend?" Sebag asked.

"You're looking at it . . . routine," an officer answered.

Sebag sensed that his presence had created a diversion. He pointed to the boy and added:

"At first, I thought he had a big vocabulary, but in the end it's always the same horrors coming out again and again. We ought to lend him a slang dictionary, that would make the conversation more interesting."

"I'd be surprised if he could read," an officer snickered.

"Screw you, you stupid cop, I fuck your mother and she sucks me . . . "

"That's a Kama Sutra position I didn't know about," Sebag joked.

Laughter mixed with insults, and the inspector disappeared, satisfied that he'd obtained a few minutes of reprieve for the young man.

In the corridor leading to his office, he met the superintendent's secretary. She was wearing a leather skirt and a flowered blouse wide open at the top. He tried to look her in the eyes when he greeted her.

"I was just on my way to see you, Mister Sebag," she said with a winning smile. "I've got mail for you this morning."

When she handed him the white envelope, Sebag stopped breathing. The address was complete this time. The envelope had come through the regular mail, as the stamp proved. But he'd recognized the typeface. To Jeanne's surprise, Sebag grabbed a tissue and took the envelope very carefully out of her hands.

It was opened in the crime lab. It contained a message consisting of a few words:

Monday 4:00 P.M. 150 million euros. Ten-euro bills.

And the message was signed:

Armed Brigade of the Surinam Bush Negroes

"This is complete nonsense," Sebag snorted.

There were four of them leaning over the laboratory bench. Pagès had temporarily put the letter under a glass slide. In the upper right, like a kind of inscription, there was a brown stain. It looked like blood.

"What can it possibly be, this 'Armed Brigade of Surinam Bush Negroes'?" Castello asked.

"Another joke," Sebag replied.

"Surinam is a country in Latin America," Lefèvre explained. "For a long time it was called Dutch Guiana."

The room fell silent. Had Lefèvre announced the winning number for the next drawing of the lottery he wouldn't have captured more attention.

"Surinam was a Dutch colony until it gained independence in the mid-1970s. Afterward there was a long civil war between a conservative guerrilla force and the Castro-inspired dictatorship that had taken power."

"What about the Bush Negroes?" Castello asked.

"They are the descendants of black slaves who had long ago fled into the forest."

"You seem to know the country very well," the superintendent remarked.

"I carried out several assignments in French Guiana. The Kourou Space Center is not far from the Maroni River, which constitutes the border with Surinam, and the French authorities have always followed the development of the situation in that country with great interest."

Pagès turned a blue light on the paper.

"Apparently there are no fingerprints. Neither on the letter nor on the envelope. On the other hand, the brown stain is in fact blood. I'll be able to tell you the blood group later today. I'm also going to ask for a DNA analysis, but that will take longer, probably several days."

"Have you received the analysis of Ingrid Raven's DNA?" the superintendent asked.

It was Lefèvre who answered.

"We have it. The Dutch police were very efficient."

"That's only a detail, anyway," Castello said, straightening up. "It's not the most important thing. Whether it's the Moluccan Resistance Front or the Surinam Bush Negroes, they've set a clear date for meeting their demands."

The afternoon was spent in the air-conditioned offices of the police headquarters. On the fourth floor, the bosses were planning strategy for Monday. In connection with Paris and Amsterdam. One floor below, the second-stringers hadn't dared leave for the weekend. They were finishing up their reports and exchanging information.

Lambert and Llach had carried out their assignment: they'd traced the paper used by the so-called Moluccan Front to the stationery section of a supermarket in North Perpignan. Thousands of people had bought this paper over the past two weeks. Thus the two inspectors' success had contributed nothing new to the investigation.

"Might as well be looking for a tanned tourist on a July afternoon on the beach at Canet," Sebag lamented.

"That's not a Catalan proverb," Llach noted.

"No, but it should be!"

Ménard had examined the headquarters log for the past

thirty days and then he'd gone to the departmental gendarmerie's office to do the same thing. He'd found three cases involving Dutch nationals: a speed-limit violation on National Route 9, a fight in a Saint-Cyprien discotheque, and the theft of a credit card.

"Hard to connect with the cases that interest us," Molina commented.

"At least this limits the scope of our investigations," Ménard said, turning toward Sebag. "We're in no danger of seeing the press come up with something we overlooked."

Then Molina made his little report.

"The case in Argelès has hit a dead-end. The gendarmes think they've questioned everyone who met Josetta Braun between her arrival in France and her death, and according to them, that already amounts to quite a few people. They questioned the people in the campground where she was staying. They collected dozens of fingerprints, but nothing came of them. No motive, no lead. The gendarmes reminded me that they haven't made any public statements about the weapon used in the crime and don't want us to talk about it either."

"Why?" Lambert said, surprised.

"To trip up the murderer if he's found," Sebag explained. "Didn't you learn that at the police academy? It's especially important when there's a confession. It's crucial to make the suspect admit details that only the killer could know. That way, even if the guy goes back on his confession a few days later, he's stuck. And then it can also enable us to eliminate people who confess to crimes they haven't committed. But for the most part, it's the less important information that isn't made public."

"The walker who found her was a retiree, is that right?" Llach asked.

Molina looked through his notes.

"Robert Vernier. Sixty-five years old. He lives in Gien, in the Loiret. He's a widower. For the past twenty years he's been spending all his vacations in the Oleanders campground, a nice little place, still very family-oriented. The owners know Vernier well and seem to like him. He goes for a walk every morning at dawn. You know the type . . . I swear, the guy is retired and can sleep as late as he wants, but he gets up every morning before the sun rises!"

Ménard thought this an opportune place for a cultural quotation.

"Anatole France said: 'The acme of laziness is to rise at four A.M. to have more time to do nothing.'"

"The acme of laziness, my ass, but the acme of stupidity, yes!" Molina snorted.

Sebag didn't want to allow himself to be distracted by his colleague's rather facile sallies.

"What impression did this retiree make on you?"

"None at all! I wasn't able to talk with him. He's gone home to Gien."

"He went home?"

"Yeah. This affair has completely disoriented him. That's what his daughter told me. He was traumatized by his discovery of the body. He stopped sleeping and hardly talked any more. He decided to return to his house in the Loiret.

"How long has he been gone?"

"Since the beginning of the week."

"It's too bad that you weren't able to talk with him," Llach said. "It seems that in 80 percent of the cases, it's the criminal who calls the police to report the crime. And that's been proven statistically."

"Proven statistically, what exactly does that mean?" Molina grumbled. "That's really the kind of thing that is completely meaningless. Watch out, Joan, your union activity is beginning to rot your brain. It always begins with the vocabulary. One hundred percent of cretins join a labor union some time or other; that's been statistically proven, too."

Annoyed, Llach took refuge in silence. Ménard put an end to the argument.

"In any event, if the gendarmes compared the prints of everyone who was nearby with the ones found on the stone, there's no point in wasting our time on vague hypotheses. What about you, Gilles, do you have anything new this morning?"

"Yes. Marc Savoy's yellow sport coupe is the car against which Anneke Verbrucke was jammed."

"This business with the car is curious," Ménard commented.

"I think so, too . . . "

Molina put an end to their cogitations.

"Well, I see that we've done a lot right here today. I propose that we move around a bit. How about a beer at the Carlit?"

His proposal was adopted unanimously. Or almost. Ménard didn't commit himself but went along with the others.

On their return, the inspectors had the unpleasant surprise of seeing themselves summoned for a last meeting with the bosses.

"Damn," Molina commented, expressing the general view.

The bosses were already in the meeting room. They went around the table asking everyone to sum up the results of his investigations.

"What good does it do to make reports," Llach grumbled.

"It maintains your spelling and vocabulary," Jacques told him in a low voice.

The atmosphere in the room was not very different from that in a middle school class before summer vacation. At the Carlit bar, Molina's round had been followed by another paid for by the owner in recognition of the devotion of French policemen who didn't hesitate to work on weekends to provide better protection for their fellow citizens.

"Raynaud and Moreno aren't here," Castello explained. "They had to go to Prades and then up to Font-Romeu to meet with two persons whose initials are B.W."

Molina had a quite different interpretation of their absence, which he whispered to his closest neighbors, Llach and Sebag.

"Those two are not as stupid as we are. They did their interrogations by telephone and stayed home in comfort."

Castello ignored his men's unruliness.

"For the moment, the BWs are leading nowhere. Raynaud and Moreno have met with about fifty of them. There are still a few they haven't yet been able to contact. For now, we've decided to omit a good dozen Wangs, Chinese and Vietnamese nationals. Pagès has just told me about an important result: the blood found on this morning's envelope belongs to the B-positive group. A rather rare group. It's not Ingrid Raven's group."

"So is it the attacker's then?" Ménard asked hopefully.

"I don't know, but let's not dream too much," Castello answered.

The superintendent paused. His eyes landed on Sebag.

"Regarding this morning's message," he went on, "I wanted to tell you that it in no way changes our approach. Instead, it confirms it. The reference to the Bush Negroes seems to us just as fanciful as the allusion to the Moluccan Front, but it reaffirms the link with Holland, the former colonizer of Surinam. Holland is more than ever a lead that we can't ignore."

The superintendent seemed to hesitate. He turned toward Lefèvre and then looked back at Sebag.

"We have another . . . , uh, connection that we can't avoid. This second message was addressed to the same person as the first. I suppose you've reflected on this aspect of our case, Gilles."

Sebag suspected that the question would rapidly be taken up again.

"I still have no explanation," he sighed.

"Cyril, you've also followed this, uh, connection. You haven't found anything conclusive, either?"

"First of all, and in order to forestall any misunderstanding, I would like to state that at no point has Gilles Sebag been considered a suspect."

A murmur was heard in the ranks of the inspectors. Some verbal precautions turn out to be more humiliating than insults.

"I have investigated and it is true that I have found nothing conclusive. Will you allow me, Gilles, to sum up briefly for your colleagues?"

"Go ahead," Sebag said, reluctantly. "I have nothing to hide."

"Fine. So you were born in Versailles and grew up in the suburbs of Paris, in Essonne, to be more precise . . . "

Llach brusquely interrupted him.

"As the union representative, I am categorically opposed to a colleague's private life being discussed in this type of meeting."

"Gilles has given his permission," Lefèvre retorted.

"You really didn't leave him any choice."

"Up to now, I don't think I've revealed any personal secrets."

"Precisely! I prefer to step in before you do."

Llach addressed himself to Castello.

"Superintendent, I repeat that I'm opposed to any poking around in a colleague's private life. This is not the place for that. Either you have discovered something useful for the investigation and you talk to us about that precise point. Or you haven't found anything and the discussion stops there."

All the inspectors applauded Llach's declarations. A revolt was brewing.

"All right, gentlemen, we'll stop there for the moment," Castello said. "I hear your protest . . . "

"Our opposition," Llach clarified.

"I hear your . . . opposition, and I'm willing to take it into account this time. Nonetheless, it is important to understand why Gilles was chosen as the contact person. We can't afford to neglect a lead."

Ménard asked for the floor.

"Things may be simpler than we think. It's true that the attacker or attackers are addressing their demands to Gilles, but that's all. Nothing in the text of the letters seems to concern him. No one seems to be settling an account or anything else with him. He's not a target, merely a privileged interlocutor."

Castello made a gesture to invite Ménard to develop his idea.

"Maybe we should look for something in Gilles's recent past. Maybe Gilles simply met the attacker a few days ago, did something for him or made a good impression on him in some matter, and that was enough."

"Maybe he also wanted to confuse us," Llach suggested. "Or even stir up ill-feeling among us."

"If that was his goal, he succeeded," Molina snickered.

Sebag hadn't brought his notebook. He swiped a piece of paper from Molina and borrowed his pen. The two ideas seemed to him interesting. Especially Llach's. While thinking about the attack on Anneke, he'd already wondered whether all the oddities he'd noticed weren't voluntary. But following that idea led to accepting the hypothesis of a connection among the three cases, which he'd refused to make up to that point. He drew a large question mark on his piece of paper.

"All these suppositions are attractive," Lefèvre commented. "But their main defect is that they advance us hardly at all. If we are looking for a strong connection between Gilles and the attackers, it's in the hope of getting a lead we can follow. And if we now assume that it's a big smoke-screen intended to lead us astray, we might as well give up that lead."

"And why shouldn't we?" Molina said provocatively.

"There is no question of doing that," Castello said. "On the contrary, we have to continue our investigations. François Ménard's idea seems to me interesting: we should also look into Gilles's very recent past. The key may be somewhere in the last few days: between Ingrid's disappearance and the first letter."

Molina snorted noisily.

"Well, if we have to question all the people Gilles may have met in the past two weeks . . . "

He turned toward his colleague.

"I hope you didn't go to a concert or a rugby game; otherwise we'll still be working on it at Christmas. We might as well be looking for a needle in a haystack."

"*O un pallagosti moreno en la platja de Canet*," Llach said, winking at Sebag.

He consented to translate for those who knew no Catalan.

"It's an old proverb here in Catalonia. It means: 'You might as well be looking for a tanned grasshopper on the beach at Canet.' 'Grasshopper' is a polite term that we use among ourselves to refer to tourists!"

CHAPTER 21

"What are you going to have?"

"I think I'll have the soup for starters, and then a grilled sole. What about you?"

"A salad, followed by lamb chops with pasta."

Gilles and Claire put the menu down on the corner of the table. A fan was blowing hot air around over their heads. There were no free tables left in the restaurant.

"A good thing we thought to make a reservation," Claire pointed out.

"For once!"

It had been a very athletic day. Leaving home at dawn, they'd parked their car near the hamlet of Lavall in a narrow valley in the Albères mountains, a range of peaks that extends the Pyrenees as far as the Mediterranean. It had taken them two hours to climb to the Tower of Massane at an altitude of 2,600 feet. Leaning against the pale, cool stone of the medieval tower, they'd eaten a snack while enjoying the view. To the north, the sandy coast of Roussillon stretched its sea ponds as far as Cap Leucate. The plain was silent; it seemed to be still asleep. To the east, the morning sun was making the Mediterranean sparkle and buried the rocky coast in a flood of light.

They'd continued their hike as far as the Roc de la Canal Grossa, a peak on the Spanish border. The south coast of Catalonia could be seen as far as the Cap de Creus. After a light picnic, it took them three hours to make the descent back down to the car.

The restaurant was small and the waiter had to watch his hips and shoulders to avoid bumping into the diners. Street signs and old shop signs decorated the walls. Antique lanterns attached to the ceiling shed a soft white light on the guests, completing an atmosphere marked by a strange urban melancholy.

"Doesn't it seem a little odd to be here, just the two of us, like we used to be?" Claire asked.

Gilles hesitated. Maybe this was the time for questions and answers.

"I have the impression that you don't much like this new freedom without children," she went on. "I like it! There's no reason to hurry home, we can follow our inspiration, decide to go to a movie, for instance, if we feel like it."

He looked at his watch.

"Ten P.M. It's already too late for a movie."

"Another time, then. But we could still go dancing in a discotheque, if we wanted."

"If we wanted, yes . . . "

Claire gently stroked his cheek with her hand. His skin was soft but he hadn't shaved since morning, and his whiskers scraped her fingers. She liked this sound composed of a mixture of tenderness and roughness.

"Don't worry, I won't drag you there against your will. I know you hate the 'nightclub' atmosphere. I don't like it much myself during the summer."

"Do you think there are too many people there as well?"

"Too many young people, especially; they make me feel old."

"Old? You're joking, I hope. You still look so young . . . "

Gilles had noticed a touch of sadness in his wife's tone. It was the first time she'd let on that she was upset by the idea that she would soon turn forty.

"You see, you added the word 'still.'"

Claire was wearing a white T-shirt that showed off her tan. Gilles took her hand and lifted it to his lips.

"Excuse me, that isn't what I meant. Youth has nothing to do with beauty. Why would you want to look young when maturity suits you so well? I think you're growing more beautiful every day."

"You're just saying that because you see me with your forty-year-old's eyes."

"So? Who do you want to please? Boys? Your students, maybe?"

She brusquely withdrew her hand and looked offended.

"Oh, please!"

The waiter brought the starters. Gilles filled their wine glasses. He'd ordered a Roussillon rosé, a light and fruity wine that Catalan winemakers had recently been marketing in an attempt to adapt to consumers' new tastes.

"Anyway, on your boat there won't be many young people."

Claire was to leave the following afternoon from Marseilles.

"The way you said that . . . 'your' boat. Are you really that angry with me for leaving?"

He shrugged.

"I can't ask you to spend the month of July at home waiting for me to come home at night. You have time off and I don't. You should do what you want . . . "

"In short, you're angry with me."

"A little, yes," he finally admitted.

Gilles put a big forkful of salad in his mouth so he wouldn't have to say more. The heart has its rancors that reason has to ignore. It had been a pleasant day. No point in ruining it. He'd made a choice: he didn't want to know. Not now. Later, after the cruise, they'd see. And rather than listing the grounds that might justify his concerns, he wanted to attend only to the signs of tenderness and love with which Claire continued to shower him, despite her absences. She could allow herself a sexual parenthesis, after all, so long as she continued to love him. Let her do what she wanted with her body on her damned boat, provided that when she came home she made love to him with the impatience and passion of a woman in love.

But Claire didn't let up on him: she wasn't a police inspector's wife for nothing.

"In fact, you seem to be jealous," she said, as if she were talking to herself.

Gilles forced himself to smile in an attempt to put her off the scent.

"You're jealous," she repeated, with a broad smile.

He frowned.

"It's all right, okay?"

The waiter came to change the plates. Sebag took advantage of this to change the subject.

"What time does 'the' boat leave, exactly?"

"At six P.M. But we have to be on board at least two hours earlier."

"And your first stop is still Bonifacio?"

"Yes, and then Naples, Palermo, Tunis, Palma de Mallorca . . . "

Claire deliberately left out the last stop in Barcelona. Ever since they'd been living in Perpignan, they'd been talking about spending a weekend in the capital of South Catalonia, but had never done it.

"I'll be back on July 22," Claire concluded. "Two weeks away: just long enough for you to miss me a little."

Gilles spoke in a low voice like a crooner's and adopted his most romantic tone.

"You know, when you're away for a few hours I already miss you."

"That's a nice thing to say," she said with a serious smile. "But you know very well that it's no longer true. Not entirely."

Gilles's eyes narrowed. His brown eyebrows fused into a single line under his forehead.

"What do you mean?"

She put her hand on his.

"Nothing in particular. But when people have known each other for twenty years, as we have, a little time apart can't do any harm, can it?"

Gilles didn't answer. He recalled their long period of separation at the time of his transfer. Fifteen months in all. He'd arrived in Perpignan in April for a temporary assignment and had been given official notice of his new posting only in November. Claire and the children had already started a new school year in Chartres, and had remained there until summer vacation, while Gilles scoured the department of Pyrénées-Orientales looking for a house. He went home only once a month. After ten years of living together, they'd rediscovered the bittersweet pleasure of missing one another. Their separation had rekindled the already lukewarm embers of desire. And when they were together, there were passionate caresses and sex; they made love by mixing the eagerness of the early days with the experience of each other they'd acquired. If her return home after two weeks on a cruise ship was going to be like that, Sebag said to himself, let her go as soon as possible. And especially let her come back to me.

The waiter brought the next course. The lamb chops were juicy and well grilled. Claire announced that she was delighted with the fish.

"In any event, with your investigation you won't have time to get bored."

They'd discussed Gilles's work at great length during their hike. Sebag liked to review with Claire the cases that posed problems for him. For her to understand, he had to explain everything, start from the beginning and not omit any details. In presenting the facts to Claire, he began to see them in a different light himself. That had often led him to re-examine elements that the whole team had too quickly considered settled. Especially when they had a lead or even a suspect. Building a case for the prosecution and for the defense was the biggest farce in the French justice system. Thesis, antithesis, specious . . .

"And this young policeman who annoys you so much, what exactly is it you don't like about him?"

"I don't know. When he doesn't say anything, his silence irritates me. And when he opens his mouth, it's even worse. You know, he's the kind of guy whose whole life must be centered on his job. He's a cop 24/7, and that necessarily makes him a jerk."

"That's how you were when you started. Have you forgotten that?"

Claire had touched a sore spot. It was true that at the beginning, Sebag had devoted himself to the police, heart and soul. At that time, he saw his work as a mission. She had often complained about it.

"You were able to cure me . . . "

She smiled. A veil of sadness fell over her eyes.

"I'm not the one who cured you. It was the children."

He couldn't disagree. It was only after Léo was born that he'd been able to distance himself a little from his work. His mission as a father had completely absorbed him.

A few tables away from them, an elderly couple were arguing in low voices. Gilles couldn't hear what they were saying, but the tension in their faces left no doubt that they were angry with each other.

"They must be in their seventies, don't you think?" he asked Claire.

"At least . . . "

"It's rare to see an old couple quarreling like that. Usually their differences of opinion arouse more irritation than anger."

"Do you think it's a good sign that they're still fighting with each other at that age?"

"Yes, probably."

"It won't end well . . . " she commented.

"It's when you give up that anger turns into irritation.

"Give up on what?"

"On changing what's wrong in the relationship."

"What would you like to change in our relationship? What's irritating you the most right now, for instance?"

The question caught him off guard. He should have seized the opportunity. But he didn't want to spoil these last moments with Claire.

"Point-blank like that, it's hard . . . I'd say, for instance, vacations! And you, are there things you've given up hope of changing in our relationship?"

"Yes, of course."

"What?"

"Do you really want to know?"

"Yes."

"The length of your cock, for instance."

"Very funny. Does that annoy you a lot?"

"No, it excites me."

CHAPTER 22

The next day would be a big one. Finally.

He'd been imagining it for a long time. He'd organized it, planned it, and then waited. The great game was about to begin. Up to now, it had all been preparation.

The most dangerous part was to come this evening. The work he had to do required coolness, discretion, and rapidity. He'd scouted out the site, rehearsed his moves, timed his actions. He mustn't allow himself to be surprised by obstacles.

He felt ready.

The house was silent. All that could be heard was the birds singing outside. A magpie and chickadees. The pair of turtle doves that had filled the yard with their stupid cooing had left. He'd been able to drive them away. With his sling. He wasn't as good with it as when he was a child, and he'd been unable to hit them. But he'd scared them enough.

He closed his eyes. Breathed slowly.

He had to summon his strength. The night would be long and tiring. But the police were in for a real surprise.

He wished he knew how far they'd gotten. He'd done what was necessary to confuse them. It wasn't going to be easy for them to figure things out. Maybe he should help them after having led them astray.

He'd counted on the press to keep him up to date on the police's investigation. He'd even given the reporters a hand, but the summertime torpor had quickly overcome them again. Nothing about the police's work had come out. Only the murder in Argelès had been given any attention in the papers.

Deep in his heart, he felt a kind of jealousy.

Chapter 23

Jesus, what a shitty fucking job!"

His head in a city trash can, digging around among the garbage, Gilles Sebag was furious. He threw an empty pizza carton on the ground, along with a half-eaten apple, plastic bags containing God knew what, and a condom whose content was only too obvious.

"What a stupid way to make a living!"

Passersby gave him hostile stares. Only the word "Police" on his red armband prevented them from expressing their disgust more clearly. Soon everything in the trash can was on the sidewalk. Sebag continued his search. In the open air, this time.

The message had arrived around 3:00 P.M. A boy, a gypsy about ten years old, had brought the usual envelope. Llach had questioned him while the rest of the team met in the superintendent's office. Castello himself had opened the envelope. Then he'd read the letter out loud. A single sentence and a proper name. The name made everyone turn and look at Gilles.

A trash can, Place de Catalogne. Inspector Sebag.

"Clearly, they really like you," Superintendent Castello commented.

Sebag already had a broadcasting radio. An earbud and a microphone attached to the collar of his jacket. He would be alone in his car, with Ménard and Molina following him at a distance of less than five hundred yards. A big blue-and-black sports bag sat prominently in the middle of the room. Lefèvre opened it to show the inspectors what was in it. It was full of crumpled newspaper.

"Why the bag, since it has been decreed from on high that we're not paying?" Llach asked.

"To make it look like we're playing the game," the Superintendent said, shrugging.

The tension in the meeting room had risen another notch. The inspectors nodded gravely, wondering what the precise rules of this sinister game might be. And especially what the kidnappers' reaction would be in the event that the trick failed.

Sebag conscientiously put all the garbage back in the trash can. He hadn't found anything that could be considered a clue or a new message. He straightened up and looked around the Place de Catalogne. In front of the prestigious building of the Dames de France, a dozen fountains made the paving stones heated by the sun seem cooler. He wiped his sweat-covered forehead. At the other end of the esplanade he saw, next to a newsstand, another trash can.

"A sucker's job, for sure!"

He left his car double-parked and crossed the esplanade. The news seller, who seemed to have been observing his activities, watched him approaching. He greeted him with a broad grin:

"Is it lots of fun being a cop?"

"It's vacation time. We keep busy however we can."

"What are you up to, anyway?"

"Playing hide and seek. But the trash can over there was too small. I'm going to try to get into this one. Do you mind if I make a bit of a mess in front of your newsstand?"

Without waiting for an answer, he started emptying the new trash can. After going through fistfuls of damp and fetid trash, he finally pulled out a white envelope. Just like the earlier ones, except that it had a lovely grease stain on its back. Sebag went up to the newsstand and waved the envelope under the merchant's nose.

"Did you see anyone throw this away?"

"If I had to keep an eye on everyone who threw stuff in the trash can . . . " the merchant replied, not repressing a look of disgust.

"But you seemed to have time to take an interest in what I was doing."

"You have to admit that it was funny."

Sebag took a business card out of his wallet.

"If by any chance your memory returns and you still feel like joking, don't hesitate to call me."

Gingerly, the news agent took the card and read it before putting it in his shirt pocket.

"Is it a now a crime to throw envelopes in the trash can?"

"It might become one . . . In any case, this is not the best way of sending a message. I know that public services don't work as well as they used to, but all the same . . . "

"In any case, that envelope was delivered, wasn't it?"

He leaned over the counter to see better.

"Moreover, it doesn't even have a stamp on it. What efficiency! Maybe all mail should be handled that way."

Sebag left the news agent to reflect on a reform of the French postal system and returned to his car. It was 4:24 P.M. Paying no attention to the bus honking its horn behind him, he tore open the envelope and read the message out loud.

Bus stop no. 27, Avenue Poincaré.

A shiver ran down his back. He moved out into traffic, went up the Boulevard des Pyrénées, then the Boulevard Mercader, and stopped his car in a spot reserved for buses. Very near the place where Anneke Verbrucke had been attacked. An old lady waiting at the bus stop looked at him ill-temperedly.

"Young man, how do you expect the bus to stop if you park there?"

He just pointed to the police armband around his bicep. He looked all around the bus shelter but didn't see anything unusual. No letter, no envelope. Just a graffito bluntly asking a girl to do a favor for one of her classmates.

"How long have you been waiting here?" he asked the old lady.

"About ten minutes," she mumbled through her mustache.

"And you haven't seen anything unusual?"

"Yes."

"What?"

"An impolite policeman who's preventing the bus from stopping."

Sebag tried to take a deep breath.

"Thank you for your valuable help, Madam," he finally said, giving her a frankly hypocritical smile.

He went around the shelter again. Nothing. His eyes then fell on line 27's schedule. There was a bus every twenty minutes from 6:00 A.M. to 10:00 P.M. One bus had been crossed out with a red pen: 4:40 P.M. He looked at his watch. It would be that time in two minutes.

"I haven't found anything so far," he said, speaking to his jacket collar. "I'm continuing the search."

"Roger," Castello answered. "We'll wait."

Sebag parked his car on the sidewalk a little further down the street.

"Disgraceful," the old woman admonished him when he rejoined her.

A bus was already coming down the avenue. The 4:40 bus; so there was one at that time. It stopped at the shelter. The doors belched air and opened. The old lady got in.

"Good-bye, dear lady!" Sebag shouted.

She did not deign to answer him. The bus drove off, leaving him alone on the sidewalk.

He turned around and looked at the schedule again. It was taped to a sheet of glass. Underneath it was another schedule. Identical, but without the crossed-out bus. He tore off the sheet of paper. On the back, a sentence was typed. He read it, gulped, and then read it out loud:

Oleanders Telephone booth 5:45 P.M.

"Son of a bitch!"

That night, going over the day in his head, Sebag could no longer remember whether it was he who had uttered this oath or if he'd heard it resound in his earbud. The Oleanders—that could only be the campground in Argelès, the one where Josetta had stayed before she was killed. They had thus come full circle. The Avenue Poincaré and Anneke Verbrucke, the Oleanders campground and Josetta Braun. This message was the missing link that bound the three cases together. It wasn't possible, Sebag said to himself. He couldn't have made such a stupid mistake. He would have sworn that these three cases had no connection.

He pulled up the collar of his jacket and asked:

"What shall we do, boss?"

Superintendent Castello's voice reached him through his earbud. Sebag could sense his disappointment.

"You head for Argelès, obviously. Molina and Ménard will continue to follow you at a distance. Don't drive too fast. I'm sending Raynaud and Moreno: they have to be in position before you get there."

Sebag returned to his car and set out for Argelès. He saw Ménard's and Molina's gray vehicle down the avenue. He didn't know what to think. The parts of the puzzle were beginning to fit together. How could he have gotten so far off track? He could imagine Lefèvre's face at this point. His smile of satisfaction making a triumphal dimple appear on his clean-shaven cheeks. He was glad he didn't have to see it. His jaw tightened and he heard his teeth grinding.

The earphone crackled:

"I've informed the gendarmes in Argelès that we need to carry out an operation on their territory," Castello explained.

Sebag took his foot off the accelerator: he was driving too fast.

Traffic was moving smoothly on Departmental 914. At this time of day, the tourists were all at the beach. Sebag went around the hilltop town of Elne, whose square bell tower overlooks hills covered with vineyards and fruit orchards. He left the departmental highway and took the smaller road that led to the Argelès beaches. In the rearview mirror he could see that Ménard and Molina were still following him.

At the Oleanders campground he parked his car next to the office. The telephone booth was by the entrance. It was empty. He went into it. In the age of the cell phone, he was the only one who dared to enter this solar furnace on a summer afternoon. He left the door half-open to avoid being dried to a crisp.

The campground was supposed to be full, but in the heat at this hour it was quiet. Sebag spotted Raynaud and Moreno parked in a shady lane next to an immaculate trailer from Germany. Smoke was coming out of the driver's-side window. He could make out a slender figure behind the windshield. Hmm, Moreno has started smoking again, Sebag thought.

"I'm in position," he said in a low voice.

He was ten minutes early.

He took out his cell phone. He'd put it on silent mode and had felt it vibrate while he was driving. He had in fact received a message. A new photo of Léo on a quad.

Two teenage girls in swimsuits walked by. They were pretty, though their thighs were a little heavy. They looked him over and he felt ridiculous with his shirt, street shoes, and jacket thrown over his shoulder, sweating heavily in an overheated telephone booth as he stood there holding a cell phone. He smiled to them,;they giggled. Kids that age had no pity.

Fortunately it was time.

The telephone in the booth rang. He picked up the receiver and heard calm breathing at the other end of the line.

"Hello," Sebag said.

No answer. Only the breathing. Deep and self-assured.

"Hello?"

"It's hot, isn't it?"

The voice that was whispering to him seemed muffled and distant. Sebag immediately recognized it from the recording of the telephone call that had accompanied the first message.

"You could have found a more comfortable place, yes. I know a bar near here where they serve very cold beer. We could meet there, if you like."

Silence again. More breathing. His interlocutor wasn't the humorous type.

"In the shade of Força Real you'll find a gift. It's all you can buy with the contents of your bag."

The mysterious caller hung up. Sebag suddenly felt cold. He went back to his car but did not immediately drive away. What did that mean? Like an echo to his thoughts, he heard Castello's voice in his earbud.

"What do you think he meant?"

Sebag wasn't the only one to foresee the worst. He didn't want to be the first to put it into words.

"What about you, what do you think?"

Castello reflected for a few seconds before answering.

"He knows there can't be 150 million euros in small bills in that bag."

"Conclusion?"

The first reply was a long sigh. Then the tense voice of his boss.

"I'm not sure that we're going to like his gift very much."

Sebag started the car, drove out of the campground, and took his place in the long line of cars slowed by the dense crowd of pedestrians. The summer visitors were starting to leave the beach.

"Damn, it's going to take an hour," he grumbled.

Castello heard him.

"The treasure hunt is over, I think. We're also leaving for the hermitage at Força Real. Join us there as soon as you can. If you need to speak to me again, use your cell phone."

Sebag was getting impatient. He'd always hated traffic jams. When he'd had enough of drumming his fingers on the steering wheel, he got out his flashing light, turned on his siren, and tried to go around the cars on the cycle path on the right. In his rearview mirror, he saw that Molina and Ménard had moved up and were following him.

When he got to Elne, Sebag decided to go through Thuir to avoid Perpignan. Bad choice. On the way they were blocked by firemen fighting a brush fire and arrived in Força Real after 7:00 P.M. The two cars stopped side by side. Sebag, Molina, and Ménard got out and headed toward a group of men among whom they had spotted Superintendent Castello's white mane.

On the summit, a light wind was blowing but the air was still muggy. The Força Real mountain has two peaks. The higher of the two is topped by a television relay antenna, the other by the hermitage. Standing in front of the little religious building, the view was splendid. At the foot of Le Canigou, Sebag immediately located the Sant-Marti chapel he liked to run up to.

Molina was talking with his childhood friend, the gendarme from Millas. Ménard was trying to make a place for himself among the officials who were talking with Castello. Sebag recognized a colonel from the gendarmerie and the director of the prefect's cabinet, a small, very neat young man who had recently graduated from the National School of Administration. This group also included Lefèvre.

Castello got away and approached his men.

"We arrived only a short time ago: I had to take care of a few formalities. The hermitage is closed for repairs. We had it opened but found nothing. Now we're going to search the surrounding area."

"What exactly are we looking for?" Molina asked.

"Anything we can find," Castello replied.

"We're looking for a gift," Sebag explained.

The colonel from the gendarmerie was directing the operations. Policemen and gendarmes deployed in a circle around the hermitage.

"First, we're going to search the accessible places," Castello explained. "If we don't find anything, then we'll go look at the base of the cliff."

"I don't think that will be necessary," Sebag said. "On the way here, I thought about what our interlocutor said. He uttered only three sentences in all. He chose his words carefully."

The sun had begun its slow descent. The summit of Le Canigou was wreathed in pink. Around the hermitage, the shadows were slowly growing longer. Lefèvre had come up. Four pairs of eyes were now fixed on Sebag.

"He said we'd find a gift in the shade of the hermitage. In my opinion, we should take what he said literally: it's in the shade of the hermitage that we'll find something. Or in what will be in the shade a few minutes from now. We might be early with respect to his estimated timetable."

All eyes turned toward the hermitage, then followed its shadow as far as a copse of live oaks alongside the asphalt parking lot. Two gendarmes were already walking over the area. One of them easily picked up a bush of dried flowers. The other scratched the earth with the tip of his boot.

"Have you found something?" Castello shouted to them.

Deep in his thoughts, the elder of the two gendarmes jumped:

"Yes . . . well, maybe . . . It looks like the soil here has recently been dug up and that the bush was pulled up and then put back."

That was the signal for action. They used pickets and an orange plastic ribbon to delimit the area to be searched. Two husky gendarmes took up their tools and set to work. The soil was dry and light. In a short time, a pickaxe tore into a piece of shiny paper. Then a piece of multi-colored ribbon appeared.

"Damn," Molina said. "It really is a gift-wrapped package."

Time seemed to stop. Policemen and gendarmes had gathered around the area. They were all silent but the birds, unperturbed, continued to sing their ode to the evening coming on.

The police lab technicians took over. Jean Pagès put on his old, faded white smock. He was supposed to retire in August. Along with his young colleague, Eva Moulin, he slowly unwrapped the present. Under the shiny paper they found a large plastic bag. They carefully opened it by cutting the top of the bag like a package of grated cheese. Sebag had prepared himself to be gagged by strong odors of putrefaction, but that didn't happen. The aroma of the brush continued to hover over the scene. An arm suddenly emerged from the opening, a muscular arm covered with brown hair. At its extremity, a large, powerful hand wore a wedding ring. Then the policemen cut the bag lengthwise. Ice crystals covered the corpse. The cold had swollen the features of the face and coils of ice had formed in the eye sockets. But the inspectors had no trouble identifying the body.

CHAPTER 24

A ssembled in the fourth-floor meeting room, the police-men listened to the coroner, Dr. Roger, present the results of the autopsy. In José Lopez's lungs, which were swollen like balloons, water mixed with mud had been found; in his stomach, dark beer and massive doses of a seda-tive. The cab driver's body bore no trace of violence apart from a black mark on his neck left by someone's fingers. The coro-ner had also noted reddish spots under the arms.

"The murderer got his victim to drink a beer containing a powerful sedative," Dr. Roger explained. "Once the victim was unconscious, he drowned him by holding his head under water with his right hand. The mark is visible but not too pro-nounced. I think the victim regained consciousness, but too late to offer any real resistance. The drowning took place in a pond or lake. The marks under the armpits suggest that the body was transported just after death. Since no similar marks were found on the ankles, we can conclude that the body was moved post mortem by one individual."

"The corpse was dragged, in fact," Jean Pagès confirmed. "I found unusual signs of wear on the back of the heels of his shoes. The murderer grabbed Lopez under the arms and pulled him."

"The victim's legs were frozen in a bent position," the coro-ner went on. "According to my calculations, the body was kept in a freezer whose length was less than five feet."

Roger also estimated that Lopez had been dead for no less than a week, and about ten days at most. He wasn't able to be more precise because freezing the body threw off the parameters. On the other hand, it was certain that the body had been taken out of the freezer the night before it was discovered.

The coroner put away his notes and tried to smile. He was a small man, puny and timid, whose only bold element was his hair: long brown bristles poked in wild tufts from his nostrils and ears.

"First, I'd like to thank Dr. Roger for having presented in person the results of his autopsy," Superintendent Castello said. "I know he doesn't much like doing this sort of thing, but it has allowed us to gain precious time. You will have his complete report, in official written form, on your desks tomorrow morning."

Dr. Roger nodded in agreement, looking down at his dirty fingernails. Sebag didn't dare imagine what materials could have blackened them that way. He'd already noted that contrary to the most elementary rules of hygiene, the coroner didn't always wear gloves while doing autopsies.

The superintendent turned to Pagès.

"Anything to add?"

"Not much. The clothes we found on the body were the ones Lopez was wearing the day he disappeared. We can therefore assume that he was killed very early."

Castello nodded his head several times.

"The main conclusion I want to draw from these first elements is reassuring," he said. "Lopez has been dead for a long time and his body was already buried at Força Real when the macabre treasure hunt began. The kidnapper wanted to make us think he was punishing us for not having brought the ransom he demanded, but that was only a maneuver. Everything was planned. To what end? Apart from driving us up the wall, I don't quite see . . . "

Sebag liked the idea put forth by the superintendent. The day before, Castello had already said something that had made him think along a certain line. Speaking of the sports bag, he'd said something like: "We have to play the game."

"The second conclusion," Castello went on, "concerns Lopez's status. If we can assume that he took part in Ingrid Raven's kidnapping in the role of an accomplice, he is now clearly a victim of the kidnapper. You'll note that I said 'kidnapper,' not 'kidnappers,' because I think we can also now say that the perpetrator was acting alone. That's my third conclusion. What else is there, in your opinion?"

The superintendent had just opened the traditional brainstorming session. The inspectors understood. They knew that when their boss appealed to their imaginations in that way, they mustn't hesitate to speak their minds. The craziest ideas were never mocked. Only silence was not acceptable.

"José Lopez knew his murderer," Llach began. "Well enough to feel like drinking the beer he gave him."

"The killer must have a van or large station wagon," Molina went on. "Lopez's frozen body wouldn't have fit in the trunk of an ordinary car."

The coroner began to give a sign expressing disagreement, but Ménard spoke first.

"Not necessarily. Dr. Roger told us that the folded-up body had probably been put in a freezer about five feet long. So it should have been possible to put it in the trunk of a sedan, shouldn't it, Doctor?"

"Yes, you're right," the coroner said. "The trunk of a large car would have been big enough."

"All the same," Molina persisted, "it's easier to get a frozen body out of a station wagon than out of the trunk of a sedan. You don't need to lift it."

"Especially if the murderer acted alone," Moreno said in a hardly audible voice.

It was Castello's turn to take notes. He wrote down all the ideas put forth, reserving the right to eliminate the less pertinent ones later on, and to take up again the discussion of the others.

Lefèvre, who had been absent up to that point, entered the room, a happy smile on his lips and a fax in his right hand. He was wearing navy blue slacks and a yellow polo shirt adorned with the famous green crocodile. Sebag said to himself that he must have brought not a suitcase but an actual trunk that would allow him to dress like a fashion model every day. No, Claire was ultimately wrong: never, even at the beginning of his career, had Sebag resembled in any way this . . . Kevin Costner.

Lambert continued:

"He's a man who's, uh, pretty strong, maybe. He must have carried Lopez several times."

"He must live on a large property," Raynaud said. "Big enough to have a pond, and isolated enough to be able to drown someone without running the risk of being seen."

"His house must have a cellar," Moreno added. "That's the most practical kind of space for holding a prisoner."

"He may have two freezers," Molina remarked.

His cynical comment momentarily extinguished the fire fed by the suggestions, and despite the heat a shiver ran through the inspectors. Lopez's frozen face still haunted their minds, with the ice crystals crushing his eyes and the stalactites sticking out of his nostrils. They'd all dreamed about it the night before, and some of them would dream about it for a long time.

After a silence, Ménard asked for the floor again.

"By the way . . . One question has been bothering me since last night and I suppose I'm not the only one: why did he choose to freeze the body?"

"Because he's a sicko," Llach replied, peremptorily. "I don't see any other explanation."

"Maybe he wanted to eat him later on."

Molina's joke was no more successful than his last one.

Nobody smiled, but neither did anyone take umbrage at his lack of taste: everyone had his own way of managing his fears.

"In general, you freeze something in order to preserve it," Moreno noted.

"But why would he want to preserve the body?" Ménard asked.

This time it was Sebag who answered the question.

"In order to be able to give it back to us at the moment he'd chosen. That was the only way to transport it in a suitable condition two weeks after the murder."

Molina was nervously drumming on the table with the pen he was holding like a cigarette. Sebag put his hand on his teammate's to make him stop drumming.

"In the superintendent's quick presentation, I noticed two things that seemed to me particularly interesting."

He glanced at his notes.

"First, you said—I'm quoting you verbatim, Superintendent—that 'everything was planned.' That's also my impression: the kidnapper is following a plan known to him alone. Then you wondered whether the main goal of the maneuver wasn't to drive us up the wall, and I think that just might be the key to understanding this whole thing."

"You have a theory," Castello smiled.

Sebag had mulled the question over and over in his head the night before. He'd ended up finding what seemed to him the right angle from which to see the case. Everything was beginning to fit together. He was fairly happy with himself, but his idea still had to pass the test of broad daylight and then the test of criticism. He knew that theoretical constructions could seem marvelous in the echo chamber of the mind and then collapse like a house of cards at the first critical comment.

"In my opinion, if this case is particularly complicated, that is no accident."

He took a few seconds to reflect on how to formulate his thought as clearly as possible.

"Fantastic claims made in the name of foreign terrorist organizations and an exorbitant sum demanded in small bills, then a kind of treasure hunt from Perpignan to Força Real by way of Argelès to finally lead us to the place to which he'd decided from the outset he'd make us go: the kidnapper is playing with us. In fact, he's putting up smokescreens with the sole objective of confusing us. I think he's having a lot of fun."

The honk of a car horn interrupted Sebag's comments. The air conditioner was on the blink *again*, and the sounds of the city were coming into the room through the half-open window.

"If the kidnapper really wanted to be paid a ransom," Sebag went on, "first, he would have asked for a reasonable sum, and second, he would have addressed the demand to Ingrid's parents, not the French police."

"You think we're playing a kind of chess game, is that it?" Lefèvre asked.

"Call it what you want. I'm just suggesting a working hypothesis."

"And so the kidnapper chose you as his adversary?"

Lefèvre's tone had become mocking. The young superintendent held his fax rolled up like a parchment and waved it at Sebag, who chose not to answer the question directly.

"Yesterday, he gave us Lopez's corpse as a 'gift.' That's one stage. He's still got the young woman, so the game can go on. Once again, this is only a hypothesis."

"And the next time it'll be Ingrid's body that we'll find?" Molina asked.

"Not necessarily. To make the game interesting, he has to give us a chance of winning."

"He's really a sicko, this guy!" Llach said again.

Lefèvre tapped the table with his fax, which was still rolled up. He seemed to be hesitating. Then he smiled broadly.

"Over the past few days, if I recall correctly, you said that the murder in Argelès and the attack in Perpignan had nothing to do with Ingrid's kidnapping. What happened yesterday proved you wrong, and yet today, despite everything, you're proposing a new theory."

Everyone turned to look at Sebag. His colleagues awaited with interest his explanations; the hunt the kidnapper had forced them to make the day before had finally convinced them that they were in fact dealing with a serial attacker.

"I don't think that what happened yesterday proved me wrong."

He had also reflected on this question at length, and he had come to conclusions he found satisfactory. But he would have preferred to keep them to himself for the time being. Lefèvre's sardonic smile made him act imprudently.

"In fact, I think the opposite."

The young cop put on an astonished look.

"You're a bold, not to say presumptuous, kind of guy. I hope you'll deign to enlighten us."

"What happened yesterday strengthened me in my convictions. I believe that if the kidnapper led us yesterday to the sites of the two other cases, it was precisely in order to make us think that everything is connected. In order to confuse us completely. He's playing with us."

"So we would be the victims of more smokescreens?"

"That's what I think."

"And how did he know about Avenue Poincaré and the Oleanders campground?"

"It was all in the newspaper," Sebag said, thinking he'd won the point. "He had only to follow the reporter's wild imaginings. The serial attacks on Dutch women must have amused him no end."

"You're very sure of yourself . . . "

Lefèvre's smile became sly.

"No. I'm not sure of myself," Sebag replied. "I have a hypothesis and I'm developing it. I'm trying to see if all the elements can be connected in the framework of this hypothesis."

"And does it work?"

"It seems to."

Sebag suddenly felt that a trap had just closed on him. He, Gilles Sebag, who was usually so circumspect, had let himself be led onto terrain where he was open to attack.

"It seems to!" Lefèvre repeated scornfully.

Sebag held his breath while Lefèvre slowly unfolded his parchment. The young Parisian cop put the fax on the table and ran his hand over it several times to smooth it out. Up to that point, he'd avoided looking at Sebag. Now he turned toward the inspector and looked him straight in the eye.

"This morning I took the liberty of calling Anneke Verbrucke and asking her what her blood type was. We'd stupidly forgotten to ask about that. Well, guess what: her blood type is B positive, like the blood found on the second message the kidnapper sent us. Does that still fit with your . . . theory?"

Sebag abstained from replying. He had not seen the blow coming, but he sensed that a second one would follow. The fax that Lefèvre was still trying to smooth out was not a blood analysis but a telephone record.

Molina reacted in Sebag's stead.

"I doubt that Anneke Verbrucke is the only person who is B positive."

"Only 8 percent of the population belongs to that group," Lefèvre said without taking his eyes off Sebag.

"That's enough so that it could be a coincidence," Molina insisted.

"Yes, that's true," Lefèvre conceded slyly. "There is one chance in ten that it's a coincidence."

"That's not negligible," Molina noted, even though his colleague's sudden silence made him uneasy.

"No, you're right, it's not negligible."

The young cop ran his hand over the wrinkled paper again.

"I have something else to tell you. Another coincidence, perhaps, but I'll let you decide how probable it is. I asked the telephone company to give me a list of the calls made on the night of July 4 from the bar where Anneke had a drink with her friends."

"I wasn't informed about that request," Castello protested.

"I hope you'll excuse me, Superintendent," Lefèvre replied with obvious hypocrisy. "The desire to be efficient sometimes forces one to take shortcuts."

"To break the rules, you mean."

"It's better to break the rules than to make serious mistakes. Because I found something very interesting: a call to police headquarters at the very time that Officer Ripoll received the anonymous call."

Sebag felt a powerful wave of heat pass over him. A trickle of sweat ran down his back. He understood what mistake Lefèvre was talking about. And he knew who had made it. He had nonetheless written in his notebook that he would need to check the timetables for that night.

"Make yourself clearer," Castello said, furiously rubbing the end of his nose. "What made you suspect that the kidnapper had telephoned from that bar?"

"Since our obsolete telephone switchboard had prevented us from determining where the kidnapper's call came from, I tried to approach the problem the other way around. The place where the call came in not giving us any information, I looked for places from which it might have proceeded. I went through all the reports and I came across Inspector Sebag's interview with Anneke Verbrucke. In it, she says that she found suspicious the behavior of a customer in the bar. On that basis, I also formed a hypothesis: I thought that if this client was the attacker and if the attacker was also the kidnapper, he had to have called from either a cell phone or the phone in the bar, for lack of time. You understand the rest . . . "

Lefèvre brandished the telephone record in front of him. All eyes moved from the fax and converged on Sebag, who sought in vain a mouse hole in which to take refuge. He was able to regain his composure only when he met the merciless eyes of Lefèvre.

"The conclusion seems to me obvious," the young superintendent went on. "The kidnapping, the attack, and the murder are all connected. Period."

Sebag understood how a groggy boxer might feel when he saw his adversary lift his gloves high and the referee announce the end of the bout. He looked at his audience and realized that his supporters had also thrown in the towel. Never had he gone so wrong in an investigation.

The sounds from the street could no longer pierce the deep silence that reigned in the room. The moment seemed to go on for an eternity. Sebag wiped his damp hands on his pants. Then Castello came to his aid by trying to obtain a certain sharing of the points.

"Efficiency is one thing, Cyril, but I would ask you not to do that again. For me, it's not a question of procedure but of teamwork. We don't fiddle around on our own."

He paused and glanced furtively at Gilles:

"And I'd like you to avoid all personal quarrels. There's too much tension for my taste. Let's be adults, please. The life of a young woman is at stake."

"We're all aware of that," Lefèvre declared in a honeyed voice.

"I hope so."

Castello dismissed his inspectors and remained alone with Lefèvre to discuss the further pursuit of the investigation. Sebag suspected that the following days were going to be among the most painful of his career.

The palm tree's fronds cut the sky into slender blue strips that the wind was shuffling. A robin warbled next to the trunk, protected by a cluster of spines sharper than daggers.

In the shade of the tree, Gilles was finishing a siesta on the chaise longue.

In the late morning, a call from Séverine had salved his heart a little. Her vacation was going well. Her friend Manon's parents were nice and gave them lots of freedom. They were making use of it, but without ever abusing it, she assured her father. They planned to go spend a few days at PortAventura, a large amusement park near Tarragona.

The neighbor's whistling drowned out the birdsong. For the past two or three days, she had often been looking for her cat. In vain, most of the time. Because the tomcat, attracted by the new calm that reigned in the yard, had taken up summer quarters in Sebag's yard. Of course, the saucer of milk that Gilles furtively set under the palm tree in the morning had something to do with this. For once, the neighbor's breathless whistling was music to his ears.

He decided to get up. His head hurt.

Before finally dozing off, he'd gone over the whole case in his mind. He still didn't understand. And in one corner of his brain there was a little, insistent voice that told him he hadn't gone off track. Not completely.

He'd put his cup down next to the chaise longue. There was still a little cold coffee in the bottom. He swallowed it.

Claire had left thirty-six hours earlier. He didn't expect to hear for her any time soon. Phone calls from the boat were very expensive, and she had decided not to take her cell phone. A trip is a chance to get away from it all, she said, and these days the first thing one has to do is break the telephone link that constantly binds us to our familiar world.

So be it.

He was still hoping to receive an e-mail from her. Today or

tomorrow. He missed Claire, but at the same time he was glad that she was far away. She would have tried to reassure him, telling him that he was the best, that if anyone could solve this case, it would be he. There are times when the confidence of your friends and family supports you, and others when it depresses you even more.

He took his cup back to the kitchen.

He had the whole afternoon before him, but he didn't know what to do with it. It was too hot to run. Take a swim and lie around in the sun? That was probably best.

Instead, he decided to go to the study. He turned on the computer and opened *Age of Kings*, Léo's favorite video game. He'd received it for his tenth birthday. Sebag had learned the rules by watching his son, and he'd begun to share Léo's passion. At one time, they'd thought about buying a second computer so they could play in a network. And then Léo had found better partners on the Net.

Gilles played until 5:00 P.M. He hadn't eaten anything at noon, and now felt a little hungry. He ate a few fresh tomatoes and opened a bottle of rosé.

After this improvised meal, he put on a swimsuit and lay down beside the pool, a glass of wine nearby. His body and his mind became coated with a sticky languor. He didn't want anything. He felt tired.

Tired of everything and everybody.

He must be coming down with something.

A cold, the stomach flu, or the beginning of a fit of depression.

After the morning meeting, Castello had called him to his office. He'd told him to go home for the rest of the day.

"You look tired to me," he'd said. "So take a break and come back tomorrow in top form."

Castello's tone was friendly, but for Sebag this was neither more nor less than a fall into disgrace. The image of Cyril

Lefèvre forced itself on him. Their relations had been electric ever since the first day. Why? It wasn't the first time he'd see this kind of Parisian cop show up. Lefèvre was no worse than others. He even seemed cleverer and less pretentious than the average one. So what was it?

He thought again about what Claire had suggested the other night in the restaurant. Yes, he'd been like Lefèvre at the beginning of his career but time had changed him. The job, too . . . The sad reality of the everyday job of the cop was the tedious, repetitive, and sometimes futile character of investigations in the field, the violence, the misery, the scorn . . . And then Léo was born and Gilles thought he'd understood that life was to be found elsewhere. He'd stopped doing too much and contented himself with doing as good a job as he could.

In his mind's eye, he saw again Lefèvre's mocking and then derisive smile. The young cop hadn't failed; Sebag had let himself be caught out like a neophyte. He couldn't understand how he'd been so mistaken.

What could have gone wrong in his reasoning?

The murder in Argelès was not a premeditated crime but an act of anger, or even a fit of madness. It had nothing in common with the resolute calm that Ingrid's kidnapper had shown. He might be prepared to recognize in Anneke's attacker the same cold-blooded qualities. But whereas the former had demonstrated his efficiency, the latter had demonstrated above all his amateurism.

Good Lord! He was doing it again. It was proven now, and in an irrefutable manner: the kidnapper and the attacker were one and the same person. That was the basis on which he had to rethink his whole argument.

Gilles got up to make a cup of coffee. He opted for a Sumatran Mocha. A coffee with a woody savor and an intense body. He stayed next to the machine. Once his cup was full, he went outside again and sat on the edge of the pool, his feet in the water.

Let's set aside for a moment the investigation into the murder in Argelès, he said to himself. Let's just look at the other two cases. They were committed by the same individual, then. In masterly fashion the first time and awkwardly the second time. Why? Had he been forced to improvise? Possibly. But for what reasons? The kidnapping of an adult cannot be improvised. So he'd never intended to commit a second kidnapping.

Sebag sensed that this was a new angle to be studied.

He felt that someone was observing him. He looked up and saw two green, almond-shaped eyes staring at him. The eyes slowly closed as a sign of confidence. Then opened again. Gilles made a long, loud kissing noise.

"Here, kitty, here, kitty."

The cat closed its eyes again but didn't move. He remained sitting on his haunches on the other side of the pool, trying to tame this strange man who, after weeks of ignoring him, had finally started giving him milk.

"Come here, kitty, come on."

Gilles suspected that the cat wouldn't budge. Not right away. The voice had to be the first contact. The first connection. He'd already had that thought recently. When? Oh, yes . . . it was the other morning near the cigarette traffickers' warehouse. When he'd succeeded in winning the boy's confidence. In getting him to put down his gun. In avoiding a tragedy. The memory did him good. He was a good cop! Maybe in the end he was also a good father. And a good husband. He had no reason to be depressed.

So where did his malaise come from?

He put down his empty cup and let himself slip slowly into the cool water. When he got out, the cat was no longer there.

Drops of water slid off his body. He lay down. A little cottony cloud was floating in the sky, lost in the immensity of the blue. Gilles wound a towel around his waist and returned to the study.

Shortly before seven o'clock, the phone rang. It was Jacques. He was on his way back from Argelès. With Anneke's description of the customer in the bar. He'd returned to the campground to question the owners and a few regulars who'd been there since June. A hard day. A useless day. The call for witnesses put out by the gendarmes had yielded nothing. The investigation into the Argelès case still seemed to have hit a dead end.

"I didn't completely waste my time, though," he said, trying to be positive. "I took my swimsuit . . . What about you, how did you spend your afternoon?"

"I also went swimming, but in the pool, and I spent some time on the computer. I kept busy."

"Yeah. In other words, you were bored stiff."

"A little, yes."

They laughed.

"Did you think about work the whole time?"

"No. Not all the time."

"How do you see things now?"

"I don't know. I don't know anymore. I have to admit that I'm floundering a little. And you?"

"To tell the truth, I'm not sure, either. You'd ended up convincing me."

"And now you're convinced by Lefèvre?"

"He struck hard, but he didn't explain everything. He's going a little too fast when he says that it's Anneke's blood on the envelope that had the ransom demand in it."

"It's disturbing, though."

"Maybe. But 8 percent of the population who belong to the B-positive group is still quite a few people."

"Not everything is just a matter of statistics."

"What do you mean by that?"

"That drop of blood didn't end up on the corner of the

envelope by accident. The kidnapper put it there on purpose to send us a message. He wanted to make us guess that he was in fact the man who attacked Anneke. I don't see any other possible explanation."

There was a silence on the other end of the line.

"The worst thing," Sebag went on, "is that I can't help wondering whether it wasn't the pleasure of contradicting . . . Kevin Costner that caused me to go off track."

"Oh, no, I'm sure it wasn't that."

Jacques's categorical tone surprised him.

"Why do you say that?"

"Listen. Since we've been working together, I've begun to know you, and if there is one thing that I've always admired in you, it's precisely your ability to set aside all personal considerations. In the South, we tend to act on the basis of our feelings. We have very pronounced likes and dislikes and we're fond of declaring them. We're too subjective, you might say. You, on the contrary, always manage to set all those parameters aside. That's impressive."

Sebag knew that Molina liked his way of working, but he'd never given him such compliments.

"Thanks."

He felt embarrassed. Molina said no more. He was probably already regretting having let that paean escape him.

"See you tomorrow?" Gilles asked.

"Of course."

"Well, until tomorrow then. Have a good evening."

After he hung up, Gilles walked around the yard, wondering how he could spend the evening. He'd had enough of the computer. A movie? Why not? But he didn't know anything about current films. It was Claire, usually, who chose for them. And then the idea of going to freeze his butt off in an overly air-conditioned theater didn't appeal to him.

He went into the garage. The back tire of his bike was flat.

He pumped it up a bit before getting on it. He rode to the video store in the center of Saint-Estève, rented an American comedy from the 1970s and a more recent porno film and slipped them into his backpack.

That evening, he was going to have some fun.

CHAPTER 25

He had to go back. One day or another. Might as well drink the bitter cup dry right away.

Sebag had the impression that everyone was looking at him strangely. With compassion. Like a person who is ill or convalescent. He was probably imagining things. Not everyone at police headquarters had heard about what happened. He'd worked up theories and had found himself suddenly contradicted by the facts. Okay. Nothing to get all upset about. This sort of thing happened every day. Only the person mainly concerned accorded that so much importance. His colleagues had probably already forgotten the incident.

He went directly to his office without passing by way of the *service de quart* or the cafeteria. He met Llach on the stairway.

"How are you?" Llach asked.

There was no more neutral question than that one. But Sebag nonetheless saw an allusion in it. He replied brusquely. Without unclenching his teeth.

"Fine. Why wouldn't I be fine?"

"I don't know. I was just saying hello."

Sebag took refuge in his office. He turned on his computer to look at his work e-mail A message from Castello gave him his assignment for the day. Meet with Brian Wayne. He was a retired English surgeon. One of the last B.W.'s who had not yet been questioned. The lead of Lopez's mysterious customer was thus still being pursued. Sebag was supposed to work on it with Lambert.

Molina came into the office. He seemed surprised to see Sebag.

"Well! How are you?" he asked.

Sebag tried to reply as decently as he could. But he felt a wave of ill humor rising up in him.

"What about you? What are you doing today?"

"After my swim at Argelès yesterday, I'm going to work on my tan at Força Real. I'm supposed to spend the day up there trying to meet people who are there often—hikers, joggers, people who go there to screw—anyone who might have noticed a suspicious individual. The kidnapper has gone to the hermitage at least twice since the beginning of the case."

"Do you think there will be many people at Força Real who go up there often? It's a little far from everything, isn't it?"

"You never know. It's a pain in the ass but it's worth a try."

Molina sat down at his desk and turned on his computer. Earlier, they'd had to share a machine, but for the past year they'd each had their own. Computers had long since become part of their daily routine. For better and for worse.

"Do you know who I got stuck working with today?" Sebag complained.

"No."

"Lambert."

"Oh, shit."

He pointed to the floor over his head.

"Looks like you're out of favor up there."

Sebag seized the opportunity.

"By the way, was there a lot of talk around headquarters yesterday?"

"Talk about what?"

"I don't know . . . About the new direction taken by the investigation, for instance."

"Ah. Not, not much. We were all surprised by the turn-about. A little annoyed, too, to have been made fools of by a young cop from Paris. But what the hell! We might have a chance to take our revenge."

Sebag nodded: he appreciated the first person plural.

Brian Wayne lived in Les Aspres, a little village in the foothills of Le Canigou. An English surgeon from Birmingham, he'd chosen to retire in the South of France. As soon as Sebag saw him, he understood that they were going to waste their time. Wayne was a quiet little old man. He was five foot two at most, with frail shoulders and a kind of doughnut around his waist.

Nonetheless, the inspectors accepted Wayne's invitation to drink an orangeade in the library, the coolest room in the large house. Sebag let Lambert run the interview. The young cop carried out his task with gravity and application.

They learned that Brian Wayne had been living in Boule d'Amont for about ten years. That he was sixty-nine years old. That he was a widower. That he had a daughter who was still living in England. Wayne had just come back from Great Britain, where he'd gone to see his second grandson, who had been born in early June. Wayne had thus "been absent at the time of the events," to use the traditional formula. The interview was quickly concluded.

However, Sebag did not come back completely empty-handed. When they explained to the old surgeon why they had come to visit him, he asked them if they were very sure that the initials BW corresponded to a true identity.

"What do you mean by that?" Sebag asked.

"They could be the letters of a nickname, couldn't they?"

Sebag was annoyed at himself for not having thought of that earlier. Had he really wanted to hide the identity of his mysterious customer, Lopez would in fact have a reason for using a double camouflage. The idea was interesting. The problem was that it led to a dead end.

How could they hope to find the nickname Lopez had

given to an unknown person? Still more difficult: how could they find that person on the basis of the nickname?

The inspectors said good-bye to their host. As they left his property, Lambert suddenly tugged Sebag's sleeve.

"Did you see that down there?"

Lambert, all excited, was pointing to a dark place at the back of the yard.

"Gilles, it's a pond."

"So?"

"Well, Lopez was drowned in a pond, right?"

Sebag told Lambert to get into the car. Then he sat down behind the wheel and started the engine. The young inspector started sulking.

"Thierry, for shit's sake!" Sebag said. "Don't you see that we've bothered Wayne for nothing? He has nothing to do with all this."

"I'm not so sure of that. He has the right initials, he's got a pond . . . You don't think we should take a sample of the water?"

"If you want to . . . but you're wasting your time! Can you imagine old man Wayne dragging Lopez's body across his yard? He wouldn't even be able to pull him out of the water."

"I've learned not to trust appearances . . . "

"You haven't learned anything at all," Sebag interrupted him. "Where have you ever seen a nice little grandpa who is transformed into a bloodthirsty beast at nightfall? At the movies?"

"I expected you to be more prudent. After what happened the other day . . . "

Sebag slammed on the brakes. The car skidded to a halt in the middle of a curve.

"What was that you just said? Can you repeat it?"

"Don't get angry, Gilles," Lambert stammered, surprised by the violence of Sebag's tone. I wasn't trying to be disagreeable. I apologize."

Sebag put the car in first gear and got back on the road.

"I apologize, too."

"It's okay, but all the same . . . Maybe you should listen to your colleagues more."

Sebag was breathing hard. He must have fallen very low for an idiot like Lambert to think he could tell him what he should do.

They drove on in silence as far as Ille-sur-Têt. After crossing the commune, Lambert asked if they could stop for five minutes. He needed to pee because of the orangeade. Sebag took advantage of the pause to send Léo a text message.

Good weather here. I'm working and thinking about my son. Lots of love. Have a good vacation.

He pushed the "Send" button and imagined the message crossing the sky to land in the left pocket of his son's jacket. There were good things about modern technology. How could he have survived far from his children without this permanent umbilical cord constituted by the cell phone?

He watched Lambert through the closed window. His right elbow moved, then his left. He was done taking a leak. But before he got back in the car, the young inspector engaged in other oscillations that Sebag couldn't immediately identify. It was only after his colleague got back in the car that he understood: Lambert had taken advantage of the stop to spray some more of his bad cologne under his arms.

Sebag held his breath for the first few kilometers and then decided to drive with the window rolled down, despite the fact that the air conditioning was on. He was ready to endure anything, but some things were beyond his strength.

"Inspector, please!"

Sebag whirled around. A motley crowd was invading the lobby at police headquarters: mugged old men, women who'd been beaten and perhaps raped, youths whose scooters had been stolen, foreigners waiting for papers they were unlikely to get, French nationals who were angry or simply annoyed. Plus a few depressed lonely people looking for a little human compassion.

Sebag hadn't been able to identify the low voice that had addressed him.

"Hello, Inspector."

A tall, slender man came up to him and held out his hand. Sebag shook his hand hesitantly. He studied the knife-edge face that was smiling at him in a friendly way. No click. He didn't know the guy.

"Would you have a few minutes for me, please? My car has been stolen."

Sebag glanced at the intern who was behind the reception desk. Even though she had her hands full with the noisy crowd, Martine had followed their conversation. She gave him a sign suggesting that she couldn't help him, and she wrapped it in a nice smile. Sebag turned back to his interlocutor.

"Sorry, but I don't deal with car thefts."

He was about to turn on his heel and leave when the man spoke to him again.

"That's too bad! Someone told me that you could help me."

"Someone? I don't know any 'someone.'"

Sebag was starting to get annoyed. He'd been given enough minor tasks lately, and he wasn't about to start investigating car thefts

"Gérard Barrère told me about you. He thought you could help me. He said you were very competent."

Sebag frowned. He was becoming distrustful and wondered if this guy wasn't making fun of him.

"It doesn't take any special competence to deal with stolen vehicles. If your car is a luxury model, it's already on the other side of the Pyrénées. Otherwise we'll find it here in a few days, all banged up at the bottom of a ravine or burned to cinders on the parking lot in a low-cost housing development. I hope you've got good insurance."

The man gave him a broad smile. His crew-cut hair made his face look even longer. A hand was suddenly put on Sebag's shoulder.

"Are you okay?"

Molina. All smiles. Relaxed. Working alone seemed to suit him.

"Yeah."

"I'll buy you a cup. I'm going to the cafeteria."

Then, addressing the owner of the car, he added:

"Excuse me, I think I interrupted you."

"We're done here," Sebag hastened to say. "This gentleman has lost his car and he's looking for a top-flight cop to conduct the investigation."

"A top-flight cop?" Molina joked. "You won't find one of those around here."

"I think I've taken enough of your time," the man replied, without ceasing to smile.

A strange glow burned in his eyes. His voice had gone down yet another note. Its timbre was enough to make the windows rattle.

"Give Mr. Barrère our greetings," Gilles said.

"I will, Inspector."

"And I hope all the same that you'll get your car back."

Gilles was beginning to regret the harshness of his reaction.

"It's an old car," the man concluded, quietly getting back in the line of people waiting to be served. "And then, I do have good insurance. I'll see you soon, I hope."

"See you soon, yes," Gilles replied mechanically.

"With or without sugar?"

"Without. That way it's less like coffee."

Molina handed him his cup without trying to understand.

"Has Barry White been annoying you for a long time?"

"Barry White? The crooner?"

It was Sebag's turn not to understand his associate. Molina tried to adopt a serious voice, which wasn't easy for him.

"I need a top-flight cop to find my old junker. I . . . "

A coughing fit prevented him from finishing his sentence. Sebag exploded in laughter.

"Did you know that I've got something new in our case?" Molina asked when he was able to speak again.

"Really?"

"I told you I was supposed to spend the day at the hermitage?"

Sebag glanced at his watch.

"You're already back? It's only three P.M."

"I'd had enough. Not much happens up there. I saw twenty-five people in all. And even then! There were eight in a single minibus. But I found a witness."

Molina put two coins in the machine and pushed the top key. Short espresso with sugar. The machine shook and noisily spit out its black juice. Jacques waited until he had his coffee in his hand before he went on with what he was saying.

"Up there I found a young kid who was bird-watching. He's writing a study on a sparrow whose name I've forgotten. He goes up to Força Real every day, occasionally even several times a day. Moreover, he noticed Lopez's abandoned taxi and was getting ready to report it to us when the gendarmes found it."

He stirred his coffee for a long time before taking an initial swallow of it. Sebag was getting impatient and didn't try to hide it. He knew that was what his colleague was waiting for.

"So?"

"So what?"

"Your witness?"

Sebag decided to speed things up.

"Your bird-watcher saw a car and the guy who went with it, is that it? And he gave you an exact description?"

"You're such a pain in the ass!"

"That makes two of us!"

Molina took another swallow of his coffee.

"You have to admit that it wasn't too hard to guess."

"No, that's true," Sebag conceded. "So what is the guy like?"

"Slim and fairly tall. Blond hair. Light complexion. Wearing a very formal outfit despite the season. That was all he could say."

"And the car?"

"A big station wagon. A Peugeot or a Volvo. He apparently doesn't know anything about cars. In any case, it was red."

"That's great! Did you find the car and arrest the suspect?"

"Uh, no, the description is still a little vague."

"That's what I was thinking, too . . . "

"In any event, it corresponds in general to the description Anneke gave of the man who attacked her."

"Go ahead, turn the knife in the wound."

"Ah . . . Excuse me, I didn't mean to make you mad."

"Too bad, it's done."

Sebag crumpled his cup. It still contained a few drops of coffee that squirted onto his pants.

The investigation was stalled, even if Castello and Lefèvre refused to admit it. The inspectors had been assigned to question the main witnesses again and to show them the improved portrait—though it was still too vague, in Sebag's view—of the suspect. He and Jacques were supposed to talk with Sylvie Lopez again. The burial of her husband was to take place the next day.

The young woman invited them into the apartment. She led them to the living room, which was very dimly lit.

"Would you like something to drink? Coffee?"

The two men accepted her offer. Jacques because he hadn't taken time to drink a cup of coffee at the Carlit, and Gilles because he was always ready to try something new. While Sylvie Lopez was busy in the kitchen, Sebag examined the changes that had taken place in the living room since their last visit. Photos had grown like mushrooms on the tables. José and Sylvie leaving the church on their wedding day; José alone in his military uniform, José sitting on a hospital bed with baby Jennifer in his arms; the same a few months later on a beach. And then, in a prominent position atop the television set, a large format photo of José sitting very proudly behind the wheel of his taxi. The corners of the frame were bordered in black cloth. Next to the TV was a long, extinguished candle. The young widow probably lit it in the evening to relieve her loneliness and pain. She was in the process of making her swine of a husband into a saint. Her marriage had failed and now she was trying to make a success of being a widow.

Sylvie returned from the kitchen carrying a tray loaded with cups. Wrapped in her dark mourning clothes, she seemed more frail and fragile than ever. She made you want to take her in your arms to console her. Sebag said to himself that if he hadn't been there, Jacques wouldn't have repressed that desire.

The coffee was without personality—a product from the lower shelves of a supermarket—but it was very strong. Drinkable. Jacques began the conversation without waiting any longer. He handed her the rough portrait of the suspect. It meant nothing to her. Gilles suggested looking at the family photo albums. He didn't have high hopes.

He found nothing remarkable. No suspicious figure, no known face. Moments of happiness like those found in all families throughout the world. Those of Sebag's family were no different. Less artificial, he hoped.

Gilles saw no reason to stay any longer. The contemplation of family photos always plunged him into a strange state.

Almost nauseous. A feeling of dizziness like the one he had when he let Claire and the kids make him get on those infernal merry-go-rounds at fairs. Jolts and speed. Life bouncing you around and slipping through your fingers. Time going too fast. Every page turned represents months, even years, of life. Buried. Fled. Forever and ever.

He suddenly stood up. Jacques seemed surprised, Sylvie Lopez frightened. She offered them another cup of coffee, a glass of fruit juice, a piece of cake . . . She was ready to do anything to keep them there a little longer. Sebag said he had an urgent call to make and took leave of his colleague.

"I'll see you back at headquarters in a little while. I need to walk a bit to think."

On his way back, Sebag took the Avenue Poincaré. That was where Anneke Verbrucke had been attacked. Marc Savoy's sport coupe was parked across from the service station. The sales rep apparently came home early on Fridays.

Unconsciously, Sebag had hoped to have an insight, or at least a new idea. He stopped for a moment, lit a cigarette. But nothing came to him. Nothing at all.

While he was saying hello to Martine at the reception desk, his cell phone rang.

"Hello, this is Gilles Sebag."

"It's me, am I disturbing you?"

"Where are you calling from?"

"A phone booth. I'm in Naples; the connection is good."

"Do you have five minutes? Give me the number. I'll go up to my office and call you back."

"Okay. Talk to you in a minute."

He hung up and climbed the stairs two at a time. When he got to his office he connected his computer and then grabbed the receiver. Claire answered immediately.

"I hope your work's not too hard?"

"So-so. And you, you aren't suffering too much?"

"Oh, yes I am! It's pretty unbearable. Swimming pool, chaise longue, reading. Magnificent cities. Bonifacio on Thursday, Naples today; this evening we're leaving for Palermo . . . "

"You're not staying very long in each city. Isn't that a little frustrating?"

"Yes, it is. But I tell myself I'm scouting out the terrain and that I'll come back with you to the places that please me most.

There was a short silence.

"What about you, you aren't feeling too lonely there in Perpignan?"

"With my job, I don't have time to get bored," he lied. "We're making progress slowly, but we're making progress."

Another silence. A little longer. It wasn't easy to find the right words. Usually they telephoned each other only when they had something precise to say. It was in the evening, as they were eating dinner, that they talked.

"Is the weather good there?" Claire asked.

"Very good. But there's a little wind, and that's nice. And you—are you having good weather?"

"Yes, more or less the same."

"Then it wasn't worth the trouble to travel so far away."

He hadn't intended to be disagreeable. It was just a harmless remark. He had to apologize. Or just go on.

"I heard from Séverine the other day. She seemed happy."

"I also had an e-mail message. One from Léo, too. He's having a great time, I think."

"That's also my impression."

They exchanged a few more banalities and then slipped in two or three tender words. It was time to finish up; Molina had just come into the office.

"I'm going to let you go, I've got to work. Thanks for calling."

"My pleasure. I don't know when I'll be able to call again. Maybe from Palermo or Tunis."

"I hope so. Talk to you soon."

"Talk to you soon. I love you."

"Me too."

He had to hang up.

"Is she okay?"

"Excuse me?"

"Is Claire okay?" Molina repeated.

"Fine."

"Are there any handsome guys on her old tub?"

"Probably."

He hastened to mount a counter-attack.

"And Mrs. Lopez—did you succeed in comforting her?"

Molina pretended he hadn't heard. He turned on his computer.

"Do our colleagues have anything new?"

"I haven't had time to look."

They glanced through their e-mails. The analysis of the blood had issued its verdict: the blood on the envelope was indeed that of Anneke Verbrucke.

"Is the last meeting this evening at six P.M.?" Molina asked.

"That's what I heard. But I don't think I'll go."

Molina looked up from his screen.

"Are you pouting?"

"A little, yeah" Sebag conceded.

"Castello isn't going to like you being absent."

"I don't give a damn!"

"That's not true."

Molina was right. Sebag wasn't fooled by his own anger.

"You know him," Jacques said. "He's waiting for you to react. You're a good cop but you've got to admit that you have to be pushed a bit sometimes."

"How about you, don't you have to be pushed, too?"

"Yes . . . But the difference is that I'll never give off sparks no matter how hard I'm pushed."

"Don't give me your modest act."

"I'm not modest, but at the age of forty-seven, I've learned to recognize my limits."

"I have, too, I know my limits."

"No, that's not true. Your problem is that you doubt yourself too much . . . "

"You sound like my wife."

"You see? If she says it too, that's because it's true."

Sebag considered the question for a few seconds.

"Are you expecting me to give off sparks?"

"Yeah."

"I wouldn't want to disappoint you, but I'm afraid I've lost my way in this investigation."

"Well, then, get back on track."

"How would I do that?"

"Start your reasoning from the beginning and think it all through again."

"But my reasoning is lousy! These cases are connected, that's been proven. And I can't start over again from that postulate."

"Stop sniveling and follow your instinct, as the boss would say. You must have had good reasons."

"We have to admit that we took a wrong turn. The blood on the letter, the telephone call from the bar . . . "

"Agreed. That proves that the guy who attacked Anneke is in fact the one who kidnapped Ingrid. But there's no connection with the murder."

"What about the treasure hunt? It wasn't chance that took us to the campground in Argelès; it was the kidnapper."

"Maybe to confuse us. As you suggested."

"I've already made myself ridiculous enough with that theory."

"It won't kill you. Just imagine Lefèvre's face if you prove that the crime in Argelès has nothing to do with the other two."

"And just how am I going to do that?"

"You find the murderer."

Sebag snapped his fingers.

"Good God, you're right, how did I manage not to think of that earlier? It's so simple: all we have to do is find the murderer! The gendarmes have been investigating for a month, you yourself have been working on the case and getting nowhere, but I, with a wave of my magic wand, will be able to find him."

"We might have missed something obvious that another more objective, sharper look would reveal."

"Thanks for your confidence, but it seems to me a little excessive."

"It doesn't cost anything to try."

"A few hours of unpaid overtime . . . "

"You'll be able to get them back some other time."

Sebag couldn't repress a smile.

"Castello will never allow me to keep pursuing that line of investigation."

Sebag's arguments were losing their pertinence, and Molina understood that he'd won.

"Why do you have to tell him what you're doing?"

"Do you expect me to work free-lance? The boss wouldn't like that."

"Lefèvre did and it worked pretty well for him."

"Lefèvre doesn't take his orders from Castello."

"I don't see what the problem is: either you don't find anything and nobody will know that you worked on your own, or you find something interesting and the boss will be forced to accept your methods. Results, comrade, results are all that matters. Besides, if you want my opinion, Castello would be very happy to see you get the better of that little cur from Paris."

"He's not like that."

"Everybody is like that."

"In short, you're suggesting that I play double or nothing?"

"So? Aren't you a gambler?"

Sebag didn't answer right away. It's difficult to say what really influences life decisions. Big ones or small ones. A smile, a look, or a phrase sometimes has more influence than fine ideas or the most conclusive arguments. Sebag often let himself be guided by the witticisms he came up with. And he'd just invented one that pleased him very much.

"You're right, pal, we have to strike Lefèvre while he's hot."

CHAPTER 26

He was almost smiling.

He couldn't remember having so much fun since he was a child. This game of hide-and-seek was turning out to be very amusing. Still, he wondered if he hadn't over-estimated his adversary. After all, he'd chosen him on an impulse. The policeman had seemed to him reliable and intel-ligent, but he'd noticed his fragility as well. Wasn't he too ten-der for the role? At police headquarters, he'd seemed nervous. His investigation must be marking time. And it wouldn't move forward much in the coming days if he insisted on ignoring the little hints he kept giving him.

Maybe he'd tried too hard to confuse things. The police were apparently getting lost in the false trails he'd put in their way.

Another concern worried him. He was obsessed with his prisoner's body. He didn't like that at all.

He hid in the large closet to watch her taking a shower. Using a knife, he enlarged a wormhole in the wood so he could see everything she did. He wasn't able to take his eyes off the washcloth that softly caressed her smooth skin. It slipped over her round shoulders, her lovely breasts, then her flat stomach. It disappeared furtively between her thighs before moving to the lower back to cover her well-rounded buttocks with white foam.

He would have so much liked to be a washcloth.

At night he dreamed of this body that was so beautiful. So accessible. He woke and got up to watch her sleep. He needed to make only one gesture: to lift the light sheet that hardly concealed her body and simply lie down on her. The young woman wouldn't have resisted. She would have limited herself to docilely spreading her thighs. She would probably even have made a few little moans to give him pleasure. And who knows, maybe also for her own pleasure.

He was the master; she was his slave.

He sensed the warmth of her body.

But he didn't want that.

His game was not a sexual game. He mustn't soil it. He didn't care if later on he was called sick or mad, but he didn't want to be called perverse. Ever. He was above all that.

So when his penis hurt too much, he took an icy shower. Once, he'd remained under the cold water for twenty minutes before he calmed down.

CHAPTER 27

The arched bridge spanned the Loire. Dominated by a kind of centaur that was half-chateau, half-church, Gien spread its façades along the river. The high, brown tile roofs bristled with large brick chimneys. A long row of sycamores lined the quays. The Loire was at its low-water mark. Only one of its branches still had enough water to allow three flat-bottomed barges with cabins to slumber there as they waited for autumn. In the distance, off to the west, a nuclear power plant was producing its daily batch of clouds.

Sebag turned left after crossing the bridge and parked his car in a lot in front of the city hall. He went into a bar, ordered coffee and a croissant, and sat down at the back. His appointment was for 10:30, so he still had about an hour to wait.

He'd spent the preceding evening going over the report on the murder committed in Argelès. Two things had troubled him. Rather late, he'd called Lieutenant Cornet of the gendarmerie's investigative team to ask him to confirm them. By midnight, he'd made his decision.

Anything was preferable to a weekend in an empty house.

He'd drunk a cup of coffee, thrown some clothes in a suitcase, and then locked up the house. Before getting on the superhighway he'd stopped at a shopping-center gas station to fill up. Then he set off for Gien. He allowed himself only one rest stop, at a service station on the Aubrac plateau. A chill wind had cooled down the inside of the car. He quickly fell asleep. He got back on the road around 3:00 A.M.

At eight o'clock, as he was getting off the superhighway at Bourges, he made a telephone call and arranged an appointment for mid-morning.

The croissant was still warm, the coffee not bad. He looked at his watch. Still a quarter of an hour. He waited. It was important not to get there early.

Bernard Palissy Street was next to the Gien earthenware factory, the owner of the bar explained. That was logical; he could have figured it out himself. He recalled learning at school the story of how Palissy, driven by his passion, burned all the furniture in his house to improve his firing techniques. He'd liked the story, and still remembered it thirty years later.

He walked to his appointment, making a detour along the banks of the Loire. He'd always like that river, which flows quietly and majestically between its dikes, concealing beneath its low and apparently peaceful waters lethal traps, whirlpools and quicksands. Every summer there were deaths. The scenario was played out over and over: a swimmer was carried away by the current, another jumped in to save him, and both disappeared in a few seconds. When he and his family were living in Chartres, they often went to spend their weekends along the river in the area around Tours or Blois.

Robert Vernier lived in a little row house. Behind a low, white wall topped with green wire fencing rose a gray stone façade decorated with brick friezes under the gutters and around the windows. A veranda extended the living space. Inside, an old rocking chair could be seen.

Sebag gently pulled a chain connected to an old bell over the gate. There was no sound. He pulled harder. Still nothing. He bent down to look under the bell: the clapper had been removed. Then he noticed a button next to the mailbox. He pushed it. A little tune could be heard inside the house. A curtain moved on the second floor.

He didn't have to wait long. Walking slowly and resignedly, Vernier came to open the gate. They greeted each other.

"The bell doesn't work any more," the retiree explained. "The neighbors found it too noisy. I could have taken it down to avoid misleading visitors. But except for you, the only people who come to see me know about it."

Sebag followed him into the yard, stroking on the way the leaves of a banana tree. They went into the house and his host asked him to sit down in the living room. The armchairs had the good smell of old tanned leather.

"Would you like a cup of coffee? It won't take long. I already made some; all I need to do is warm it up."

Sebag barely repressed a grimace of disgust. Warmed-up coffee was like Coke without carbonation, beer without alcohol, *chili* without *carne*.

"Perhaps you'd prefer something else?" Robert Vernier asked. "Some lemonade?"

Sebag accepted this new offer with pleasure. It had been years since he'd drunk lemonade. He'd tried to go back to that old-fashioned drink when he got to Perpignan, because there was a local producer whose reputation was well-deserved. But the children hadn't taken to it, preferring something more carbonated, and lemonade had quickly disappeared from their refrigerator.

His glass was sparkling with coolness. He took a sip. Vernier put his coffee cup on the low table between them. Then he fidgeted in his armchair.

"Did you have something you wanted to ask me about?" he finally dared to ask.

"Yes. Two or three little details."

He minimized the importance of their meeting. Without trying to be credible. Vernier couldn't for a moment imagine that he'd driven five hundred miles to get a few details he could have obtained by telephone.

Sebag asked him to begin at the beginning and tell him everything all over again. His bouts of insomnia, his morning walk, the beach, the thicket of reeds. The account of the discovery of the body was painful for both of them. Vernier's voice broke several times, but his words remained coherent. As in a story often told. Or well learned.

Silence reigned. Robert Vernier had finished. He was waiting for questions. His eyes were tired; his lips trembled. Throughout his life as a worker, he must have dreamed about a peaceful retirement. The inspector took a drink of his lemonade. It was time to take up the first point to be clarified.

"Josetta Braun's body was not visible from the path to the beach. According to the gendarmerie's report, you heard a sound and went toward it. What kind of sound?"

"A kind of slipping sound in the grass."

"What kind of slipping?"

"A furtive slipping, the kind you sometimes hear when you're walking. Especially in the morning. It must have been a snake. Or maybe just a lizard."

Little animals that took off through the grass as soon as anyone approached. Sebag often heard them when he was running on trails. If he'd had to go looking for them every time, he'd have spent more time in the underbrush than on the trails.

"And that was enough to make you go look around in the reeds?"

Vernier's breathing sped up imperceptibly. His weary eyes rested on the policeman for a moment before moving on to stare at something behind him.

"Do we always know why we do things?" he said evasively. "The noise must have seemed to me louder than usual . . . "

While hardened criminals accustomed to lying have a tendency try to make their interlocutors believe what they're saying by looking them straight in the eye, others always have a moment of weakness when they're telling a lie. As if they feared that an experienced policeman could read them like a book. In almost twenty years with the police, Sebag had seldom misinterpreted what people did with their eyes.

"Did you know Josetta Braun well?"

"Well? Uh . . . no," Vernier stammered. "I wouldn't say that. I'd met her a few times in the campground. I believe she was a nice girl. It's . . . terrible, what happened to her."

"The gendarmes' investigation isn't making progress. You, who . . . met Josetta and who were the first to be on the scene of the crime, might you have some idea about this murder?"

The question seemed to frighten Vernier. His eyes shifted away again and looked over Sebag's left shoulder.

"There was some talk about the crime being committed by a vagrant, I think."

"Yes. That's what the gendarmes say when they don't have a lead."

"I see."

The conversation was bogging down. Robert Vernier didn't want to go where Sebag was trying to lead him.

"Would you like a little more lemonade?"

His glass wasn't yet empty. He declined the diversion with a wave of his hand.

"You were saying that it was a terrible crime. Probably the work of a sadist."

Vernier nodded mechanically.

"How could anyone do that to the face of such a young, pretty girl? She was almost disfigured. Her mouth was crushed, her temple cracked open. I've seen the photos: she was genuinely butchered."

The retiree shrank into his armchair.

"No, really: a sadist did that."

Vernier's cup clattered as he set it back on the saucer. His hands were shaking.

"You had no difficulty recognizing her?" Sebag continued.

Without breathing, Vernier answered him. His voice was toneless.

"No . . . Her eyes were still open. Her beautiful blue eyes . . . Empty."

"The worst of it is thinking that the last thing they've seen is the twisted face of a murderer. Yes, that is truly horrible. What a bastard!"

"You're right," Vernier admitted. "Only a bastard could do that."

"To beat in the face of a young woman with a rock . . . "

Robert Vernier was very pale. He'd aged ten years. His lower lip sagged.

"It was a huge stone. Five pounds at least. You'd have to be sick to hit somebody with that. Besides, it must have made a strange sound."

The old man put his hand to his mouth and jumped to his feet. He mumbled an excuse and disappeared. Sebag had a moment of fright: if he was wrong, he wasn't just an imbecile but the worst sort of scum.

He finished his lemonade.

Vernier hadn't batted an eye when he'd mentioned the stone. However, the gendarmes had been deliberately vague regarding the murder weapon, and had even gone so far as to suggest to the reporters that it might be a hammer. The murderer had thrown the stone far away, and it had been discovered by investigators only later on. Vernier couldn't have seen it next to the body.

Sebag heard a toilet flush somewhere in the house. A few seconds later, Vernier reappeared, wiping his mouth with a paper tissue.

"Pardon me . . . I still find it very difficult to discuss that painful moment."

"I'm the one who should ask your pardon, Mr. Vernier. I shouldn't have stirred up those memories."

Sebag rose as well.

"I'm going to leave you now; I've disturbed you for no reason. I think we're going to have to close this case. All that remains is for me to bid you good-bye . . . "

"You're leaving?"

Vernier extended his soft, damp hand. Sebag turned around and saw, on a piano pushed up against the wall, the photo of an elderly woman smiling rather sadly in front of the Great Pyramid of Giza. It was that photo that Vernier had been looking at during much of their conversation.

"Your wife?" he asked.

"Yes. She died three years ago. After a long illness, as they say on the news. Cancer."

"You went to Egypt?"

"It was our last trip. She was already sick, but she wanted to go there before she died. She'd dreamed about it all her life."

Sebag took the photo in his hands and examined it more closely. Mrs. Vernier looked tired. It wasn't only her smile that hollowed her cheeks.

"I'm sure she must have loved that last happy time spent with you," he said, putting the photo back on the piano.

He ran his fingers over the keyboard of the piano. He'd also dreamed of going to Egypt. Were they going to have to wait until he was dying to finally make the trip?

"Was she the one who played the piano?"

"Yes. She also sang. She sang very well; she even belonged to a chorus."

Vernier was beginning to perk up.

"My wife also sings in a chorus," Sebag said.

"She does?"

"You loved her a lot, didn't you?"

"To tell the truth, until she fell ill I'd never really realized it. That's stupid, isn't it? But we were living together; we got along well. We didn't really talk about love."

"You miss her, don't you?"

He tried to reply but his voice broke again. Sebag put his hand on the old man's shoulder. He was determined to go all the way. You can't be a cop without being a bit of a bastard.

"I imagine Josetta's parents are also weeping in front of their daughter's photo. The loss of a daughter must be even harder. You have a daughter, don't you? And every day, Josetta's parents ask "why?" I know they're calling the gendarmes all the time, asking whether the investigation is getting anywhere. It's impossible to grieve when too many questions remain unanswered."

He paused for a moment; his hand was still on Vernier's shoulder. He'd reserved for the end the second, more important reason for his visit.

"By the way, I was about to forget! Looking through the file, I noticed that something was lacking. A detail. The gendarmes got fingerprints from almost a hundred people, but they forgot to get yours. That was stupid on their part, and it might cause a problem when we finally have a real suspect. The defense could rush into that breach. You don't mind going through that formality, do you?"

"No," Vernier mumbled faintly.

"Fine, fine. So I'll ask the gendarmes here in Gien to come see you. I'm not allowed to take your fingerprints myself. I'm outside my own territory . . . "

He let go of the old man's shoulder and took his hand, which was hanging inert alongside his body. He shook it again.

"Don't bother to see me out, Mr. Vernier. I can find my own way."

Three boys were roller-skating on a vast esplanade bordered by high sycamores with twisting trunks. They were weaving between posts and jumping over the chains that kept cars out of the area. Sebag sat down on a bench. Using a cane, an old man was trying to cross the esplanade. He walked hesitantly, frightened by the daring roller-skaters. The kids paid him no heed; for them, he was merely another obstacle providing new challenges. Their pants legs crumpled over their shoes, baseball caps worn backwards on their heads, and MP3 headphones screwed into their ears, they swept past him several times but never actually touched him. The old man walked on; his mouth was open and he was short of breath. He raised his cane, grumbled two or three curses the kids couldn't hear. Having perfectly mastered their art, they had no idea of the fear they were arousing, and probably took his raised cane as a friendly salute. Sebag stood up to escort the old man to the end of the esplanade.

"Little jerks!" the old man said.

Instead of thanking his rescuer, he spluttered his oaths in his face.

"Forgive them, for they know not what they do," Sebag replied, himself astonished by this sudden recollection of the Gospels.

The old man looked at him in surprise, while he punctuated his sentence with an enigmatic hand gesture halfway between a greeting and a blessing. Proud that he'd tried to slow the growth of misunderstanding between generations and the rise in the feeling of insecurity, Sebag sat down again. He lit a cigarette. The kids were now swooping around a baby carriage pushed by a young woman.

The inspector glanced at his watch. "After having vigorously stirred the sauce and brought it to a boil, let it simmer for ten minutes and serve it hot." He took a last drag on his cigarette and threw the butt on the asphalt. Then he went back to Vernier's house and rang the bell.

He didn't have to wait as long as the first time. It was as if Vernier had been watching for him through the curtains.

"I think we still have things to say to each other . . . "

Vernier did not respond, but he stood aside to let Sebag come in. In the living room, before they sat down, Sebag took the photo of the late Mrs. Vernier and put it face down on the piano. The gesture did not go unnoticed by Vernier.

"This time, I'd like something stronger than lemonade. Whisky, if you have any."

Vernier opened the doors of an old wooden dish cabinet and came back with two bottles and two elegantly decorated glasses. He poured Sebag a healthy dose of whisky and gave himself a little Banyuls dessert wine. They took a first sip in silence.

"You were right not to take Banyuls," Vernier forced himself to say to fill the gap. "It isn't very good. When I'm in Argelès, I usually buy six bottles of it at the Domaine de La Tour Vieille, and that lasts me all year. This year I didn't have time to buy it, so I got some at the supermarket in Gien. It's another brand, and it's less expensive, but it isn't as good."

Sebag waited another few seconds. He knew what he wanted to say, but he was trying to find exactly the right tone. Vernier gave him a hand.

"I can't sleep without drinking two or three glasses."

He raised his glass and took another drink. Sebag cleared his throat.

"I'm sure you didn't mean to kill her . . . "

The old man was expecting it, but Sebag's assertion nonetheless hit him hard. A punch in the stomach hurts, even if you've been forewarned. He put his hands to his mouth. He eyes sought something in the room that he could look at. He gasped several times. Like someone who's suddenly catching his breath after having been under water too long. Then his eyes came back and met Sebag's. And he began to talk. He talked without the inspector having to ask any questions.

He told him everything and then some.

He'd met Josetta for the first time very early one morning,

on the beach near the campground. It was still dark. He was taking his usual pre-dawn walk. He'd seen them hidden in a hollow in the sand only when he was already upon them. The man who was busy on top of Josetta hadn't noticed, but the young woman had seen him. He'd even had the impression that she'd started breathing faster when their eyes met. She'd looked at him without hostility and even, it had seemed, kindly. As if she was making him a gift of her pleasure. She'd smiled. He'd run away.

Then he'd seen her again in the campground. Her tent was pitched only a few yards from his trailer. Josetta's image had begun to haunt him. All the more because the young woman wasn't very prudish. She often came out of the shower half-naked, and Robert hadn't needed to peek at her very long to see her little breasts before she decided to put them in her bra. He had the feeling that she was aware of his presence. Several nights in a row, he'd gone to stand near her tent. Once he'd even heard her moans. He knew that she was alone that night. Robert couldn't sleep. His desire was too strong. Contrary to what he'd thought, the volcano was not extinct.

One evening, he'd followed her to the beach. It was almost midnight. She'd undressed and gone swimming naked. When she came out of the water, Robert was still there. Sitting two yards from her clothes. She'd dried off in the moonlight. She'd put on her T-shirt. Only her T-shirt. The erect nipples of her still-wet breasts had immediately formed halos on the fabric. She'd taken his hand and led him away. He'd walked one step behind her, hypnotized by the moonlight and a pair of very firm buttocks.

She'd lain down in the reeds. Smiled at him. Kissed him.

But while she was unbuttoning his pants, he'd felt his body betraying him. His desire was still there, however. "It's okay," she'd murmured, understanding his problem. She'd taken his hand and guided it toward her vagina. "It's okay," she'd repeated. And she'd smiled at him again. Her smile made her cheeks swell, and her white teeth glimmered in the moonlight. A beautiful smile. Unbearable.

That's when he'd lost his head. He'd grabbed a stone and had made that smile disappear forever. He didn't remember having hit her several times. He'd read that in the newspapers, and it was surely true. He didn't doubt that he was capable of having done it. He hadn't recovered consciousness until he was on his way back to the campground. But he knew she was dead when he'd left her there.

Vernier swirled his Banyuls around in his glass before drinking it down at a single draft. Sebag took a long swig of his whisky in order to respect his silence. He had before him a broken man. Already dead. It wasn't the first time, and it certainly wouldn't be the last. He knew he'd never get used to it. You couldn't get used to it. People who say you can are either liars or madmen.

Robert resumed his confession. What he had to say now was not necessarily easier to admit than the murder itself.

As a young man, he'd had sexual difficulties on several occasions. The most difficult to endure had been the compassion those women had thought they had to show, whereas he was well aware that it was mainly pity, or even scorn, that they were feeling. These failures had kept him at a distance from women. And then Solange had come along. She knew what she wanted. She proved to be enterprising, and she succeeded in overcoming his shyness. And his so-called impotence. A real miracle: with her, everything had always worked fine. He'd been faithful and ended up forgetting his earlier misadventures.

The failure with Josetta erased at a single blow all the years of peace with Solange. It cast him back into the sad memories of his adolescence. He'd reacted in a bestial manner to Josetta's smile. The smile of all women. He'd since thought a great deal about that terrible night and that was all he'd found to explain his barbarity. He saw no other way to understand it. But that was not a justification. Nothing could ever cleanse him of that monstrous act. It was as if sixty-five years of repressed violence had been set free in a single sentence.

Vernier took out handkerchief. He wiped his eyes and blew his nose at length. Sebag took advantage of this to look at his watch. It was after 1:00 P.M., and they still weren't completely done.

"It's horrible," Vernier went on, "horrible to realize how lives can be turned upside down in a moment. Josetta's life, of course. Mine, too, though that doesn't matter. I'm thinking especially of my children and grandchildren. What a disaster! What shame! To find out that their father, their dear old grandpa, is nothing but a murderer. Worse than that: a murderer who's a dirty old man. It was because of them, you see, that I didn't go turn myself in at the gendarmerie. I wanted to do that. If it could have brought Josetta back to life, I'd have done it. Without any hesitation. But after all, it wouldn't have changed anything. So since no one seemed to suspect me, I didn't say anything. It was all over for her, and for me too, but by keeping quiet I could still let my family live a normal life. And when I died, the secret would die with me."

He poured himself another glass of Banyuls, which he drank more rapidly than the first.

"I still have one question, Mr. Vernier: why did you pretend to have discovered the body? You could have waited until someone else came across it by accident."

"I was afraid it would be too long. She was off the path. I didn't want animals . . . or the sun . . . you see what I mean, I wanted her to be found quickly and put out of harm's way."

The telephone rang in the entry hall. Vernier started but didn't get up.

"That's probably my daughter," he explained. "If I answer, I won't be able to lie to her. I don't have the strength for that anymore. If I can still grant her a little reprieve . . . "

Vernier himself was going to be granted a reprieve. Sebag had come to Gien on his own initiative, and had no power. He would first have to call Castello, who would notify the prosecutor in Perpignan and the local gendarmes. He finished his glass of whisky. It was not very good, but it was better that way. He got up.

"Aren't you going to arrest me?" Vernier asked, also rising.

"No, not right now. I can't. I'll come back to take you to the gendarmerie. We'll make an official deposition there. You have until tomorrow."

"You're going to leave me alone? All alone . . . "

His features had sagged, his wrinkles deepened. He looked extremely tired. His eyes were empty. Sebag was aware of the risk.

"May I ask how you guessed?" Vernier asked.

"I didn't guess anything. Nothing at all. I just managed to figure out what you no longer wanted to hide."

"But if you came here, it was because you had an idea at the back of your mind."

Sebag shrugged. He was not completely sure he'd acted for the right reasons. Under normal circumstances, the things that had bothered him in the gendarmes' report would not have justified a trip of over five hundred miles. But the desire to take revenge had won out. He wasn't proud of that.

"When I come back to get you, it would be good if you'd prepared a few things to take with you."

He shook Vernier's hand for a long time. As he walked past the piano, he pointed to the photo, which was still face down on the varnished wood.

"Don't hesitate to take souvenirs you care about. They're very helpful for getting through the hard parts. Especially since in the coming days your wife will be the only person not judging you."

"She has already judged me," retorted the enigmatic old man.

Sebag ate a chicken sandwich at the bar in a brasserie. He hadn't found anything better. It was almost 3:00 P.M., and lunch was no longer being served. To wash down the sandwich, he made do with a bottle of sparkling mineral water. It was all he could allow himself after an almost sleepless night. Vernier's whisky had already made him a little dizzy. His confessions too, perhaps.

The owner of the bar suggested a hotel in the pedestrian zone. Not very far away. The carpet was worn and the wallpaper faded, but the room was large and the bathtub clean. He set the alarm on his watch to let him sleep an hour and sat down in an armchair. He preferred not to fall into a deep sleep so that it would not be too difficult to wake up.

After his nap, he put on his running clothes and went out. The air was still warm; a little breeze was blowing off the river. Built on a hill alongside the Loire, Gien offered courageous runners a few steep inclines. He allowed himself little accelerations. His jersey was soon damp with sweat.

In a narrow, deserted street he came across a young woman. She was black. A Walkman headset on her head, she was clapping the beat on her generous thighs. The music she was listening to accentuated the natural swaying of her hips. After he had passed by her, he couldn't help turning around. Running a few paces backward was a great way to build up your quadriceps.

He waited until evening to call Castello. He talked to him on his cell phone, and could hear the clatter of dishes behind their conversation. The superintendent started to get angry when he learned about what Sebag had done but, as Molina had foreseen, he rapidly calmed down when he found out the results. He set aside his reprimands and promised to do the maximum to legalize Sebag's initiative.

"I'll arrange matters with the gendarmes. I'm sure they'll do all they can to smooth things out; they've allowed the perpetrator to get away and we're bringing him in all tied up. I just need a little time. Officially, you don't arrive until tomorrow. In the course of the morning, you can come to the gendarmerie with your suspect."

Sebag sat down on the Loire levee. The sun was going down behind the nuclear power plant.

"Are you sure about your suspect?" Castello asked. "He's not going to retract his confession between now and tomorrow?"

"No, I don't think so. He was relieved to be able to confess. And then in any case, we can always use his fingerprints to prove that he did it."

"Oh yes, that's true, the fingerprints, you're right to remind me of that. I'll emphasize that detail in the event the gendarmes complain. If they'd done their work the way they should have, we wouldn't find ourselves in this position."

Sebag abstained from making any comments. It was easy criticize after the fact. To err is human. So human.

"One last thing, Gilles. Can I inform Lefèvre, or would you prefer to wait until you're here and can do it yourself?"

Sebag chose to be generous.

"I think it would be better for you to do it. As you said the other day, we have to be able to move beyond personal quarrels."

"If I'm not mistaken, that's called an excess of zeal."

Whether it was a matter of being generous or sucking up depended on your point of view.

He slept deeply. Nine hours of slumber without dreams or nightmares. When he awoke he allowed himself a half-hour workout on the worn-out carpet of his hotel room: stretching and ab exercises. After breakfast, he had the pleasure of receiving a telephone call from Séverine. She was fine, the weather was beautiful, her girlfriend's parents were really very nice, they'd gone on a boat trip the day before, and on Sunday they were leaving for PortAventura. Everything was great. Séverine was even thoughtful enough to say that she missed her dear papa.

A delicious lie.

He checked out of the hotel and drove to Vernier's home. Behind its closed shutters, the little house seemed to be still asleep. He rang the doorbell and waited.

No response. He rang again.

Bernard Palissy Street was calm. Sunny. A curtain moved, but it was behind the window of a neighboring house. He hardly had time to glimpse an old lady's emaciated face.

Still no answer. He dialed Vernier's number on his cell phone. He heard the phone ring inside the house. He counted to ten.

There was no answer.

He decided to open the gate. It was not locked. He walked through the yard. The earth was still damp around the flowers; it had been irrigated the preceding evening. Even the banana tree seemed to have gotten a few drops of water.

He went into the little veranda that served as a vestibule in front of the entrance to the house. He put his hand on the handle, but the door didn't open. He put his shoulder against the wood and pushed. The door moved a little; it was not bolted.

He hesitated. He had a passkey but he'd already violated a lot of rules.

He put the passkey in the lock anyway. The door opened. Almost by itself. "It really did, I assure you." He already saw the gendarmes laughing. He wouldn't want to present things to them that way later on.

From the entry, he called.

His call faded away into the upper stories. On the low table, in the living room where they had talked, the bottle of Banyuls was empty. The photo had disappeared from the piano.

He looked in the kitchen, then in the study. There was no one on the ground floor.

He went over to the stairway. Called again. The wooden steps creaked under his feet. Even though he was climbing slowly.

On the landing, he found four doors. The two facing him must be those of the bedrooms that looked out on the street. He reflected. It was undoubtedly the curtain of the bedroom on the right that he'd seen move the day before when he'd rung the bell. He opened the door.

A bed occupied most of the room. It was covered with a yellow quilt decorated with blue birds. Between the two pillows, an old teddy bear without eyes was dozing while waiting for the impossible return of a child who had disappeared into maturity. At the foot of the bed, the quilt had preserved an imprint. Someone had no doubt recently sat down there. On the wall above the bed there was a poster. For Jean-Jacques Beineix's film *Diva*. The Verniers had two or three children—Sebag didn't remember exactly, the old man had mentioned only his daughter—and this bedroom had probably belonged to one of them. What would Séverine's and Léo's rooms look like after they had left home? He and Claire would certainly use one of them to set up a second study. The other would become a guest room. They would surely also leave, on the bed or elsewhere, a stuffed animal or a security blanket as a souvenir of a bygone period.

The other bedroom belonged to the parents. Wallpaper with large flowers, lace curtains on the window, varnished furniture. On a bed made of dark wood, Robert Vernier seemed to be asleep. He'd lain down fully clothed; he'd taken off only his shoes, which he'd sensibly put at the foot of the bed. On the night table, next to the photo of his wife—the one that had been on the piano—there was a note and an empty container of sleeping pills. He took the old man's pulse.

Robert Vernier had succeeded in forgetting his remorse.

Sebag went back down to the living room to telephone the

gendarmes in Gien. It was high time to do so. Then he called his boss. Castello couldn't hide his annoyance. Vernier's suicide was going to cause the case to be prematurely closed and would leave questions unanswered. The family of the victim would certainly suffer from the absence of a trial.

Sebag knew all that, but he felt no regrets.

He sat down in the armchair where he'd sat the day before. He resisted the desire to pour himself a whisky. That wouldn't have been right. Even to drink to Vernier's health.

Three gendarmes came into the Verniers' house, breaking the silence that reigned there. Sebag summed up the situation for two of them, one of whom was a corporal, while the third scrupulously examined the front door. They had been informed of his arrival this morning and were already familiar with the main lines of the Josetta Braun case. Sebag decided not to tell them that he'd visited Vernier the day before.

"He must have guessed that I suspected him. His remorse probably became unbearable. He left a letter upstairs."

In this letter, Vernier clearly acknowledged his guilt. He said he was sorry to flee his responsibilities but explained his act by the desire to abbreviate his family's suffering. Without a trial or a prison sentence, the shame wouldn't be as great, he wrote. Finally, he begged the pardon of Josetta's parents. Fortunately for Sebag, he did not mention their talk. He limited himself to saying that he felt relieved but knew that the feeling was temporary.

The corporal went upstairs with a gendarme. The gendarme who had examined the front door approached Sebag.

"Was the door to the house open?" he asked.

"Yes, of course, Sebag answered, trying to remain natural.

"And the gate and the veranda as well?"

"Yes."

The gendarme studied him for a few seconds.

"That's curious," he commented.

Sebag pretended he hadn't heard.

"Are there a lot of tourists in Gien?" he asked to divert attention.

"A few," the gendarme answered after a long silence. "Mainly just passing through. People stop here for a day or two, hardly more than that."

There was a lilt in his voice.

"You're not from here, are you? Or else you're from the southern part of the region."

The gendarme gave him a brief smile.

"I'm from Bordeaux."

Sebag tried to play the southerner card to get him on his side.

"You don't find it too hard being here? As for myself, I lived a few years in Chartres. As the kids say: it's not a lot of fun."

"That's for sure," he replied in a resigned tone. "I'd really like to go back to the Bordeaux region. But my wife is from Normandy and my son was born here in Gien. They don't really want to leave."

The gendarme must have been about Sebag's age. Maybe two or three years younger. He still had no gray hair, but his uniform couldn't entirely conceal the beginning of a pot belly.

The corporal came back downstairs.

"It doesn't get any clearer than that," he said. "The note, the drugs. That completely closes the case. A little suddenly, perhaps, but our colleagues in Argelès will be happy."

"They're pretty overworked in the summertime."

"That's the impression I got on the telephone. We have a period like that ourselves. It's terrible in May and June every year."

"Tourists?" Sebag asked, not being able to resist glancing at the other gendarme.

"No, not here, as you can imagine. It's just a meeting of gypsies. It's a religious thing: at Pentecost they do baptisms. Their association owns a big piece of land in the country a couple of miles from Gien. There are about twenty thousand of them, after all . . . For a few days, the canton's population increases by a factor of two or three and the number of crimes naturally follows the same curve."

"And the number of gendarmes is the only thing that doesn't change, I suppose?"

"We do receive a few reinforcements, but never enough. We have to hope that nothing very serious happens during that period."

The gendarme from Bordeaux broke into the conversation. He hadn't given up on his first idea.

"Do you have a passkey?"

"I do have one. Not on me, but in my car. Why?"

"No particular reason. I just wanted to know."

The corporal understood the situation.

"Gérard, could you call Dr. Béraud? I asked him to come by to certify the death but it seems to me he's being a little slow getting here. I'd like to wind this case up quickly."

He'd emphasized the last sentence. Gérard reluctantly went away. The corporal addressed Sebag again.

"He's the tenacious type. It's a good quality for an investigator to have, but the problem is that he sometimes gets lost in details that aren't important."

Sebag smiled but took care not to thank him.

"Regarding details," he said, "there are a few that we mustn't forget even if everything seems clear. We absolutely have to take Mr. Vernier's fingerprints. It's the only material proof that we'll be able to get."

"The other colleague is still upstairs. He must be taking the prints right now."

"That's perfect."

Sebag held out his hand. He was suddenly in a hurry to get out of the house.

Outside, he drew a deep breath. The day was only starting and Sebag still had a long drive ahead of him. But the hardest part was over.

The murder of Josetta Braun had been solved. Even though they had been deprived of the prospect of a trial, the young woman's parents could begin their grieving. That was the most important point. The Perpignan newspapers would soon write the epilogue to the case, but with a little luck few people outside the department of Pyrénées-Orientales would read their articles. In Gien, the memory of Robert Vernier could remain intact, and once their sorrow had faded a little, his children wouldn't have to bear an additional burden.

Sebag felt sad but relieved. Like a doctor after performing a euthanasia.

CHAPTER 28

C ontrary to what Sebag hoped, the denouement of
Josetta Braun's murder was going to be covered in both
the local and the national press.

The next day, in fact, the daily *Le Parisien-Aujourd'hui en
France*, which still had not learned of the results of Sebag's
investigation, devoted its front page to "the serial criminal"
who was attacking young Dutch women in the department of
Pyrénées-Orientales. This time, the writer abandoned all precautions and in a sidebar whose tone was extremely violent, he
strongly criticized the Perpignan police for its lack of effective-
ness. As soon as the newspaper came out, the radio and television stations got involved, and so did the Dutch press. Police
headquarters had been overwhelmed by demands for information and interviews. And within the pack, the local reporters,
furious at having been scooped, were not the least aggressive.

A press conference was supposed to be held Monday morning, just before noon. Superintendent Castello was jubilant. All
the more because the comparison of the fingerprints had supported Vernier's confession.

"I'm going to give those assholes what for," he exclaimed,
abandoning polished language for once. "They won't be disappointed this time."

Castello slapped the newspaper with the back of his hand.

"I'll show them who the incompetents are!"

From the boss's window, Sebag was observing a cameraman
who was filming the headquarters.

"The whole national press corps will be forced to recognize the quality of our work. Of your work, Gilles."

Sebag was savoring his return to grace. The morning had begun with an update in the boss's office. Castello, Lefèvre, and himself. Bernard Petit, the cop from Montpellier, had joined them in the course of the meeting. The superintendent began with his usual song and dance about teamwork, personal quarrels, and efficiency. Then he gave Sebag the floor. The inspector told them about his weekend. First his deductions from the reading of the gendarmes' report, then his trip to Gien, his meeting with Vernier, how he'd led him to confess his crime. He didn't mention finding the corpse the following day. And no one asked him about it. The fact that the guilty party had committed suicide was now a mere detail.

Sebag had chosen his words carefully. He wanted his triumph to be modest. During his account, Lefèvre did not look up. He limited himself to taking notes in his electronic agenda. At one point, he swore under his breath: his battery had gone dead.

At the end of Sebag's presentation, the two men had looked at each other for some time. Without hostility, but also without liking. Lefèvre had won a point in the Verbrucke case, and Sebag had just evened the score by solving the murder in Argelès. They were tied. What about the endgame?

"If I were you, I'd remain prudent in dealing with the media," Lefèvre suggested to Castello.

"You would? Why?" the superintendent asked, visibly disappointed.

"We still have two cases to deal with. Two kidnappings by the same individual."

"Two cases hardly make a series," Petit objected.

"True, but the summer isn't over yet," Lefèvre replied.

"You think he might do it again?" Castello asked.

Lefèvre threw up his hands.

"There's no way I can say, but it can legitimately be feared that he might. Especially since he failed with Anneke . . . "

Castello took his lower lip between his teeth.

"Damn, I hadn't seen things like that. I'm completely at sea in that case. So we're still at the same point?"

"In a way, yes," Lefèvre replied. "We've clarified one point—an important one," he said, looking at Sebag"—but fundamentally nothing has changed. On June 26, a man kidnapped Ingrid Raven and killed José Lopez. Two weeks later, he tried to do it again with Anneke Verbrucke."

In addition to disappointing him, Lefèvre's analysis plunged Castello into perplexity. After a moment of reflection he turned to Sebag.

"Is that also your assessment, Gilles?"

"There is a risk," he said evasively. "Nonetheless . . . "

"What?" Castello said, full of hope.

"Do you have a new theory?" Lefèvre asked apprehensively.

"Not a new one, no," Sebag replied.

He said nothing more. The two superintendents glanced at each other in surprise.

"And would you agree to present it to us?" Castello questioned.

"It's more a matter of reminding you of it."

"Let's not play on words, go ahead."

"If you insist . . . "

"Yes, I insist, Sebag, get on with it."

"It's that . . . "

Castello scratched the end of his nose and snorted.

"Come on, Gilles, what game are you playing? Stop all this childishness."

"That's fair," Lefèvre interceded.

"If you get involved here, too, we'll never get anywhere. I'm wondering if I wouldn't prefer the earlier situation. Divide and rule, that's as old as the world but it can sometimes be good. Go ahead, Gilles."

"As you wish, superintendent. But this may take a while!"

"We'll be patient."

"Okay. In fact, I think the kidnapper has always had just one goal: to kidnap Ingrid Raven. All the rest is just a smokescreen."

"What about the attack on Anneke?" Lefèvre asked.

"Same thing. A smokescreen!"

"But you just said that there was still a danger of another kidnapping," Petit retorted.

"I didn't say there was a risk of a kidnapping . . . "

Castello slammed the flat of his hand on his desk.

"Now listen, Gilles, you're out of your mind, we all heard you say that."

Sebag looked at his interlocutors, one after the other, then smiled.

"I think in fact there is still a risk of an *attempted* kidnapping.

Bernard Petit opened his mouth, but was so astonished he couldn't close it again. Lefèvre turned to Castello.

"It's my turn to be completely mystified."

"Explain yourself, Gilles," the superintendent begged.

"That's what I'm doing."

"Then do it more clearly, please."

"I'll try . . . As we now know, Josetta Braun was killed by Robert Vernier in a fit of madness and our kidnapper has nothing to do with this murder. Are we agreed about that?"

"Completely," Castello assured him.

"Good. However, the other day, during his little treasure hunt, the kidnapper led us—after a stop on the Avenue Poincaré—to the Oleanders campground in Argelès. Why? To make us think that he was also responsible for that murder."

"You did talk about a smokescreen," Castello remembered.

"In fact, I suggested the other day that the kidnapper was taking pleasure in confusing us and that he was spreading smokescreens all around us. Outlandish demands, the excessive amount of the ransom . . . "

"You also claimed that the attempted kidnapping of Anneke was a smokescreen," Lefèvre slipped in.

Sebag hesitated. He would have preferred to take up that point later on. But since he was being pressed on it—too bad!

"And I still maintain that."

Sebag's assertion cast a chill on the room. The superintendents stared at the inspector, searching his face for signs of a sudden attack of insanity.

"Come now, Gilles, that's absurd," Castello spluttered. "It has now been proven that Ingrid's kidnapper is the same as Anneke's attacker. We aren't going to go back over all that, after all . . . "

"I have no intention of contesting what has been proven, no. I was mistaken on that point, but it's only a detail."

"Detail, detail," Lefèvre protested. "You minimize things very easily when it suits your purpose."

"I thought the two cases were unrelated, and I was wrong; I recognize that. That mistake bothered me a great deal, but on reflection, it doesn't affect my hypothesis. On the contrary, it supports it."

"When is this going to start getting clearer?" Petit complained.

Sebag smiled.

"The other day, I said that in order to confuse us, the kidnapper had claimed two crimes he hadn't committed, the murder of Josetta and the attack on Anneke. Today, I'm still persuaded that the kidnapper's goal is to sow confusion in our minds, but I can be more precise: to confuse us, he tried to claim the murder for himself, and in Anneke's case he committed, not an attempted kidnapping, but a simulated kidnapping."

The three superintendents frowned simultaneously.

"Do you mean to say that he never intended to kidnap Anneke?" Castello asked.

Sebag nodded.

"That's a daring theory," Castello commented.

"I'd call it over-complicated," Petit protested.

"Can you prove what you're saying?" Lefèvre asked.

"Unfortunately, no. But this theory has the advantage of explaining the odd things we all noticed in the Avenue Poincaré attack."

"Can you remind us of them?" Petit implored him.

"There were actually two things. To understand, we have to go back to the facts. On July 4, Anneke Verbrucke spends the evening with friends in a bar in Perpignan. Her attacker is also there. He's watching her. Anneke leaves around three A.M. and heads for home alone. The man follows her. On the Avenue Poincaré, he slams her up against a car and puts a knife to her throat. Then, strangely enough, nothing happens. What exactly does he want? To steal from her? To rape her? To kidnap her? At the time, Anneke asked this question, and she still doesn't know the answer. The man doesn't do anything, doesn't start to do anything, he seems to be waiting. How long? It's hard to say. Then Anneke sees the headlights of a car coming down the avenue, and that's the moment the individual chooses to try to make her get into the car he's pinned her against. He relaxes his pressure, she fights with him, manages to push him away, and takes off. End of the episode and the first question: how could the attacker hope to make Anneke get into a car that wasn't his and whose keys he didn't have?"

"It wasn't his car?" Petit asked.

"No. Reread the file, and you'll see that the car belongs to Marc Savoy, a sales rep with no record who lives nearby. The car was parked in the neighborhood as it is every night. It was locked and has an excellent alarm system."

"That is strange, in fact," Petit conceded.

"And what do you conclude from that?" Castello asked.

"Well, precisely that our man never intended to kidnap Anneke Verbrucke. At the moment that seemed to him most favorable, he pinned the young woman against the first car available and waited."

"Waited for what?"

"That is the second question I asked myself. The answer now seems to me obvious: he waited until a car came along. That's all. And what seemed to be clumsy blunder turns out to be a very clever trick."

Sebag didn't see any lights go on in the superintendents' eyes. He was going to have to be more explicit.

"He made sure the young woman had seen the car coming and at that moment, on the pretext of opening the car door, he relaxed his pressure on her. Reassured by the car that was approaching, Anneke took advantage of this to get away from him and run toward her rescuers."

A deep silence followed Sebag's demonstration. The inspector gave his interlocutors time to think. The superintendents were looking for a flaw in his reasoning. Apparently the couldn't find one. Sebag's throat was dry.

Bernard Petit was the first to speak.

"All that seems coherent, but nonetheless it's hard to accept."

"It's more like a crime novel," Lefèvre said, half in jest, half in earnest. "Still, we can't exclude the possibility that the kidnapper is a fan of thrillers. In fact, I have to admit that I find your theory seductive, but all the same I have an objection to make to it, Sebag: how could the kidnapper be sure that we would make the connection between the three cases?"

He'd been expecting that question. He'd thought about it while he was driving back to Perpignan and had found an answer only when he saw the front pages of the daily newspapers.

"He wasn't sure, and that's why he helped us. Through the intermediary of the press."

"The first article in *Le Parisien*, of course!" Castello exclaimed. "Do you mean to say that he's the one who informed the paper's correspondent the other day?"

"I think so. And he's probably also the source for the article that appeared this morning."

Sebag's answer dissipated Lefèvre's last doubts.

"The dirty bastard has really led us in a merry dance. I hope we're going to catch him . . . "

Castello looked at his watch.

"So what do I tell the reporters?"

Sebag sat back in his chair. In his view, that question did not fall into his domain.

"I think we should limit it to the murder in Argelès," Lefèvre proposed. "That case has been solved, and you can give all the details the reporters want. And you absolutely refuse to answer questions about the other two cases. You can say that they're under investigation and that you don't wish to say anything about them at this time."

"What if they ask me if the other two cases are connected?"

"You simply don't answer. After the revelations regarding Argelès, the reporters will have to be more careful. They'll no longer dare to talk about serial crimes."

"The reporter from *Le Parisien* is going to get bawled out by his colleagues," Petit commented.

"He should have done a better job of checking his sources," Castello replied. "I'm planning to have a private talk with him after the press conference. I've got a few questions to ask him."

Lefèvre agreed:

"If he tells you that someone suggested this idea of serial crimes, that will confirm Sebag's theory."

"And if he knows who that someone is, that will give us a new lead," Petit said hopefully.

"Let's not count on that too much," Lefèvre said.

Castello rose, signaling that it was time to go. He went up to Sebag and put his hand on his shoulder.

"You must be tired, Gilles, huh?"

"A little, yes."

"Vernier's death didn't affect you too much?"

"For his family, it's probably a good thing."

"I'm inclined to share that view but it mustn't be repeated. Go and rest up, Gilles, you need it. But stay close to your cell phone. At least we've learned something about the kidnapper. He has good judgment: in you, he chose a tough adversary."

After leaving headquarters, Sebag did some errands. He bought some roasted chicken thighs, tomatoes, rice, pasta, a melon, and peaches. Enough to make himself a few bachelor's feasts. When he got home he found in the mailbox a postcard from Claire that had been sent from Bonifacio the preceding week. The news was out of date but the thoughtfulness pleased him. In fact it was this time lag that made the card valuable, as if the words had mellowed in the space of a few days. The e-mails were precious because they provided almost instantaneous reports, but they would never have that slightly aged flavor. On a postcard, the words had been weighed while staring into space and chewing on the pen. They were laid down with care and measure, since there was limited room. The cards were redolent of coffee and fruit juice drunk on a terrace, the perfume of flowers in the shade of a public park. The e-mails smelled of a dirty keyboard and a poorly venti-lated office.

Claire's card contained its share of banalities and loving words. These could even be synonymous. But three words moved Sebag. They had been slipped in after the signature.

"I miss you."

He placed the card in a prominent place on the living room

bookcase. He ran a finger over the bookcase. It was dusty. He'd have to clean the house. He realized that he hadn't done anything in the house since Claire left. Usually, he didn't mind doing housework and often went at household chores with more zeal than his wife did. An ideal father and husband. It was as if the role had been tailor-made for him. It fit him well and he'd constantly sought to live up to it. But the cloth had gotten old and the seams were coming out everywhere.

He drove away his negative thoughts and settled comfortably into the chaise longue in the yard. So his superiors had authorized him to take another nap during his work day. The second in three days. The first one had been a punishment; this one was a reward. He fell asleep meditating on the precarious nature of honors in the French police force.

In the late afternoon he went back to headquarters, booted up his computer, and saw that his colleagues hadn't been loafing.

They'd started over from the beginning, the teams cross-testing for greater security: what escaped one of them might attract the attention of others. Lambert and Llach had finished the list of "BWs," including in their search all the Wangs and Wongs in the Vietnamese community who had been previously set aside. Molina had interviewed Anneke Verbrucke, Ménard had met with Sylvie Lopez and the Revel couple, while Raynaud and Moreno had taken on Gérard Barrère and Fabrice Gasch.

For his part, Lefèvre had listened over and over to the recordings of the kidnapper's telephone calls. He'd gotten everything possible out of them, but it still wasn't much. Despite the caller's whispering, he concluded that the man had a deep, toneless voice. His breathing was strong and slow, clearly audible: that could indicate that he was greatly overweight, but contradicted the physical description of the suspect. Lefèvre assumed that the heavy breathing must reflect an effort to control a strong internal tension. The voice had no trace of an accent, but the slow delivery might have been intended to conceal it.

The police had done a great deal of work. But they hadn't found anything new.

They'd made hardly any progress.

Sebag had searched his memory all afternoon. But not a single face or name had risen to the surface. He couldn't imagine who the kidnapper might be. And still less why he had chosen him as his chief contact.

It was almost 8:00 P.M. when Castello came into his office.

"I knew I'd find you here. Once you've started, it's impossible to stop you."

The superintendent sat down in Molina's chair.

"It's too bad that sometimes it's so hard to get you to start working."

Sebag tried to protest but his boss stopped him.

"I'm not here to criticize you. This is not the time. I know you'll give me other opportunities for that . . . "

He pushed aside the papers on Molina's desk so he could rest his elbows on it.

"I wanted to tell you about my conversation with the reporter from *Le Parisien*. He had an appointment in the late morning and I had to dangle an exclusive in front of him to get him to agree to come back to headquarters this afternoon. So far as the exclusive is concerned, he got it."

Mechanically, he lifted the sheets of paper he'd piled up on the side of the desk and abstained from any remark on seeing an issue of a sports magazine.

"All that to tell you that you were right," he continued. "The reporter didn't want to admit it right away, but he was in fact contacted. He received an anonymous letter, typed and mailed from a post office in Perpignan. At first, he claimed to have thrown the letter away, but then he acknowledged that he'd kept it and argued that it was a matter of respecting the privacy of his sources. In short, he doesn't want to give it to us."

"That doesn't matter. There won't be a clue in that letter any more than in the others."

"That's what we thought. However, he was willing to look at several fonts that we showed him, and he definitely recognized the one used for the letters making claims."

"That amounts to a signature."

"We're in agreement about that."

"I think this validates my theory, doesn't it?"

"Looks like it. I have to offer you, for the second time today, my warmest congratulations. I hope you'll develop a taste for that sort of thing. We still have work to do to find Ingrid."

CHAPTER 29

How long had she been pacing around her cage? Twenty minutes, an hour, two days, a month? She was losing all sense of time. Only meals and showers punctuated her solitude. Night and day were the same: endless hours that she usually spent lying on her old, damp mattress, hovering between consciousness and somnolence.

The fear and boredom had made her bulimic. Everything her jailer brought her to eat she wolfed down without ever leaving even a crumb. Thoughtfully, he increased the portions but could never satiate her. She would have eaten forever. And without hunger. She thought she must have gained at least six or seven pounds. She felt plump.

Plump like a sow being fattened up for slaughter.

She didn't need a mirror or a scale to see what was happening. The rolls of fat on her belly provided the best evidence. She was familiar with these little rings around her waist: they returned from time to time. Every time she had an exam at school or was depressed about her love life.

She'd decided to do exercises. She'd begun by doing standing warm-ups. Stretching her arms, relaxing her back, then running in place. She'd rapidly gotten out of breath. She'd always hated sports.

She took the time to recuperate by walking up and down before beginning a series of abdominal exercises on the floor. Pain appeared very quickly, but she gritted her teeth. She recalled the last time she'd suffered so much. She'd been six-

teen years old and was in love—like all her girlfriends—with a
well-built high-school student, the regional gymnastic champion. The girls admired the athlete's rippling muscles and his
broad chest, but it was especially his feline way of walking that
captivated Ingrid. He moved through the school corridors
slowly, with a powerful and supple gait. The crowds of students opened up before him as the Red Sea opened before
Moses. Ingrid had persuaded a girlfriend to go with her to
enroll in the same club. During their first—and only—training
session, she'd endured the abominable torture without attracting a single glance from the champion. Her nascent love had
not been equal to the atrocious cramps that had followed. Her
girlfriend had been more persistent, and Ingrid seemed to
remember that for a time she had been on their hero's list of
favorites.

After working on her abs, Ingrid started walking up and
down in her cell. Five paces in one direction, turn around at
the wall, five paces in the other direction.

Her head was spinning but she no longer wanted to stop.

Five paces in one direction, turn around at the wall, five
paces in the other direction.

She was going back and forth in her cage imagining that each
step took her a little closer to her parents. Papa . . . Mama . . .
The words escaped her lips. She didn't even notice.

Her head was spinning more and more, she was beginning
to feel sick, but she could no longer stop.

Five paces in one direction, turn around at the wall, five
paces in the other direction.

She told herself that if she ever managed to get out of this
cellar, she would be capable of walking three hundred miles
to escape her tormentor. That was absurd. But she didn't
care.

Five paces in one direction, turn around at the wall, five
paces in the other direction.

She finally had the feeling that she was doing something useful.

She had to cling to that.

Five paces in one direction, turn around at the wall, five paces in the other direction.

CHAPTER 30

Gilles Sebag was looking for inspiration on site. After roaming around the cab stand at the Perpignan rail station and then strolling down Avenue Poincaré, he got into his car. He drove as far as Força Real, admired the view once again, and then took off for Canet. But at the hotel where Ingrid had stayed after she left Collioure, no one remembered seeing the young woman.

Toward noon, Sebag allowed himself the pleasure of drinking an orgeat soda on the terrace of a restaurant on the Place de la Méditerranée. Then he decided to eat lunch there.

At a nearby table, two lovers were holding hands and smiling at each other with their eyes as much as with their lips. They were both over forty. The man was wearing a wedding ring. An adulterous couple, Sebag thought, making fun of that old-fashioned term that his mother might have used. Weren't they right to want to experience several love affairs? And wasn't it nonsensical, not to say perverted, to hope to spend one's whole life with the same person? Who could claim to stand the test of time?

By early afternoon, he was back in the old center of Perpignan. The Deux Margots bar had just opened. It was kept by two women who had been prostitutes on the Place Blanche in Paris. They'd chosen to retire in Roussillon and had kept their stage names to pun on that of a famous café-théâtre in Paris.

Sebag observed with care the place where a few days earlier the kidnapper had chosen his prey. His bait. He went up to the bar.

"What would you like, darling?"

With her drawl verging on vulgarity, her voice made hoarse by alcohol and cigarettes, her bleached blond hair, and her enormous mouth smeared with bright red lipstick, this Margot flaunted her past as a hooker. Sebag slammed his badge on the bar.

"Excuse . . . uh, excuse me, I didn't know. But your colleagues already came by last week."

He nodded to signify that he was aware of that. Raynaud and Moreno had gone to talk to the two owners as soon as it was learned that the kidnapper had called headquarters from this bar.

"They gave you a description of a suspect, right?"

"Yeah. Some description: a big skinny guy at least forty . . . "

"And if I add that he had a very deep voice and breathed heavily?"

Margot limited herself to an eloquent frown.

"Sorry, no, that doesn't help."

Sebag took out his wallet. He laid out a few photographs on the bar. José Lopez, Ingrid Raven, Anneke Verbrucke. After hesitating for a moment, he also put down a photo of Claire. He thought it was better to add to the sample someone who had nothing to do with the case.

"Do you recognize one of these people?"

Margot bent over the photographs. She squinted.

"Excuse me," she said, going to take a pair of glasses from a drawer.

She put them on her nose.

"I can see better like this."

She examined the images attentively. When her finger fell on one of them, Sebag couldn't hide his surprise.

"I seem to remember this woman. She came here at least once."

Her chubby finger was pointing to Claire's face.

"Are you sure?"

"Sure? Let's not exaggerate. A lot of people come here. We can't remember everybody. Do you want me to call my partner? Margot!"

"What?" a voice replied from the back of the room.

"Can you come up here? It's the . . . uh . . . it's important."

Margot 2 didn't have to be asked twice. She'd understood. She looked just like her partner, except that she was a brunette.

"This gentleman would like to know if you recognize someone. I told him that this face was familiar."

Margot 2 took the photo and held it at arm's length, but she didn't need to put on glasses.

"Yes, I've seen this woman. Several times, in fact. One evening, she knocked over a glass."

Sebag felt his stomach being tied in knots. He thought again about the couple in the restaurant.

"Was there someone with her?" he asked in an expressionless voice.

Margot 1 looked at him over her glasses.

"Women rarely go to bars alone at night," she replied. "At least in the provinces."

"I seem to recall that she came mainly with other women," Margot 2 added.

Gilles began to breathe again. His reprieve didn't last.

"But the night she knocked over a glass, she was with a man. I remember: she spilled the glass on his suit and I sort of had a feeling that she'd done it on purpose."

"It wasn't that man," Margot 2 explained, pointing to José Lopez.

Sebag gulped painfully.

"And . . . what did they look like? I mean, the man and the woman, did they seem to be . . . "

He couldn't get the word out.

"Lovers?" Margot 2 said, helping him.

"For example."

"I don't know but if they were, they were about to have a fight."

"When a man comes here with a woman, if he hasn't already slept with her he's hoping to do it," Margot 1 said, philosophically.

"Or to do *her*," her comrade added, bursting into loud stage laughter.

Sebag forced himself to return to his investigation.

"And you really haven't seen any of these other people?"

The two Margots confirmed their initial judgment.

"No, we'd have liked to be able to help you, but we don't see how."

"Okay, thanks anyway."

He was about to pick up the photos when the brunette put her finger on Claire's again.

"On the other hand, I might know who the other man is."

"What other man?"

"The one who was with the little lady with the curly hair."

Sebag almost choked. The man who was with Claire . . .

He felt his cell phone vibrate in his pocket. He took the call before it began to ring.

"Hello Inspector Sebag. It's Martine at the reception desk. I'm sorry to disturb you but there was a telephone call for you. I think it's important. The man who called said it was urgent, that he wanted to speak only to you, and that he would call back in half an hour."

"Did he give his name?"

"He refused. He told me you would understand. At first, I didn't take the call very seriously; I thought it was the guy from the other day."

"Who?"

"The one whose car was stolen."

"And it wasn't?"

"Apparently not. He said several times that it was urgent. He said something about a treasure hunt, that's why I thought at first it was a joke. And also, I had a hard time understanding what he was saying. It was weird: he was whispering."

Sebag felt a kind of electric shock.

"How long ago did he call?"

"Five minutes. I had another call right afterward."

"Good. Tell Superintendent Castello, I'll be there in a few minutes."

He hung up. The two Margots had listened to every word of his conversation.

"I've got to go. Thanks for your help, ladies."

To their great surprise, he immediately turned on his heel and left.

"But . . . don't you want to know?"

He stopped. He already had his hand on the door.

"Know what?"

"The name of the man that was with the lady."

He thought. Just three seconds.

"Another time. It's not as important as I thought."

The responsiveness of the police was astonishing. As soon as he returned, Sebag noticed that the whole headquarters was ready for action. Officers in uniform or in mufti were already fanning out over the city to set up surveillance on telephone booths. With the exception of Raynaud, Moreno, and Llach, who were still under way, the inspectors had come to the meeting room to receive instructions. While Castello was speaking, members of the crime lab staff were equipping Sebag as they had the last time. Gilles hoped that the kidnapper would show some imagination and that he wouldn't send them out to search the neighborhood garbage cans again.

"This time, we're not trying to pretend," Castello explained. "There's no need to put crumpled newspaper in a big sports bag. Since it's a treasure hunt, we'll just play the game, and hope to win. We'll see where that takes us."

Concerned faces were looking at him. Everyone remembered the outcome of the first inning. Castello chose to address the collective anxiety:

"Hoping that it doesn't lead us to another corpse."

But he abstained from giving a name to this corpse. The ring of a telephone resounded in the room. Conversations stopped. People stopped breathing, as well. Castello signaled to Sebag to answer the phone.

"Hello?"

"It's for you," Martine said. "It's the guy who called a little while ago. I'm connecting you."

There was a silence, and then slow, heavy breathing. The superintendent turned on the loudspeaker.

"Hello?" Sebag said again.

"Hello, Inspector."

A muffled whisper.

"Hello, everyone. Is everything ready? Can we begin?"

"Whenever you're ready."

Silence. Breathing.

"Good. The Moulin à vent housing development. A mailbox. You can guess which one."

Another silence. Then the shrill sound of the dial tone. In unison, the inspectors started breathing again at the same time.

Castello roused his troops.

"Is the rendezvous clear to everyone? José Lopez lived in Moulin à vent. We're going to contact his wife immediately."

Castello leaned over to speak into the microphone in front of him.

"Gilles, you're up."

That sentence crackled in Sebag's earphone, and he gave a thumb's up to confirm that the system was working properly. They all stood up immediately.

Sebag drove back up the Boulevard des Pyrénées, then started once again down the Avenue Poincaré. In the Moulin à vent quarter, he found a parking place in front of the building where the Lopez's had lived, almost happily. The young widow was waiting for them in front of the door to the building, holding a white envelope in her hand. The inspector's name was written on it

"I found it in the mailbox a little while ago. It wasn't there this morning. I was going to call you when your superintendent called me."

Sebag tore open the envelope. Hôtel du Sud, Canet. Still the same type face. Still the same economy of expression.

"It's odd. You'd think it was a game," Sylvie Lopez commented. She'd read the message over Sebag's shoulder.

"It is a kind of game, yes. But it isn't fun."

"Are you going to arrest him?"

Sebag noticed the doubt in the young woman's voice.

"It's just a matter of time."

"And you're going to save her?"

"I hope so."

She nodded, pensively.

"I hope so, too. It's strange, I should probably be angry with her. But I have the feeling that if she dies, it will be as if José died a second time. Do you understand?"

Sebag thought of his own situation. He now knew that Claire had a lover, but he felt no resentment. All he felt was pain.

"Yes, I understand."

"What the hell are you doing?" Castello interrupted, through the earphone. "We have other things to do."

Sebag said good-bye to Sylvie Lopez and got back in his car. He headed for Canet and the hotel where he'd stopped a few hours earlier. On the way, Castello brought him up to date on the latest information.

"We know that the kidnapper is calling us from a cell phone. We have the number, and we're looking for the owner. But I'm continuing the surveillance of the phone booths; you can never tell. Raynaud and Moreno have just returned to headquarters. I'm going to send them to Moulin à vent to question the neighbors. People don't put envelopes in mailboxes in the middle of the afternoon every day, and somebody might have noticed."

Sebag put his rotating light on the roof of his car and drove at high speed down the four-lane road that connected Perpignan with Canet. The Hôtel du Sud looked out on the sea, and was separated from the beach only by the street. He parked in front of it. He unfolded the sun-shade on the back of which the word "POLICE" appeared in capital letters. He locked the car and went into the coolness of the lobby.

The employee at the reception desk recognized him.

"You seem to like our hotel," he said.

"It's all right. But I've got a meeting here. I don't suppose you have a message for me? Inspector Sebag."

"Not so far as I know. Ask my colleague."

The young woman he pointed to was on the telephone. He listened to what she was saying.

"I'm sorry, but we don't have a guest by that name, you must be mistaken . . . What do you mean, in the lobby? But . . . "

Sebag handed her his business card and took the receiver out of her hands.

"Hello?"

The same heavy breathing.

"You aren't too warm this time?"

"No, thanks for asking. The hotel is air-conditioned. It's better than the telephone booth at the campground."

"I think I'm treating you too kindly."

"If you say so . . . "

He sensed that at the other end of the line the kidnapper was dying to continue the conversation. He was the one who had designated him as his main contact. He must have had his reasons. Sebag decided to ask him the question directly.

"Why me?"

" . . . "

"Why did you choose me? Do we know each other?"

Sebag had the impression that the man began breathing faster.

Imperceptibly.

"Not really."

"Then why?"

"Because I think you're a good cop."

"What makes you say that?"

"An impression. Am I wrong?"

"It's not for me to say."

"I have to admit that at one point I had my doubts. But you reassured me."

"When?"

"When you solved the murder in Argelès. That was good."

"I also understood about the attack on Avenue Poincaré."

Silence. This time, Sebag was sure: he was breathing faster.

"Do you think it was committed by a third party?"

Sebag discerned a certain disappointment in the whisper.

"No. It was you who attacked Anneke Verbrucke. But you did it only to put us on the wrong track."

The breathing seemed to stop. The kidnapper must have taken the receiver away from his mouth.

"Are you still there?" Sebag joked.

The breathing resumed.

"I wasn't mistaken. The game is interesting."

Sebag decided to pursue his counter-attack. He was tired of being on the defensive.

"We're going to arrest you, you know."

"That's possible. That's part of the game."

"You'll spend the rest of your life in prison."

"That would surprise me."

"You've already lost."

"You're very presumptuous."

"If we find Ingrid's body, I promise you that we'll never quit. I won't leave you any peace."

"The time for peace will come soon. I can't lose."

"Now it's your turn to be presumptuous."

"I don't think so."

"Why?"

"Because that depends on the goal of the game. And I'm the one who determines the goal and the rules. I alone. I can't lose, but you can win all the same."

The kidnapper paused, then said one last thing before he hung up. Something that made a shiver run down Sebag's back. And certainly down the backs of all the policemen who were listening to their conversation. Castello was the first to recover.

"He said the parking lot at Força Real. We're all going. We'll meet up there."

Sebag rushed out of the hotel and jumped into his car. Starting the engine, he put the transmission in first gear but stalled as he tried to pull away. Instead of restarting, he got out of the car.

He crossed the street and went over to the beach. He was beginning to understand something.

The telephone at the hotel had rung as soon as Sebag crossed the threshold. However, no precise time had been set for the rendezvous. It couldn't have been accidental. The kidnapper was there. Somewhere. Very nearby.

When Sebag arrived, the kidnapper had seen him get out of the car and go into the hotel. It was only then that he'd dialed the hotel's number.

"Goddamn it," Sebag swore out loud, causing two ladies sitting on a bench in the shade of a palm tree to jump. He was there and I didn't see him!

He spoke to the two women.

"Did you see a man make a telephone call here a few minutes ago—about forty, tall, slender, with light brown hair?"

The women looked at each other. They seemed to be hesitating as to whether they should answer this strange and rude individual.

"No. We're sorry. We were talking. We paid no attention."

He looked out over the beach one last time. He couldn't help thinking that the kidnapper was still there and was smiling as he observed him. He got back into his car and set out for Força Real. On the way, Castello informed him that he had just learned that the cell phone the kidnapper had used belonged to Lopez.

Just as he was leaving Millas and was starting up the switchbacks that led to the hermitage, his telephone rang. It was Léo.

"Hello, son. How's it going?"

"Fine. How about you?"

"Work. Routine."

"You're not too bored, being all alone?"

So much concern was concealing something. Gilles was aware of that, but the call still pleased him.

"No, not at all. I've begun to rather like it. Freedom, you know, no limits. And you, are you still having as much fun?"

"More and more. Yesterday, we had an all-day outing. On the bike from eleven in the morning until seven in the evening."

A car from the gendarmerie passed him at high speed. Its tires squealed on the turn. To keep the conversation from bogging down, Gilles helped out his son.

"Did you have something you wanted to ask me?"

"No, no. I was calling just to see how you were doing . . . But, well, since you mention it, I've got a great buddy here, he's from Toulon. His parents have a yacht on the Côte d'Azur. They've offered to take me along for a couple of days this summer . . . if you're willing to let me go."

Sebag tried to avoid making a decision.

"We'll have to ask your mother."

"I already did. I called her on the phone."

The first rule for obtaining parental authorization is to start with the more flexible parent. Léo was clever, and had perfected his technique.

"And your mother said she had no objection if I agreed . . . "

"Right, papa. You know what? You should have been a cop."

Gilles didn't like his son to use that word. He wasn't so clever after all, this son of his; he'd violated the second rule: don't rub your father the wrong way, especially if he was reluctant from the start.

"So?" Léo timidly asked, concerned about his father's silence, which he feared was hostile.

"I promise you to think about it, but for the moment I've got work to do. Can you call me again tomorrow?"

"Okay, papa. Talk to you tomorrow."

"Bye, Léo. Love you."

Gilles wasn't unhappy with himself. Not only had he not yielded immediately, but he had forced his son to call him the next day.

He parked his car in the lot below the hermitage. What were they going to find this time? On the way from Canet, he'd avoided asking himself that question, but when he saw the grim faces of his colleagues, he understood that they were fearing the worst as well. That was also why he'd taken the call from Léo. A breath of life before the horror.

As it had been the preceding week, the parking lot was full of cars, the dark blue of the gendarmerie's vehicles harmonizing with the white of those belonging to the national police. The collaboration between the two branches could perhaps be seen in this color compatibility, Sebag said to himself, while noting that the red of a big station wagon disturbed the pattern. As they had the preceding week, the gendarmes fanned out over the area, kicking up tufts of dry grass looking for earth that had recently been dug up. Sebag felt like he was watching a flashback. He recalled a movie he'd seen a few years earlier. *Groundhog Day*, that was the title of this film, in which the hero was forced to relive the same events, over and over. But it was certainly not Lopez's corpse wrapped in a plastic bag that they were going to find today.

Castello came up to him.

"For the moment, we haven't seen anything. The other day, he said 'in the shade of the hermitage.' Am I wrong, or has he failed to give us any clue this time?"

Sebag tried to recall the kidnapper's last sentence, the words that had made a shiver run down his back.

"He said: 'Last stage, for today,' didn't he?

"Preciscly."

"And you didn't notice anything in the rest of the conversation, either?"

"No. I listened to it again several times on the way here with Lefèvre, and we didn't notice anything in particular."

"Can we listen to it in your car?" Sebag asked.

"Of course. Come on."

Castello led him to his car. Lefèvre was leaning against it. The superintendent opened the driver's side door. He picked up the radio microphone and asked that the tape be replayed for him.

"Put the headset on—you'll hear better."

Sebag sat down. It was warm inside the car. He put on the headset and listened attentively to the recording.

"Well?" Lefèvre asked when he got out of the car.

"I didn't notice anything in particular. I have to say that I didn't let him run the conversation."

"I thought you did pretty well," the young Parisian cop said. "You brought him down a peg or two."

Castello seemed delighted by this thaw in the two men's relations. Sebag, for his part, appeared not to have heard the compliment.

"It's odd that he didn't give us a clue. I thought he liked to play."

"Maybe there's a clue that we're not seeing," Lefèvre suggested.

"If there is, it's well hidden," Castello groaned.

"Or it's so obvious that we don't see it," Lefèvre said.

Sebag thought out loud.

"If there is a clue, it can only be in the last sentence. However, all he said was: 'The parking lot at Força Real, last stage, for today.'"

He repeated the sentence slowly, as if to himself.

"'For today . . . ' I think that's rather reassuring: the game isn't over."

The gendarmes were still searching the area around the hermitage. One of them suddenly looked up and called to one of his colleagues. The other man quickly came up to him. He took a packet of cigarettes out of his pocket and threw it to him. Sebag went back to his thoughts.

"The parking lot at Força Real . . . "

His eyes swept over the parking lot and stopped at the red splotch made by the station wagon. Then he recalled the testimony Molina had taken right there a few days earlier. An ornithologist had told him he'd seen a big red station wagon several times.

"I thought that car belonged to tourists or hikers," Castello said. He'd seen what Sebag was looking at.

"That's what I thought, too," said Lefèvre.

"He's clever," the inspector commented. "He knew that we'd be obsessed by the idea of finding a body buried up here, and that it would take us a while to see what should have jumped out at us immediately."

As they talked, the three men had approached the car. It was a big Volvo station wagon.

Castello called an officer over. He asked him to send the car's license number to headquarters.

"I want an answer within one minute," he ordered.

Lefèvre was walking around the car. He stopped in front of the driver's window.

"It looks like it was started without a key," he said excitedly, pointing to wires that were hanging down under the steering wheel.

He continued to inspect the car. He pressed his head against the back window. Sebag saw him shudder.

"There's a tarp hiding something . . . "

Castello approached, but the inspector preferred to keep his distance. He'd thought he saw a vague form under the covering and nausea was already roiling his stomach. He saw again in his mind's eye the photos of Ingrid Raven. The young woman's perfect body. Her shining eyes and her smile full of life.

The officer soon came back.

"The vehicle belongs to a certain Didier Coll, who lives in La Fusterie Street in Perpignan. It was reported stolen last Thursday."

Castello gave the signal. The police officers began to examine the vehicle's body. They noted a few dents, but they all seemed to have been made long ago. They took fingerprints off the door handles, and then took samples of earth from the wheels and the underside of the car.

Then it was time to open the trunk.

Wearing gloves, Jean Pagès pushed on the latch. It offered no resistance and the trunk slowly opened. The head of the crime lab waited for his co-worker to take a few photographs and then caught hold of the tarp. He drew a deep breath and slowly pulled. Instinctively, the policemen crowded around the

318 · PHILIPPE GEORGET

trunk of the car. Castello had to remind his men to observe a minimum of decency.

The tarp slipped off. They all held their breaths.

The trunk contained nothing but a few women's clothes.

And a large cushion to deceive them.

CHAPTER 31

Sebag slept very badly.

He'd gotten home late. Tired and frazzled by the day's tension. It had been a warm night; at midnight it was still 80 degrees outside, without a breath of wind.

The dark aroused pain and doubts. Up to that point, he'd succeeded in not thinking about what the two Margots had told him. But it had remained hidden in his mind like arthritis in an old body.

Claire had a lover.

His reaction had surprised the two Margots. He hadn't wanted to know more. Why? He was still asking himself the same question.

He'd taken this revelation as if it had been an inevitable fact: it had to happen sooner or later. When he'd realized one day that Claire could dream about other men, he'd already felt betrayed. Don't we give ourselves away as much in our dreams as in our acts?

Where did adultery begin? It wasn't a new debate. There were several possible answers to the question. He had to find his own.

He woke up repeatedly, sweating heavily. Since summer had really set in, the walls of the house no longer remained cool. Toward three in the morning, he finally got up and did a couple of laps in the pool. He swam under the water to avoid making noise. Then he went back to bed, all wet.

Dawn woke him out of his agitated dreams long before six o'clock.

Even though he'd had a bad night, he went for a run anyway. But he limited himself to jogging for half an hour. Keep exercising without increasing fatigue.

To drive his professional and conjugal preoccupations out of his mind, he tried to think about Léo. What was he going to tell him when he called back to ask again about sailing on the Côte d'Azur with his friend's parents? He didn't want to let him leave in August, but he had no valid reason to refuse. He couldn't say to his son: "No, you can't go to your pal's home because your father wants to keep you close to him. Keep you for himself."

He took advantage of the time on his hands to do a little housework. He ran the vacuum cleaner around the kitchen and living room and mopped the floor. The dust on the furniture could wait a little while longer. Before leaving, he started a load of laundry that he would take out when he got home that evening. If he wanted to wear decent-looking shirts, he would also have to do some ironing. A real chore with heat like this.

He got to headquarters long before Molina. From home, he'd called the Revels, the artist couple in Collioure, to ask them to stop by and identify the clothing found in the car. They'd promised to come early.

Sebag brought the clothes to his office. They had been put separately into transparent plastic bags. There was a pair of sky-blue pirate pants and a pink tunic with half-length sleeves whose opening in front could be adjusted by a series of small straps. There was also a pair of sandals with pink and green laces that crossed under a white flower. In the absence of a label, it was not clear where the shoes came from, but the clothes had been bought in France. The tunic and the pants had been washed before being left in the car, and no fingerprints could be taken from them. Nothing indicated that they belonged to Ingrid Raven.

Molina suddenly appeared behind Sebag.

"He sure fooled us, the bastard! I really thought the girl's body was in that trunk."

"Everybody thought that," Sebag said. "He'd foreseen our reactions and knew how to play on our nerves."

"It's terrible to say it, but I was almost disappointed not to find a corpse in the car."

Sebag did not comment, but at the time he'd shared this disagreeable feeling of frustration. Relief had come only later in the evening. It was followed by a furious desire to get this over with, to arrest the guy before it was too late.

Someone knocked twice on the door.

"Come in!" Molina shouted.

An officer in uniform appeared on the threshold.

"Mr. and Mrs. Revel are here. They have an appointment, I think."

Molina had the couple come in. Sebag put the clothes on his desk. Before asking the question, he already knew the answer. He'd seen Martine Revel's glance and the trembling of her lips that followed it.

"Do you recognize these clothes?"

"Has something happened to Ingrid?" she asked instead of replying.

"So far as we know, she is still alive."

"We've heard about the cab driver," Gérard Revel said. "That is . . . We read in the newspaper about his murder and we made the connection with Ingrid. Are you sure she's alive?"

"In this case, we're not sure about anything," Molina admitted. "But right now there's no reason to think that her kidnapper has killed her."

The Revels didn't look convinced. Sebag pointed to the clothes on his desk.

"I need an official response, Mrs. Revel. Did these clothes belong to Ingrid?"

"Yes. She was wearing them the day I met her at the museum in Céret. The tunic suited her well. It showed off the whiteness of her skin."

"Are you certain about that?"

"As certain as one can be," she said, annoyed. "These are not the only clothes of this kind, I suppose. Let's say that she had clothes just like these."

Sebag quickly typed out the report and had them sign it.

"Is that all?" the Revels said as they reluctantly rose to their feet.

"That's all, yes."

"Are you going to find her?" the woman asked.

"I'm sure we will," Sebag said as firmly as possible.

The Revels were satisfied by that answer and left the office, not without adding that the police could contact them at any time, day or night, if they needed any further information.

"They're afraid they're partly responsible," Sebag noted after their departure. "That's normal. They feel like they handed her over to the wolves."

Molina nodded pensively.

"You mean that if Martine hadn't been so stuck up and refused the threesome, none of this would have happened?"

"Who can say? Maybe she would have had her throat cut a few days later in the streets of Amsterdam as she came out of a movie theater."

"Yeah. I'm going down to drink some coffee. Do you want something?"

Sebag declined the offer and called Pagès's office to find out if he'd finished examining the red station wagon. The telephone rang but no one answered.

For the moment, the previous day's treasure hunt had not advanced the investigation. The kidnapper had led them to a car. There must be a clue. The clothes? For Sebag, they were more in the nature of a proof. In case the police had difficulty making the connection between this abandoned vehicle and the kidnapping of Ingrid. But there must be something else.

On the telephone the day before, Sebag had laid his cards on the table, and the situation was now clear for everyone: the smokescreens had been dissipated. Sebag and the kidnapper were now face to face. The game was under way. The life of a young woman was at stake.

They couldn't make any mistakes.

Sebag's cell phone vibrated. It was Léo calling to learn his father's decision.

"Have you thought about what I asked yesterday, Papa?"

"Yes, a bit."

"And?"

"I'm not very enthusiastic . . . but I'm not opposed to it."

"Great . . . "

"On one condition."

"What?"

"I want to meet your pal's parents."

"Okay, fine, that shouldn't be any problem. But why?"

"To get to know them. And thank them, that's the least I can do. I'll come get you as planned at the end of your stay there, and I'll drive you to Toulon myself. Is that all right?"

"Why not . . . "

"You talk to your friend, he talks to his parents, and then you call me, okay?"

"Okay, fine."

Jacques returned to the office. Holding a cup of coffee in one hand and a bag of candies in the other, and with Ménard right behind him.

"Apart from that, is there anything new, son?" Sebag continued.

"No. We're going swimming in a lake this afternoon."

"That will be a change for you."

"We'll also be doing some jet-skiing."

"I wondered about that . . . Okay, good, I've got to let you go. Take care of yourself, son. See you soon."

Ménard's face looked tired, his complexion waxy. Sebag understood that he wasn't the only one who'd slept badly. He also realized that his colleague was supposed to have left on vacation at the beginning of the week. Castello had certainly asked him to delay his vacation. Unless Ménard himself had offered to stay another week. The old bugger was very capable of that.

Vacation . . . In any case, his had been put in jeopardy.

Molina and Ménard were pursuing a conversation that had probably begun in the cafeteria.

"Well?" Jacques asked. "Was your guy glad to get his car back?"

Ménard had just met with the owner of the stolen station wagon.

"He didn't seem euphoric. It was an old car and he had very good insurance on it, he told me."

He took out his notebook and started to summarize his notes for them.

"Didier Coll bought the car about ten years ago from his mother, who was too old to drive that big wagon. Coll lives and works downtown. So he uses the car very little. He noticed that the car was gone last Thursday about eight in the morning, when he was getting ready to leave for a long weekend. It wasn't where he'd left it. At first he was afraid that it had been towed away—he often parks in streets with alternate-side parking, and he'd already forgotten more than once the days when you're supposed to change sides—but after he looked into it, he came to headquarters to file a complaint."

"The theft could have taken place long before last Thursday," Molina noted.

"Right. Coll hadn't touched his car for more than two weeks. Since June 24, to be exact."

"So it could have been used on the first day of the kidnapping?"

"It's possible."

Sebag was mulling over his dark thoughts. He heard the discussion vaguely, but without being able to take an interest in it. Ménard spoke to him:

"By the way, Gilles, why didn't you tell me that you knew the owner of the car?"

Sebag jumped. He stared at his colleague, astonished.

"I know him? What did you say his name was?"

"Didier Coll."

"Didier Coll . . . Coll, Didier. The name means nothing to me. Are you sure I know him?"

"That's what he told me."

"He did?"

"He asked me to give you his greetings, in fact."

"Thanks. That's nice. But his name really doesn't mean anything to me."

His cell phone rang again.

"Hi there, it's me." Claire sounded cheerful and affectionate.

"Uh . . . Hello."

"Am I disturbing you?"

"Yes, a little. It's complicated just now at work."

Claire's voice became coaxing. And slightly mocking.

"My poor darling! And you don't have five little minutes to spare that you can devote to the woman of your life?"

Gilles didn't have the heart to pretend. But this was neither the time nor the place to unload all he had on his chest. And then there were too many witnesses.

"No, not for the moment."

Sebag's cold tone dampened Claire's spirits.

"The problem is that I'm calling you from a telephone booth in Palma de Mallorca and I don't know if I'll be able to call back later."

It would have been so much easier if she'd taken her cell phone, Sebag thought irritably. She had so much wanted to be left alone . . . He felt his anger rising.

"Try this evening if you're still on land. Or send me an e-mail. You can also call me from the boat; it can't be that expensive. But right now, I really can't talk."

"Okay, too bad," Claire said, put out. "Talk to you later. I love you."

"Me too. Later."

Sebag turned off his cell phone and put it on the table. Looking up, his eyes met Molina's for a moment. His colleague hadn't missed a word of the whole conversation, even though he'd been trying to pay attention to what Ménard was saying to him.

"All right, what's next?" Sebag asked with annoyance.

"We have a meeting with the boss at two P.M.," Ménard answered.

Molina glanced at his watch.

"Great, we have time to eat, then. The Carlit has *cargolade* at noon today. You coming with me?"

Jean Pagès, the head of the crime lab, spoke first at the afternoon meeting. He made no effort to hide his irritation.

"One thing is sure: we haven't found in this car what the kidnapper wanted us to find there."

The last investigation of his career was giving him a hard time.

"We went over the car with a fine-toothed comb. It was spotless, without any trace of dust on the dashboard, or even dirt on the pedals. And yet, we were able to find the fingerprints of the owner, José Lopez, on the driver's side and especially on the inside door handle on the passenger side. In the trunk, there were a few dried stains: mud completely identical with that we found in Lopez's lungs and on his clothes."

When he spoke, two furrows danced between his eyebrows.

Jean Pagès had retained his youthful figure. He was short and thin, all skin and bone. Only the deep wrinkles on his face betrayed his age. He was supposed to have retired two or three years ago.

"In the trunk, we found a hair—just one!—a blond hair. The DNA analysis is under way but the length and the color of this hair suggest that it belongs to Ingrid Raven. There was also earth stuck to the tires. A heavy, chalky soil, the kind found all over this region. We also found three pink chunks of gravel, pink, very common, stuck in the treads. They could provide us with evidence once we have a suspect, but they're not enough to help us locate the site where Ingrid is being held. That's it, that's all I can tell you."

Pagès's presentation was over, and the inspectors had no questions. Their faces were grim and tired. This case was beginning to obsess them. Concerned that discouragement might set in, Castello spoke up.

"We are moving ahead. Slowly, but we're moving ahead. The identikit portrait of the kidnapper is being confirmed if not made more precise. Raynaud and Moreno have gathered information in the Moulin à vent area. One of the Lopez's neighbors—a retiree who does . . . what do you call that?"

"Sudoku," Moreno said.

"That's right. In any case, this retiree was sitting in his loggia when he noticed an individual handing out leaflets late in the afternoon. Surprised that this individual went into only one stairway, he followed the suspect with his eyes for a few moments until he disappeared behind a group of buildings. He didn't see him get into a car, but his description of the individual matches in every respect the one we already had: a tall, slender man in his forties. He couldn't say what color the man's hair was because he was wearing a cap."

The superintendent saw that he had not aroused even a glimmer of interest among his men.

"Probably more interesting, Llach and Lambert called in Pascal Daniel this morning. The name no doubt means nothing to you, but he is the ornithologist that Molina met a few days ago—I don't know if you all remember that detail of the investigation. Daniel's favorite bird-watching point is not very far from the hermitage, and he told us that on several occasions he saw a big red station wagon in the parking lot at Força Real. This morning, he said he was sure he recognized the Volvo."

Sebag saw Lefèvre squirming on his chair. Their eyes met and they understood each other. Although all the clues fit together ideally, they didn't allow the investigation to advance. Molina was also on the same wave length. Faithful to the role that everyone expected him to play, he put it bluntly and plainly.

"To make a long story short, Superintendent, and with all due respect, we have our asses in a sling."

"You can choose your own expressions," Castello said with annoyance, "but we mustn't forget that we are also working for what follows: we're accumulating facts so that we can construct a solid indictment when we finally have a suspect . . . "

"*If* we finally have one."

"Please, let's not scoff. We're doing all we can. If you have an idea as to how we can advance the investigation, tell us about it."

A cold silence followed these words. Superintendent Castello took the time to look at each of his inspectors, one after the other. They avoided his eyes. After long seconds, Ménard broke the silence.

"A red Volvo station wagon is not inconspicuous. We should launch a neighborhood investigation."

"Which neighborhood? That's the problem!" Llach remarked.

"We can begin with the streets where Coll parked his car." Castello approved.

"That's a good idea, François. We'll also ask the gendarmes to gather information."

The atmosphere was warming. But Moreno suddenly cooled it down with his cavernous voice.

"Who says Ingrid Raven is still alive?" he asked.

Sebag felt a shiver run down his spine.

"After all, Lopez freed up a place in the freezer," Molina breathed.

Lambert tried to suppress a nervous laugh. Llach elbowed him in the ribs, which had the effect of making the laugh escape from him in a series of childish squeaks. Sebag decided to speak up.

"In my opinion, Ingrid is alive . . . If not . . . "

He hesitated and then smiled.

"If not, as the kids say: 'it's not a game.'"

Lefèvre nodded gravely and then asked:

"Do you still think the kidnapper is playing with us?"

"If I still had any doubts, today would have completely dispelled them. He played marvelously well on our nerves, don't you think?"

"That's clear," the young superintendent agreed.

"The game can amuse the kidnapper only if we have a real chance of winning," Sebag explained.

"In Lopez's case, he didn't give us a chance," Moreno persisted.

"That has nothing to do with it. Lopez wasn't part of the game. He got in his way, and so he immediately disposed of him."

"I hope you're right," Lefèvre said. "I had the Dutch police on the line a little while ago. Mrs. Raven was hospitalized yesterday. She's no longer eating and hasn't slept for two weeks. The waiting has gone on too long for her."

"For us, too," Castello concluded, "for us, too."

CHAPTER 32

He was disappointed.

He'd received a visit from a policeman with a sad face who had asked him banal questions. Inspector Sebag had not come.

No one suspected him yet.

It wasn't funny.

Perhaps he'd overestimated the policemen's abilities? Or maybe he hadn't given them enough signs? In a game, the hardest part was finding the right balance. It reminded him of the crossword puzzles he'd invented when he was a teenager. He'd always found it difficult to gauge the difficulty of the puzzles that rose out of his knowledge and his imagination. And even though he constructed one after another, he didn't feel that he was making progress.

If only someone had tried at least once to solve them!

Today, he had a partner. But no rehearsal had been possible. And there would be no second attempt.

They were entering the home stretch. He had to be doubly prudent. He must never come to this house directly. The police mustn't discover its existence too quickly.

Ingrid was becoming more submissive every day, and he continued to reward her. A table, a lamp, a book, a chair. She'd asked for paper and pen. He was considering satisfying that desire in the near future.

The young woman's behavior never ceased to surprise him. He wondered what he would do in such a situation. But he'd never undergo the same fate. He wouldn't be a captive. He wouldn't even go to prison.

Never.

He was finding it increasingly difficult to control his desire. That annoyed him. The young woman's body haunted his mind day and night. It was his cross, his burden. His punishment. This suffering would end only when the game was over.

He mustn't touch this body. He didn't have the right. It was one of the rules. He had set it at the beginning. When he still thought he didn't like women.

He didn't love anybody.

And nobody loved him.

Perhaps his mother loved him. No! In fact, she had loved the boy she believed he was. The boy she wanted him to be. She'd always refused to accept the truth.

He'd tried to act as if he were that boy. Then he'd tried to make her understand. No use. She fled from reality. And when her husband left, she didn't want to hear about it. She'd believed what the policemen told her.

What he'd succeeded in making them believe.

Already at that time, he'd been the stronger.

The game was coming to its end. He mustn't sink into the sordid. He wouldn't touch this body. Otherwise people would no longer see the beauty of this gratuitous game. That's all they would remember.

People were so nasty.

CHAPTER 33

Gilles Sebag printed out all the documents in the Raven file, from Sylvie Lopez's deposition three weeks earlier to Ménard's account of his conversation with the owner of the Volvo. The file was available in digital form on each computer, but Sebag, to feel comfortable, felt the need to have contact with the paper.

He hoped that light would emerge from all these pages blackened with information.

Molina, who was rather late, made his entrance into the office. He threw his jacket on his chair and sat down at his desk. He turned on his PC and finally consented to stop gritting his teeth.

"Damn it," he said before explaining himself. "I'm looking for things for my sons to do. They're arriving this weekend to spend two weeks with me. I was supposed to go on vacation next Friday, but I don't believe Castello will let me leave."

He started tapping on his keyboard.

"Do you have any ideas about what your sons can do?"

"I just had one, yeah. I went to see a pal who runs a riding club. He's willing to take them for at least a few days. They'll give him a hand with grooming the horses, feeding them, changing the straw in their stalls. In exchange, he'll let them go for some rides."

"Good plan!"

"Yeah, I think they might like that."

"In any case, I notice that you're not exactly optimistic regarding the further course of our investigation."

"Why? Are you optimistic?"

"Not especially, but I'm trying to keep in mind that in every investigation there are times when nothing is happening and times when things move very fast."

"Maybe. In this case I think we are more likely to stop dead than to get a ticket for speeding."

"That's clear."

Molina started reading his e-mail. Sebag bent over his keyboard. While it was all still fresh in his memory, he wanted to compose a more or less coherent account of the whole case.

He began writing.

"Ingrid Raven and José Lopez disappear on the night of June 26, when they go to the Força Real parking lot to see a mysterious customer who has asked them to come there. The customer, BW, has paid two thousand euros in advance for the services of the young woman, who is preparing to start a career as a call-girl. Ingrid and José leave the taxi near the hermitage and get into the customer's vehicle. Maybe the Volvo station wagon. Once they are at his place, the kidnapper—at this point in the story, he's beginning to deserve that name—has Lopez drink the beer containing a powerful sedative.

"The kidnapper, who owns an isolated house surrounded by extensive grounds including a lake or pond and a pink gravel driveway, imprisons Ingrid in a room or cellar. He drags the cab driver as far as the pond, where he holds his head under water. Lopez struggles but not enough to save his skin. The kidnapper—who is now also a murderer—puts the corpse in a freezer.

"What does he do next? He attends to his prisoner and waits until the police begin to take an interest in the two people who have disappeared. During this period, he lives normally, going to work as usual. One day, he hears people talking about the murder in Argelès. Then it occurs to him that he can use the nationality of the two women to put the police on the wrong track. He writes the first ransom letter in the name of the Moluccan Front.

"During the night of July 4, he puts an anonymous letter in the mailbox at police headquarters. Then he goes to the Deux Margots bar. Sitting near a table where a group of young people are talking, he notices a young woman's foreign accent. He immediately identifies it. She's a Dutch girl, like Ingrid. When the young people leave the bar, he plans to follow them. In the meantime, he slips out for a few minutes to call police headquarters to be sure that they will find his letter that very night.

"The Dutch girl leaves her friends and goes off on her own. A lucky break for our man. He follows her, waiting for a favorable moment, and pins her against a car. He simulates a failed attempt at kidnapping and disappears. But before he does, he takes on the sharpened point of his knife a drop of the young woman's blood that he will use for his second letter. After having caused the police to focus their investigation on international terrorism, he tries to make them adopt the hypothesis of a serial criminal. He hopes to lead them into utter confusion. And he succeeds in doing so."

Sebag stopped writing. Certain things didn't fit very well. The kidnapper sometimes proved clever in misleading them—the drop of blood, for example—at other times he sent grotesque ransom letters. It was a cat and mouse game. With a cat who constantly hesitated regarding the degree of freedom to be accorded to his victim.

He returned to his narrative.

"On July 9, the kidnapper leads the police on a treasure hunt to Perpignan and Argelès. He persists in wanting to make them believe in the existence of a serial criminal, and at the conclusion of the hunt provides a token of his seriousness and determination.

"On July 17, a second treasure hunt. Informed—probably by the press—that the murder of Josetta Braun has been solved, the kidnapper, after dropping the far-fetched terrorist demands, also abandons the false lead of the serial criminal. In the new itinerary he imposes on the police, the stages are all connected with Ingrid Raven and José Lopez. Playing on the investigators' nerves, he does everything he can to make them think they're going to find a corpse, but gives them only a car. A Volvo that was used to transport José Lopez's cadaver, and in which he has deposited clothing belonging to his prisoner."

Again, Sebag hesitated. He looked up. Watched for a moment Molina reading his e-mail. Then he bent over his keyboard again to write in boldface letters a few questions that remained unanswered.

"Why the car? Why abandon it just then? What is the message?"

Then he reread what he'd written, corrected a few errors, erased the words "probably" and "maybe." What he'd worked out wasn't the truth, but it must come close to it. He checked to be sure he'd saved the text before sending it to his colleagues, asking them to point out any incoherencies.

"I've just sent you an e-mail. Can you have a look at it?"

"Okay, no problem," Molina mumbled without taking his eyes off his screen.

"I'm going to drink a cup of coffee across the street."

"Fine. I'll stay here and hold down the fort."

"*Com vas?*" ("How are you?")

"*Be, gracies. I tu?*" ("Fine, thanks. And you?")

"*Comme sempre. Vols un cafè?*" ("As usual. You want a coffee?")

"*Amb molt de gust.*" ("Love one.")

Rafel Puig disappeared long enough to make the drink Sebag had ordered. Emanations of garlic were already mixing with the perfumes of hops and anise. Sebag didn't need to look at the clock. He knew that noon was approaching.

He drank his coffee rapidly, put two coins on the bar, and returned to police headquarters. The short break he'd allowed himself had not refreshed his mind. The sentences he'd written that morning continued to get tangled up in his head.

"You've come at the right time. I was just going to go eat," Molina said when he came into the office. "I wanted to leave a note for you. As I was talking with Ménard a minute ago, I made the connection. You remember, Didier Coll, the owner of the Volvo? Who claimed he knew you?"

Standing in front of his desk, Sebag moved his mouse to wake up his computer.

"Yes, but that still doesn't mean anything to me," he said distractedly.

The sound of a diesel engine made Sebag's office shake. A white flash crossed the computer's screen. Colors gradually appeared, creating the image of two smiling children.

"And yet you do know him. Didier Coll, the famous owner of the Volvo station wagon found on the parking lot at Força Real knows you, and you know him, too. Didier Coll is . . . Barry White . . . "

Sebag's eyes moved away from the screen and settled on his colleague. He frowned.

"What's all this about Barry White?"

Molina's voice descended a few tones below its normal timbre.

"You don't remember me, Mr. Sebag? The other day, I needed a top-flight cop for my old junker."

Sebag bit his lip.

"Don't tell me . . . "

"Yes!"

"Oh, shit!"

"You can say that again!"

"That guy's car was the Volvo station wagon . . . "

"Bravo, Mr. Top-flight cop," Molina laughed. "Good reasoning. A little late, though."

Sebag suddenly got up and started walking up and down the office. He was thinking about what could have changed if he'd agreed to deal with this theft as soon as the owner came to seek him out.

"Don't fret," Molina said. "That wouldn't have helped us advance more quickly. You couldn't have known that that car was used for Ingrid's kidnapping."

"You're probably right. All the same . . . It doesn't look good."

"I find it pretty funny."

"I can see that. You'll excuse me for not sharing your gaiety."

"No problem. I promise I'll be as quiet as a tomb. Nobody will know about this. Except me."

"That's already too many," Sebag said, aware that his colleague would probably regularly remind him of his blunder. For the next twenty years at least.

Sebag had planned to take advantage of the noon break to do some errands at a shopping center. His fridge was empty. Claire was coming home in three days.

He left Molina, who still hadn't gone to eat lunch. His ex-wife had called him and they'd gotten into a tense discussion. Since their divorce, they'd never been able to talk with each other in a friendly way.

"What a pity," Sebag moaned, "never that."

In the reception area, two women were waiting on a bench. There was no one in front of the desk. Martine was taking the opportunity to watch television. When he saw her, Sebag stopped short. In his mind's eye, he saw himself again in the same place a few days earlier: himself, Martine, and . . . Barry White.

He had the feeling that he was close to something essential.

"Have you forgotten something, Mr. Sebag?" Martine asked.

"No, no . . . "

He dug into his pants pocket and pulled out his keys.

"I've got my car keys after all, it's okay. Have a good lunch, Martine."

"You too, sir."

His car was roasting in the sun. He turned on the fan for a few minutes before starting the air conditioning. Then he switched on the radio. He took Arago Bridge and headed north. The radio station was playing an old American hit from the 1970s. Barry White.

Life certainly produced some astonishing coincidences. Today, it was Barry White. He didn't remember the title of the song. But he was sure he'd heard it recently.

He was bothered by a piece of white paper on the dashboard that was being reflected on the windshield. It was his shopping list. He stuck it in his pocket.

The last notes of the song were fading away when he felt a new idea being born. Still intangible. Like the glow of a candle flame flickering in the wind at the end of a tunnel. He slowed down.

He felt something. He had to let it come. He emptied his mind of static and let the melody resound.

The answer was there.

In Barry White's warm, deep voice, maybe. Yes, he'd heard this song recently. It was at the Lopez's home! While he was searching the apartment . . .

So he'd found it.

Now what? Where could this discovery take him?

This time, he decided to pull over. He slowed down and stopped the car on the shoulder.

In the tunnel of his thoughts, the light had grown stronger. He could try to move forward. Lopez had a complete set of Barry White in his collection. Sebag had put a CD in the player . . .

It was coming!

It was almost there.

There was a connection between the singer and the kidnapping of Ingrid Raven. No, that was impossible; he was nuts. This case was making his head spin.

And then suddenly . . .

"Shit! Barry White, of course, it's Barry White!"

He looked in the rearview mirror. A truck was coming but he had time. He made a U-turn in front of the truck and roared off. The driver didn't miss the opportunity to honk at him for making such a crazy maneuver.

Sebag double parked in the lot at police headquarters.

"Back already?" Martine said.

Sebag replied with a broad smile.

Martine.

There, too, he understood. Martine . . . on the telephone . . . a voice that was whispering. Without knowing it, she'd found the answer before he did.

Everything was fitting together.

He bounded up the stairs and ran to his office.

Jacques had left. He called his cell phone.

"Where are you?"

"At the Carlit."

"What are you doing?"

"What do you think?"

"Eating?"

"Bravo, champ! You're definitely in top form, Sherlock: it's half-past twelve, I'm in a restaurant, and I'm eating. Or more precisely, I'm about to order. As soon as I've hung up."

"Can I join you?"

"Uh.. sure, if you want."

Sebag noticed his colleague's hesitation.

"Are you alone?"

"No . . . But you can come anyway."

"I need to talk to you alone."

"Okay. As soon as I've finished, I'll be there. Are you at headquarters? You haven't already done your errands, have you?"

"No, I haven't done them yet. I just had an idea Jacques, and I need to talk to you right away."

"What do you mean, right away?"

"Right away means immediately. I have to talk to you, now! And one on one. Please . . . "

"Shit, you're a pain in the ass. What's going on?"

Sebag thought about what he could say. He hesitated. And then to overcome his colleague's resistance he said out loud the sentence he hadn't yet dared utter in his head:

"Jacques, I know who Ingrid Raven's kidnapper is."

Sitting at his desk, Molina was waiting for an explanation. He still smelled like food. Sebag was trying to decide what to say. If his colleague had come so quickly, that was because he had confidence in him. He didn't want to disappoint him, but how could he explain his intuitions?

"It's about Barry White . . . "

"Excuse me?"

He was off to a bad start. Molina was already getting annoyed.

"Let me explain. It's complicated."

"If it's too complicated for me, I can go back and eat, you know. I can handle that."

"Wait! It's . . . You know, your comparison with Barry White. That's what you called Didier Coll, the owner of the Volvo, because he had a deep, serious voice . . . "

"You want to tell me that you liked my joke? I'm touched, but that could have waited until I'd finished eating."

"Please shut up. I don't find your joke funny. I find it brilliant!"

"Uh, there you're going a little too far . . . "

"No, not at all. It's thanks to you that I made the discovery. You're brilliant, pal!"

"Okay, if that's the way you want it, I'm quite willing to be brilliant. But I'm not brilliant all the time, and right now I need you to explain yourself a little more clearly."

"Barry White, he's the kidnapper. The famous BW."

"No, are you kidding? You think he doesn't sell enough albums and he needs money? By the way, did you know he's dead?"

"I'm explaining myself badly. As we thought for a while, the initials BW probably don't correspond to a real name but to a nickname. Barry White, in this case. Lopez was a fan, he had all White's disks in his collection."

"What are you getting at? I'm not sure I understand where you're going, as Ménard would say. You think that Lopez made the same joke as I did and that he nicknamed his mysterious customer Barry White because he had a particularly deep voice? Why not . . . It's an idea we could pursue. The identikit sketch is getting more precise, but that still leaves a lot of suspects."

"No, now there's only one!"

"There is?"

"Yes. Your train of thought followed the same lines as Lopez's, and regarding the same person. Didier Coll . . . He's the kidnapper."

Molina's eyes and mouth became round simultaneously.

"Uh . . . there, you're going a little too fast, aren't you? What's the connection between Coll and Lopez, apart from the car?"

"Barrère! When he came to see me here, Coll gave his name as a reference."

"If it's really him, he's got nerve!"

"You bet he's got nerve. We've known that for a long time. He's seeking us out, provoking us."

He paused. His reasoning was moving forward as he talked.

"And I thought there must be a clue in the car that we'd missed. A red Volvo station wagon, his own car: that was the clue!"

Molina scratched his chin. He was puzzled.

"This Coll is rather tall and slender, even thin," Sebag went on. "He's between forty and fifty years old, has light brown hair, dark eyes. He corresponds to the identikit sketch."

"You were the first one to say that thousands of people correspond to that description."

"That's true, but on the contrary there are also tens of thousands who don't correspond to it. If Coll had been short and fat, I'd have had to revise my hypothesis. But not here. And then there's his voice."

"Barry White . . . "

"Yes . . . His voice is so characteristic that he's forced to whisper on the phone to mask it."

"Anybody making an anonymous telephone call would try to disguise his voice. The kidnapper couldn't have been unaware that we were recording the messages and that we would analyze his voice."

"That's true, you're right, but he also whispered when he was talking with the receptionist at the hotel in Canet."

Sebag sensed that Molina was starting to weaken. He'd kept the best arguments for last.

"Tuesday, when the kidnapper called headquarters for his second treasure hunt, he got Martine, who was on the switchboard. And Martine, who didn't know she was dealing with the kidnapper, at first thought it was Coll trying to get me to look for his car again. That's curious, isn't it? Don't you think that's too many coincidences?"

Molina looked at his colleague. Sweat was beading on his forehead, his cheeks were red, his upper lip was trembling slightly. Sebag had spoken with fervor, and it was as much his passionate tone as his reasoning that was convincing. During the seven years they'd been working together, he'd seen Sebag two or three times in this state of excitement that he would call—were it not for his profound aversion to religious matters—prophetic ecstasy. And each time he'd allowed himself to be possessed by his intuition that way, Sebag had been right all down the line.

Sebag had *la vista*.

"That might hold up, it's true," Molina recognized. "It would also explain why the kidnapper wasn't afraid to use a stolen car for several days. Coll was well placed to know that the owner hadn't filed a complaint right away."

Molina ran his hands through his hair.

"The problem is that we will never convince the prosecutor with that! There aren't enough tangible facts. And that means: no search warrant, no phone taps . . . "

"You think?"

"I know you, and I have confidence in you. But if somebody starts being hyper-critical, believe me, the business with Barry White could look pretty ridiculous."

"Too bad about the prosecutor. In any case, we can't proceed to investigate too overtly. If the guy thinks we've figured him out, he could very quickly call an end to the game."

"Wait . . . I see where you're going. In a few moments, you're going to ask me to work on the quiet, day and night, without overtime pay."

"You're really brilliant, Molina. Barry White, working on the quiet, overtime . . . What intuition! Bravo."

Sebag gave his colleague a big pat on the back.

"I knew I could count on you. How about grabbing a quick pizza?"

CHAPTER 34

B its of pizza were still scattered all over their desks, and a tomato stain adorned Molina's flowered shirt, adding an inappropriate red petal to a white rose. The two men were in the grip of an extreme concentration.

As he ate, Sebag had reread more attentively all the statements Didier Coll had made when Ménard interviewed him the day before. He hadn't learned much; the conversation with the owner of the Volvo had been merely a formality. Coll was a personnel officer in a large company specializing in public works. He was forty-three and lived alone in an apartment in the heart of Perpignan's downtown pedestrian zone. He'd bought the Volvo from his mother when she moved into a retirement home, but he didn't use it much, because he went to work on his scooter. He parked the car rather far from his home, on the few streets downtown that didn't have parking meters. He left it parked there for days, even for weeks, without using it.

Sebag picked up his phone and made a call.

"Hello, Ménard here."

"Hi, it's Gilles."

"How's it going? I read your synthesis at noon. The scenario seems valid. Which doesn't mean that it's the only possible one."

"I agree with you, it's a starting point. Apart from that, I was calling especially about the owner of the Volvo. Didier Coll. I'd like to know precisely what he said to you about me."

"Meaning?"

"Did he tell you that he knew me?"

"Yes."

"And that he'd had dealings with me, professionally?"

"No, he didn't go into detail. He asked me to give you his greetings."

"That's all?"

"Not entirely. He added that you were a good policeman."

"He said that?"

"More or less, yes. I can't guarantee that those were his exact words, but that's what he meant."

Sebag fell silent and thought. If he'd been merely the owner of a stolen car, logically Coll should have complained to Ménard that Sebag had brushed him off a few days earlier. On the contrary, he sent his greetings and praised his qualities as a policeman.

"Were his compliments ironic?"

"No, not at all. Why?"

Sebag didn't answer.

"Does this have something to do with the investigation?" Ménard asked.

"Nothing at all," Sebag lied. "Yesterday I was preoccupied with other things when you came to talk to us about that conversation and I didn't react. It's true that I met the guy, but I'd forgotten. Thanks for the further explanations."

"No problem, Gilles . . . We work as a team, as you know very well."

The last words showed that he hadn't been taken in by the lie. Sebag didn't like playing a solo game, but Ménard was too devoted to the rules to be taken into his confidence.

Sebag opened the Internet phone directory site.

"If Coll is in fact our man," he explained to Molina, "he must have another address. He can't be holding Ingrid in his downtown apartment."

Coll was a fairly common Catalan name, but the directory had only two listings with the first name Didier. The first was on La Fusterie Street, the second in the Les Fenouillèdes area. Sebag felt his pulse speed up.

"I might have something. In Fenouillèdes. I'll call the mayor's office right now."

However, the lead he was hoping he'd found didn't pan out.

"No dice," he said as he hung up. "According to the records in the mayor's office, that Coll is a wine grower. Married, two children. He's fifty-four."

"Why didn't you call the phone company right away? He might have an unlisted number."

Molina grabbed his phone. It took him only a few minutes to get an answer. Also negative.

"Coll might have rented a house," he suggested.

"That's possible. But if we have to contact all the real estate agencies, it'll take us all day."

"Not to mention that quite a few rentals are not handled by the agencies . . . "

"Great!"

Molina was trying to finish off one by one the crumbs that were still lying in the pizza carton. Then he put his finger on a drop of tomato sauce and licked it.

"If you want my opinion," he said, "there's only one thing to do."

"Namely?"

"Follow him. If he's holding Ingrid somewhere, he has to go see her every day . . . "

"I'm afraid it's a little early to tail him: he mustn't suspect anything."

"I'll be careful."

"Why you?"

"He doesn't know me."

"He saw you the other day here, at headquarters."

"That's true. So let's say that he knows me less than he knows you."

"It's risky . . . "

"No doubt, but I'll be very cautious. I'll follow him at a distance, and if I lose him, too bad: I'll find him again later at his workplace or his home."

Molina was right. They couldn't limit themselves to investigating from their office. And then it wouldn't necessarily be a bad thing if the kidnapper realized that they were investigating him. It might even please him. The thrill of the game . . . The essential point was that he never guess that he had become their main suspect.

"Okay," Sebag finally said. "You go to his office, wait until he comes out, and then follow him. Let's hope he's still taking us for idiots and isn't on his guard."

"What about you, what are you going to do?"

"Investigate without moving out of this chair and remain in permanent contact with you."

"Cool!"

"I'd rather be in your place."

"Waiting for hours in an over-heated car until Mr. Coll has finished sending out pay slips and a few dismissal notices? That would surprise me!"

As soon as Molina was gone, Sebag contacted the tax office. Didier Coll did in fact pay property tax and residence tax, but only as the owner and occupant of a two-room apartment in Perpignan.

Then he looked at the real estate agencies. There were dozens of them in the department. He sighed. What else could he do while he waited?

He kept at it for at least two hours. Made about fifty calls, often having to wait to speak to a boss, then negotiating, deceiving, threatening, whining, sometimes inventing some outlandish fiction. Some agencies gave him the information without hesitation, but others protested and demanded an official request. By the middle of the afternoon he'd made little progress.

At least he'd tried.

It occurred to him to try an Internet search for the name Didier Coll. Two persons came up often, a Didier Coll who was an artist, and another who was a hairdresser. He also got some weird hits. He noticed that the search engine had selected almost 400,000 sites and decided to reformulate his search. Using quotation marks judiciously, he managed to limit the results to 2,000 sites. But they were still confused, "Coll" being understood by the search engine as an abbreviation of "collection."

After spending an hour on the Net, he'd found only one site that mentioned "his" Didier Coll. That of the Chamber of Commerce and Industry in Pyrénées-Orientales, which presented the organizational chart of the company the suspect worked for. Sebag had the painful feeling that he'd wasted his afternoon.

He decided to allow himself a little break, and took out of his drawer a news magazine he'd bought that same morning. It contained a series of articles about the Sanch. That traditional procession on Good Friday fascinated him. He'd gone several times to watch the parade of penitents, hidden under their *caparutxe*, a long, conical hood that before he came to Perpignan he'd associated exclusively with the American Ku Klux Klan.

His cell phone rang, putting an end to his break. It was Molina.

"Barry White got off work twenty minutes ago. He went by scooter to the Mailloles quarter where he's gone into a retirement home."

"He's probably visiting his mother. You didn't have too much trouble following his scooter in your car?"

"Do you take me for a greenhorn? It's in the manual. I took precautions. I've got a pal who sells used motorcycles. He lent me one."

"Congratulations!"

An idea suddenly occurred to him. An idea they should have had a long time ago.

"Your cell phone takes photos, doesn't it? Could you take a picture of Coll that we could show to Anneke?"

"The problem is that I'm not going to get too close to him. And a long-distance photo taken on a cell phone won't be very good."

"We can always try."

"Okay. How about you, are you getting anywhere?"

"No, I haven't found any trace of a house. But that doesn't prove anything. I hope you'll be luckier than I've been."

"Let's hope!"

"Hello, is this the Joffre retirement home in the Mailloles quarter, Perpignan?"

"Yes. What can I do for you, sir?"

"Let me introduce myself: my name is Damien Gourrault. I work for the Ray Barreto Institute, and the Ministry of Senior Citizens has asked us to conduct a study of family care for retirees. I'd like to speak with the head of the home, please."

"Please hold on, I'll see if Mrs. Raynald is available."

She was available.

"Hello, madam. This is Damien Gourrault of the Ray Barreto Institute. We have been asked to conduct a study for the Ministry of Senior Citizens in the context of the plan for coping with extreme heat. To make families more aware of the needs of old . . . uh . . . Senior Citizens, we are looking for children, sons or daughters who care particularly well for their relatives who have been placed in retirement homes. We would like to honor one family in each department of France. That's why I'm calling you. I am currently making the rounds of retirement homes in Pyrénées-Orientales to ask each establishment to name one or two persons who might be candidates for the title of "Super Son" or "Super Daughter." The exact title hasn't yet been decided upon, but the principle is to give a prize. Deserving children will win a trip for two, on the assumption, of course, that they will travel with their mother or father."

"That seems to me to be an interesting idea," the directress said politely.

"Thank you. Could I ask you then if you might have a few people to propose to us?"

"Certainly, yes, we have residents whose children visit them daily. But you've caught me somewhat unprepared. I'll have to think about the matter."

"I realize that. I don't need an immediate response. I can call you tomorrow."

"Tomorrow?"

"Yes, I know, that's quick, but the ministry is in a hurry. We have to be able to award the prizes before the end of the summer. Above all, don't waste time contacting the families, we'll take care of that ourselves. Is tomorrow possible?"

"I'll do my best."

"Wuhnnderful! One last thing before I let you go. We already have many women candidates, and since we'd like to present a rather broad spectrum of winners, we are especially looking for a man. The ideal person would be a bachelor in his forties who holds a position of responsibility. Do you think that's possible?"

"Maybe, yes . . . I already have an idea of who that might be."

"Wuhnnderful. So, I'm counting on you. Until tomorrow, Mrs. Reynald."

Sebag hung up. He wasn't sure what his initiative might produce but he was smiling like a kid who has just made a good joke.

The little hand of the clock on his desk was now almost pointing to the eight. Molina hadn't called back yet. Did that mean that Coll was still at his mother's bedside? He glanced at the screen on his telephone to be sure that his colleague hadn't tried to call him. There was no message.

Sebag decided it was time to eat dinner. He put his computer on standby and left the office. The reception area was empty, with the exception of an old alcoholic who was chatting quietly with Ripoll.

Sebag crossed the street and went into the Carlit. Behind his bar, Rafel Puig was reading *El Punt*, a weekly published in South Catalonia. Sebag ordered '*un entrepas amb pernil i formatge*' ("a ham and cheese sandwich"). And a *pastis* to drink while he waited. In the bar, near him, two men in their thirties were talking in Catalan about regional politics. He recognized members of a small regionalist party to which the owner of the Carlit also belonged. The bar was where they held their cell meetings.

A few minutes later Sebag left to return to headquarters, his meal under his arm and the veins in his brain delightfully irrigated with anise.

His cell phone rang while he was in the stairway. It was Séverine. She was on her way back from PortAventura, where she'd had "loads of fun."

"Are you back in Calella, then?"

"Yes, we went to the beach today."

"That's something new and different."

Sebag opened the door to his office.

"Isn't it? Have you heard from Léo?"

"He's ecstatic," he said, moved that Séverine cared about her big brother.

"He's planning to go to Toulon with a friend after his camp is over. He'll probably stay there until the end of the month."

"So, do you and Mama have plans for August?"

"*Non*, we haven't talked about it again."

"Huh," Séverine said, without trying to hide her disappointment.

"I've got a lot of work just now," he said to justify himself. "You see, I'm still at work this evening. And then I'm not sure if your mother will have things she particularly wants to do after her cruise."

"What about you, do you have things you particularly want to do, apart from running and loafing around?"

The signal for another incoming call sounded in his ear. Molina was trying to reach him.

"No, not really," he replied anyway, "I haven't really thought about it."

"You should."

"Think so?"

"I think it would please Mama if you proposed something. Not necessarily something big, but a little trip in France that you cooked up just for the two of you."

"Are you sure you wouldn't want to go with us, then?"

He heard Séverine sigh at the other end of the line and realized he hadn't understood what his daughter was trying to tell him. She'd matured a great deal these last months, but he wasn't prepared to see her play the role of marriage counselor. Did she suspect something?

"No, as I told you, I'd rather stay in Saint-Estève. But think about what I said regarding the month of August, that would really please Mama."

Annoyed, he said to himself: *Why should I please her?* But he didn't want to let his daughter see anything.

"I'll think about it," he managed to say.

The signal for an incoming call sounded again.

"Somebody's trying to reach me. I've got to let you go. Love you."

"I love you too, Papa."

Séverine's tone had the sweetness of acacia honey. Molina's was more like rotten ketchup.

"Nice of you to let me cool my heels here. Was your mouth full? I hope I'm not disturbing you too much?"

Sebag looked at his untouched sandwich lying on the desk between the lamp and the computer mouse.

"I'm sorry, I'm here now. Anything new?"

"What do you think . . . if I'm calling you?"

Sebag took care not to reply.

"Coll left his mother's retirement home ten minutes ago. He stopped to buy bread in a bakery and then went home, on La Fusterie Street. What should we do now?"

"What do you think?"

Sebag knew very well what they should do, but he preferred to let Molina make the decision himself.

"He might decide to go see Ingrid at any time. We can't let up on the surveillance."

"All night?"

"If necessary, yes."

Sebag let a few seconds go by as if he were weighing the pros and cons.

"Fine. You're undoubtedly right. Do you have a good place to wait?"

"Are you kidding? It's a pedestrian zone!"

Sebag translated: Molina couldn't do the stakeout in his car.

"Is there a bar nearby?"

"Fifty yards away, on the Place Rigaud. But I can't see the door to the building from there."

"That doesn't sound good! Do you have a drainpipe to lean on, at least?"

"A fairly large carriage entrance about ten yards away."

"Oh, terrific!"

"Don't worry too much about it, okay?"

"I can cover for you tonight."

"That wouldn't be prudent."

Sebag knew Jacques was right, but he had reservations. Even in the summer, nights could be long under a carriage entrance.

There was a silence. Sebag thought the line had gone dead.

"Are you sure it's him?" Molina finally asked.

"I think so."

"You think it's him or you think you're sure?"

"We have to follow this lead all the way to the end; it's the best one we have."

"You can say that again. It's the only one."

"It's the right one, you'll see."

Sebag would have liked to be more convincing but his own conviction hadn't been fed for several hours and he could feel it fading. He had to find something tangible very soon. A little fuel for the machine. Molina's motivation wouldn't last through a long, fruitless night.

"Did you get the photo?"

"Yes, but it's not good. Even I would have difficulty recognizing him."

"Stay there, I'm coming."

He had an idea for relieving his colleague, for an hour at least . . . *I want to play too*, he said to himself as he left headquarters.

In Dalle Arago, the restaurant terraces were buzzing with activity. A gypsy was making his way among the tables vigorously strumming his guitar, but there were only a few English tourists to listen to the lamentations of his strings. Sebag strode rapidly across the square and entered the narrow pedestrian streets of the city center.

He easily located the entrance to Didier Coll's apartment building, and then some ten yards away, on the same side of the street, the carriage entrance where Molina was waiting.

Molina was wearing a clean shirt—without a pizza stain—

shorts, and leather sandals. A yellow sun hat completed his disguise. Sebag passed in front of the carriage entrance without saying anything and stopped a few yards farther on. Molina waited a moment before joining him. Sebag frowned.

"Isn't the sun hat a little too much?"

"You think?"

"Frankly, yes. These days only retirees on organized trips are bold enough to sport that kind of headwear."

Molina didn't resist. He put the sun hat in his pocket.

"You're right; I swiped it from my father. He brought it back from a trip to Turkey . . . "

"Otherwise?"

"Still nothing. An employee and a model son, apparently."

"What did he do with his scooter?"

"He put it in the hall."

"Are there no other exits from the building?"

"No, I checked. He has to come out here."

Sebag looked at his watch. It was almost nine-thirty.

"Do you think he's going to come out?"

"I'd be surprised. With his baguette under his arm, he looked more like someone who was going to eat supper in front of the TV set. And then he had trouble getting his scooter through the door, and he wouldn't have done that if he was going to leave again in ten minutes."

Sebag reflected.

"Maybe he has another way of getting around. He could have bought a car. Or rented one."

"Didn't you check?"

"I didn't think of it until just now. I'll look into it tomorrow. Have you got the photo?"

Molina handed him his cell phone. It was hard to see the face, but the figure was recognizable.

"That'll do," he commented. Before coming, I left a message for Anneke. I'm waiting for her to call me back."

A roar in the streets made them turn around. First they saw an enormous green trash can fall over on the street about fifty yards from them. The top came off and a flood of refuse flowed noisily out onto the pavement. A bottle broke when it hit the ground, followed by a can that rolled down the street until an iron post diverted its course toward the gutter. Then a dark figure slowly detached itself from the trash can. The man stood up. He was tall, hairy, and seemed to be extremely angry. He walked off without even looking at his victim. He swung side to side, offbeat. When he came to another trash can, he froze for a moment before uttering another roar. Then he lunged, throwing his adversary to the ground.

"Nice technique," Molina commented.

"I've heard about a guy who attacked windmills, that was classier!"

The man got up. He was now only ten yards from them, and gave them a furious look before moving on toward a third trash can.

"You should call headquarters," Sebag suggested. Otherwise the streets of Perpignan are going to look like a huge garbage dump. Afterward, you can go get something to eat. I'm going to go up to Coll's apartment. I'll meet you here in an hour."

"You're going to Coll's apartment? Do you think that's smart?"

"We'll find out. We worked all day without finding any convincing evidence. We can't wait anymore. That's what wouldn't be smart."

CHAPTER 35

W hat surprised Sebag first about the apartment was its emptiness. And immediately afterward, its silence.

The room was large, with two tall windows looking out on the street. It was furnished with two armchairs separated by a low table on which a book lay. The Bible. A simple lamp—a translucent ball on a long, gray metal base—illuminated the scene. The walls were pale pink, undecorated except for blue-figured wainscoting about halfway up. The green shag carpet muffled the sound of footsteps. You felt more like mowing it than vacuuming it.

Coll was wearing sky-blue pants and a mustard-colored polo shirt. He was about the same height as Sebag, but thinner. His dark eyes stared into the inspector's. His hand did not tremble when he pointed to the armchair.

"Please sit down."

His deep voice seemed to be swallowed up by the perfectly sound-proofed walls and ceiling. Sebag sat down. The brown leather chair was comfortable. He put his arms on the mahogany armrests.

"You read wholesome books," Sebag complimented him, alluding to the Bible in front of him."

"It's the only novel I can stand," Coll replied, sitting down in turn. "Do you know the Bible?"

"By name. I know the main lines. Especially the end."

Sebag listened, but he couldn't hear any of the usual street noise. In this apartment, the silence was as deep as in a recording studio.

"You don't like noise?"

"I am especially fond of silence."

"Then why don't you live in the countryside?"

"The countryside isn't silent. There's nothing noisier than nature."

Sebag contemplated the emptiness around him. Not a single knick-knack or photo. He suddenly had the feeling that the apartment had been set up this way specifically for this meeting. His host had said nothing about his visiting so late. He hadn't even seemed surprised. He'd buzzed open the ground floor door without protest and he'd come out on the landing to greet him. As if he were a friend who'd been expected.

"How can I help you?"

"Do you know why I'm here?" Sebag was deliberately elliptical.

Coll did not immediately respond. He seemed to be sizing up his adversary.

"You've ended up being interested in my car, haven't you?"

Sebag nodded.

"Did someone explain how it was useful?"

"Your colleague told me. A case of kidnapping, I believe."

"Kidnapping and murder," Sebag said.

"I thought kidnappings were rare in France these days. I recall several famous cases in the 1970s, but I thought they'd gone out of fashion."

"You know how fashion . . . "

"Yes, it comes and goes."

"Exactly."

One might have been listening to two old acquaintances talking over a cocktail. It was a good sign. Still, Sebag felt ill at ease. The muffled sound of a door slamming reached them

from the landing. The silence ceased for a moment. Coll grimaced with annoyance.

"Did my colleague show you some photos the other day?"

"No. Should he have?"

Sebag took his wallet out of his jacket pocket.

"He didn't have to, no. Let's say that I like to do it as a matter of course. You never know. Chance always plays a role in
investigations, but not necessarily where you expect it. Maybe
there's a good reason why it should be precisely your car that
was used in this case. Maybe, without knowing it, you are connected with this case."

"You're scaring me, Inspector."

Sebag opened his wallet. He hesitated for a second, then
decided not to add Claire's picture. He handed the photos to
Didier Coll, who took his time looking at them. Sebag had the
impression that this was a calculated pause. Coll was waiting,
not reflecting.

"No, I really don't recognize these faces," Coll finally answered.

He put the photos on the table alongside the Bible. Sebag
finally took out Claire's photo.

"How about this one?"

Coll took the photo and held it up to his eyes. This time, he
really looked at the photo.

"Who is it?"

Sebag did not reply.

"You know Gérard Barrère well, I think?"

"I wouldn't say I know him well."

"You gave him as a reference when you came to see me at
police headquarters."

"I thought that would help me keep your attention."

"Are you doing business with him?"

"Our directors like to reward our best managers every year.
I'm the one who has been assigned to handle contacts with
Perpign'And Co. to organize parties."

"Do you participate in these parties?"

"As infrequently as possible."

"Why?"

"I don't like leisure activities in groups. Besides, I never leave Perpignan. Because of my mother."

He spoke slowly, punctuating his sentences with deep breaths. Sebag pretended not to know.

"Is your mother ill?"

"Ill, no. Let's say that she's elderly and is losing her mind. She's in a retirement home."

"Do you visit her regularly?"

"I try to go there every day."

Sebag gave him an admiring look.

"You're a model son."

Coll refused the compliment.

"No. Not at all. If I were a model son, I wouldn't have put her in a retirement home."

"What else could you do? You work . . . "

"One can always get help."

Sebag gestured with his hand to indicate the apartment.

"And then here, it wouldn't be very practical."

"That's true," Coll replied with surprise, as if he'd never thought of that argument. "But that's not what you're here to talk about."

"You're right. Let's get back to Gérard Barrère. It happens that José Lopez, the man whose photo I showed you, worked for Barrère from time to time. You might have had occasion to meet him . . . "

Coll put down Claire's photo, which he was still holding in his hands, and looked again at the photo of Lopez.

"No. Truly not. His face means nothing to me."

Sebag then slipped in a few questions about the Volvo. He asked again where Coll had parked it, when he'd used it the last time, how he'd realized it had been stolen, and so on. Coll gave the same answers as he'd given to Ménard. Sebag noticed that he often even used the same words and expressions that had appeared in the interview report.

"Have you bought another car?"

"No, not yet. I was hoping to get the old one back."

"Don't count on it: it's evidence. Are you currently renting a car?"

"No. I . . . don't really need one. I might rent one for a weekend. But for everyday, from work to my apartment by way of the retirement home, I can do all that on my scooter."

Sebag felt that something wasn't right. Coll was speaking correctly but his hesitations lacked spontaneity.

Silence took possession of the room again. Sebag wrote a few things in his notebook. He took his time. He was thinking about what he would do after the conversation and tried to observe Coll without his noticing. The periods of silence were the hardest ones for suspects to manage, because they left them alone with their fears. Coll, however, showed neither concern nor tension. He limited himself to breathing. Calmly.

"Were you satisfied with that car?" Sebag abruptly asked him.

"What do you mean?" Coll said, surprised.

"It interests me personally, excuse me," Sebag lied. "I'd like to buy a new car and I'm looking for a station wagon. When you have a house with a yard, a wagon is more practical for going to the dump, for example. You can't put anything in the trunk of a sedan. So, was the Volvo a good car?"

"It's reliable. Though not very comfortable."

"How many miles does it have on it?"

"A hundred and ten thousand."

"Has it run well?"

"I never had any problems."

"How old is it?"

"It's over twenty years old."

Sebag seemed to be making a rapid calculation.

"It's true that you don't drive much. That's something I was wondering about: why did you buy a car like that when you live in town?"

"I didn't buy it, I took it over from my mother when she went into the retirement home."

"Did your mother live in the countryside?"

Sebag had spoken faster than he'd thought and it was only as he asked the question that he had what might be called a revelation. He tried not to let Coll see that.

"Yes," Coll replied in a voice that seemed to Sebag even more toneless. "In fact, it was my father who bought the car."

Sebag jumped on the opportunity. He had to change the subject.

"Is your father no longer with us?"

"In a manner of speaking. He took off without leaving a forwarding address a little over twenty years ago. He'd just bought the car."

Sebag adopted a tone he hoped would be anodyne.

"Now I understand better. I said to myself: such a big car for an elderly lady, that seems odd. Did she keep it as a souvenir, maybe?"

"In a way."

Sebag smiled. A bit foolishly, but not too much.

"So . . . to sum up, would you advise me to buy a car like that?"

"I don't know. Do you have children?"

"Two grown-up ones, yes."

"Well, why not? You'd have plenty of room for going on vacations."

Sebag imagined his whole family in the Volvo. A car like that might have been useful. Before. He asked a few more questions about the case and tried to take an interest in the answers. Then he got up and said good-bye.

"I'm sorry to have disturbed you so late."

"It's all right. I hope I've been useful to you."

The two men shook hands. As they had at the beginning of the conversation, Coll's eyes looked into the Inspector's. They were trying to read his thoughts. The scene reminded Sebag of a black-and-white movie he'd seen when he was a kid. The story of a class of schoolchildren who were evil and exceptionally gifted. Children who were killers. Endowed with supernatural powers and capable of reading other people's thoughts. At the end, their teacher tries to exterminate them. He hides a bomb in the classroom, but the kids very quickly guess that he's hiding something from them. They come up to him. Blue eyes, blond hair, angelic faces surround him and try to discover what he's trying to conceal. Then the teacher concentrates. He focuses his mind on a brick wall. The children decipher his thoughts but can see nothing but this brick wall.

And the bomb explodes.

"As much as you could," Sebag replied, trying to think about a brick wall.

The door closed behind him. He thought each of them had gotten what he expected out of the conversation. Coll had gotten the thrill of the game, and he'd gotten a new lead that he was eager to follow the next day. He went down the stairs slowly, trying to relive in his thoughts the meeting he'd just had with his suspect. Coll hadn't betrayed himself; he hadn't let Sebag see anything. And yet, Sebag felt growing within him a diffuse but powerful feeling: the certainty that he was not mistaken.

CHAPTER 36

The door had just closed and he didn't know what to think.

But he was finally having fun.

He'd enjoyed the conversation. A highpoint, so long awaited. Raskolnikov confronting Porfiry. He thought he'd been remarkable. Calm and relaxed. He hadn't discerned any false note in his replies.

Inspector Sebag had done well, too. Pertinent questions. Especially when he was talking about the house. But he'd missed the bus, passing on too quickly to something else.

Unless . . .

He wasn't sure what to think, and that was delicious.

He had to remain wary and be ready for the last stage.

Already . . .

He was beginning to have second thoughts about the end he'd imagined. He couldn't lose, but how would he know if he'd won?

Too bad!

He'd granted himself the right to improvise regarding the form, but not the content. The end had been set long ago: he had to stick to that. One didn't have the right to change the rules in the middle of the game.

So far as the young woman was concerned, there was still nothing to be feared. He'd gone to see her after work: she was calm, patient, and resigned. The sedative he put into her pitcher of water every day promoted that state of mind, but it didn't explain everything. Despite appearing to be a free woman, she was ultimately very docile. Wanting to be prudent, he limited his visits to one per day.

Scarcely an hour.

And he forced himself to go back to his apartment to spend the night. The advantage was that he slept better far away from that body.

It had been a red-letter day. This conversation with the inspector, and then a little earlier . . . the message left on his cell phone by the directress of the retirement home.

Somebody from a ministry had called the home. They were looking for a model son. Devoted. Loving. Attentive. "I immediately thought of you," the directress had told him.

He'd almost laughed.

A model son . . . The inspector had used that expression, too. A model son. I who go to visit my mother only for the pleasure of contemplating her decline . . .

She no longer understood anything, and he confessed to her all the terrible things he'd done as a child. The thefts of money from her purse, the cats whose eyes he'd put out, the dog shit mixed into the morning marmalade. He also talked to her about her husband. His father. He'd left a little too soon, unfortunately.

He particularly liked to feed his mother. She chewed slowly because her false teeth were poorly fitted to her rotting gums, and he enjoyed shoveling food into her mouth. The poor woman spat out half of it. It was disgusting.

He made her drink a lot, too. To the point that she ended up wetting her diaper. Then he changed her. Before the admiring—and grateful—eyes of the young women who worked in the retirement home.

He wouldn't have spent a day far from his mother for anything in the world.

He breathed. Counted slowly up to ten. Breathing was his

sole gymnastics. His sole philosophy. Absolute self-control could be acquired only through absolute control over his breathing.

All the same, he did feel that he had a tendency to allow his thoughts to get out of control as the fated result approached.

He had only one regret: not having played earlier. Why did he have to wait until his mother fell ill? As if he could have feared that she would one day be ashamed of him. He hated her so much.

He would never experience other days like this one. Too bad. He had really almost laughed.

Suddenly he understood that all this would not have happened if he had ever proven capable, even once, of laughing.

CHAPTER 37

Sebag had slept fitfully, his head resting on his desk. His body felt tired but his mind was clear. Lucid. He'd given himself the morning to make a significant advance. He hoped that at noon he'd be able to give Castello proof of Coll's involvement.

Anneke Verbrucke hadn't called him back. He dialed her number, but after the phone rang a dozen times he got her answering machine again.

Molina had staked out Coll's building until 7:00 A.M. before going home to bed. By common accord, they'd asked Lambert to take over. That was risky. But they had no choice. Llach was attending a meeting of his union in Montpellier and Ménard would have refused to play along.

Sebag's eyes were stinging. They were bloodshot. He'd noticed it when he went to the lavatory to throw some cold water on his face.

He had to hold on. They were in the final stretch.

He called Barrère and had the pleasure of awakening him. Barrère complained on principle, but ever since the police had brought to light some of his activities, he could no longer refuse them anything. To conceal the precise objective of his call, Sebag took care to begin with various questions concerning Barrère's last deposition. Then he took up the question that preoccupied him.

"Didier Coll, you say? Yes, I know him, of course. But I don't recall having recommended you to him. Why would I have done that, anyway? I don't feel like I've exactly made friends in the police department lately."

"I must have been mistaken, then. It's not important."

He immediately went on to other minor questions. It was Barrère who returned to the subject at the end of their conversation.

"That reminds me . . . About Coll. You met him at my office the other day."

"I did? Are you sure you're not confusing me with my colleague Ménard?"

"No, no. I had an appointment with him and I was forced to make him wait in order to talk with you."

Could this be the link he'd been looking for? He'd looked so hard. In Coll's past. In his relationships. The question had tormented him night and day; he'd even felt guilty at times. And the answer might be right there. He'd met Coll by accident at Barrère's office. And that was how Coll had chosen him as his contact person. This guy is sick, Sebag thought.

Barrère was still on the line. He had just said something.

"Excuse me?" Sebag said.

"I was asking whether this is all that urgent."

"What?"

"Well, this telephone call!"

Sebag didn't want to put a bug in his ear. Barrère was quite capable of warning Coll.

"No, you're right. This is a matter of unimportant details. Mr. Coll's car was stolen, and we're trying to find it. But you know what they say, there's no rest for the wicked . . . "

He hung up.

Sebag went downstairs to get some coffee. Clutching his cup, he stopped at the reception desk to talk with Martine. The young woman remembered the telephone call the other day but was unable to say why, when she heard the kidnapper whispering, she'd thought he was the owner of the stolen car.

"You saw him just the one time?" Sebag asked.

"Yes, but he called back the next day—or the day after that, I'm not sure."

"So you'd already talked to him on the phone?"

"Yes."

Sebag nodded but said nothing. He looked at Martine, and she smiled without understanding. He decided he could rely on her impression.

Back in his office, he called the Joffre retirement home. It was still too early to contact the car rental companies or the tax office. The directress was surprised that he was calling at that hour but she was already at her desk and had thought about his request.

"I would like to propose a candidate whom I haven't yet been able to contact. I've left a message and am waiting for a reply."

"I hope it's a man, as I asked?"

"Yes, of course. A bachelor, so far as I know, and in any case he's not married. In his forties. He comes to see his mother every day and won't let anyone else take care of her while he's there. In fact, I thought he was with her when you called, and I went to see right away, but didn't find him. He's a very good person and . . . "

Sebag paid no attention to the rest of what she said. Coll must have been in his mother's room during the phone call, but then he had disappeared. Could he have left the retirement home without Molina seeing him? That could turn out to be important. Unless the directress was talking about someone else. He had to be sure about that. Didier Coll might not be the model son she had chosen.

"If you'll give me his name, I can put him down as a candidate right away . . . "

"I'm not sure it's wise to rush things. He's a very discreet gentleman. I don't know if he'll agree to participate."

"He'll do it to please his mother, surely. What mother wouldn't be happy and proud to see her son honored in that way?"

"Oh, you know, his mother . . . "

"What do you mean?"

"She's completely senile, the poor thing, and for the past several weeks she hasn't recognized anyone. Not even her son."

"Is that right? And he takes care of her anyway? What devotion! The minister will absolutely want to reward this fellow. Give me his name, please. If he's reluctant, we can always work it out afterward. I'm seeing the minister this morning, and he'll be very happy."

The directress finally gave in.

"It's Mr. Coll."

"And what is Mr. Coll's first name?"

"Didier. But note that his last name is spelled C-o-l-l, though it's pronounced 'Coye.' It's a local name."

"And you say that you were unable to reach this Mr. Coll yesterday? I called you around seven P.M., didn't I?"

"It was exactly 7:07 when I hung up."

"You were in your office after seven P.M. yesterday and you are still there before eight A.M. . . . on a Saturday . . . Well! I'll know where to go when the ministry decides to reward the best administrators of retirement homes. So at 7:07 Mr. Coll had left, is that right? He couldn't have just gone to the rest room or outside to smoke a cigarette?"

"Uh . . . No, I don't think so. I stayed in his mother's room for a quarter of an hour and I didn't see him come back . . . Afterward, I had to go home, my children were waiting for me . . . "

"Of course, of course, that doesn't matter."

Sebag would have had other questions for the directress, but he couldn't ask them without running the risk of making her suspicious. He promised to sing her praises to the minister.

He consulted the map of Perpignan that he always kept at hand in his desk drawer. The Joffre retirement home occupied a full city block. The map wasn't detailed enough to tell, but he could imagine that there was an additional exit on the other side of the building. He redialed the retirement home's number, identifying himself by his real name this time, and trying to disguise his voice.

"Yes, of course we have a service entrance on Le Couchant Street," the young woman on the reception desk told him. It's used by our suppliers."

"It isn't guarded? Some of your patients are senile; isn't there a risk that they would try to get out that way?"

"The door is always locked. The guard's booth is right next to it, and he's the one who has the key."

"Do visitors sometimes use that exit?"

"No, that's not allowed, precisely for security reasons. If you want, I can connect you with the guard; he'll confirm what I said."

Sebag reflected rapidly. It was too early to ask such direct questions. There were other things he had to check first.

The most important task was to locate the house where Coll could be holding Ingrid. He called one of their contacts at the local tax office, a fairly high official for whom they had done a favor in a case involving his daughter. Possession of marijuana. The girl had been arrested during a routine check. She didn't have much on her, in fact.

"It's a question of life and death," Sebag explained, "and a matter of hours as well."

The girl's father didn't raise many objections, and promised to provide the information before noon. The final sprint had started. Sebag was enormously excited and abruptly stood up. He would have liked to have another coffee in the cafeteria but knew that wouldn't be smart. So he limited himself to going into the hall to fill a glass of water at the drinking fountain. He heard Castello's big voice resounding in the stairway. He left his glass of water behind and took refuge in the rest room. Sitting on the toilet, he felt he was being childish, but he didn't want to talk to the superintendent just yet. It was still too soon. In a few hours—or maybe a few minutes.

Back in his office, he locked himself in and then grabbed his telephone again. He had before him a long list of car rental agencies. About sixty of them. He began with the largest. The law of probabilities required it, and so did logic: it would be easier for someone renting a car to conceal questionable activities by dealing with a large agency rather than a small one. The same reasoning led Sebag to look first at the agencies that had an office at the airport. Hoping to avoid being refused information as often as he'd been when he called real estate agencies, he invented a little story about a hit-and-run driver.

With his ninth call, he hit pay dirt.

"Yes, I've got a record in the name of Didier Coll, residing in Perpignan. Last week he rented a Renault Mégane station wagon for two weeks."

Sebag wrote down the dates and the vehicle's license plate number.

"Was the accident serious?" the manager of the agency asked.

"Not very," Sebag said. "But for the sake of the investigation I need you to keep this confidential. If your vehicle was involved in this accident, we'll have to play by the rules. Is that clear?"

"Completely," the manager replied.

Sebag felt a tingling in his fingertips. Finally . . . he had proof that Coll had lied. The pieces of the puzzle were beginning to come together. Coll had probably parked his rented car behind the retirement home to foil a possible tail. While people thought he was with his mother, he went to the place where he was holding Ingrid. Sebag needed a confirmation.

He called the guard at the retirement home.

"Do the residents' relatives sometimes use the service entrance, the one for which you hold the key?"

"No," the guard replied. That's forbidden."

"Never ever?" Sebag asked. "This question could turn out to be crucial in a very important investigation, so I'll ask it in an official manner and your answer will be recorded in a formal statement: Do visitors sometimes leave the building through the service entrance?"

There was a silence of a few seconds.

"Uh . . . That might have happened," the guard finally decided to answer. "That might have happened a few times."

Sebag imagined him squirming at the other end of the line.

"That might have happened or it did happen?"

"It did happen a few times, I think."

"Yesterday, for example?"

Another silence. Sebag was more precise:

"What time did Mr. Coll leave through that door?"

Still no reply.

"Are you still there?"

"Yes, uh, excuse me, but I can't answer your question just now. Can you call back later?"

The rogue was exhausting Sebag's patience.

"Maybe you'd prefer that I send two officers down to get you? The management would surely like that . . . "

"I . . . uh, one second, I mean, a moment. Please."

Sebag heard disagreeable sounds in the receiver. As if it had been slammed down. Then he heard people talking in the distance. Finally he heard the guard's voice again.

"Hello, what were you asking me again?"

Sebag felt a serious desire to go down there and read the jerk the riot act.

"I was asking you what time Mr. Coll left by that door that is normally closed."

"Shortly before seven P.M."

"And he came back when?"

"A little after eight."

"Are you sure?"

"I was watching the news on television and it must have been the third or fourth story when he rang."

"Does Mr. Coll often go through that door?"

"He's been doing it for a few days. He goes out to do an errand and then comes back."

"And why does he use that door?"

"He parks behind the building. He told me he finds it easier to park there."

The guard seemed to have had no trouble accepting a justification that wasn't very plausible.

"But when he first comes in and the last time he leaves, he still goes through the main entrance?"

"Yes. It's just when he needs go out for a while that he asks me."

"And he goes out often."

"Lately, every day."

"And each time, he gives you a little tip, doesn't he?"

"He's . . . uh, he's a very nice fellow."

"I imagine he is, yes. I hope you've taken full advantage of his generosity because you're going to have some problems."

"I . . . I don't see . . . what . . . "

"I'm afraid Mrs. Raynald won't appreciate that way of supplementing your pay."

"But . . . I . . . you . . . Do you have to tell her?"

Sebag let the guard stew in his own juices for a few seconds. He had a proposal to make to him.

"I'm a nice fellow too, you know. I'm willing to forget about it this time. On one condition."

"Yes?" the guard said eagerly.

"On condition that you inform me immediately the next time Mr. Coll uses that exit, okay?"

A deep silence followed his offer.

"Well?"

"It's that . . . "

"Would you prefer that I tell the directress?"

"No, no, it's not that. It's that . . . "

The guard gulped and finally got it out.

"I couldn't talk to you right away because Mr. Coll was just then leaving."

"Goddamn it to hell!"

In his rage, Sebag almost threw his telephone against the wall. But he got control of himself and dialed Lambert's cell phone.

"The weather good in front of the retirement home?"

"How do you know?"

"A little bird told me. You could have informed me that he'd left his apartment."

"I was going to do that, but I didn't have time . . . I followed him as discreetly as possible, but it isn't easy. Is there a problem?"

"You might say that . . . "

Sebag quickly brought him up to date on what he'd just learned.

"Listen, now you're going to forget the main entrance and go stake out the service entrance on Le Couchant Street. As soon as you see him park his Mégane, call me and go back to the front of the building. Understood?"

"Okay. Do you think it's serious?"

"I don't know. Are you sure he didn't make you?"

"I hope not. But it isn't easy to follow a scooter with a car."

"Didn't Molina leave you his motorcycle?"

"He offered to, but I've never driven one, so I'm stuck with the car."

Sebag snorted. He was getting uneasy. His cell phone rang. A private number. It was his contact at the tax office.

"I've got your info."

Everything was definitely going very fast.

"As you suspected, Marguerite Coll owns a house in Le Soler. According to what it says here, it's an old farmhouse with about three-quarters of an acre of land."

Sebag took down the address and thanked him.

He contemplated the bit of paper for a few seconds. He was savoring the moment. He now knew enough to inform Castello.

He decided to let Molina know first. He deserved that. The telephone rang but no one answered, and the answering machine came on. Sebag dialed the number again. In the meantime, he'd opened the white pages on the Internet. He knew there would be no telephone at the farmhouse, but he looked for a neighboring address. When he found one, he clicked on the aerial view option. He was zooming in on the photo when Molina finally answered his phone. A few words of explanation sufficed to wake him up.

"I'm coming. Go see Castello, I'll meet you there."

Sebag didn't hang up immediately. The computer had focused as closely as possible on the aerial view and showed the whole property owned by the Coll family. At the back of the grounds, there was a large, dark area that could easily be a pond.

Castello was on the telephone when Sebag entered his office. Gilles sat down across from him. Borrowed a pencil and a piece of paper from him. He wrote a single word and showed it to the superintendent, who cut short his conversation.

"Is it really that 'urgent'?" he asked.

"Even more."

Before going upstairs, Sebag had taken time to write a summary, and he was now ready to make a clear and organized presentation of his evidence.

He didn't beat around the bush. The time for "perhaps" and "probably" was past. "Didier Coll is Ingrid Raven's kidnapper and José Lopez's murderer," he told the superintendent. "He's forty-three years old, he's tall and slender, he has light brown hair and dark eyes. His voice is serious and deep, easily recognizable on the telephone except when he whispers and conceals its timbre. This very distinctive voice reminds some people of Barry White, of whom Lopez was a fan. To hide the identity of his mysterious customer, the cab driver gave him the initials of his favorite singer: BW."

Sebag felt Castello's eyes looking at him more and more intensely as he talked, and he saw a thin smile beginning to form on his lips.

"As the director of human resources for a company specializing in public works," he went on, "Didier Coll has regular contacts with Perpign'And Co. That was where he met José Lopez, and it was also where he saw the policeman whom he later chose as his contact person. After the alleged theft of his car, he addressed himself to this policeman. Just to challenge him. He even went so far as to call him up and try to get him to look into the case.

"Didier Coll lives in an apartment in the city center, but he didn't tell investigators that he also has the use of a property in Le Soler. A farmhouse that belongs to his mother and is suitable for holding a prisoner, it stands in the middle of a large, private lot and has"—here Sebag hesitated for an instant—"a rather large pond."

"Another of the suspect's lies: he claims to have traveled exclusively by scooter since the theft—or rather the abandonment—of his Volvo, whereas in reality he has rented another vehicle. Also a station wagon," Sebag added, his voice trembling a little. "This rented vehicle is parked in a street in the Mailloles quarter in front of the service entrance to the retirement home where his senile mother resides. This subterfuge allowed him to lose a tail yesterday. He was gone for a little more than an hour, which gave him time to go back and forth to Le Soler to visit his prisoner."

Sebag had finished. Castello nodded enthusiastically. He was getting ready to congratulate his inspector when the latter cut him off.

"He's with Ingrid right now. He probably realizes that we know. We have to act quickly, Superintendent."

CHAPTER 38

So it would never end.

A thin ray of golden light made its way under the planks that closed off the cellar window. A new day had begun. A sunny day. The kind she would have liked to spend sunbathing instead of rotting in her dungeon . . .

She couldn't stand her passivity any more. She felt submissive, tamed, defeated. She was no longer able to react. Fear was destroying her. And yet what could she be afraid of?

Death?

Death would be far preferable to living this way, like a moribund woodlouse.

She could no longer bear to look at her reflection. Her eyes were empty and had bags under them, and she had the transparent complexion of a cadaver.

She was already dead.

She slept all day. Dragged herself from her bed to the slop pail, sometimes taking a shower on the way. She now had free access to the shower. The door from the cellar to the shower was always open. Her jail had doubled in size. What luxury! She cursed herself for having rejoiced when she realized that this door would never be closed again. If her tormentor gave her his hand she would kiss it happily. If he offered her his cock she would lick it avidly. Where could such a renunciation come from? She would have slapped herself if she'd had the strength to do it.

His visits had become less frequent recently. She was pained by that.

She heard a sound behind the door. It wasn't time for him to come, however. The last few days he'd come only in the evening.

The key squealed in the lock. The door of the vestibule creaked as it opened. He was there, on the other side. She threw herself on her bed and buried her head in the pillow.

He approached her slowly. She didn't dare turn over. She heard the sound of a glass being set down on the tiled floor.

"Drink this, please."

The angelic voice was warm and coaxing. Mesmerizing. The angel of death.

She turned over but couldn't raise her head. She saw a big glass at the angel's feet. It contained an amber liquid rimmed with foam.

"Drink it," he repeated. "It won't hurt you."

She took the glass and put it to her lips. The glass clicked against the enamel of her teeth. She drank. It was beer.

A nice cool dark beer.

Had Socrates felt the same inner peace when he swallowed the hemlock?

She handed the empty glass back to him. He took it and then knelt down to put it on the floor. The angel had a face. Neither ugly nor handsome. He opened his arms. She took refuge in them and began to cry. An unknown serenity was flowing through her veins.

Before slowly falling asleep, she had the impression that the destroying angel was weeping with her.

CHAPTER 39

The game would go on without him.

That was one of the rules. He now regretted it, but that was the way he'd wanted it. It was what made the game beautiful.

He would soon lack the strength to go on.

Everything had happened as planned. Or almost. He wasn't sure that he'd completely controlled the tempo. A little too slow at the beginning. A little too rapid toward the end. Inspector Sebag had succeeded in giving him the impression that the investigation was stalled, whereas in fact he had succeeded in identifying him. He'd understood that only this morning, when he noticed he was being followed. The police had won this inning.

Would he win the last one? Deep inside, he hoped he would.

He'd been forced to rush the end, but still in accord with the scenario he'd foreseen from the beginning. He'd stuck to the line he'd decided on. It was his victory. Everything was set now, the police could come, they wouldn't find anything. If they persevered, they would have one more chance. Otherwise, too bad for them.

Too bad for her.

He felt a twinge in his heart when he thought again about Ingrid. She'd slipped into unconsciousness as he held her in his arms. Peacefully. He'd told her she wouldn't suffer, and she had trusted him. He'd rocked her like a child.

Good-bye, Ingrid.

He would have liked to hold her in his arms longer, but time was short. She'd had to make the last journey before they arrived. He'd succeeded. He was ready.

They could come.

His limbs were gradually becoming numb. Especially his right arm.

He felt at peace. As he hadn't been for centuries. People had always said he was a tranquil man; no one had perceived the tumult that murmured in his head. His movements were slow and measured; he had a low voice and calm breathing. They didn't look deeper.

He was the only one who knew that his thin body sheltered a volcano.

Fatigue was overcoming him. It was the origin of this unfamiliar calming. His eyelids weighed tons. Soon he would fall asleep.

And sleep without nightmares.

He would leave so many questions behind him. The policemen would find some answers, but not all of them. The press would also ask questions. For a few days, he would be all people talked about.

Why?

He imagined journalists debating that question indefinitely.

Yes, why? He who could say would be a clever man. He himself didn't have all the answers. The only thing he knew for sure was that he wouldn't have wanted to die as he had lived. In silence. For once, he wanted to be surrounded by a little sound and fury.

His head was spinning. It seemed to him that he already heard them coming.

Let me have a little more time, Mama, please.

He was happy. He was leaving before the din enveloped the house.

His father's image occasionally disturbed his serenity. So the old bastard was going to bug him right to the end.

"The bastard!"

He'd said the word out loud. He was astonished by this. He was getting vulgar at the end. Even when Papa . . . left, I didn't dare tell him that he . . . that he . . . that he was a . . .

A bastard.

His ribcage shook. His breathing became irregular. An unfamiliar sound escaped his open mouth.

So that was it. Laughing.

Chapter 40

The pitiless sun scorched the Roussillon plain with it burning rays. Far off to the southwest, the summits of Le Canigou were disappearing in a haze of heat. At the edge of an orchard, a wooden shed sheltered an old man with a leathery face. He was dozing, his head resting between two empty baskets. He no longer had any peaches to sell. He'd been cleaned out.

Leaning against a tree, Sebag listened to the locusts chanting their summer song in rhythm. Sweat was running from his armpits down his sides. He wasn't the only one suffering. Dark rings were spreading over his colleagues' shirts as well. Even the plainest were becoming two-tone.

The policemen had surrounded the road that led to the Colls' farmhouse. The dirt tracks were blocked. An officer had discreetly sneaked along the property's perimeter wall and made his way toward the gate. At the end of a driveway paved with pink gravel he'd seen the rented Mégane station wagon. Castello had decided to wait for Coll to come out before arresting him.

A cloud of flies was buzzing over a peach pit someone had recently thrown away. The old peasant's fruit had provided most of the lunch eaten by the thirty or so policemen and gendarmes who'd been waiting in the sun for almost two hours. Sebag deftly tossed the peach pit and the flies into the ditch. He was beginning to get impatient. And not only because of the heat.

He thought they'd taken too long to get going. It would have been better to immediately send a small team to arrest the kidnapper, who would surely not have resisted.

On the way from Perpignan to Le Soler, Sebag had fallen asleep on the back seat for a few minutes. Ménard was driving, with Molina sitting at his side.

Gilles had dreamed about Claire. She was supposed to return the next evening. They hadn't spoken since Wednesday, when he'd brusquely rebuffed her on the telephone. She hadn't called back. But he'd received another letter. Mailed earlier, from Tunis. A letter full of sweetness and love.

He didn't want to think about Claire. Not now. This wasn't the time. But the wait was long and the breeze was carrying to him aromas that reminded him of his wife's perfume. Was it peach, rosemary, or star anise?

He wondered what he should do when he saw her again.

He turned the question over and over in his head.

One answer struck him as absolutely clear.

It was peach!

That was the fragrance that constantly took him back to Claire. To restore the shine to her hair dulled by the sun, the sea, and the chlorine in pools, in the summer she used a peach shampoo. He closed his eyes and took a deep breath of it. The ripe, juicy, soft fruit. That was it. He felt relieved. He was going to be able to control his thoughts again.

The Colls' property was hidden behind a thick wall made of *cayrou*, a mixture of stones and bricks that was typical of the region. Alongside the old wall, a hedge of laurels in flower made the place even more secluded. The white petals danced slightly in the breeze. All that could be seen of the house were the tiles at the crest of the roof standing out against a cloudless sky. No sound came from the property; there was no movement. No sign of life.

Sitting next to Sebag, Molina lit a cigarette. His face raised toward the sky, he blew out a long, voluptuous stream of smoke. His eyes were bloodshot and tired. At the back of his dilated pupil there was a glimmer of uneasiness.

"This doesn't smell good," Sebag murmured.

Molina misunderstood him.

"I couldn't hold out any longer: it's my first cigarette since we've been on the stake-out."

"I wasn't talking about that . . . Anyway, give me a drag, please."

Molina smoked mentholated cigarettes. The puff Sebag took did away with the peach fragrance.

"It's going on too long, he should have come back out long ago."

"That's what I was thinking, too," Molina confirmed, taking back his cigarette. "His scooter is still in front of the retirement home; he's supposed to still be with his mother. If he was trying to shake off a tail, he failed."

Sebag glanced at Lambert. The best place he'd been able to find to take a leak discreetly was a nearby bush.

The young inspector had just joined them. Before, he'd gone to show Anneke and the owners of the Deux Margots bar a photo of Coll taken from his mother's bedside table. The three women had been able to identify their suspect as the solitary drinker who'd been sitting a few tables away from the Dutch girl the night she was attacked.

If they needed further proof, they had it.

"He must have noticed we were tailing him," Sebag said.

"What the hell is he doing in there?"

"He's preparing a surprise for us."

"What kind of surprise?"

"I don't know, because it's a surprise. He must have foreseen this visit. The game isn't over."

"You mean we're not going to find anything in that house? Neither him nor Ingrid?"

"Lack of sleep doesn't make you more optimistic, it seems."

"And how do you think this damned game is going to end? Are you optimistic about it?"

Sebag reflected and didn't find anything reassuring to say.

"Me? I didn't sleep much either."

Molina carefully crushed out his cigarette on his heel. The vegetation was dry, and a spark would be enough to set it on fire. Castello slowly approached them. He smelled the mentholated fragrance in the air. He took a deep breath. His right hand was clenched, with his index finger and his thumb sticking straight up.

"We're going in. Lefèvre is getting impatient, and the gendarmes too."

"There's no point in waiting any longer," Molina confirmed.

Sebag nodded. Castello addressed him directly.

"Would it be dangerous, in your opinion?"

"No, I don't think so."

Castello went off to talk with Lefèvre. Then he came back to them.

"We're going to send four men onto the property. Two in front and two behind the house. When they're in position, you'll go ring at the gate."

Sebag returned to the car, switched on his walkie-talkie and hooked it on his belt. Around him, the policemen were putting on their equipment. They adjusted their bullet-proof vests and checked their weapons.

"You should take your gun," Molina advised him.

Sebag opened the glove box and looked at his service weapon for a moment, then changed his mind. The policemen accompanying him were all armed. That was more than enough.

He got out of the car and went up to the cast-iron gate.

Castello and Lefèvre followed him but took care to keep hidden behind the stone wall.

They waited. Then a voice whispered in the walkie-talkies. "We're in position."

Laurent Massart was directing the operations inside the property. He was a shooting instructor. He'd taken his best men with him. Castello signaled to Sebag.

"Go ahead!"

Gilles pushed the button. No reply. He pushed again. With no more success.

The walkie-talkie crackled.

"We hear the bell but no sound inside the house."

Sebag glanced furtively toward the superintendent.

"Ring again," Castello said.

Sebag obeyed, even though they all knew it was futile.

"Still no sign of life," Massart's voice replied.

Sebag turned off his walkie-talkie and pushed open the gate, which creaked over the gravel. He went in and was careful to leave the gate open behind him.

Protected by a flourishing palm tree, the farmhouse was surrounded by a poorly maintained lawn composed chiefly of dried moss and yellowed grass. The pink gravel driveway climbed slowly toward the house. Sebag moved forward. He felt calm and relaxed. The fear would come later. So long as they were in action, the concentration kept fear at a distance.

He stopped in front of the Mégane station wagon parked in front of a large wooden garage door. In the trunk, there was only an old road sign: "Road Closed—Repairs."

The old farmhouse seemed to be dozing behind its wooden shutters. On the roof, the cascade of ochre-colored tiles was interrupted only by a little skylight, which was closed. A green ceramic gutter bordered the roof, then ran down the corner of a wall to its spout above the driveway. The gentle slope down to the road was sufficient to carry off rainwater.

Sebag took up his position in front of the main entrance. Two policemen came and stood on either side of him. Sebag knocked. Three quick blows. The officers leaned against the wall. Their revolvers raised to face level, they no longer moved. They were listening. They had the house's silence in one ear, the conversation on the walkie-talkies in the other, through their earphones. Their colleagues posted on the other side of the building confirmed the absence of sound.

Sebag put his hand on the door handle. He pushed. The door opened silently. The interior was dark, and his eyes needed time to adjust. Suddenly he saw himself a few days earlier, standing on the threshold of Robert Vernier's house in Gien. The same lugubrious atmosphere. The same profound silence. And here, also a warm, sugary odor that he could not immediately identify.

IIis eyes first distinguished an inert mass slumped on a chair. Then two legs stretched out. Finally, two arms hanging limply over the armrests.

Sebag opened a shutter while the two other policemen started exploring the house. A ray of light penetrated the living room. Contrary to the apartment in La Fusterie Street, this room was full of old furniture and knick-knacks.

Didier Coll was smiling. He was extremely pale and seemed to be asleep. A sticky puddle covered the floor from the chair to the fireplace. Sebag approached the body. The legs were resting on a low table, where an empty glass held up a handwritten sheet of paper. Sebag bent down. The glass had contained alcohol. As for the message, it was a short poem in verse. A few stanzas and a refrain. Castello's figure appeared in the doorway.

"Is he dead?"

Sebag put his head on Coll's chest. To his great surprise, he heard a distant heartbeat.

"It looks like he isn't," he said, standing up.

"Then let's get the emergency team working on him."

Castello went away. Before launching the operation, he'd alerted the emergency medical service. A young woman doctor entered the house. Two nurses were following her, a stretcher under their arms. All the inspectors waited outside. Without saying anything. The crackling of the walkie-talkies reported the exploration of the house.

"Nothing found upstairs. It's an attic. There are only cardboard boxes containing old clothes, papers, and photo albums."

"There's an unmade bed in one of the two bedrooms on the ground floor. A few clothes in a closet and books on a kind of secretary. That's all."

"The kitchen has been used recently. There's an empty bottle of vodka in the sink and fresh food in the fridge."

Jean Pagès and his assistant made their way through the inspectors. Castello put his walkie-talkie to his mouth to speak with the policemen inside the house.

"If you don't find anyone, come back out again. And be careful especially on the ground floor, there's blood everywhere."

Pagès granted him a smile in place of thanks. Before going in, he had to let the stretcher pass. He questioned the young doctor. She rolled her eyes.

"He's lost a lot of blood," she said. "He's in a coma. We'll rush him to the hospital. I can't say right now whether he'll make it."

The walkie-talkie cut her off. There was more crackling, and the voice was more excited.

"I'm in the cellar. It's empty, but it's clear that somebody has been held here."

Sebag went back inside. When he saw him, Pagès gave him a dirty look.

"Don't get upset, I'm not going to touch anything," Sebag said.

While he was going down the stone steps that led to the cellar, he heard footsteps behind him. He turned around. It was Lefèvre.

At the bottom of the stairs, a hall led to a door. At the midpoint, a freezer narrowed the passage. Long and wide, it looked like a white tomb. The policemen stopped, hesitating. Lefèvre put his hand on the lid, took a deep breath, and lifted it.

The freezer was empty.

Sebag and Lefèvre followed the hall to the door. They found a first room converted into a bathroom. A bare, dim bulb gave a pale light. Across from a large closet there was a shower pan. A policeman in uniform was already there examining the place, his revolver still raised.

"That's good, you can take off," Sebag told him. "There's no point in too many of us being here."

He went into the other room. The odor of wine still filled the atmosphere, but far less than the stale smell of a wild animal.

"It smells like dirty underpants and sweaty armpits," Lefèvre coldly summed up.

Sebag preferred to say nothing. Aside from its brutality, Lefèvre's remark stated the obvious.

The room was plunged in semi-darkness. It had a small, high window that let only a slender ray of sun come in. Sebag, feeling his way, found a light switch. He flipped it, but nothing happened. Lefèvre crossed the room with small, cautious steps. He opened the window and with a well-aimed blow of his fist knocked away the pile of planks and cardboard that obstructed the opening. An old mattress, a table, a chair, and a slop pail were the cell's only furnishings.

Sebag went over to the mattress. He sniffed it. Examined it without touching it. There were damp spots on the pillow. Tears or sweat. He felt dizzy. A profound fatigue came over him.

He sat down against the wall. Exhausted. It wasn't over. The game went on.

Ingrid must have undergone a terrible ordeal during her three weeks in this horrible prison. She had experienced solitude, darkness, filth. Fear and anxiety. The total absence of hope in this damp dungeon. He recalled bits of a poem by Baudelaire. In it there was something about a damp dungeon. He no longer remembered the beginning, but it went something like:

"Hope, like a bat, goes beating against the walls with its timid wing and hitting its head on rotten ceilings."

The end, on the other hand, he remembered only too well. Opening his lips, he murmured:

" . . . Hope, defeated, weeps and atrocious, despotic Fear plants its black flag on my bowed skull."

He buried his face in his hands and lost consciousness for a few fractions of a second.

A hammering sound drew him out of his torpor. He looked up. Lefèvre was tapping the wall with the butt of his gun.

"What exactly are you looking for?" Sebag asked him.

"A cavity . . . a hiding place . . . a secret room, I don't know, some weird thing."

Sebag gave up on trying to hide his puzzlement. Lefèvre felt obliged to explain.

"Do you remember the case of Dutroux, the Belgian pedophile?

"In its main outlines, yes."

"When the gendarmes who were investigating the disappearance of two girls searched Marc Dutroux's house the first time, they inspected the notorious cellar where they had been imprisoned, but didn't find anything. The girls were just a few centimeters away from them, in a cavity hidden behind a wall, but gendarmes didn't see or hear anything. I wouldn't like something like that to happen to me someday."

Sebag leaned against the wall to stand up. He rubbed his hands and brushed off his clothes whitened by the saltpeter that was oozing out of the concrete blocks. Then he took out his lighter and also started tapping the wall. Elsa Moulin, Pagès's assistant, found them hard at it when she silently entered the room. They jumped. She smiled at them.

"You rehearsing for a concert?"

"I wish we were, yes," Sebag replied, "but this damned wall refuses to produce more than one note."

"Jean is getting impatient about you being here. He'd like you to leave the site. This is our job, and he's pretty touchy about that."

Sebag put his hand of Lefèvre's shoulder.

"We've gone all the way around, haven't we?"

"Yeah. Apparently there isn't anything."

The young superintendent turned to Elsa.

"I'd like you to examine this room first."

"No problem. We've already finished in the living room. I'll go talk to Jean; if I propose it, he won't object."

Sebag was glad to get out into the daylight. His fatigue was visible on his face.

"You should go rest," Castello advised him. "You can't do anything more for the moment. In that condition you won't be of any use to us. We'll stay here. We're going to examine every square centimeter of this house and if necessary we'll dig up the yard."

Sebag was shifting his weight from one foot to the other. He couldn't make up his mind to leave. He knew Castello was right. But it wasn't easy to let go.

"I also told Molina to go," the superintendent insisted. "You've both done good work. It's for us to take over now. Go home, take a nice shower, and lie down. I promise to let you know if we find something. Otherwise, we'll meet at eight A.M. tomorrow at headquarters."

As he was talking, the superintendent had started walking down the driveway. Sebag followed him. Molina was waiting in front of the gate.

"Jacques, take Gilles home and then you keep the car."

His hand on the car door, Sebag was still hesitating. He looked at the house for a long time. Molina came up to him.

"Nobody is indispensable. We've done all we could. It's the others' turn now."

Sebag turned back toward his colleague.

"He left a note on a coffee table. I read it but I can't remember a single word. It's probably important."

"Give yourself a couple of hours' sleep in your bed, and afterward you'll be fresher to launch into a new puzzle."

On the way, Molina and Sebag didn't try to make conversation. They were thinking only about Ingrid. The young woman's smiling face danced before Sebag's eyes: what had happened to her? Were they now going to have to look for her corpse?

At the La Garrigole traffic circle, Sebag advised Molina to take the ford to pass over the Têt River.

Somehow, Sebag sensed that the young woman was still alive. Coll had planned for the game to go on after his death. That thought produced a feeling of urgency. Did he have the right to go rest while Ingrid was waiting for him somewhere? He reproached himself for giving up too quickly, and then for taking this too much to heart. As Molina had said, no one is indispensable. He no more than anyone else. The investigation could move ahead without him.

They drove by the Saint-Estève rugby stadium and arrived in front of the water tower. They were no longer very far from his home.

Molina stopped the car in front of the gate to the house. Sebag opened the car door and then held out his hand to his colleague.

"By the way, weren't you supposed to see your sons today?"

"I was. But my wife agreed to keep them again this weekend. Monday it'll all be over, won't it?"

Sebag nodded.

"Yes. One way or another."

The solitude and silence of the house were a relief to him.

He took a beer out of the fridge, drank it out of the bottle, and collapsed in an armchair in the living room. Sebag thought he was not doing a good job of handling the shock of staying up all night. He felt old.

He took his cell phone out of his pocket and dialed Castello's number. A dull fear had started twisting his stomach. But the superintendent quickly reassured him. The pond had been rapidly dragged. They'd found only three frogs and a whistling toad.

He left the empty beer bottle on the coffee table and slipped between the sheets on his bed—they were dirty, he'd have to change them.

It didn't take him long to lose the thread of his thoughts. He slept long and deeply, even though his sleep was full of unpleasant dreams. Chained in the hold of a decommissioned ocean liner, Claire was desperately calling to him for help, but he couldn't move. He'd drunk too much, and his excessively heavy body was incapable of responding.

He woke up screaming.

CHAPTER 41

Intrepid mouse sang, content to wait,
But cruel cat's paw set its fate
For ill-trained dog t'was check and mate.

Down in damp hell, mouse at bay
Slept, and had naught to say
While cat found himself a hairy prey.

Who does what, who catches who?
Who's the cat, who the mouse, who?

Tired of being cat, greedy mouse was fain
to play, make his prey first lose, then gain.
He chooses a day to sit, opens a vein.

Mouse found it amusing you to use
You found me, but I didn't lose.
Beyond the passage the game renews.

Who does what, who catches who?
Who's the cat, who the mouse, who?

The die is cast, the cat's run away
The mouse remains on a summer day
For other cats' survival, she must stay.

In shade of a mast bobbing o'er the wave
She waits and waits, a patient slave
The house of stone will be her grave.

Who does what, who catches who?
Who's the cat, who the mouse, who?

CHAPTER 42

Sunday morning, eight o'clock. No one was absent from the roll call. Even Llach was back. Informed of the latest developments, he'd left his union buddies and returned to be with his teammates.

Sebag had lost count of the meetings they'd had regarding the Ingrid Raven case. All he knew was that there had been too many of them. Far too many. Three weeks of intense work on a single investigation—he'd never seen that since he'd been in Perpignan.

One thing was sure: this Sunday meeting was one of the last, if not the last. If anyone still had any illusions, Castello dispelled them at the outset:

"As the hours go by, our chances of finding Ingrid alive are getting slimmer."

Jeanne distributed to everyone a posthumous poem by Didier Coll, taking care to make her red miniskirt flutter among the tables. But the lovely muleta waved in front of their eyes did not succeed in distracting the inspectors from their somber thoughts.

"I've just talked to the head of intensive care at the Perpignan hospital: Didier Coll is still in a coma, his condition is considered stable, but the doctors remain pessimistic. In any case, even if he wakes up, we can't count on getting any information out of him."

Ménard was the first to present his report. The preceding day he'd gone to the retirement home to question Didier Coll's mother. His report was brief: the old woman was completely senile. He hadn't noticed immediately, and had even been surprised by how coherent some of her remarks were. She spoke well; her words were precise and clear. Except that all the events she was talking about dated from the 1970s. In her world, Didier was a turbulent adolescent loner who spent his leisure time exasperating his father.

"She thinks her husband is still living with them, for example. She constantly repeats that he's going to return soon, even though he disappeared in 1988."

"Is he dead?" Castello asked.

"No one knows, in fact. One fine day he went to a professional meeting and was never seen again. At the time, the investigators thought he probably just took off: he had a mistress and had just withdrawn a large sum of cash from his bank account."

Cyril Lefèvre came into the room without knocking. After quickly greeting everyone, he sat down on the superintendent's right and passed him a bundle of papers. Sebag recognized Jean Pagès's format. Castello thanked Ménard and started to sum up the work done by the police lab on the Colls' property.

"Our colleagues are still there, they're going to deal with the yard now. The examination of the house confirms what we assumed, namely that Ingrid was in fact held in the cellar from the beginning of her imprisonment until yesterday morning."

He turned to Lefèvre for further details.

"Pagès and Moulin examined that cellar as well, and didn't find any secret hiding place. Moreover, after inspecting the rental car during the afternoon, they conclude that the young woman was moved just before we arrived. She was transported to some place that we assume to be relatively close to the house in Le Soler. Not more than two and a half hours separated the time when Coll abandoned his scooter in front of the retirement home and the time we surrounded the property. Traces of sweat were found in the station wagon's trunk. Even in the absence of DNA analyses—they will arrive too late in any case—Pagès says he's convinced that it is in fact Ingrid Raven's sweat."

Castello took the time to look at each member of his audience.

"And that indicates that the young woman was still alive when she was transported. As you know, a corpse doesn't sweat."

A heavy silence reigned in the room. A little fly was buzzing in the air, indifferent to the thickness of the atmosphere. Castello went on.

"We have to start out from the principle that at this precise moment, Ingrid is alive. Still a prisoner somewhere, but *alive*. Unfortunately, as I told you when I began, we may now have only a few hours to find her."

"So long as the referee hasn't blown the whistle, the game's not over," Molina said approvingly.

Castello liked what he said, and not being used to agreeing with Molina, he willingly said so. Sebag had just read and reread Coll's poem, and thought he'd deciphered as least its general meaning.

"For me, it's obvious. Ingrid Raven isn't dead. Otherwise the game Coll invented wouldn't be meaningful."

He picked up the copy of the poem he had in front of him and waved it at his colleagues.

"Besides, Coll wrote it in black and white: 'You found me, but I didn't lose, beyond the passage, the game renews.' It's clear: for the game to continue, Ingrid has to be alive."

Eight faces simultaneously bent over the copies of the poem. Castello whisked away the fly that had just landed on his hand, then read out loud the whole stanza Sebag was citing.

"And 'beyond the passage,' what does that mean exactly?" Molina asked.

"Oh, that's a way of saying 'beyond death' and more precisely 'beyond his own death,'" Sebag replied. "That kind of image is often found in poems written by adolescents who want to believe that everything will be easy after death."

"Really? Do your kids write morbid stuff like that?"

"No, not my kids."

Sebag didn't have to say more. Lefèvre agreed with his interpretation.

"That's how I read that stanza, too."

"What if it's a false lead?" Raynaud interrupted. "Coll showed himself to be particularly sly and he's been able to throw us off track several times since this case began."

"He was also able to put us on the right track," Sebag said.

"'Play, make his prey first lose, then gain,'" Lefèvre recited.

"Cyril has read Coll's poem very attentively," Castello explained, "and at this point I'd like to ask him to give us his interpretation of the text."

Lefèvre didn't have to be asked twice.

"You will have noted that in this poem there are six different stanzas plus a sort of refrain that returns three times: 'Who does what, who catches who? Who's the cat, who the mouse, who?' Four questions that recur as in a nursery rhyme and that ask about the place of each actor in this case."

He pointed to the first lines of the text.

"At first, the characters seem easy to identify: the 'intrepid mouse content to wait' is Ingrid Raven. Her situation is perfectly described in the second stanza, where he says she was held "down in damp hell," which represents the cellar of the house, as you've all understood. The cat whose cruel paw sets the mouse's fate is Coll himself. No major problems there, either. On the other hand, the "ill-trained dog" mentioned in line three raises more difficulties. At first I thought it referred to us, policemen often being represented by dogs in stories."

"Oh yes . . . police dogs," Lambert thought it useful to explain.

"But on reflection, I think it refers to José Lopez," Lefèvre went on. "'For this ill-trained dog t'was check and mate,' that is, he was removed from the game. And he would also be the 'hairy prey' mentioned a little further on."

Sebag felt like he'd gone back twenty years to his high school years, when he listened to his French teacher commenting on the great texts of French literature. Lefèvre's memories were more recent: the young superintendent's presentation was clear and didactic. He was doing very well.

"We—that is, the police—appear later in the poem. First in the form of another prey, one that he 'makes first lose, then gain. Then we are the 'you' used in the fourth stanza. Finally, we appear again in the next-to-last stanza: in my opinion, the other cats' again refers to us."

"I think I'm no longer following you," Ménard said, perplexed. "It seemed to me that the cat was Coll."

Lefèvre looked up at Ménard for a moment and smiled at him.

"'Who's the cat, who the mouse?' The questions are clearly addressed to us in the refrain, and they are asked throughout the poem. Coll is sometimes the cat and sometimes the mouse: incontestably the cat with Ingrid, but both cat and mouse with us. 'Who does what, who catches who?' We're the ones who are supposed to chase the kidnapper but he's the one who came to seek us out, to challenge us, he's the one who's playing with us. We may be cats, but we're his prey."

"And, from a certain point of view, maybe he's the one who will end up catching us," Ménard went on.

"That remains an open question," Lefèvre concluded.

The little fly collided violently with the windowpane, but its flight was hardly affected. It buzzed over their heads, sounding like a revving scooter, but then chose to land on the paper in front of Molina. The former rugby player slowly brought up his big hand and then suddenly captured the fly before it could escape. He got up, opened the window, and threw the fly outside.

"Remarkable technique," Lambert commented as Molina sat down.

Llach cleared his throat and pointed to a line in the poem with his index finger.

"In the third stanza, it says that the mouse 'chooses a day to sit, opens a vein.' Doesn't that suggest that Ingrid Raven has in fact been killed? Her vein would be opened, just like Didier Coll's."

"The answer is in your question," Lefèvre replied triumphantly. "You're misinterpreting the text. In this stanza Coll isn't the cat but the mouse; he calls himself a 'greedy mouse.' And he chooses a day to open his veins in an attempt to kill himself."

"Except that it wasn't really he who chose the day. It was our raid that triggered everything," Raynaud quibbled.

"Yes, that's true. Coll was probably a little pretentious there . . . "

In general, Sebag agreed with Lefèvre's analysis.

"Coll isn't pretentious," he said. "He really did choose the time of his death. He'd undoubtedly planned from the outset to commit suicide on the day we came to get him. In that sense, as he wrote, he didn't lose: he did what he'd set out to do."

Molina tapped on his sheet of paper with his fingers.

"All that's perfect. Clear and brilliant. But if we want to have a good grade on the final exam, we have to find the place where Coll hid Ingrid. I suppose the answer is in the text?"

"Absolutely," Lefèvre sighed. "The last two stanzas refer to that. The message is clear: Ingrid is waiting for us patiently, but the 'house of stone' will also be her tomb."

Molina was impatient and pursued his point.

"Fine, so where is the girl hidden? Have you discovered that, yes or no?"

"In a 'house of stone.' 'In the shade of a mast bobbing o'er the wave.'"

"And that means . . . ?"

"The mast, the wave . . . naturally, that makes us think of the sea."

"So Ingrid is being held in a stone house near a boat?" Llach asked. "That's not very precise."

"There are two places near the sea that are connected with this investigation," Lefèvre replied. "The Revels' house in Collioure and the Hôtel du Sud in Canet."

Castello turned to Sebag.

"Is the Revels' house built of stone?"

"The façade is stuccoed," Gilles answered. "I don't know what's underneath it."

Ménard spoke up. He had an idea.

"I investigated the murder in Argelès. There was a *casot* between the Oleanders campground and the beach."

"A what?" Lefèvre asked.

"A *casot*," Castello explained, "is a cabin where vineyard workers store their tools and sometimes spend the night."

"A stone cabin," Ménard added.

"Stone . . . " Lefèvre repeated in a low voice. "That interesting, but I don't see why the campground in Argelès would be brought back in here. Ingrid has nothing to do with that."

"There are lots of *casots* in the department, Raynaud said. "And some of them are not very far from the sea."

"There are vineyards in Collioure, and thus also *casots*," Moreno added.

Lefèvre glanced at Castello questioningly. He wanted to urge him to make a rapid decision.

"I'm not very convinced but we've got to do something. And since we don't have any other ideas . . . Raynaud and

Moreno, you'll go to Canet to have a look at the Hôtel du Sud. Molina, Llach and Lambert, you'll go see the Revels in Collioure. In the meantime, I'll call the gendarmes, and they'll give you a hand examining all the *casots* in that area tomorrow. And finally, Ménard, just to be sure, I'm sending you back to Argelès anyway. We mustn't overlook anything."

The superintendent turned to Sebag.

"You stay here, Gilles. While your colleagues are running all over hell and gone, I want you to think about other leads."

The inspectors got up and went out, one after the other. Lefèvre followed them. He had decided to go to Collioure as well.

When Castello was alone with Sebag, he telephoned his secretary to ask her to bring them some coffee. He sank down on his chair and gave his dejection free rein.

"You don't believe it either, do you?"

"No. I didn't feel anything click."

"Your instinct didn't tickle you?"

Sebag just smiled. The two men continued to sit in silence, each lost in his somber thoughts, until Jeanne came in. She put two steaming cups on the table, along with two spoons and a plastic glass in which she'd put a few lumps of sugar. Then she went out again.

"Go ahead," Castello said. "I don't like it when it's too hot."

Sebag didn't have to be asked twice. The coffee was weak but acceptable.

"By the way, are your kids doing all right?" the superintendent asked him.

"I think so. Léo is roaring around on a quad in the Cévennes and Séverine is in Spain with the parents of one of her girlfriends."

"And your wife is on a cruise in the Mediterranean, if I'm not mistaken?"

"She is. She's coming home in a little while, incidentally."

"If I know you, you must be feeling a little lonely, right?"

"Oh, I really haven't had the time . . . "

Sebag preferred to avoid the subject. But Castello was in a mood for confidences. He put two lumps of sugar in his cup and stirred it slowly. He continued while staring sadly at his coffee.

"It's going to be six months since I saw Charles. Charles is my eldest, he's studying medicine in Paris."

He suddenly got up and opened the window. He took out a cigarette and began to smoke. He took two long drags before turning back toward Sebag.

"Plus I'm getting old and I think family is the most important thing in the world. I say that with force and conviction even though I'm well aware that I'm preaching to the choir: family values have become fashionable again."

A plane passed far overhead, leaving its white contrail across the blue sky.

"What isn't said often enough is that what holds the family together is the couple. Without a stable couple, there is no solid family."

Sebag hurried to finish his coffee. He put the cup down on the table and got up, pushing back his chair noisily.

"Let's hope our colleagues' investigations will be success-ful . . . "

It took the superintendent a while to understand what Sebag was talking about. Then he shrugged.

"Don't count on it too much."

Sitting in his office, he contemplated his computer. His hand flitted over the blackened keys. The machine couldn't do anything for him.

No machine could.

Electronic circuits, even very complex and powerful ones,

turned out to be too primitive to follow the corrupt twists and turns of human neural pathways.

He couldn't concentrate on that damned poem. He read it. Reread it. He just couldn't keep his mind on it. Nonetheless, behind these clumsy verses and sad rhymes the life of a nineteen-year-old woman was hidden. But the blond Ingrid's smile was effaced behind that of a brunette almost twenty years her elder. Claire would be home in a few hours . . .

He wanted another cup of coffee.

"The die is cast, the cat's run away."

He'd put the poem down on the computer's keyboard and turned the desk lamp on it. But it was his brain that needed light, not his eyes.

"The mouse remains on a summer day, for other cats' survival, she must stay."

He tried to get around the obstacle. Go back to the simple stanzas. Use them to get started. Land by surprise on the obscure lines. Make them spit out their poison.

"In the shade of a mast bobbing o'er the wave."

Claire with her suitcases on the platform at the train station.

"She waits and waits . . . "

Claire with her soft eyes, her face without makeup.

"The house of stone will be her grave."

To rid himself of irrelevant thoughts, he tried to imagine Ingrid Raven lying on the cold marble of a tomb.

He looked at his watch. 10:30. He couldn't concentrate.

The cruise ship should be approaching the port of Marseilles. The arrival was scheduled for a little before noon. How long would it take such a boat to land? Would it have to wait off the coast for a while first?

He got up from his chair, swearing. He had to get hold of himself. Ingrid Raven's life depended on it.

Pretentious idiot! he said to himself. *Do you think you're the only one who can find her?*

He thought about his colleagues who were searching the *casots* near the seacoast and finally answered "yes," he might in fact be the only one who could save her.

Unfortunately for her.

In seven hours, Claire would arrive at the station in Perpignan. And he still hadn't made a decision. He'd see when the time came. Everything would depend on her attitude. If she was still resentful about their last phone call, things would certainly be easier. But if she threw herself into his arms and murmured words of love in his ear, he was capable of forgetting everything.

He loved her. That was the only thing he was sure about.

"The couple is what holds the family together," Castello had said.

By asking Claire for an explanation, he was taking the risk of destroying everything. Of course, if she loved somebody else, it would be better to get it over with right away. Force her to choose.

To divorce him.

Separation. Alternating custody. A few words exchanged between two doors at each meeting. Angry fights, perhaps. Bitterness, for sure.

Weeks without them. A life without her.

But if Claire's affair was a simple fling after twenty years of fidelity . . . What good would it do to bring it out into the open? I'm a cuckold, I know it, you ask my pardon and I absolve you. Ridiculous and vain. If he was ready to forget everything, why not push the logic all the way?

Not say anything. Not do anything.

Accept?

The other day, at the Deux Margots cafe, he could have learned more about Claire's lover. He hadn't wanted to. Instinctively, he'd already decided. When he had felt himself ready to pardon her, he'd been scared. He thought that was a bad sign, a sign that he no longer loved his wife enough. But jealousy is not a proof of love.

He sat down on his chair again. Settled himself firmly against its back.

Ingrid Raven.

The house of stone.

An image had come to him a little while ago when he'd thought about the young woman stretched out on the marble tomb. The cold marble. Slabs. Stone walls. A house. A church. The house of God . . .

In his mind's eye, he saw again Didier Coll's apartment. A coffee table between two armchairs. The Bible lying on the table.

"You read wholesome books," he'd said.

"It's the only novel I can stand," Coll had replied.

Ingrid Raven was being held prisoner in a church.

"In the shade of a mast bobbing o'er the wave."

A church at the seaside. The church in Collioure? He put his hand on his telephone to suggest that his colleagues also have a look at the church in Collioure. He felt it vibrate before it rang. It was Jeanne.

"The superintendent is waiting for you downstairs. A body has been discovered at the house in Le Soler."

They didn't exchange a word during the trip to Le Soler. When Pagès had called, the superintendent was on the phone. Pagès had left a brief message that contained no more details than those Jeanne had given him.

A cadaver had been found at the back of the yard behind a copse of reeds.

Castello was driving too fast. He'd turned on the siren and floored the accelerator. Fortunately, the road to Le Soler had few curves. Sebag didn't want to believe it: Coll actually killed Ingrid before killing himself. The traces of sweat in the car, the poem: all that was just meant to deceive them.

Impossible!

"Beyond the passage the game renews."

The meaning of this line in the poem was clear. And without a prize, there could be no game. And the prize had to be finding Ingrid alive, not discovering her body under a layer of earth. He tried again and again to reach Pagès, but each time got his answering machine. He checked his list of phone numbers but didn't find one for Elsa Moulin.

The superintendent had to slow down as he came into the village. He drove down the main street, passed the city hall, then turned left on the road to Thuir. Now Coll's house was not far away.

A midnight-blue car was parked in front of the entrance to the property. Castello and Sebag greeted the gendarmes before going through the gate. They went around the house and approached the back of the yard. A red backhoe was holding its powerful arm over a pile of ochre-colored soil. Alongside it, Jean Pagès's bald head was sticking out of a hole. They went up to the hole and bent down. They were totally surprised to see what the crime lab men had unearthed.

"What the hell is that?" Castello exclaimed.

Pagès stood up, holding a trowel in one hand and a toothbrush in the other. He wiped his brow with the back of his hand. His face was sweaty and dirty. He'd already managed to excavate the lower half of a skeleton.

"That's not Ingrid," Castello observed.

"No, that's highly unlikely," Pagès replied. "This guy's been here for at least twenty years."

The head of the crime lab put the toothbrush in the pocket of his shirt spattered with dirt and handed the trowel to his assistant. Then he held out his arm to Sebag so he could help him climb out of the hole.

"Who is it, then?" Castello asked.

"It's a little too early to say, Superintendent. The shape of the pubic bone tells us that it's a male and the size of his femur tells us that he was about five foot eleven. Finally, the presence of osteoarthritic calcifications on the toes suggests that the individual was at least fifty years old, maybe sixty, but that's an initial estimate. If we can excavate the whole of the skeleton today, we might be able to identify him by examining the jawbone."

"Assuming that we already have some idea of who he is. And that we can find the right dentist. So in your opinion he's been buried here for twenty years?"

"Give or take five years, yes. And what's strange is that he's been buried here from the outset. We're almost sure that the body has never been moved."

"And why is that strange?" Castello asked.

Elsa Moulin climbed out of the whole in turn. She was the one who replied.

"We decided to look here because we noticed that the earth had been recently dug up. We don't know why. It's an odd coincidence!"

"In this case," Sebag remarked, "every time we think we're dealing with a coincidence, Coll is behind it. To help us or to lead us astray."

"You think he dug up this patch of earth on purpose, so we'd find this body?"

"He's quite capable of that, don't you think? It's very clever. He's killing two birds with one stone: helping us and leading us astray at the same time."

"Meaning?"

"He's helping us discover another of his crimes, and at the same time distracting us from our main search. Ingrid isn't in this yard. The game goes on."

"Do you think the man buried here was killed by Coll?"

Sebag turned toward his colleagues.

"Do you have any idea how he died?"

"Absolutely not," Pagès replied. "You're asking too much of us for the moment."

"I hope we're not going to find other bodies in this yard," Castello sighed.

Sebag shrugged. He was hoping that too, but he didn't think it was very important. If there were other bodies, they had been dead for a long time. Ingrid, however, was still alive.

They returned to headquarters. In less than three hours, Claire would arrive. If his work allowed him to, Sebag would go to meet her at the station.

Before leaving the farmhouse, he'd made a little tour of the yard with Castello, but they hadn't found anything suspicious: no other patches of earth recently dug. If Coll had other crimes on his conscience, he wanted to keep them secret.

Raynaud and Moreno had just come back from Canet. Empty-handed. The Hôtel du Sud was fully booked and the manager hadn't appreciated this police raid on his establishment. At first he tried to oppose it, but Moreno had been able to convince him to cooperate fully. In two hours, everything had been searched: the forty-five rooms as well as the common areas, the kitchen, the stockrooms, and the laundry. With the exception of some rotten food in the fridge and a Moroccan chambermaid without a work permit, they hadn't found anything in particular. Ménard's investigations in Argelès had been no more fruitful. The famous *casot* wasn't one. It was a small brick building used for gathering meteorological data. Ménard had nonetheless stayed there to explore the surrounding area. He'd discovered two other *casots*—real ones, this time—that served as public toilets for vacationers and that contained nothing but more or less fresh turds. For the moment the other policemen had also drawn blanks. They had found nothing at the Revels' home and were now searching, under a leaden sky, the steep slopes of the Collioure vineyards.

For his part, Sebag was assembling the various bits of information collected regarding Didier Coll's life in order to put together a personal and familial biography. One fact had very quickly attracted his attention. He was distracted from his work by a phone call from Castello.

"I've just talked to the hospital. It's over: Coll is dead."

Sebag was staggered by the blow. Their only connection with Ingrid had just been broken.

Time was passing too quickly. Each minute that passed diminished their chances of finding the young woman alive. Sebag felt as if he had a stopwatch perpetually hanging over his head. He'd never liked cop shows in which the action was a race against the clock. Tick-tock, tick-tock. At the last second, the hero always won. Tick-tock, tick . . .

However, this time he had serious doubts about the hero and he found the suspense unbearable.

He went into the office that Ménard shared with Llach and Lambert. His colleague had told him that he'd put the file he'd gotten the day before from the archives in the top drawer of his desk. Sebag found it easily and went back to his cave to study it.

Maurice Coll had disappeared on March 21, 1988. As he did every morning, he'd left the family home around seven o'clock to go to the public works business he ran. Around mid-morning, he'd gone to the bank to withdraw fifty thousand francs in cash—a hefty sum at the time—and then chaired a construction project meeting in Cabestany. He'd left at eleven-thirty. That was the point at which he disappeared. No one had ever seen him again.

Maurice Coll was a well-known figure in Roussillon. In 1943, at the age of twenty, he had joined the Resistance. Like his comrades in the Resistance, he'd barely escaped being killed in the village of Valmanya. On August 1, 1944, German troops raided that village on the slopes of Le Canigou, and to punish its inhabitants, who supported the Resistance, burned it to the ground. After Liberation came, Maurice Coll had held a few local offices before retiring from political life to devote himself to his business. It was widely rumored that he was a Freemason.

Maurice Coll had married Juliette Pujol in Perpignan on June 12, 1956. From this marriage was born just one child: Didier, who came into the world on September 5, 1961.

Sixty-five years old at the time he disappeared, Maurice had been involved for several years in an adulterous relationship with a certain Marie Cardona, a Spanish teacher in a private high school who was fifteen years younger than he. She'd told the police that she'd had no word from her lover, either, but a few days later she'd left her residence and her job—right in the middle of the school year—to go back to live in South Catalonia, the region from which her parents had come. This sudden departure had convinced the police that Maurice Coll had left his family to live in Spain with his mistress. His disappearance was thus considered voluntary, and the case was closed.

Sebag wondered whether Maurice Coll's dental records still existed somewhere.

He asked Martine to get him Elsa Moulin's telephone number, entered it into his address book, and called her.

"Hi, it's Sebag. How far have you gotten?"

"We've just finished excavating the body. I can confirm the estimates we gave you earlier regarding the height—five-eleven—and the gender. So far as age is concerned, we can now say that he was over sixty."

Sebag felt his fingertips tingling.

"We found something interesting that will help us identify him," Elsa went on. "There are traces of fractures on the left side of the clavicle. Two fractures. Jean thinks they were caused by bullets. But it's difficult to be sure, we'll have to wait for the coroner's examination."

"So our man was probably killed, then?"

"No, we can't go that far yet. The wounds I mentioned occurred before death. Long before, even. The calcification is complete. He must have had an accident when he was twenty or thirty."

"Are you practically done there?" Sebag asked.

"Almost. Jean is just finishing up, and I'm having a beer with the gendarmes. I think we're going to put a tarp over the site and wait for the coroner."

"Could you do something for me?"

"Sure."

"When you searched the house yesterday, did you find any photos? I mean family photos, an album . . . "

"Yes. In fact, there were a lot of old photos in a trunk in the attic."

Sebag told her about his suspicions and she promised to go—as soon as she'd finished her beer—have a look at the pictures of the papa. After he hung up, he called Castello, who gave him the telephone numbers of a few former members of the Resistance he knew.

In less than an hour, Sebag was able to collect some precious information, though it was not always very precise. Maurice Coll had been wounded during the last skirmishes with the occupying forces. One of his former comrades in combat recalled having visited him once or twice in the hospital in Perpignan after Liberation. Another had been able to provide additional information: Maurice had been shot in the arm—or maybe the shoulder—by a French militiaman collaborating with the Germans.

"I can still see him with his arm in sling during a ceremony to award medals," Charles Jouhandeau told him in a voice that was as emotional as it was quavering.

"Which arm?"

"Umm . . . I think it was his right arm. Unless . . . oh, I don't know any more. Is that important?"

"Yes. It might be."

"In fact, I'm not sure. I said it was the right arm because I recall that he found it very difficult to write. But maybe he was left-handed. Because when I imagine the ceremony, it seems to me that the general who decorated him had to slip the medal underneath his bandage. And as you know, medals are always pinned on the left."

Sebag thanked him and hung up. He was hot. He was thirsty. He went down to the cafeteria to get a can of Perrier. The clock in the hall reminded him of other things he had on his mind.

In an hour and a half. Claire. At the Perpignan train station. The center of his universe.

He went back to his office, opened the can, and called Elsa. She picked up immediately. She'd taken the trunk out of the attic and sat down on the grass in the shade to look at the photos.

"It's moving, you know, to dive into the past of a family like that. When you see Coll as a baby, with his curly hair and angelic smile, in his parents' arms, it's hard to imagine that he could later become a murderer. It's crazy! You'd like to know at what point things started to go wrong. When the perfect little boy—he's very cute, you'll see, at the age of five with his magician's outfit—had his first bad impulses. And I think especially about his mother: in most of the photos, she looks totally infatuated with her little kid. Is she still alive?"

"Yes and no. The body's still there, but the mind is gone."

"Alzheimer's?"

"No, just an ordinary case of senility. So, did you find any photos of the father?"

"Absolutely. A tall man. Slender. Fairly good-looking. Lots of presence. Except I don't like his mustache."

Sebag laughed heartily. He liked Elsa's spontaneity.

"So do you think he could be your stiff?"

"Maybe . . . I found a photo taken in front of the house.

That served as a reference point for me: I think daddy Maurice was about five-eleven. That doesn't mean he's our man, but for the moment we can't rule him out."

He summed up the information he'd gathered from the veterans.

"Do you really think Didier Coll could have killed his father?" Elsa asked.

"I wasn't around him long enough to be sure."

"Why would he have killed him?"

"I don't know whether we'll find out someday, but family hatreds are often the most violent ones. Statistically, you're more likely to be murdered by a member of your family than by a stranger."

"Is that right? Are you sure your numbers are right?"

"Absolutely."

"Well! I'm no longer sorry to spend my Sunday working. I'm running fewer risks."

They laughed again and hung up. That did him good. He knew no music sweeter than a woman's laugh. And he wondered if he would someday laugh again with Claire.

He quickly wrote up his initial conclusions and then e-mailed them to all his colleagues. He printed a version of them and took it to Castello.

The superintendent read it attentively and approved it in general. However, he regretted that it didn't advance them. Ingrid Raven was more than ever beyond their reach.

"Your colleagues are coming back from Collioure soon. I'm going to hold a last meeting for today and then . . . and then there'll be nothing to do but hope for a miracle."

Sebag ostentatiously glanced at his watch. It was 7:00 P.M. Castello understood easily.

"Claire?"

"She'll be at the train station in less than half and hour."

The superintendent sighed.

"Go ahead, old man. I'll let you know if we have anything new."

Sebag thanked him, but Castello cut him off.

"I'm going to set up an ongoing watch, anyway. Ménard and Lefèvre will stay until midnight. Then Raynaud and Moreno will take over. It'd be good if you could come in at six. You'll be with Molina."

Standing on the platform, Sebag waited. The train wasn't going to be late. In ten minutes, Claire would be getting out of it. He'd soon know. He'd act in accord with his feelings. His cop's instinct had never failed him. Why not let his man's instinct guide him this time?

A loudspeaker crackled, then a familiar female voice droned the usual announcements. The train from Marseilles was coming into the station; travelers were asked to stand back from the edge of the platform, please.

The train stopped with a great deal of hissing and clanking. The passengers got out one by one. The platform was already almost deserted when he finally saw her.

She was scanning people like a worried doe. She was wearing a short skirt and white T-shirt that set off her tanned skin.

She was beautiful.

Her dark, curly hair danced around her face as she was looking for him. She'd had her hair cut, not too much, probably in the ship's beauty salon. Her earrings sparkled in the sun. Two garnet teardrops on white gold hoops. She'd long dreamed of having earrings like that. He'd given them to her for their tenth anniversary.

Claire's blue eyes lit up when she saw him.

Words can lie, he thought. Not that look.

A second later, she was in his arms. When she'd run toward him, dropping her suitcase, her arms had spread all by themselves and she'd plastered herself against him. Thigh to thigh, belly to belly. Their lips smashed together in a passionate kiss.

Words can lie. Not bodies.

She caressed his tired-looking face with her fingers.

"I missed you," she said.

"Is that lie true?"

"It's not a lie."

She put her lips on his scratchy cheek.

"So, did you miss me, too?"

"No. Not at all."

She pretended to be offended.

"Is that lie true?"

He put his hands on her cheeks and looked into her eyes.

"It's true . . . yes. It's true that it's a lie."

On the way home in the car, she asked him about his investigation. He recounted the latest developments in the case. Identifying Coll, surrounding the house, discovering the body in the yard, and so on. He didn't hide his anxiety about Ingrid.

"That's a horrible story . . . The poor girl. I understand why you look so tired. It must be awful to feel so powerless that way. You really don't have any idea where she might be?"

"Not the slightest, no."

He parked the car in the driveway. As she got out, Claire glanced at the yard.

"I can see that it has been hot. I'll water in a little while."

"I was planning to do it but then I didn't have time."

"I understand," she said. "For the moment, I'll take care of the watering. I'm going to have a shower. It was warm in the train."

He took her suitcase out of the trunk of the car and carried it into the bedroom. So everything was going to return to normal. He felt a cowardly relief. He didn't know if that was the right solution. What he did know was that for the moment, that solution made him happy.

The water was running in the shower. He opened the bathroom door a little way.

Claire was soaping her body. The suds made her skin glow. He was fascinated. He liked every part of her body. She noticed that he was looking at her.

"What about you, weren't you too hot at work today?" she asked.

"No more than other days, why?"

"You smell . . . ripe."

"Ah," he said, a little annoyed.

"You should take a shower," she said, with a risqué twinkle in her eyes.

He didn't have to be asked twice. In a moment, he was naked. His saber at attention, he got into the shower.

After they got out, they had dinner on the terrace. Since the children weren't there, no one complained about the tomato salad. Moreover, it was excellent. Claire had garnished it with hard-boiled eggs and tuna. Gilles had insisted on spicing it with marjoram leaves from the garden. After the meal, they smoked a cigarette together.

Then they went swimming naked without waiting for midnight.

They made love alongside the pool. With less eagerness than the first time, but still with great appetite. Gilles felt that Claire was forcing herself not to cry out.

They went to bed around eleven. In the dark, Sebag listened to Claire's breathing. He heard it slow. In less than a minute, she fell asleep.

He remained awake.

Sleep eluded him, despite his fatigue. He lifted the sheet to look at Claire's body. Other eyes had admired it recently; other hands had probably been put on it. That evil thought irritated his wounded soul. He'd have to live with that. It was possible.

The pain had already turned into a prickling sensation. Like a backache, it would return to haunt him from time to time. To remind him of the fragility of these small happinesses, which are never so threatened as when we think they are not.

Life could go on.

When he thought about it, he hadn't been guided by his instinct, but by his heart. He had long believed that this apparent resignation was a bad sign for their relationship. Watching Claire sleep, he realized that he'd been wrong.

He didn't love his wife less: he loved her better.

He got up as discreetly as he could and went into the dining room to pour himself some whisky. The thermometer still read 80 degrees. He sat down naked on the sofa and stroked the old tanned leather with the flat of his hand.

The leather was old but in good condition. The whole family's buttocks had polished it over the years. It had suffered the children's shoes, sometimes served as a gymnastics mat or even a trampoline, and absorbed, on certain evenings, a furious thumping. Sebag ran his hand over an armrest. Léo had scratched it a few years before with the sharp steel of a toy pistol he'd received as a Christmas present. His finger passed lightly over the old scar. It was smooth, like the rest. Like all the scrapes. Time had covered it over with a patina that was inimitable. Inestimable. This sofa told the story of their lives. There was no other like it anywhere.

Their love resembled this old leather. It hadn't grown weaker over time. Just a little more flexible. You could get rid of it, throw it away, destroy it. You could never replace it. Gilles and Claire had twenty years of closeness behind them. Two children. A family. What Claire had experienced with him she would never experience with anyone else. That certainty lent him strength.

He was proud of their love.

Happiness, after all, was compatible with a few compromises.

He stood up, filled with a new energy.

He poured himself another glass of whisky and went outside to drink it. The moon had come up and was bathing the yard in an unreal pale light. They hadn't watered the lawn. They'd do it tomorrow.

Tomorrow . . .

Tomorrow, Ingrid might be dead. He looked at his watch. It was already tomorrow.

He knew he wouldn't be able to sleep that night.

A person in good condition could go almost seven days without eating or drinking. But how long could Ingrid hold out? Her three weeks of captivity had doubtless already exhausted her. And for her, it was more a question of hours than of days. Where could she be at this advanced time of night? Was she able to sleep, or had she already slipped into a semi-coma?

A sea breeze was carrying sound to Saint-Estève from the superhighway a few miles farther east.

He heard whistling sounds. Followed by a hoarse cough. The neighbor woman was calling her cat. Gilles saw two green, almond-shaped eyes looking at him. The tomcat was hiding out.

He decided to go inside.

He took a sheet of paper, sat down at the dining room table, and rewrote Didier Coll's poem from memory. He studied his notes for a long time, his head full of awkward rhymes.

He didn't find the solution.

During the afternoon, he'd thought for a moment that he was getting close to the truth. He tried to re-create the atmosphere of that moment, but failed.

He felt an imperious need to move. The clock in the living room showed 3:00 A.M. He still had time before he had to go to headquarters. He grabbed the car keys and went out.

Sebag started the engine and slowly backed up. He turned on the headlights only after he'd left the driveway. He drove through the empty streets of Saint-Estève, crossed the Têt and headed for the chapel of Sant-Marti de la Roca.

He passed through Thuir, followed the highway toward Ille-sur-Têt for a mile or so, then turned off on a little road that led to Camélas. At the entrance to the village, he parked in the lot next to the cemetery. His first steps were accompanied by the lugubrious hooting of an owl. He walked through the sleeping village. The moon shone on the carefully maintained façades of the houses. Sebag looked up. Two hundred yards farther on, atop its pointed hill, the chapel was waiting for him.

The little paved road became a forest path. He followed it as far as the La Roque saddle. From there, the path led back down toward the medieval village of Castelnou. Sebag left it and took instead a rocky trail that set out courageously for the summit of the hill. Sebag usually ran up this last steep climb.

The last time he'd been up to Sant Marti, he was still blissfully ignorant of everything that was going to spoil his summer. Didier Coll had kidnapped Ingrid Raven, but no one knew it.

The chapel soon appeared, sitting peacefully on its stone foundation. More enchanting than ever in the moonlight.

Sebag wished he believed in God.

He slowly approached the church. The door was locked. He went around the building and leaned against a rock. The lights of a series of villages gleamed on the plain below. In the distance, the coming dawn was already brightening the sky, separating it from the dark waters of the sea.

Sebag took out of his backpack the bottle of mineral water he'd brought with him. He drank at least two-thirds of it before taking another breath.

The horizon was on fire, casting bright glows on the azure sky. The sun was coming up for Ingrid, too, somewhere on that plain. Perhaps quite nearby.

Sebag spotted the windmill that dominated the Perpignan area. He looked down on the Têt and tried to follow its course upstream. Le Soler, Saint-Féliu d'Avall, Millas. Above, the hill of Força Real proudly displayed its two camel humps, one for the hermitage, the other for the television relay antenna. The Middle Ages had scattered chapels, hermitages, and watch-towers on most of the summits in Roussillon; on the others, the twentieth century had erected its wretched masts that spread their evil waves on all the homes below.

Sebag froze. He stopped breathing. By casting its rays on the metallic parts of the antenna and making them sparkle, the sun was giving him a wink.

The evil waves . . .

How could he have failed to see the obvious?

He swallowed with difficulty. Breathed in again the early morning air. And a broad smile spread across his face. It wasn't yet time for reproaches.

There was a hope.

He jumped to his feet and put his bottle in the backpack, which he then attached firmly to his back. Then he rushed down the rocky path.

On his way down, he twisted his ankle twice, but he ignored the pain. Nothing, no one, could have stopped him. Never had he run so fast. On his bristly cheeks, tears mixed with sweat. She was going to live; he was certain of it. His pant-ing was punctuated by laughter and words that surged out of his mouth involuntarily. His steps resounded on the asphalt of the little streets of Camélas. Fortunately, he met no one in the village. This early morning runner who was muttering abstruse words would have been taken for a madman.

"House of stone," "Mast bobbing o'er the wave." Coll had been clever. The clue, far from helping them, had led them astray.

But everything was clear to him now.

He roared off in a cloud of dust. The tires squealed on the curves. He took shortcuts by way of small roads to go directly to Millas, which he crossed at full speed. He still hadn't caught his breath when he parked his car in the lot at Força Real.

In his view, the hermitage lacked the charm of the chapel of Sant-Marti. To renovate the walls of the building, the masons had plastered them with great loads of mortar that not only bound the stones together but partly covered them. The result was that the whole now looked like a cheap nougat candy.

Sebag climbed a flight of stairs. The entry porch sheltered three doors. All locked. A sign indicated that restoration would soon begin inside the building. The work was supposed to begin in September, and the building was closed to visitors for the whole summer.

By examining the main entrance more carefully, Sebag noted that the lock had recently been broken. A chain and a padlock now blocked the way in. A brand-new chain and padlock. Anyone could have put them there and thus made the hermitage his personal property during the summer. Or his substitute prison.

Sebag put his ear against the thick wood of the old door. But he could hear no sound.

He went back down the stairs and searched the area around the hermitage. It was now getting light and he easily found what he was looking for. He returned to the big door with a large, pointed stone. A few powerful blows rapidly sufficed to split his finger but also broke the padlock.

Sebag pushed the heavy door open. A ray of light passed through the opening, but he had to wait a few seconds for his eyes to get used to the darkness. He still didn't hear anything.

He flicked his lighter and, protecting the flame with one hand, advanced cautiously into the nave. He looked between the rows of pews, but saw nothing suspect. A clatter of beating wings made him jump. Flying out of a dark corner of the choir, a bat crossed overhead and found refuge in a cavity hidden by the stone vault. Sebag turned around. He thought he'd heard something like a rustling of fabric behind the altar, where the bat had come from.

An old, moth-eaten cloth covered the ancient stone table. The greasy drippings from a candle had completed the soiling of the fabric. Sebag went around the altar and made out a dark form lying behind it.

Made red-hot by the flame, the flint of his lighter burned his thumb. Sebag swore. Just on principle. He was no longer capable of feeling pain. He'd reached the goal of his quest. The dark form had just moved.

He bent down and flicked his lighter again.

The body was lying on its side, bound from head to foot. A rough canvas sack concealed the head, but by the light of his flame, Sebag could see a bird tattooed on the bare shoulder. With trembling hands, he removed the sack. He saw an emaciated face with terrified eyes.

"It's over," he said softly as he started undoing her bonds one by one. "It's over. I'm a policeman. I'm going to take you home. Your parents are waiting for you."

EPILOGUE

The house was silent but it had recovered its soul.

Gilles put on the kitchen table a fresh baguette, a paper sack containing two hot croissants, and a national newspaper. He opened the French doors in the living room and went out onto the terrace. The neighbor's cat came to rub against his legs, meowing raucously.

"Are you hungry? You should go home to your mommy, that would be better for everyone. You know that you and I, that would never work."

He firmly pushed the cat away with his foot, then walked on into the yard. The sky was a pitiless blue. It was already hot. Gilles crouched at the edge of the pool and lifted the basket of the skimmer. He'd have to put in some more chlorine.

He went back toward the house, and the cat, running between his legs, almost tripped him. He took the carton of milk out of the refrigerator. He poured himself a big glass. And also put a few drops in a dish that he put on the terrace.

Gently, he opened the door to the bedroom. The sun was filtering into the room despite the closed shutters. A ray drew a golden line from Claire's shoulders down to the small of her back. Gilles sat down beside his wife and ran his finger along the ray of sunlight. Claire turned her head toward him, opened her eyes, and smiled.

Gilles's finger moved back up to her face. Caressed her rounded chin. Lingered on her lips. Traced their curve.

"Did you sleep well?

"Very well. It's good to be home."

He nodded pensively. His finger brushed across the soft furrows her smile made in her cheeks.

"How about you?" she asked. "Did you sleep a little?"

"Not really."

His finger had stopped on a hollow between her pink lips and her pointed nose. She put her hand on it to urge him to continue caressing her.

"What did you do?"

He traced the contour of her nose to the sweet place between her eyes. Caressed her eyelids. Slipped over her temples. Stopped on an earlobe. Then he went back to her mouth.

"I found her."

He felt Claire's lips tremble. His finger caressed the swell of her cheeks. Returned to the eyelids. "I drove her to the hospital. She's going to live."

The crow's feet around her eyes lengthened. There was more than love in the dark eyes that were staring at him.

No, that look couldn't lie.

He felt his vision blurring and closed his eyes.

Claire sat up in the bed. She put her lips on his eyes and wet them with the nascent tears.

"I love you," she whispered.

They'd devoured the two croissants and all that was left of the baguette was a few crumbs. The pages of the newspaper bore the marks of this morning orgy. Butter, jam, and a little honey on the Culture section.

Claire stretched with the voluptuousness of a cat in the sun. Gilles filled two big cups with a mellow, fruity aroma. A Colombian coffee. Léo had called while they were in the shower. He'd left a message. He was no longer going to Toulon. He'd had a fight with his friend. So he'd be coming home as planned, the day after next.

"He's not going to spend the rest of the summer here, I hope," Claire said.

"That might seem a little long," Gilles agreed.

"But if he doesn't stay there . . . "

"It's out of the question for Séverine to be all alone in the house."

Claire seemed as delighted as Gilles was at this prospect. A summer, another summer. All together.

"What do you suggest?"

"Everybody gets in the car, we throw our stuff in the trunk, and we leave."

With her elbows on the table, Claire rested her chin on her hands.

"To go where?"

"To see your parents?"

A light went out in her eyes. She stood up and crossed her arms.

"I was joking . . . I'd like to go to Central Europe: Vienna, Prague, Budapest . . . "

"Warsaw?"

"*Si vols.*"

"Is that Polish?"

"Almost."

"Are you sure?"

"In any case, the other day, at Le Perthus, I met a Polish truck driver who spoke like that."

"We're not getting anywhere . . . "

"No one can be dissected to do the implausible."

She frowned.

"That's ridiculous, it doesn't mean anything."

"I know, but I like it. Don't you?"

ABOUT THE AUTHOR

Philippe Georget was born in Épinay-sur-Seine in 1962. He works as a TV news anchorman for France-3. A passionate traveler, in 2001 he traveled the entire length of the Mediterranean shoreline with his wife and their three children in an RV. He lives in Perpignan. *Summertime, All the Cats Are Bored*, his debut novel, won the SNCF Crime Fiction Prize and the City of Lens First Crime Novel Prize